INFINITE SHORES

ALSO BY PASCALE LACELLE

Curious Tides
Stranger Skies

INFINITE SHORES

PASCALE LACELLE

SIMON & SCHUSTER
London New York Amsterdam/Antwerp Sydney/Melbourne Toronto New Delhi

First published in Great Britain in 2026 by Simon & Schuster UK Ltd
First published in the USA in 2026 by Margaret K. McElderry Books,
an imprint of Simon & Schuster Children's Publishing Division,
1230 Avenue of the Americas, New York, New York 10020

Text copyright © Pascale Lacelle 2026

Jacket illustrations by channarongsds/iStock (hourglass), seijirooooooooooo/iStock (whirlpool), Tori Art/iStock (galaxy), DaryaGribovskaya/iStock (hands),
and Tolchik/iStock (burst)
Jacket design by Greg Stadnyk
Map illustrations © 2023 by Francesca Baerald

This book is copyright under the Berne Convention.
No reproduction without permission.
All rights reserved.

The right of Pascale Lacelle to be identified as the author of this work
has been asserted by her in accordance with sections 77 and 78
of the Copyright, Designs and Patents Act, 1988.

1 3 5 7 9 10 8 6 4 2

Simon & Schuster UK Ltd, 1st Floor
222 Gray's Inn Road, London WC1X 8HB

For more than 100 years, Simon & Schuster has championed authors and the
stories they create. By respecting the copyright of an author's intellectual property,
you enable Simon & Schuster and the author to continue publishing exceptional
books for years to come. We thank you for supporting the author's copyright
by purchasing an authorized edition of this book.
No amount of this book may be reproduced or stored in any format, nor may it
be uploaded to any website, database, language-learning model, or other repository,
retrieval, or artificial intelligence system without express permission. All rights
reserved. Inquiries may be directed to Simon & Schuster, 222 Gray's Inn Road,
London WC1X 8HB or RightsMailbox@simonandschuster.co.uk

Simon & Schuster Australia, Sydney
Simon & Schuster India, New Delhi

www.simonandschuster.co.uk
www.simonandschuster.com.au
www.simonandschuster.co.in

The authorised representative in the EEA is Simon & Schuster Netherlands BV,
Herculesplein 96, 3584 AA Utrecht, Netherlands. info@simonandschuster.nl

Simon & Schuster strongly believes in freedom of expression and stands against
censorship in all its forms. For more information, visit BooksBelong.com.

A CIP catalogue record for this book is available from the British Library.

ISBN: 978-1-3985-5501-3
eBook ISBN: 978-1-3985-5514-3
eAudio ISBN: 978-1-3985-5500-6

This book is a work of fiction. Names, characters, places and incidents are either
a product of the author's imagination or are used fictitiously. Any resemblance
to actual people living or dead, events or locales is entirely coincidental.

Interior design by Irene Metaxatos
The text for this book was set in Haboro.
Printed and bound in the UK using 100% Renewable Electricity
at CPI Group (UK) Ltd

FOR MY DEAR READERS, WHO SAILED
WITH ME TO DISTANT SHORES. HERE'S
TO WHEREVER THE TIDE TAKES US NEXT.

AND FOR ANYONE STRUGGLING TO
FIND THEIR WAY OUT OF THE DARK:
I HOPE YOU REMEMBER THE LIGHT
ALWAYS COMES. *POST TENEBRAS LUX;
ITERUM ATQUE ITERUM.*

AUTHOR'S NOTE

PLEASE BE ADVISED that this book deals with and portrays a number of difficult subjects, including death, murder, grief, guilt, branding/tattoos, body horror, suicide ideation, bloodletting, self-harm, alcohol, violence, magical asylum/prison, and torture. If at any point you find the material distressing or triggering, please take a breather and return to the book only if you feel ready. Your well-being matters.

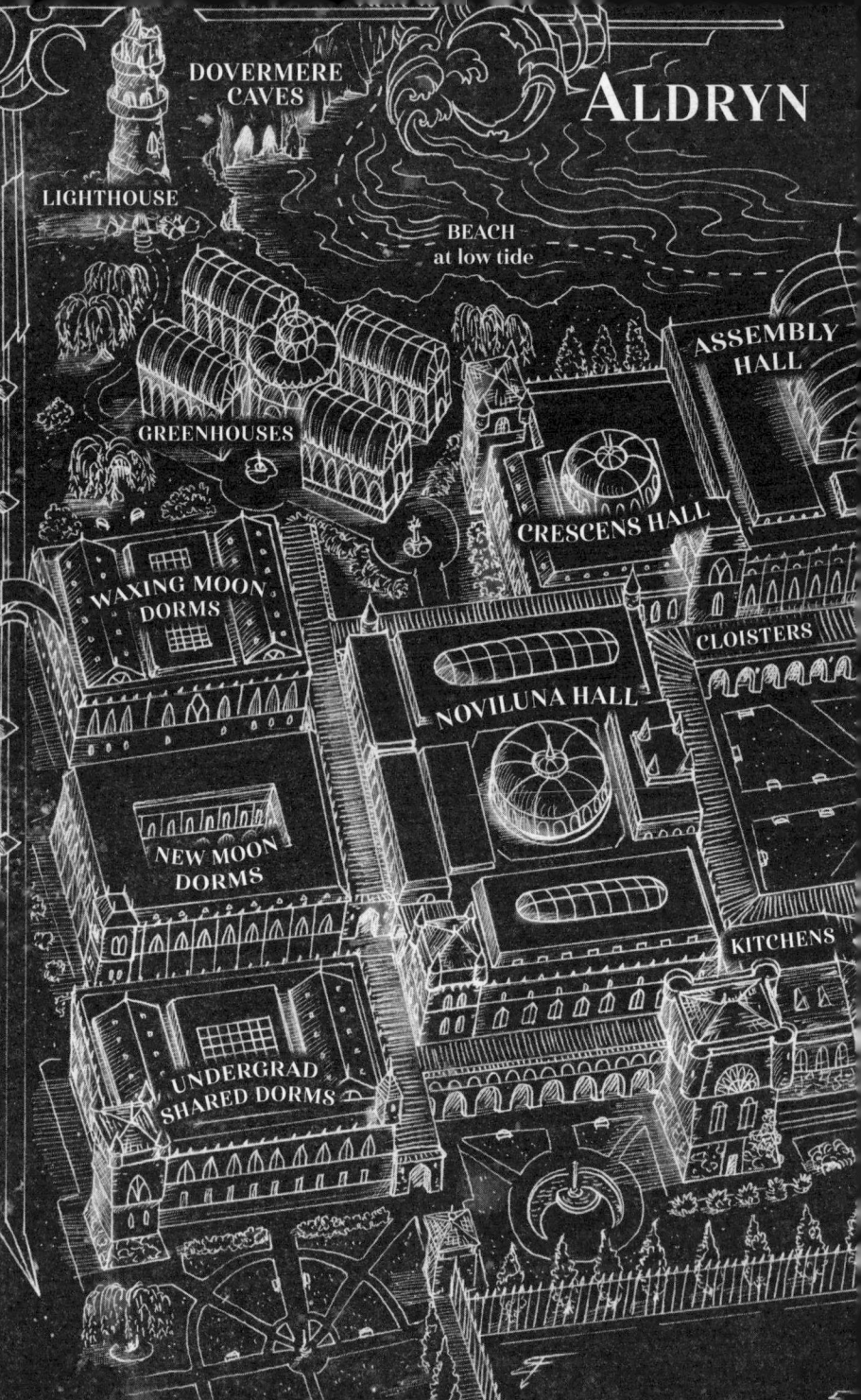

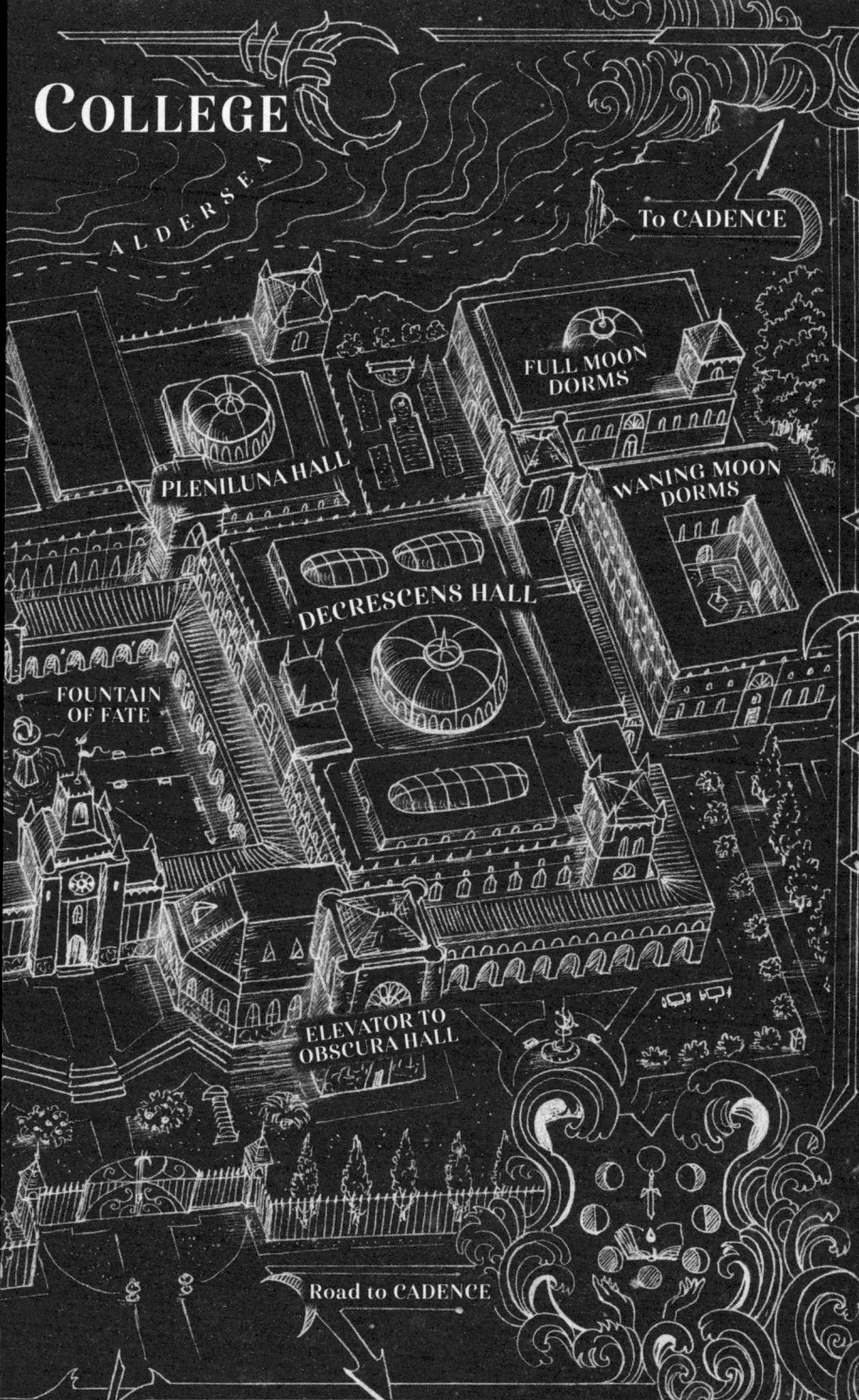

The Sacred Lunar Houses
& Their Tidal Alignments

HOUSE NEW MOON
Noviluna Hall

HEALERS (*Rising Tide*)
–ability to heal themselves and others

SEERS (*Ebbing Tide*)
–gift of prophecy and psychic visions

SHADOWGUIDES (*Rising Tide*)
–ability to see beyond the veil, commune with spirits

DARKBEARERS (*Ebbing Tide*)
–darkness manipulation

HOUSE WAXING MOON
Crescens Hall

SOWERS *(Rising Tide)*
–ability to grow and alter plants and other small organisms

GLAMOURS *(Ebbing Tide)*
–compulsion; charisma and influence over others

AMPLIFIERS *(Rising Tide)*
–ability to amplify the scope and range of other magics

WORDSMITHS *(Ebbing Tide)*
–ability to manifest things into being

HOUSE FULL MOON
Pleniluna Hall

SOULTENDERS *(Rising Tide)*
–emotion manipulation; empaths and aura-seers

WARDCRAFTERS *(Ebbing Tide)*
–ability to weave protection spells and ward magic

PURIFIERS *(Rising Tide)*
–ability to perform cleanses, balance energies

LIGHTKEEPERS *(Ebbing Tide)*
–light manipulation

HOUSE WANING MOON
Decrescens Hall

DREAMERS *(Rising Tide)*
–dream manipulation, dream walking; ability to induce sleep

UNRAVELERS *(Ebbing Tide)*
–ability to unveil secrets and decipher codes;
breaking through wards and spells

MEMORISTS *(Rising Tide)*
–ability to see and manipulate memories

REAPERS *(Ebbing Tide)*
–ability to reap life; death-touched

HOUSE ECLIPSE
Obscura Hall

Lunar eclipses produce variations
of other lunar magics

Solar eclipses produce rare new gifts
beyond other lunar magics

PART I
THE FALSE GOD

THERE ONCE WAS A SCHOLAR WHO BELIEVED HIMself a saint. He had the kind of rare magic that others viewed as a curse, but he knew to be a blessing. A power that would help him become the savior his world so desperately needed, for he had seen the end that would come with the fading of magic, that would destroy his beloved shores, and he believed only he could stop it.

It was a responsibility he shouldered with righteous fervor as he left the college that had shaped him to journey across worlds, a saint embarking on a holy mission.

But his pilgrimage wound up sullying his sainthood. He was a monster now, with an appetite so insatiable that not even the exquisite, hearty life forces he had gorged himself on could sustain him. It seemed like the more he fed on power, the hungrier for it he became. He was ravenous by the time he stepped into the godsworld, this place at the center of all things that was not yet a sea of ash but a lush paradise.

His appetite sharpened to a vicious ache as he beheld the mighty gods who dwelled here, safe from the rot slowly devouring the worlds they claimed to care for. They did not deserve this haven of peace nor the fountain at its heart that overflowed with such delectable power, a heavenly nectar so pure and abundant it could end all suffering if it were allowed to flow freely beyond this place.

The once-scholar turned monster knew something of greed, but his intentions, he believed, were not as self-serving as those of these gilded gods languishing on their gilded thrones. If their power were his, he would share it widely with the malnourished and the starved and the eternally eager, for he knew how it felt to want a seat at the table.

Yet what could one famished monster do against four ever-sated gods? Even the most cunning predator knew it could not feed on a pack of wolves four times its size. But sever them from their source of power—claim the fountain for himself—and he might stand a chance.

They were curious about him, at first. Intrigued by this unusual visitor in whom they could sense conflicting and impossible powers: the Tidecaller blood they believed had been purged from the world and the unified fragments of a lesser deity they thought would never be whole again. They did not know what to do with him but ask questions, sniffing him out like strange prey.

I have come to seek your help, the monster proclaimed, appeasing the gods with lies he had once believed, when he had still only been a scholar who fancied himself a saint, looking to petition those holier than him for their help saving the world.

But these lies were a diversion. He did not want their aid; he wanted to become them. And so, before they could stop him, he funneled their fountain's power into himself.

It was like ambrosia on his tongue, divinity flooding his veins. The more he took, the closer to godlike he grew, while the four gods dimmed, their might dwindling to nourish his own.

But before he could finish them off, drain them of every last morsel of divinity, the gods vanished.

The world trembled with their leaving, and in the ensuing silence, the near-god found that he was only that: *almost* divine, *not quite* exalted, his deification halted by his unfinished feast.

And now he was trapped here with a hunger that would inevitably return and a fountain that trickled ever so faintly on, as good as spent.

He knew, then, that he would never be a god in full until he finished what he started. Until he ended the cowardly beings who had ruled the living and took their place as the one true god.

EMORY

EVERY DREAM EMORY HAD OF LATE INEVITABLY TURNED into a nightmare.

There wasn't a single peaceful memory that wasn't marred by darkness. When she dreamed of home, her father's lighthouse was swallowed by the sea, his bones sinking toward the Deep. When she dreamed of Aldryn, all the students who'd once been her peers clamored for her death, their hissed accusations of *Tidethief* and *Shadow reborn* like lashes against her skin.

When she dreamed of three kids laughing by the seaside, the gulls overhead plummeted lifeless into the water, and the sea dragged the kids into its depths. Emory screamed for Baz and Romie as water filled her lungs, but the current was pulling them all in different directions, and she knew they would never see each other again.

Tonight, Emory dreamed of the Hourglass. Not as it was in real life—the slender stalagmite and stalactite that melded into each other—but as it had often appeared to her in sleep. An actual hourglass, silver and towering and full of fine black sand that fell from one elongated bulb to the other.

She walked barefoot on the damp, slick ground of Dovermere as she approached it, feeling like she'd been here a thousand times before. Every step she took made flowers bloom in her wake. Narcissus, hollyhock, orchid, poppy. When she ran fingers along the cave wall, vines sprouted at her touch. A breeze played in her hair, the sound of it like music to her ears. Sparks danced all around her, like embers from a fire or lightning bugs in a summer field, illuminating the oppressive dark.

Emory, Emory.

The hourglass called to her. Inside it was a door set at the bottom, an opening through which the black sand vanished, sinking and swirling until it disappeared. Emory set her hands on the cool glass. Shadows gathered inside the bulbs, lifting the sand as if there were a sudden gust of wind trapped within. The black sand shimmered like stars in the dark, rearranging into something vaguely familiar. When the shadows dissipated, a tree was trapped in the hourglass, filling every inch of space. Its branches full of healthy green leaves filled the top bulb, and its trunk squeezed tight in the narrow space leading to the bottom bulb, where its dead-looking roots twisted and twined onto one another.

Emory's hand moved of its own volition as it tightened into a fist and punched through the glass.

The tree dissipated into black sand and shadows once more, which burst out of the shattered glass like an exploding star. Emory wanted to shield her eyes but couldn't look away, not as shadows and sand and glass pulled back, leaving her untouched, and remade themselves into a shape she knew well.

An umbra wearing a wicked crown of obsidian.

Sidraeus. The deity she'd once known as the Shadow.

Emory's sleeping consciousness sharpened at his presence. This

was no longer a mindless dream; she was *dreaming*, her Waning Moon magic making her suddenly lucid. Fear shot through her like adrenaline. She'd been trying to find Sidraeus in dreams for a while now, without any luck. Now here he was.

It was odd, seeing him in his umbra form. She'd become so used to seeing him wearing Keiran's face. Sidraeus had possessed him to escape the sleepscape, where the deity had been imprisoned for centuries by the mighty god who ruled over the realm of sleep and death. Now Sidraeus was trapped again in the dark between stars, bodiless, after he'd lost his vessel.

That was the last time Emory saw him. When he, in Keiran's body, had put himself between her and Cornus Clover, saving her from a killing blow that ended Keiran's life—for good this time—and left Sidraeus as the crowned umbra that stood before her now.

He did not seem to recognize her. Or if he did, whatever tentative truce they had found vanished as his shadowed hand shot out to wrap around her neck.

Emory flinched, her body going rigid. She wasn't sure if it was the deity towering over her she feared or the echo of Keiran the gesture conjured. "Sid—Sidraeus," she sputtered as his clawed hands dug deeper into her skin. "Let go of me."

Those fathomless eyes drank her in, a flicker of hatred burning deep within.

You're the reason I'm here, Tidecaller. Why should I not kill you?

He had no mouth to speak with, the words echoing instead in Emory's mind. He spoke in a tongue that was rough yet ethereal, something she felt certain she had heard before but never understood until now. His hold on her tightened, and she grappled with the arm choking her, her hands connecting with what felt like exposed bone, those swirling shadows making her fingers go numb with cold.

"Please," she managed painfully. *Pitifully.* "You need me."

Cold laughter in her mind. Lungs burning as they ached for breath. Her vision started to go dark, and she truly believed he would kill her then. Would she become an eternal sleeper? Her consciousness trapped among the stars while her body remained behind, vacant until it eventually withered?

All at once, Sidraeus let her go. Emory gasped for breath and grasped her neck, scrambling away from the umbra's towering form. The shadows around him lengthened to follow her. They wound around her middle as if to keep her from escaping.

His voice sounded in her mind again: *We've played this game before, and you had me captured. You betrayed me, yet still I chose to sacrifice myself for you.*

"I never asked you to." Her voice was raw, her throat burning with every word. "And you betrayed me first. You were going to make me siphon all the power of the gods' fountain to you, knowing it would have killed me."

A pity you still breathe, and I paid the price for it. Spin it however you want, Tidecaller, but you owe me. A clawed finger of shadow brushed against the bruises on her neck. A threat; a promise. *Rest assured I'll find a way to collect.*

Fear settled in her bones. She was, perhaps for the first time, truly scared of him. It was as if whatever shred of humanity she'd come to glimpse in him had been filed away to nothing, stripped from him the same way his body had been. Before her stood not Sidraeus but the Shadow of Ruin, the ruthless deity she had always heard of in stories.

A chill went through her as she realized they were no longer in the dream-Dovermere but in the black, glittering sleepscape, empty save for the two of them. There was nothing but darkness and stars, but it felt to her like there were a thousand eyes on them, countless whispering voices on a nonexistent breeze. And it was her name they were calling.

The souls of the dead are restless, the Shadow said. *How eager they are for you to join them.*

Her gaze snapped to his fathomless one. The swirling shadows around him receded until she could see the bony outline of his ribs, the abyss that lived between them, the obsidian thing that beat in his middle. His heart. She wondered if all umbrae were like this beneath the billowing shadows, or if this was a particularity of his, a king amongst umbrae. A deity stripped of his body, reduced to this creature that was as much overseer as prisoner in this slumbering realm.

"Does this mean you're back to ferrying the souls of the dead, then?" Emory asked.

I cannot help them so long as the fountain remains depleted. There is no resting place for them now.

Dread crept along Emory's spine. If the souls of the dead couldn't be put to rest, if all the power from the fountain had been extinguished by Clover, were they all trapped here in the place between worlds? A purgatory of sorts. Maybe they were overspilling, slipping through cracks between worlds. It would explain why Emory was still plagued by ghosts whenever she used magic, she supposed.

Tell me, have you been visited by his *ghost yet, or can I assume his soul is burning in the infernal abyss?*

His voice dripped with cold disdain, and Emory knew he meant Keiran.

"I haven't seen him," she said. She was grateful Keiran's ghost seemed to be gone for good. She puzzled over Sidraeus's cruel contentment over this. She knew there had been no love between Shadow and vessel, but surely the prison of Keiran's body had been better than the one he now found himself in. "But it's not him I care about right now. I need to know if you've heard anything from my friends. From the keys."

Emory wasn't sure how Sidraeus's imprisonment here worked. Clearly, she could contact him through dreams. Perhaps Romie could as well, and he'd gotten to talk to her—something Emory hadn't been able to do since the last time she'd seen her best friend, when Clover's creatures had taken Romie, Aspen, and Tol to the sea of ash, where they would be sacrificed to revive Atheia—the deity known in Emory's world as the Tides, the opposite of everything Sidraeus was.

They are shielded from me, as they are shielded from you, Sidraeus said. At the way she deflated, his voice became almost gleeful. *You cannot stop what's coming. Clover will sacrifice them. Atheia will be whole again, I will have my body back, and you—*

"I won't let my friends die. There has to be a way to stop Clover."

A cruel, cold laugh. *Even if you were to reach the godsworld in time, how do you plan to stop him? If his power is an entire sea of ash, yours is but a tiny speck of dust. You stand no chance against him.*

He was right. And this was the conundrum they found themselves in, wasn't it? Because the only one who might stand a chance against Clover was Sidraeus, but he was trapped here. The only way he could regain his true form was if Atheia came back to life, and for that, Emory's friends needed to die. Which meant that as long as Sidraeus was in here, Romie, Aspen, and Tol still lived . . . but so did Clover.

There had to be another way. Sidraeus had done it before, had escaped his prison by slithering into Keiran's revived corpse. If all it took was another body . . .

That feeling of being watched slithered along Emory's spine again. She felt properly cold now, goose bumps running along her skin. Or maybe that was the dawning of consciousness, the chill of where she lay asleep seeping into her dream. Calling her back to herself.

Emory, Emory, the unseen souls of the dead whispered, as if trying to tell her a secret. As if hungering for her own soul.

Sidraeus withdrew into the darkness. *When you're ready to pay your debt, Tidecaller, you know where to find me.*

A trail of shadows caressing her neck was the last thing she felt before waking.

Storms raced across dark dawn skies like a grim omen of the day ahead. It hadn't stopped storming since they'd gotten here, rain falling in sporadic bursts, then quickly turning to snow, before the skies cleared for a blissful few minutes of sunshine that never lasted long enough.

Emory tried to keep her mind off the bone-deep cold that seeped through her damp clothes, but the clacking of her teeth wouldn't let her think of much else. This world was too quiet. There was only the howling wind, the distant thunder, and her own trembling. It was unsettling for a world that was supposed to be full of song.

Emory and the others had taken shelter under the sloped wall of a mossy cliff. Not quite a cave, but it offered enough protection from the elements. They'd managed to keep a fire going through most of the night, huddling next to it with woolly blankets they'd found in an abandoned village a ways back. They'd slept two to a blanket—Emory with Virgil, Nisha with Vera—too exhausted from the previous day's journey to mind the fact that their clothes were still damp and their bellies mostly empty.

A noise had them all tensing, but it was only Vivyan and Ivayne returning to their makeshift camp. The mother and daughter duo had accompanied them to this world—the fourth and final one before they reached the sea of ash. And thank the Tides they were here, or Emory and her friends never would have made it this far. The two women were draconics, able to sprout dragon wings from their backs, and seasoned warriors, too. They'd taken it upon themselves to stand lookout and scout the surrounding areas. And best of all, to hunt.

Ivayne held up a dead rabbit with a wide grin. "Breakfast," she proclaimed.

Emory felt her stomach rumbling at the sight, too hungry to despair over the cute bunny's death.

Today marked a week since they'd first arrived in this world. They'd come into it with a splash, stepping through this world's door, which had been a slab of ice-covered rock, only to fall into a scalding pool. For a moment, Emory had imagined they'd fallen into a fiery pit, the very belly of the sleeping volcano they'd left behind. But the warmth was actually pleasant and not flame at all but water a shade of turquoise so vivid, it looked unnatural. Steam wafted up in the air, which was, in contrast, completely frigid.

They'd all heaved themselves out of the steaming pool onto a mossy bank and immediately regretted leaving the warmth behind. The pool was set in a mountainous ridge of black rock and lush grass interspersed with patches of snow. In the distance, high, scraggy peaks glittered white against an angry sky the color of a deep bruise, all blue and black and purple. Lightning split the skies, the rumbling of thunder threatening to break the world apart.

Ever since, they'd been walking toward that distant mountain range. It was where the compass-watch pointed them to, and so they had to assume it was where they'd find the last door—the one that would bring them into the sea of ash where Clover had brought the keys. Where he planned to sacrifice Romie and Aspen and Tol to bring Atheia back.

It hadn't happened yet. Emory would have known this with certainty even if she hadn't just seen Sidraeus in the sleepscape, because whenever she used her magic, she could feel the pull of the keys from far away, as if her Tidecaller power were desperately seeking a source to fuel itself on. They were still alive. Which meant either Clover hadn't found the guardian yet—the last piece of Atheia, the soul to bind her blood and heart and bones—or he had but was biding his time, for whatever reason.

As they ate a meager breakfast of grilled rabbit, Emory told her friends of her encounter with Sidraeus. All of them took it as proof that the keys were still alive, if Sidraeus was still without his true form. They debated, for what felt like the hundredth time, why Clover hadn't sacrificed them yet.

"It's almost like he's waiting for us," Nisha said ominously. Her face was drawn, her eyes red-rimmed. "Like maybe he's luring us to the sea of ash, just like in the book."

Emory's heart lurched as their gazes met over the fire. If anyone here understood the desperation and premature grief she herself felt, it was Nisha, who had only just rekindled her romance with Romie. Some days, it felt like there was no point to keep going; that they would never be able to reach Clover in time to stop him from killing Romie and the others. And then they would have to mourn Romie all over again. Only this time, she'd be gone for good.

"If he were luring us to the sea of ash," Virgil said darkly, "you'd think he'd help us get there, not try to hinder us at every turn by sending his ash monsters after us."

They all glanced at the open wilderness outside their shelter, as if expecting said monsters to appear, conjured by Virgil's words. The ash-umbrae, they'd taken to calling them. The same creatures Clover had manifested back at the Sunforge, umbrae-like wraiths he'd created out of a mound of bones and dust.

Ever since they'd gotten here, ash-umbrae would sprout from the storms and the darkness, as if born of the lightning itself, and attack them relentlessly. Clover was nowhere in sight, but surely he had to be commanding them from afar.

And because the creatures were made of ash, no blade or physical weapon of any kind could impede them. Virgil's Reaper magic was useless too—ash itself was dead, so what good was it to try to kill what was already lifeless?

Only Emory's magic seemed to have any effect on them, and even that took a while to get right. She used the same principle as when she'd healed the umbrae in the sleepscape the first time she'd gone through the door in Dovermere. Unmaking them. Returning the ash to where it came from.

Without Sidraeus here to alleviate the dark side effects of her Tidecaller magic, without the keys nearby for her to borrow power from, Emory let herself dive fully into the depths of her power. No holds barred, side effects be damned. There were no limits to what she would do to reach that Godsgate in time. And she didn't mind the ghosts that appeared after she used magic anymore. Keiran's ghost was gone. She still saw Lizaveta, Travers, Jordyn, Lia, and all the other Selenic Order initiates who had perished in Dovermere, but most ghosts that flocked to her were faceless, unknowable. She found their presence comforting. Almost.

The souls of the dead are restless.

Sidraeus's words prickled unpleasantly along her skin.

As they erased all evidence of their camp and prepared to leave for another long day of trekking under hostile skies, Vera held the compass-watch in her lap, fixated on it as if to engrain the direction they needed to go in her mind. The compass had belonged to Emory's mother, and though it was technically Emory's now, she'd let Vera have it, thinking her cousin was more attached to it than she was.

Her *cousin*. Emory still couldn't wrap her head around it. If one good thing came out of this ordeal, it would be this expansion of her family. Getting close to Vera and hearing all about the Kazans had awakened a sense of belonging in her that she hadn't realized was lacking before.

It had always been just her and her father, but now, not only did she have a cousin, she had *three* aunts, too. Thanks to Vera's vivid stories, Emory felt like she personally knew Alya, Agata, and Ava, the three older Kazan sisters. Agata and Ava, the latter of which was Vera's mother, both still lived in Trevel, while Alya lived in Cadence, steps away from Aldryn College. It was a wonder Emory had never crossed paths with her—or maybe she had without even knowing.

Vera had also told her what little she remembered of Adriana, the youngest Kazan and Emory's mother, whom Emory knew as Luce Meraude. Though *knew* was putting it mildly, since she'd never met her mother and probably never would. This way, at least, she was no longer something so mythical.

"We've veered off path again," Vera noted, her eyes lifting to Emory. "I swear, each ash-umbra attack pushes us farther away from where we're supposed to go."

"It's a good thing we have that compass to stay the course, then."

As soon as they left their shelter, rain fell upon them, thunder rumbling overhead. Even without the ash-umbrae to impede their journey, it seemed the world itself was always against them: landslides, flash storms, anything to slow down their progress.

"I hate this place," Virgil grumbled as they walked, miserable and cold and already exhausted at the thought of another long day ahead of them.

Emory had to agree with him. This world might have been beautiful if it weren't so desolate. During the week they'd been here, they hadn't come across a single person. They'd stumbled upon one village, and it had been abandoned, most of it destroyed by some storm, or perhaps by something worse, like the ash-umbrae.

The silence, the emptiness, the raging storms . . . it was crushing their spirits. Especially since the mountain range still looked so distant.

But today, it seemed, they were given a bit of a reprieve.

Around midday, Ivayne returned from scouting ahead, her draconic wings unfurled, with a smile on her face. "There's shelter up ahead, not very far. Some kind of ruins."

The discovery couldn't have come at a better time as hail started pelting them. The ruins in question were at the foot of a waterfall, half-submerged in the flooded river that wound through the desolate landscape. The site was impressive: great carved pillars and broken sculptures, what could have been some sort of shrine, part of a wall that still stood with carvings of winged horses and great peaks among the clouds.

"Looks like this might have been a temple," Vera said with awe.

Emory could feel the ley line beneath them, corrupted as it was by Clover. It would have made sense to build a temple to the Celestials— this world's version of the deity that was Atheia—atop such a source of power. Part of the ceiling was still there, protecting them from the hail. The howling wind seemed not to reach them here either. True silence reigned, making Emory realize the constant wind had become so normal to her ears that she hadn't really heard it anymore. It was eerie. In her mind she heard those whispers from her nightmare, the souls of the dead calling her name.

Emory, Emory.

There was a sudden, earsplitting crack like the earth was splitting apart as a shaft of lightning hit the waterfall a mere few feet away from the temple. Ivayne already had her sword drawn in case the ash-umbrae showed up, despite it being useless against the monsters. Emory hurried to the draconic's side, magic at the ready. Another fork of bluish lightning split the skies, but not a single ash-umbrae appeared.

Something else did.

Across the river, a man sat astride a horse of pure white. Emory's first thought was that it was Clover, but the man's stature was too bulky, the frame of a seasoned warrior. He wore a navy jacket embroidered with silver details of lightning bolts and wind gusts, and had a heavy cloak draped over his shoulders, the hood drawn over his head. Gloved hands gripped the reins of his steed, which had feathered wings just like the creatures carved on the temple ruins. As beautiful and ethereal as Emory would have imagined a winged horse to be.

Except for the eyes. They were gaping, dark hollows ringed by knotted veins of black that spread all along its face and neck, marred its beautiful wings, too. As if it were corrupted from within. A ghostly, tainted version of what it once might have been.

The man held a hand to the skies and caught a bolt of lightning that fashioned itself into a wicked lance. In one swift motion, he threw the lance at the temple. It whirred past Emory, so close she felt it singe her cheek, and embedded itself in one of the carved pillars, crackling and sparking until the lance disappeared in a wisp of smoke. From that smoke appeared another man dressed in a similar outfit, holding a sword of lightning and moving on silent feet. They hadn't noticed him coming into the temple from the opposite side.

Vivyan threw herself at him with a battle cry, her metal sword meeting his lightning one in a thunderous clash. The man's lightning sword pierced through Vivyan's shoulder, making her scream. The smell of burning flesh filled the air. Before Emory could think of helping Vivyan with magic, before any of them could go after the man, a horde of ash-umbrae descended upon the temple swifter than the wind. The man disappeared among them, only to jump across the river with inhuman strength and settle behind the other warrior astride the winged horse.

As Ivayne and Vivyan swung their swords to no effect at the dozens of ash-umbrae that encircled their group, Emory opened herself up to the power of the ley line. Silver veins danced along her skin. She felt it burning inside her, power coursing through her like the cold burn of a distant star, and she unleashed herself to unmake the ash-umbrae.

She tried to reach farther still to the two men across the river, but she was burning out, depleting herself too quickly. Ash-umbrae fell around her, but more seemed to rise in their wake. Distantly, she felt the call of the pieces of Atheia, blood and bones and heart and soul, but they were too far away and felt shielded from her somehow.

The ley line tore through her. Ghosts sprung up around her. She tasted blood in her mouth, heard someone screaming in her ears— her own screams?—and felt her vision blur as unconsciousness pulled at her, seeking to plunge her into the dark.

Suddenly there was music.

A voice singing loud and clear, achingly beautiful. The dark skies above them split open, sunlight piercing through to chase away what was left of the ash-umbrae, which seemed to disintegrate to dust under the light.

Emory fell limp to the ground. Before darkness could claim her, she searched the riverbank, but the two men were no longer there, their infernal steed carrying them toward darker skies.

BAZ

I T WAS IRONIC, BAZ THOUGHT, THAT TIME SHOULD LOSE all meaning here, in the very place where it was spun.

He was surrounded by more clocks than he'd ever seen in his life, time-measuring instruments of all sorts, shapes, and sizes, and yet it felt to Baz like time stood frozen. Days and years might have passed without him knowing, were it not for the incessant ticking of clocks, a constant hum that followed him even in sleep. But they indicated the passing of time *out there*—in the four realms of the living where time flowed differently for each according to careful sets of rules.

In here, though, time was an endless loop.

Here was the workshop of a god Baz had magically stumbled upon. Maybe he should have been used to it by now, being dragged unsuspectedly through strange doorways. He'd traveled back in time to an Aldryn College of the past, had spent a lifetime obsessing over a book about a scholar who went to other worlds through a portal on a page, and still it had come as a shock to fall into one such portal. To find himself here, at the center of all worlds, in the presence of divinity.

Assisting the god of balance was meticulous work, tedious and time-consuming—or so Baz assumed; he knew time passed in here only by the hunger that seized him and the sleep he would fall prey to. He woke, filled his belly with whatever the god conjured out of thin air for him—the endless supply of coffee and tea was nothing to complain about—then got to work. Filled his belly again. Slept again. And again, the loop went on.

There was always something for him to do, whether it was dusting astrolabes or marking the pace of pendulums of different clocks for comparison. Tasks that felt useless to Baz, though they seemed like the most crucial of things to the frazzled god of balance. (If he had a name, he would not divulge it to Baz, who thought of him simply as *the god* and referred to him politely as *sir*, like he would any other professor.)

The real work revolved around the giant loom in the center of the god's workshop, which spun threads not only of time, Baz learned, but of *fate*—working past, present, and future into a great big tapestry that was the universe itself.

"I'm here to ensure all things happen as they should," the god had told Baz upon his arrival. There'd been an air of self-importance to his demeanor, a note of gravity to his voice that Baz would come to be familiar with. "Otherwise," the god had continued in this dramatic way of his, "the tapestry of fate would be ripped to shreds, the worlds forever skewed off-balance. Thrown into chaos."

Which was, understandably, the last thing a god who served balance wanted.

"But sir," Baz had asked, running a nervous hand along the nape of his neck, "why am *I* here?"

He'd wondered if his tinkering with time—all the tiny little threads he'd pulled throughout his life, all the bigger ones he'd more recently dared to mess with, like mending the Hourglass when he ventured into the past—had done something to anger the god and landed him here to face the consequences.

"Why, you're here to help me, of course," the god had replied with a gruff chuckle and a clap on Baz's back. "Time runs through your veins, and I'm here to show you how to use it to its full potential."

So the god showed Baz how the loom worked. He taught him how to use the warping board to measure and organize individual threads for weaving; how to work out small snags in the loom; how to properly gather the woven tapestry that piled onto the floor, shaking the fabric out flat as if he were making up his bed and watching it billow up and out into the stars beyond the workshop, where it disappeared into the dark.

"Where does it go?" Baz had asked, mesmerized.

"Into the universe," the god had replied, "and back again." At this, he'd pointed to the warping board where individual threads waited to be woven. "Past, present, and future are always being woven and unwoven and on and on. Time is a never-ending thing, you see."

Time hurt Baz's brain and only added to the misery he felt over not knowing how those he loved were faring. Images of that last moment with Kai haunted him often, how the Hourglass had barred Baz from following Kai through the door. He needed to know what awaited Kai and Luce and Clover, if the vision Luce and Clover had both seen about the worlds being reduced to ash—by a Tidecaller they had believed was Emory but was in fact Clover himself—would prove true. If this horrid fate could be changed.

But no matter how much Baz begged for answers, the god of balance would not tell him their fates, always keeping his replies short and vague and infuriating. "Mortals are better off not knowing the ins and outs of fate's design."

The god's responses only made Baz more desperate for the truth. And if the god would not share with him Kai's fate, then Baz would find out on his own.

So he set about studying, eager to excel at every lesson and task the god threw his way. Baz learned how to use his magic to manipulate the threads of time in ways he never had before, like unspooling them forward so that he might view an object's future. The principle was the same as pulling them back, but it was harder to do in practice.

"The past is easier to make sense of," the god explained, "because it has already happened and cannot be changed." When Baz argued that he and Kai had ended up in the past, and surely that meant they had changed it, the god shook his head. "You were always meant to travel to the past; and so the past always involved you. There has never been a version in which you did not find yourself there by some means. Fate's design can never be broken."

"So then isn't the future also set in stone, if fate is already written?" Baz asked.

"Well, yes," the god faltered, fiddling with the buttons of his waistcoat—a very loud floral print that he'd paired with a plaid jacket and brown tweed pants, a mismatched ensemble that should have been an eyesore but somehow worked for him. "But there can be variables in the road leading up to that fate," he continued, "which is why the threads multiply and unravel in ways your mortal mind could not keep up with. You would have to follow each thread separately to see the several different ways in which a thing might happen, but it will always lead to the same outcome."

Baz slumped in defeat. "Then what am I doing here? If nothing at all can be changed, what's the point of doing any of this?"

"The point," the god said, "is for you to learn. You have yet a part to play in your world. What knowledge you acquire here will serve you when you go back."

Baz asked the more pertinent question: "Back when?"

He had come here from the past—Aldryn College as it was in its two hundredth year of existence. But there was nothing left for him there. After being separated from Kai and the others who had gone through the door, Baz had intended to find a time rift that might bring him back to present-day Aldryn. Instead he had inadvertently found himself *here*, at the center of the universe, in the presence of a god who would not give him a straight answer.

"Back to your own time, of course," the god said as if it were obvious. He looked at the silver pocket watch he carried—one of four pocket watches attached to his vest, each one representing one of the four worlds, though if they told time or something else, Baz did not know. "Things there are getting worse," the god continued conversationally, as if he were discussing something as trivial as the weather. "Your arrival will be due soon."

"And what exactly am I meant to do there?"

"It would not be wise of me to say. Your part will play out the way it is meant to. You'll know what it is when it comes to you."

Frustration sang through Baz's veins. It wasn't that he did not want to return to present-day Aldryn and help however he could—especially if things were getting worse. But he couldn't help this sinking feeling in his gut, this unshakeable idea that, if he left this place and went back to the present, he would lose Kai for good.

Kai, whom he had last seen in the past. Kai, whose fate remained unknown.

It was clear to him that what Clover had set out to do—wake the Tides and the Shadow, save their worlds from being plunged into darkness—had not happened. *Would* not happen. Clover would bring them to ruin as his vision foretold. Baz himself had seen this in Thames's memory, a nightmare of Clover's where he and

Emory faced off against each other, two Tidecallers at the end of the world, one wretchedly evil, the other a source of light.

But if Clover was still alive in the present—having found a way to make himself immortal, perhaps—what would become of Kai and Luce? Surely they would not exist in Baz's time given that they'd left with Clover two hundred years ago.

If Baz left the past behind, he would never see Kai again.

It was not unusual for the god of balance to step away from the loom and become so engrossed with the workings of one instrument or another that he seemed to forget about Baz entirely.

Today what held his attention was a large piece of canvas he was hunched over, sketching like a man possessed. There were sketches scattered everywhere in the god's workshop, plans and designs for fancy clocks and whimsical gadgets and instruments of all kinds. Baz had never seen him quite so invested as he was now. With his thick black hair disheveled, his peculiar goggles covering his eyes, he looked like a mad scientist.

However tempted he was to get a closer look, Baz seized the opportunity to find the answers he was searching for. He approached the loom on quiet feet, and, after making sure the god was still preoccupied, put into practice what he had learned.

There were as many threads spun on the loom as there were living beings in the universe, each one showing how a singular life played into the larger tapestry of fate. Baz found the thread connected to Kai by feel alone, and with his magic followed it all the way to its beginning.

Warmth spread through him as Kai's life unspooled in his mind's eye: his birth, his first steps; the taste of his favorite Luaguan dish on his tongue; the ease with which he learned languages; the love he had for his parents, never diminished despite how abandoned he felt whenever they dropped him off at a new school and left him there while they traveled the seas for their trading business; the pride of getting the Luaguan symbols tattooed on his chest, his father explaining what they meant; the taste of nightmares, of Baz's specifically, how it felt to pull all the darkness away from the printing press scene.

Kai's first kiss. His first love. His first heartbreak.

Baz, a beacon in the dark.

All the thousand little moments they'd shared together in the Eclipse commons, past and present. And then: Kai going through the Hourglass after Clover and Luce, his hand ripped from Baz's as Baz was thrown back, barred entry, the door shutting between them with grim finality.

From here the thread of Kai's fate split into multiple thinner strands, each one harder for Baz to grasp. They unspooled in different directions, weaving through darkness and stars, sentient forests, what looked like the bottom of an ocean, a spiraling path of obsidian–

And then nothing.

All the threads frayed as if they had been cut off. Cleaved. Ripped at the seams.

Baz opened his eyes with a gasp, letting go of his magic as if it had burned him. His head and heart raced wildly, and he had to remember to breathe. In, out, in again.

He couldn't stop now.

Determinedly, he found the thread of Luce's fate and discovered it ended the same as Kai's. And Clover's . . . That one, he could not see the end of; it went too far beyond his reach, leaving him gasping for breath until he let go of it.

"There's a reason I kept this from you."

Baz whirled around at the god's voice. The god peered at him with sad, gray eyes, his goggles resting atop his head.

"What does it mean?" Baz didn't realize he was trembling

until he heard the words spill shakily from his mouth.

The god let out a heaving sigh. "Is it not obvious?"

Baz shook his head through tears. "They can't be dead. I know what death looks like, and that was not it."

The god had shown him before, what happened to a person's thread when they died. The bright, glowing thread simply became dark and kept going, unmoored, until it eventually returned to the warping board, shining once more.

"You're right. Death does not cleave one's thread," the god said. "When a life ends, one's soul is repurposed. Returned to the fabric of the universe. Think of an hourglass being flipped over, sand filling a previously empty bulb. An end becoming a beginning."

"So then why are Kai's and Luce's threads cut off?"

The god shifted uncomfortably. "There are things worse than death. I'm afraid the end of the Dreamer and the Nightmare Weaver is . . . an unmaking, if you will. Oblivion. That's all I will say on the matter."

"But how? That's not possible, not *natural* . . ."

The god looked at him with a quiet sort of pity, as if the answer were clear enough for him to grasp. And it was.

Whatever happened to Kai and Luce could only be one person's doing: Clover.

Guilt speared through Baz at the realization. Kai and Luce hadn't known what he now knew of Clover—all the horrible things Clover had done back at Aldryn, the people he had killed. They'd traveled with him to the Wychwood thinking he was a friend and ally, only to meet an abrupt end.

An unmaking. Oblivion.

If Baz gave in to the grief and despair gnawing at his heart, he felt he would suffer such a fate himself from the pain alone.

"There has to be a way to stop it," he begged. "A way I can change things. What good is my magic if I can't—if it means Kai—" He bit the inside of his cheek to stop from crying. "Send me back to the past. I can convince Kai not to go through the door. I can fix this."

"You can't."

Baz looked beyond the workshop, remembering all the doors to other worlds he'd passed on his way here. "Then I'll go after him through the Wychwood door. I'll help him stop Clover before–"

"This place we are in exists outside of time, boy," the god snapped. "You are no longer in the past. If you were to walk through that door, *any* door, you would find yourself back in your own time, where you belong. Kai is in the past, and there is nothing you can do for him. Fate cannot be changed."

"But–"

"Clocks," the god exclaimed, throwing his hands up in exasperation. "Let me show you, if you're so insistent, what would happen if you were to pick at the threads of the past."

He rifled through a pile of stray pendulums and gears and abacuses, grumbling to himself before he handed Baz an intricate brass scale.

"This," the god said, "allows you to explore different possibilities without actually disturbing the tapestry itself. I use it to interpret patterns, see all the different ways a thread might work itself into fate's design. See what might happen if someone were to change something here, erase something there."

"If the past can't be changed, then what's the point?"

"The point," the god growled, setting the instrument between them with an indignant thud, "is that even gods get curious."

Baz stared at the scale. "So how does it work?"

"Think of a significant moment from your past. A catalyst that would fundamentally change the course of your life had it not happened."

"The printing press," Baz said with confidence. "The day I Collapsed."

The god nodded and, with an enthusiastic flourish, produced two intricately carved wooden beads from one of his many pockets, one white, one black.

"This is your life as it is," he said, putting the white stone on one side of the scale, "and this is your life as it might have unfolded if you had not Collapsed." He set the black stone on the other side of the scale. "Hold that day in your mind. Now, watch the pendulum here in the middle of the scale . . . and let it show you what might have been."

The god gave the pendulum a little nudge, and Baz was hypnotized by the steady rocking motion. The god disappeared, the workshop, too, and he found himself in the printing press he so vividly remembered, almost as if he were in one of his nightmares. But Kai wasn't here, and this wasn't a nightmare. The scale was still in front of him, the pendulum swinging rhythmically, but the scene around him played out in rapid motion, a blur of color.

He saw himself as a boy with his father and Jae Ahn in their printing press. He saw Keiran's parents and Lizaveta and Artem's father enter. He saw the altercation between them and Jae just as he remembered it. But Baz did not Collapse. Keiran's parents and the Orlov siblings' father did not die.

A sliver of hope bloomed in Baz's chest. If he hadn't Collapsed, hadn't killed anyone that day . . . then surely Keiran would not have become obsessed with bringing back the Tides, would never have gone after Emory. Baz's own father wouldn't have ended up at the Institute. None of this would have ever happened.

But then the rest of the scene unfolded. No Collapsing on his part meant there was no stopping Keiran's parents from going after Jae, who was the reason they'd come to the printing press to begin with. A fight ensued, and in the chaos, Baz's father told him to run. He hid in a shop across the street. And when all was said and done, it was Jae who was brought to the Institute, hands bound in damper cuffs. Their secret–that they had been Collapsed for years–had come to light, and they would now receive the Unhallowed Seal.

The scale skewed off-balance. Fate thrown off course.

The scene shifted before Baz's eyes, the years speeding up as he followed the thread of everyone's life who had been at the printing press that day.

He saw Jae at the Institute, where they became a shade of themself, wholly unrecognizable. He saw his own father, a free man, but a haunted one; in the wake of Jae's arrest, Theodore closed up shop, the printing press long forgotten, and lost himself in obscure work trying to understand the Nullifying magic used in damper cuffs and the Unhallowed Seal to find a way to reverse the damage. His work ruffled some feathers, and he, too, ended up at the Institute for misusing his magic.

Baz followed the other threads, seeing Keiran at his parents' funeral years later, after another tragedy led to their deaths. Keiran still wound up on his quest to bring back the Tides, still went after Emory, still died in Dovermere.

Baz saw himself Collapsing years later to even more catastrophic results. It happened in Dovermere, on that fateful day he saw Emory slip through the Hourglass. Here he called on his time magic to try to stop Keiran from going after her, but since Baz hadn't Collapsed, since his magic was not yet limitless . . . This is where it finally happened. A great blast of silver light flooding the Belly of the Beast, killing everyone who was there as the cave crumbled onto itself–Virgil, Nisha, and the rest of the Selenic Order.

Leaving only Baz and Kai alive, their only way out through the Hourglass–where they were pulled, once more, back in time.

The pendulum suddenly stopped, and Baz found himself in the

god's workshop again, everything around him coming back into sharp, dizzying focus.

"You see?" the god said with a defeated, sad smile. The scale was completely off-balance, even though all of their fates had remained the same—or worse. "Changing the past is pointless. You might be able to sway individual threads, make things like death and destruction happen sooner or later than they should, but the larger picture remains an immovable outcome. Fate will always autocorrect, leading you down different paths that will still inevitably get you to the same destination. You can't unwrite what is already written."

There was a wistful note to his voice, as if he'd tried to do just that but could not.

Baz righted his glasses. "I can't accept that. I have to try."

The god sighed, muttering something to the darkness above them. He looked at Baz, studying him intently before saying, "If I do send you back to the past. If I give you the chance to try changing history. Will you let this go and return home?"

Baz gulped. "Yes."

Another sigh. "So be it. I will entertain this naive determination of yours." He rifled through his pockets. "If you reach the end of the sequence of events and fail to alter the outcome, you'll be brought back here, and the timeline will reset to what it originally was. You can then attempt to go back if you wish, however many times you deem necessary. But be warned—every time we reset, whatever change you did make may leave ripple effects. Small snags in the tapestry, not of fate in the larger sense, but in the threads of individuals you interact with. The more directly you try to change things, the more knotted their threads might become, which could lead to all kinds of, ah, unpleasantries in their future."

Baz blanched. "Unpleasantries?"

"Drastic changes in behavior, hallucinations, delusions, loss of touch with reality, distorted memories. That sort of thing."

The god handed Baz a pocket watch that fit in his palm, and for a moment Baz thought it was like the Veiled Atlas compass watch that Emory's mother had left her. It was similar, but made of bronze, not silver, its clockface full of symbols and lines and words Baz didn't recognize.

"You will need this to navigate to the past," the god explained.

He showed Baz how to manipulate the pocket watch. At the flick of a finger, a little magnifying glass popped out on the side, which would allow him to view past events, see how threads were connected in time. There was a dial he could turn to make time speed up, so that he wouldn't need to relive every second of the past and would be able to jump between key moments and locations as needed. Another dial made the symbols on the clockface come alive, which would render Baz invisible to unwanted eyes–his former self, especially.

"The repercussions of a past version of yourself coming face-to-face with the current version would be . . ." The god shuddered. "Just don't let past Baz see you. And for clocks' sake, don't lose the pocket watch. You lose it, you lose yourself."

"Meaning?"

"Ever seen a ship caught in a storm? That'll be you, adrift in the currents of time, and good luck finding your way back here then." The god closed Baz's fingers over the pocket watch. "Don't. Lose. It."

Baz's hands felt unbearably clammy. "Thank you," he said, trying to put on a brave face.

"Well." The god gave him a curious look. "Don't thank me just yet."

The god snapped his fingers, and shimmering threads of light pulled Baz back into the past.

EMORY

Emory must only have been out for a few seconds. She opened her eyes to Virgil hovering above her, saying something she couldn't hear, his voice muffled, distant. Above him, the sky had started to darken again. Emory sat up with a start, Virgil keeping her steady as she scanned their surroundings.

Not a single ash-umbra was left. The winged horse was nowhere to be seen.

Ivayne crouched over her mother, whose arm was badly hurt where the lightning lance had pierced flesh. Emory sent a wave of feeble healing power to mend the wound. Her magic still felt depleted, and she realized with new clarity that she hadn't been the one to chase away the ash-umbrae or the strange men.

That voice . . .

Her eyes caught movement nearby, where a child was staring at them, half-hidden behind a mossy mound of rocks.

The girl couldn't be more than seven or eight. She had red hair braided in a crown atop her head and wore a fur coat that was several sizes too big for her. Her eyes widened when she saw them all looking at her.

"Hello?" Nisha called out to her. "Who are you?"

The girl put a finger to her lips, then beckoned them over.

"Yeah, like that's not creepy at all," Virgil muttered.

"Should we . . . follow her?" Vera asked.

The child motioned for them to come with more persistence. And so, with little other choice, they did.

Storm clouds had gathered, angrier than before. Lightning the likes of which Emory had never seen lit the skies in neon blues and purples. The girl picked up speed as the wind did, great gusts of it winnowing around them in whirlwinds that picked up grass and dirt and snow and rain that lashed at their cheeks like arrows in a battlefield. Just when Emory thought the wind would knock them all flat on their backs, the girl fell over a ridge.

No, not a ridge–she'd jumped down into a trench, its sides made up of those basalt columns they'd found beneath the tree cavern back in the Wychwood. The girl pressed on one of the columns, which was no column at all but a door that looked like one, revealing an opening through which a grown man could just barely fit. She motioned again for them to follow, and this time they did without hesitation. It was either follow the creepy child or suffer the eerie storm, as Virgil pointed out.

As soon as they were all inside, the girl shut the door soundlessly behind her, and for a moment they were in utter darkness. Then– hundreds of tiny blue lights shone above their heads, illuminating the tunnel they found themselves in like a ceiling of stars. Nisha reached out a finger toward the pretty lights, only to draw back with a sound of disgust. Upon closer inspection, Emory realized why: the lights were glowworms.

"Over here."

This came from the girl, her voice barely above a whisper.

"Oh, so she does speak," Virgil grumbled.

And she wasn't the only one. Sound came alive down here, their own voices echoing against the rock walls. And farther down, the chatter and hum of voices reached their ears, along with the clash of pots and pans and the crackling of embers and the raindrop patter of some kind of cascade.

The tunnel opened onto a vast grotto that was in fact an entire village. Houses built into the walls, communal areas spread out between them. And though the people were indeed talking, they did so quietly. As if they were scared to make too much noise—which only begged the question why.

Their group got strange looks and murmurs thrown their way as the girl brought them to an elderly woman with silver hair and deep laugh lines who greeted them with a smile.

"Welcome, travelers. I'm Inga." Her voice and accent were lilting, musical. "We're glad you've made it this far. We've been expecting you."

Emory frowned. "How do you . . ."

"Know who you are?" Inga finished with a mischievous grin. "We have eyes up above. Saw you coming. Please, sit. Eat."

They didn't need to be told twice. Their group sat around a fire and devoured the bowls of stew that were handed to them. Inga was clearly these people's leader; they treated their elder with deference, and she exuded serenity and wisdom.

"What is this place?" Ivayne asked around a bite of food. "You're the first people we've seen all week—well, other than those men who just tried to kill us."

Inga nodded grimly. "The Songless. We do not claim them as our own." She motioned to the people around her. "We are what's left of our world, at least in these parts where the storms rage on. We left our homes to seek shelter here. From the storms—and the Soulless One's creatures." Her gray eyes peered at Emory intently.

"It's no easy feat to vanquish these beasts of ash the way you have been doing. You have power in you."

Emory squirmed under her gaze. "I wasn't alone in defeating them this time." She looked over at the redheaded girl who'd sat down next to Inga. "You're the one who sang out there, weren't you?"

The girl gave Emory a gap-toothed smile in answer. "They don't like it when I sing."

"Elín is one of the few of us still able to call on the Celestials' magic through song," Inga explained. She leaned in close to Elín and, in a slightly chastising voice, added, "But she must use that power sparingly so as not to anger the Soulless One."

Elín pouted but answered with a respectful, "Yes, elder."

"The Celestials," Emory began tentatively, "they're gods of yours?"

"They ruled the skies, long ago," Inga said, "forming a great pantheon of gods whose power we could call upon with music."

"Music is what gives a soul to the universe," Elín recited proudly, "so the Celestials give miracles in return for us feeding that soul."

Inga pinched her cheek. "That's right. Songs were like bargaining chips. Different instruments and melodies were associated with different Celestials. There were innocent songs, the ones that called on the more benevolent Celestials who powered us with small magics. Speed and strength, courage and love, talent and renown. Heightened tracking skills. The ability to not grow cold in winters. Protection over one's flock. A talent for storytelling or dancing. Then there were the songs one dared not play unless willing to accept the consequences that came with the more powerful Celestials' magic. Stopping avalanches from swallowing villages whole. Diverting storms. Healing abilities that could pull someone from the brink of death. These types of magics came with consequences."

"What kind of consequences?" asked Emory, eyeing Elín.

"It varied depending on the Celestial who answered. Some had to give years off their life. Others would simply find themselves quickly depleted of energy after wielding their miracle."

"I get headaches," Elín said. "But they don't last too long. At least the Soulless One hasn't taken my voice."

"*Yet*," Inga said pointedly, and Elín's smug smile faltered. "The Soulless One was once part of the same pantheon of gods as the Celestials. If the Celestials were gods of peaceful skies and order, responsible for things such as the turning of the seasons and the small miracles of life, then the Soulless One was the god of storms and mayhem. Disruption of nature. They worked in tandem with one another. Equally revered and respected. But then something changed. All we remember is that the Soulless One brought down the entire pantheon of Celestials, silencing them forever. He made himself into the sole deity of our world, ushering in this dark, songless reign of storms and terror."

"You mean he still lives?" Virgil asked, frowning.

"Oh yes," Inga said gravely. "Who do you think is responsible for these endless storms? Who controls the creatures who terrorize our world, those soulless beasts made of storm and dust and death? The Soulless One is hunting for songs, for power. Has been for as long as I can remember."

Virgil met Emory's eye, and she knew what he was thinking. The Soulless One was supposed to be this world's version of Sidraeus. But how could that be, if Sidraeus had been trapped in the sleepscape for centuries?

"What about those men we encountered who wielded lightning bolts and rode winged horses?" Vera asked.

Inga seemed to consider her words. "We call them the Songless. Back in the age of Celestials, they were considered . . . different. Blessed, by some standards, because they did not have to call on any god with music to wield magic. Cursed, some would say, for their power was that of the Soulless One: the ability to call on storms. It's no wonder they still follow the Soulless One today. They are his faithful warriors, terrorizing any who come in their way."

It sounded like the Songless were the equivalent of the Eclipseborn, the result of Sidraeus's magic, like the hellwraiths in the Wychwood and the eldritch beasts in the Heartland.

"Has no one been able to stop the Soulless One and his followers?" Emory asked.

Inga sighed. "We had thought–hoped–that one of our own would defeat the Soulless One and bring back the Celestials, but . . ."

"Orfeyi!" Elín exclaimed. "He's my cousin and his song healed his mother, but he was struck by lightning and survived, which means he's Godstouched, and then he took the lyre up the mountain and–"

Inga laughed, stopping Elín's excited rambling. "Take a breath, child." Her gaze trailed over to a woman sitting alone not too far from them, her face drawn, her eyes red-rimmed. "Orfeyi healed his mother with magic more powerful than anything we've seen in a long time. So we sent him to the Godsgate not so long ago, but he never returned to us. And since the storms have kept raging and the Soulless One seems to have grown more powerful . . ."

She didn't finish her thought, eyes darting to an unsuspecting Elín with profound sadness. Emory understood. Orfeyi clearly hadn't defeated the Soulless One.

"Did Orfeyi have a mark like this?" she asked, showing Inga the spiral scar on her wrist.

Inga's eyes went wide. "Yes. That–you are Godstouched too?"

"Sort of. We're not exactly from around here."

Virgil choked on a laugh. "That's a subtle way of saying we're from another world."

Emory shot him a look. But Inga didn't seem fazed by this in the slightest.

She gave them a sly smile. "I know where you're from. Travelers from other worlds. The Veiled Atlas." She pointed to Vera, then Vivyan—who both had a Veiled Atlas compass hanging from their neck. Inga produced her own identical compass. "This was passed down from elder to elder, each of us tasked with watching over the door that leads into our world, waiting for the travelers we knew would one day come and help us stop the Soulless One."

Emory put the pieces together in her mind. If Orfeyi had the mark and, supposedly, a power unlike anyone else, he had to be this world's key, called to the sea of ash to bring back the Celestials—Atheia—the same way all the other keys had been called there too.

A realization struck her. The Soulless One that Inga described... if it wasn't Sidraeus—couldn't possibly be—then it had to be Clover. He must have stepped into the Soulless One's shoes, so to speak; made himself into the villain of these people's mythology. Taken Sidraeus's place and twisted his role into something entirely evil.

Clover had wormed his way into the sea of ash, absorbed all the power from the original keys, then from the gods' fountain itself, growing into this monstrous thing he now was. Then, unable to reopen the doors back to other worlds, he must have found a way to at least keep the Godsgate open between the sea of ash and this world that was so intricately connected to it. An extension of his prison, which he'd then lorded over for years as the Soulless One.

The original Soulless One, the real Sidraeus, was never feared here. When he and Atheia disappeared—he, imprisoned in the sleeping realm, and she, splintered across worlds—the magic in this world remained in the Songless, with their ability to wield lightning bolts, and in those who sang to the skies, calling on the magic of whom they believed to be the Celestials. The same way people from Emory's world still had magic from the Tides and the

Shadow, even after the deities had left their shores. The same way witches were blessed by the Sculptress, and some, like Bryony, were hellwraiths touched by a netherdemon, the dark rival of the Sculptress. The same way the draconic knights were given hearts of gold made of dragon flame, this gift created by their Forger, and the Night Bringer's eldritch beasts still roamed the Heartland.

Sidraeus and Atheia's magics lived on in these worlds without them. A legacy unbroken.

Until Clover.

Because now that the worlds were dying, now that magic was on the verge of extinction, that legacy would fade. There would be nothing left but Clover and his reign of terror.

Unless they found a way to stop him.

"We're trying to get to the Godsgate," Emory said. "To stop the Soulless One from making himself into something even more evil. If he succeeds . . . Orfeyi will die. Along with three of our friends who've been taken captive with him."

Inga went pale but gave a resolute nod. "We will send our best rangers to guide you to the foot of the mountains. But only those who are Godstouched can go up the mountains themselves. You will have to go the rest of the way alone."

They talked of preparations and logistics, deciding they would stay the night to get properly warm and rested for the first time since they'd arrived in this world. In the morning, they would leave.

"One last thing," Inga said. "Orfeyi has with him a golden lyre. The instrument is ancient, hailing from the era when our pantheon of gods still ruled the skies. Back then, there was a myriad of such instruments, each one tied to a different Celestial, all lost or broken now like the temples they were forged in. But this lyre is something we have kept safe for centuries. It is rumored to have been the original instrument with which the Celestials gave life to the universe. We believe it to have many powers, one of them being the ability to bring back the Celestials and ask for their favor in healing our world. In the hands of someone like Orfeyi, it has the potential to do wonders. But in the hands of the Soulless One . . ." Her face was ashen. "It could spell the end of everything."

"This lyre," Nisha said, "it sounds like the one the guardian has in the book."

The beginning of an idea formed in Emory's mind. "Are there other such instruments? One that might have been tied to the Soulless One as he once was?"

When Inga hesitated, Emory told the elder her theory. That the one terrorizing their world now wasn't the Soulless One of old, but Clover, someone from her own world. That the real Soulless One was gone, just as the Celestials were.

Inga sat with this information for a few minutes. Slowly, she said, "There are rumors of a great number of powerful instruments hidden in the ruins of old temples to the gods like the one you found up there. Most of these temples are high in the mountains you will travel through to reach the Godsgate. If what you say is true . . . well, there are stories of a syrinx."

"Did she say a *syringe*?" Virgil whispered in Vera's ear. She swatted him with an annoyed *shh*.

"A *syrinx* is a pan flute," Inga said with an indulgent smile. "It is said to be made entirely of glass, formed by lightning striking sand. According to legend, it once was able to tame even the most destructive storms and quell all chaos."

Lightning. Storms. Chaos. This had to be tied to the Soulless One.

The elder peered at Emory. "Be careful in the temples. The Songless have been drawn to them of late, as you witnessed firsthand. We do not know what power resides in these ruins. Evil loves to fill the empty spaces left by divinity."

Emory understood that better than Inga knew.

She thought of what the Selenic Order had believed about whoever managed to bring back the Tides. That they would earn the Tides' favor, be able to use it for whatever they desired. If the people in this world believed something similar about the Celestials, that whoever brought them back might earn their favor . . . What if it was all true? What if, by bringing Atheia back, Clover would have control over her? And by bringing Sidraeus back, he'd have control over him, too. Over both deities, who would then be powerless against him as he used them to make himself into a god.

Unless someone else brought Sidraeus back first—earned his favor.

And wielded it against Clover.

Emory found the crowned umbra in the sleepscape again.

The dream was the same as last time. Dovermere. The hourglass. The tree trapped inside. Glass shattering, Sidraeus appearing in his shadow form. And again, they were in that empty space surrounded by the chilling presence of a thousand invisible eyes.

This time, at least, Sidraeus did not attack her.

Back so soon? his voice crooned. *Can I take this to mean you're ready to repay your debt?*

Emory hugged her arms to ward against the cold and the unsettling feeling of being watched. "You keep talking about this debt I owe you," she said, "but what about yours?"

Mine? came his baffled reply.

"All those Tidecallers you sacrificed."

The ones whose blood had been spilled to seal the doors between worlds—Sidraeus's own creations, whom the gods had viewed as such a threat to their godhood, they'd been ready to burn down their realms and rebuild them from scratch just to ensure such a power never saw the light of day.

"Saving my life doesn't make up for what you did to them."

Emory regretted saying anything at all as the swirling shadows around Sidraeus thickened dangerously, those fathomless eyes of his sucking her in like black holes.

I've already told you their sacrifice was inevitable, he said, low and threatening. *And this isn't about them. This is about what you can do for me.*

"What exactly do you have in mind?" she asked, if only to defuse the tension, indulge him for a second.

The shadows seemed to retract a bit. *I would have asked that you bring a body into the sleeping realm so that I might possess it as I did Keiran,* Sidraeus said. *But I suspect you're too far from the door to reach me in time.*

"Is there no other way to reunite you with your true form? Without Atheia being brought back first, I mean." Or her friends having to die.

If there was, do you really think I'd still be wasting away here?

"The people in this world believe there are ancient instruments able to summon their gods," Emory pushed, watching for his reaction. "A lyre that might bring back the Celestials and earn their favor. A pan flute that could do the same for the Soulless One. They call it the syrinx."

Ghostly voices rose in an incoherent cacophony, as if summoned by the name. Emory had the distinct impression they were trying to tell her something, but her focus remained on Sidraeus—and the cold fury that emanated from him as shadows thickened around his form.

The syrinx, he repeated, *is said to be lost.*

He didn't deny the potential it had to summon him, and Emory latched onto this wild hope dawning inside her. "What if I find it? If I bring you back with it and—"

No. If you find that cursed instrument, you must destroy it.

There was something hiding beneath the strain of his voice that she hadn't expected. Fear, she thought. From the ruler of nightmares himself.

"Why?" she asked.

Because if it were to fall in Clover's hands, he would use it to bind me to his will, rendering me powerless. But break the syrinx, and I will help you defeat him once I regain my true form.

Emory shook her head. "It'll be too late by then."

His voice lashed out in exasperated anger. *Your friends will die, Tidecaller. The sooner you accept that you cannot save them, the better.*

"I can't do that."

Then you condemn us both to die too.

He spoke it as incontestable fact, but Emory knew it to be a lie. The fear in his voice at her mention of the syrinx, the ghosts' agitated whispers in the dark—they were proof of this instrument's power, of what she now knew with utter certainty she must do with it.

"No one has to die if I find the syrinx," she told Sidraeus. "Not to break it, but to use it as you say Clover would."

To bind Sidraeus to her own will.

As the weight of her words settled between them, Emory willed her subconscious to wake, leaving the dream and him behind before the angry, swirling shadows that lashed out of him could reach her.

BAZ

ONE SECOND, BAZ WAS IN THE GOD'S WORKSHOP, AND the next, he was once again standing on the windswept cove of Dovermere, half-hidden behind a rocky outcrop as he watched himself emerge from the sea.

It was the oddest thing in the world to see himself not as a reflection in a mirror or a face in someone's memories, but the *real* him as he had been the night he and Kai appeared in the past. Glasses askew, drenched and shivering from the cold, so pale as he fought for breath.

From his vantage point, Baz couldn't hear the words his past self and Kai exchanged, holding on to each other so tightly as the rising tide rolled in around them, but he remembered in vivid detail how Kai had calmed him. He ached to have that now–Kai's soothing, solid presence at his side.

But he was alone, and he had no Tides-damned idea what he was doing.

As he watched them retreat down the beach toward Cadence,

Baz thought to follow them. Maybe he could stop them before they even set foot at Aldryn.

Just don't let past Baz see you.

Maybe not, then.

Finally tearing his eyes away from the boy he'd been and the boy he was trying to save, Baz made his way up the secret stairs to the Eclipse commons. He needed a plan, and he needed to be smart about it.

Things he did not wish to change: his relationship with Kai. All the tiny, beautiful moments that had made butterflies flutter against his ribs, that had sent his heart into a racing gait, that had set all his nerves aflame. He could not bear a reality in which they never kissed. A reality in which Kai never peeled off his armor to lay bare his feelings for Baz. A reality in which Baz never realized that what he felt for Kai had been there all along, slowly evolving into something undeniable.

Things he must change: Kai going through the door with the murderer that was Clover.

One way or another, he had to prevent this one thing.

The Eclipse commons were thankfully empty, Thames and Polina probably at the Bicentennial's opening ceremony. Baz paced in front of the fireplace, trying to come up with a plan.

He could start small. Leave Kai a note telling him not to go through the door, not to trust Clover—which Kai never really did to begin with, come to think of it. But would Kai be confused by this so early on? Be even more suspicious of some ominous note telling him *not* to do something? That would probably only entice him to do it more.

Baz could set crumbs. Pave the way for Kai deciding not to follow Clover. Or he could outright expose Clover for what he was. That would solve it. It would solve everything.

But Clover was cunning. He'd left no evidence of what he'd been doing. Even his journal, which Baz had studied at length, gave nothing away, or was too obscure to make sense of. Baz would have to catch him in the act. He knew from Thames's memories about the atrocities Clover had committed: the four students he had killed the night of the velleity party. Louka, Cordie's boyfriend, whom he had killed not long after.

If he could make past-Kai and past-Baz see the kind of monster Clover was . . .

All his pacing made him lose track of time. Voices outside the commons had Baz scrambling to hide behind the curtains just as Polina came in with his past self and Kai. Heart pounding wildly in his chest, he stared at the pocket watch in his hand, forgetting which dial would make him invisible. Was it the one on the left? Or was that the dial that sped up time?

He looked up to see Polina had gone to bed, leaving his past self alone with Kai in front of the fireplace, with Kai staring at him so longingly that it was a wonder past-Baz had ever questioned Kai's feelings for him.

Baz's heart swelled to see that look. But it plummeted as he thought of everything the god had said. Maybe he was right, and the past couldn't be changed, and Baz would never see Kai look at him like this again.

And if this time was all they had together, who was he to change it?

No. I have to try.

Baz turned the knob on the right of the pocket watch—and the scene before him sped up, night bleeding into day, over and over again, until he glimpsed a flash of navy and copper. He abruptly let go of the knob, and time returned to normal. In the middle of the commons, his past self stood in a copper suit, and Kai in a navy one.

He recognized these outfits, the trepidation on his own face.

This was the night of the velleity party.

The first of Clover's murders.

The invisibility worked. It let him pass by Kai and Baz, still getting ready to leave for the party, without them even blinking his way. Brushing past his own face, seeing how nervous he'd been . . . Tides, this was strange. But he couldn't linger, had no time to waste.

Baz rushed to the Decrescens library ahead of them, desperately trying to remember where Clover and Thames had hidden the unconscious bodies of the four students they would kill in a twisted experiment once the party ended.

But Baz couldn't find the bodies. He recalled Clover putting up a ward to shield them from unwanted eyes. If he could pull back the threads of time to before that ward was up, if he could draw past-Baz and Kai's attention to the bodies . . . Surely they'd find out Clover had had a hand in this.

Except he was running out of time, knowing full well that past-Baz and Kai would show up any minute now. He eyed the pocket watch, suddenly remembering the magnifying glass that flicked open on the side. If it allowed him to view past events, could it show him where Clover and Thames had stashed the bodies?

He brought the magnifying glass up to his eye and peered at the library through it, focusing on the velleity painting that opened onto the secret ballroom beyond it. It didn't seem to do anything until he started to see students walking backward out of the secret room, the threads of time unraveling, playing out the scene in reverse for him. Finally he saw Clover and Thames coming out of the room and followed this strange, rewinding vision of them through the library until they were huddled in a dark corner, standing over the unconscious bodies of Wulfrid and his Eclipse-hating friends.

Baz withdrew the magnifying glass and headed for that same

dark corner, where he tripped over something invisible and fell face-first to the floor, the pocket watch shooting out of his hand. He fumbled to get it back, his hands coming up against something fleshy and warm instead. A body, most definitely. Dread sluiced through him. He pulled back the threads of time around what he knew to be four unconscious bodies, until the ward was no longer around them, and they were plainly visible.

But without the pocket watch, Baz was *also* visible. And those were footsteps coming his way—and his and Kai's voices drifting toward him.

Baz paused time. Found the pocket watch. Activated the invisibility knob, then unpaused time and, panicking about how to get Baz and Kai's attention, knocked a few books to the floor, wincing at the damage. He couldn't help himself—he felt like he was hurting the books. But the resulting noise had the desired effect:

"What was that?"

His past self's voice, a slight tremor of fear laced through it.

Baz could see himself through the shelves. His past self's hand had shot out to grab Kai's arm upon hearing the noise.

"Dark corner of a library where a party's going on?" Kai said, a sultry note beneath the teasing in his voice. "Isn't hard to imagine what that was."

His midnight eyes lingered on Baz's hand on his arm, before slowly raking up to look at him. They stood so close. Past-Baz looked flustered, cheeks burning red. He quickly removed his hand and cleared his throat.

Tides, even present Baz felt flustered, even as part of him wanted to wrest Kai's mind out of the gutter. This was serious—and more importantly, this was *new*. He didn't remember this conversation happening, which must mean he *could* change the past.

And yet . . .

"I don't like this," he heard his past self saying.

"The fact that you, Basil Brysden, are going to an actual party? Or the fact that said party goes against the rules?"

"Both."

This, he remembered.

And as present-Baz watched the scene unfurl, a gutting thought occurred to him. If he did manage to get past-Baz and Kai's attention, if they did see the bodies, their night would be over before it could start. Baz wouldn't find himself dancing close with Kai, wouldn't finally come to terms with this attraction between them. And if not tonight, then when? Would he ever realize he had feelings for Kai or be confident enough to act on them? Would they ever kiss?

Did it matter, if he managed to save Kai in the process?

He glanced at the unconscious students beside him, rethinking his entire plan. Past-Baz and Kai seeing them here would prove nothing. Even if Wulfrid were to talk, it wasn't enough to prove that Clover and Thames had meant to actually *kill* them.

This whole thing suddenly felt beyond him. Baz stood frozen with fear, the way he used to be before. Unable to act as a thousand different scenarios ran through his mind, each worse than the last.

What if he messed everything up?

It was the image of the threads of Kai's fate severing that finally got him moving. He threw another pile of books on the floor, more forcefully this time, just as past-Baz and Kai reached the velleity painting. They looked at each other.

"Now tell me that wasn't creepy," past-Baz said.

Kai frowned at the shelves, taking a step toward them.

Yes, just come and have a look, you ass, present-Baz thought, face smushed between the shelves.

A soft sound made him whip around, thinking Wulfrid or one of his friends had regained consciousness. But it wasn't them. It was Clover, standing over the four of them with a mildly panicked look on his face, puzzling over why his ward had vanished. Clover threw a glance over his shoulder, then quickly used his magic to make them invisible once more.

Damn it, Baz thought as Clover sidestepped the bodies.

Clover stopped with his foot in the air, tensing as if he'd heard something. As if he'd heard *Baz*. Clover's gaze went to the fallen books. He bent to pick one up, and his eyes slowly traveled up, searching the empty space where Baz stood, invisible.

As if he knew Baz was there.

An edge of fear. Something darker honing to a sharp point. Because as Baz stood there, a foot from the man who had betrayed everything he believed in, who was a murderer and the source of all chaos to come, a wicked thought crossed his mind.

If Baz were a killer, he could end this here, now.

He already *was* a killer, wasn't he? Had killed before, an accident, yes, but would it be so different now if he did so intentionally, if it was for the greater good?

"So you're the one making all that noise."

Kai's voice tore Baz from his thoughts. His heart stopped, thinking he'd been discovered. But Kai didn't see him. He inspected the fallen books Clover crouched over, then looked around for someone else. He raised a brow. "Having fun all on your lonesome?"

Clover slapped on one of his easy smiles. "Something like that." He put the books back on their shelves and casually leaned against the frame. "Truth be told, I was waiting for someone." He looked Kai over as if to say, *Not who I was expecting, but you'll do.*

A hint of jealousy reared its head up in Baz before he saw the flat, uninterested look Kai gave Clover. "Party's that way," he said before rejoining past-Baz.

And just like that, the bodies were forgotten, an opportunity missed.

Despite being invisible, Baz couldn't risk going into the ballroom after them. Too many dancing bodies to weave through undetected. But as he paced around the empty Decrescens library thinking of his next move, Thames came barging through the hidden door looking like he was going to be sick.

And that's when Baz remembered the bloodstain on Thames's jacket—and the doubts that would be creeping into Thames's mind right about now. He had seen this before through Thames's own eyes, from the memory Polina had extracted from his dead body. And this doubt, he might be able to use to his advantage. Get him to turn Clover in.

Baz started to follow Thames, but a sudden prickling sensation on the back of his neck made him stop dead. He turned, peering around the dark, empty library. He had the distinct impression someone was watching him.

When he turned back, Thames was gone.

Baz deflated. It probably wouldn't have mattered anyway. Despite all his doubts, Thames was too enamored of Clover to turn his back on him. It was the great tragedy that would lead to his own death.

A string of more failures followed.

First Baz tried to keep his past self and Kai at the party after hours so that they could catch Clover and Thames in the act of killing Wulfrid and his friends, to no avail.

Next he sped time up to the night he and Kai had caught Clover emerging from the Vault—which also happened to be the night Clover and Thames brought the bodies up into the library to make it look like Wulfrid and his friends had been killed by the Vault's vicious wards. But he failed to alert past-Baz and Kai to Thames's presence, and Clover seamlessly managed to divert their attention so they never saw him handling the bodies.

Before the authorities were alerted and the bodies moved, Baz decided to damn the risk and seek out Polina. She was the first person his present self interacted with, pretending to be past-Baz, and he hoped she wouldn't look too closely at the slightly longer length of his hair or the different clothes he wore. If she noticed anything off with him, she didn't say, and eagerly agreed to come with him to the library, where he convinced her to use her Enshriner magic on the corpses of the four students to extract their memories so Clover would be ousted.

But Polina came up blank. "It's as if their memories have been wiped clean," she said, frowning at the bodies. "Could the wards have done that?"

Baz grumbled a noncommittal response. He knew without a doubt that Clover had wiped the corpses' memories using his magic. Covering all his tracks like the clever fox he was.

Everything Baz tried backfired. But he kept going. Had to.

Wondering if the changes he sought to enact were too direct, he shifted gears and tried leaving subtle clues instead. And when neither Kai nor past-Baz picked up on any of them, and time kept ticking forward until it was the night they were to break through the wards and disappear behind the door in Dovermere, Baz resorted to blatant desperation.

He found Kai alone while past-Baz had gone to tell Cordie the truth about what they were doing. If Kai knew he was not *his* Baz– at least, not exactly–he did not show it. Kai only looked at him with an arched brow, dark eyes glinting with amusement.

"Back so soon?" Kai asked.

"I, uh . . ." Words escaped him. Because here he was actually talking to Kai again, and for a moment, he could pretend everything was right. He wanted to draw Kai close, pull him in for a kiss. Get lost in his eyes, his voice.

But all he saw in the back of his mind was the thread of Kai's life, cleaved by a fate worse than death.

Whatever you do, don't go through the door. The warning was stuck in his throat. Would Kai believe him, if he were to speak to him so bluntly?

"Brysden." Kai's brows were knit together. "What's wrong?"

"I think you were right not to trust Clover," Baz said, opting for the truth—as much as he felt he could divulge of it.

Kai immediately grew tense. "What did he do?"

"It's what he's going to do. What he said about Emory bringing about the destruction of the worlds . . . It's not true. It's *Clover* who will do that, not Emory."

Kai studied him for a moment, expression unreadable. "Look, I know I gave Clover a hard time," he said tersely, "and I know you're dead set on thinking there's no way Emory could do this, but you have to face the facts here."

"What if we don't have all the facts? What if Clover manipulated the facts to make himself look like the hero?"

"What about Luce, then? She had the same vision as Clover. I don't see how both of them could be wrong about this." He frowned at Baz. "What prompted this, anyway? You were team Clover a minute ago. What changed?"

I saw how it ends. "I just have a bad feeling."

"About tonight?"

And what comes after.

"I know you're nervous," Kai continued. "You don't have to be. But if you don't want to do this, I'm with you. We'll head to Harebell Cove, try to go through this time rift Luce spoke of. We'll find another way. But Baz? I know you can do this."

Baz wanted to cry. *Lie,* a voice in his head said. *Tell him anything that will stop him from going through that door.*

Tell him the truth.

It's what Kai would do.

"Don't freak out," Baz said slowly, "but I've seen this all happen before. Because I'm . . . I'm from the future."

Kai gave him an odd look. "Yeah, you and me both."

"No, I mean, I'm not the same Baz who came here with you." He took a deep breath. "In a few minutes, Baz is—*I* am going to walk in here, and I'm going to tell you that Cordie's coming with us tonight. And then we're all going to go unpick the Vault's wards, and I need you to listen to me, because something really terrible is going to happen."

"You're freaking me out here, Brysden."

"I know, but—just listen, please."

And Kai did. He listened without interrupting as Baz told him everything that would happen, how they would get separated by the Hourglass, how Baz would later find out everything Clover and Thames had done, the murders, the Tidecaller synth. How Baz would pen their favorite book and be transported to the very center of the sleepscape, where he would meet the god of balance and learn of the grim fate that awaited Kai and Luce.

Kai was quiet for a while after, making Baz think maybe he'd broken his brain. Was there a rule the god forgot to tell him against divulging someone's future?

"I know it's a lot to take in," Baz said. "I know you probably don't believe me, but—"

"I believe you."

He met Kai's eyes, so stark and bright with trust.

"You do?"

A muscle feathered in Kai's jaw. "I swear, if that piece of shit Clover thinks he's getting away with this . . ."

"Kai?"

Baz's voice drifted toward them—*past*-Baz's voice. He was back.

Panic seized present-Baz. He gripped Kai's hands. "No matter what you do, promise me you won't go through the door. Please, I can't lose you."

Before Kai could reply, before his own past self could see them together, Baz turned the dial on the pocket watch, the symbols on its surface coming alive to make him invisible. Kai frowned at the space where he disappeared, then at Baz's invisible hand as it squeezed Kai's arm. His eyes fluttered shut.

"I promise," Kai whispered.

For the first time, Baz thought there might actually be a chance to change both past and future—and save the boy he loved.

KAI

KAI SALONGA HELD ON TO ANGER THE WAY MOST PEOPLE kept once-treasured souvenirs long after they'd lost any meaning. It was a permanent bitterness in his mouth, a taste he could never wash out. Whatever fleeting peace he had experienced at Baz's side during their time at Aldryn—both in the past they'd been pulled into and the present they'd left behind—had only been that: brief delusions of sweetness he would never get back.

If Kai weren't so angry at the world, he might have been able to appreciate the enchantment of the Wychwood. Even with the rot that had started to spread, the beauty of the woods persisted, and the witches, for their part, remained absurdly optimistic and steadfastly rooted in community spirit despite the so-called netherdemon possessions that had become all too common among them.

Tonight the witch twins' estate gardens were all aglow with candlelight and music and the sound of merry laughter. A celebration thrown in honor of Oleander and Asphodel, the twin sisters who ruled the coven–and Clover, who'd made himself into their white knight. The would-be savior of the Wychwood.

This story they were living out had all the makings of a fairy tale, but Kai knew better than to be fooled by pretty facades. And though this was *reality*–at least, Kai assumed it was, but who could say nowadays?–darkness seeped into him as if it were the sleepscape and he were pulling all the shadows from a nightmare.

It clung to him now, that darkness, as he sat alone in a shaded corner of the garden. Two older witches walked by him murmuring behind their hands and throwing wary glances his way.

Kai glowered at them. *"What?"* he snapped.

The effect was instant; the witches scurried off, leaving him in Tides-damned peace. Kai knew all these witches wondered if *he* was a hellwraith–if a demon might have taken his soul, given his perpetually foul mood and the way his magic made him act out. The only reason no one ever said anything to his face was because he was Clover's right-hand man, and no one dared to reproach Clover and his entourage.

It had started when they'd first come through the door, leaving Bicentennial-era Aldryn behind to step into this version of the Wychwood that was eerily similar to the one from *Song of the Drowned Gods*. They'd stumbled upon the ascension of a witch, an adolescent boy emerging from the earth where he'd been buried alive for the Sculptress to unlock his magic. The boy's eyes had gone pitch-black and his body had floated in the air, throat bared to the night sky as he took a great, gasping breath. This had set the witches into a frenzy. They'd screamed about netherdemons tainting the boy's soul, had marked themselves as if to ward off evil, their fear growing rampant as fallen leaves and dirt and branches floated off the ground to swirl around the boy's levitating form.

That's when Clover had stepped in, shining bright with magic.

Kai still wasn't sure what happened, what magic Clover used, but it got the boy to come down, the leaves and dirt and branches too, and everyone grew calm as the boy's eyes went back to normal, then closed peacefully, as if he'd been lulled to sleep.

The witches hailed Clover for pacifying the boy—the hellwraith, they called him, a witch who'd been touched by a netherdemon while he was buried. Netherdemons, they believed, were hellish forces from the underworld that sought to claim a witch's essence. They were the antagonist to the Sculptress. The Shadow to the Tides, as Kai understood it. When a hellwraith ascended, they did so with magic that defied the usual scrying of witches. Magic that was deemed wrong.

A witch's magic was always rooted in the earth. They tethered their essence to the physical world through one of the five bodily senses, while their sixth sense, or third eye, wandered what they called the astral plane. A hellwraith was different. They did not need bodily anchors, because their magic did not come from the earth, but from the astral plane itself. It allowed them to leave their bodies entirely, to possess others, *control* others; to move matter with their minds and levitate and even commune with the dead.

While the Sculptress's magic was a passive thing, acts of clairvoyance that did not interfere with the natural world, magic influenced by the netherdemons was all about manipulation. Disruption. And because so many witchlings were suddenly ascending as hellwraiths, the coven feared that the netherdemons were getting stronger. That they were trying to slip through the cracks of the astral plane and into the Wychwood. The rot that had started was proof that something was amiss.

And so hellwraiths were being pushed to the brink of society, forced to form their own dark coven of sorts, with Clover as the mediator between the two groups, the light-touched hero who could appease a hellwraith's possession by taming the netherdemon within.

"Are any of them actually possessed?" Kai had asked Clover, with all the skepticism of someone well acquainted with fear and hatred from people who viewed his own magic as other. The look Clover had given him all but confirmed his suspicions: a hellwraith was only this world's equivalent of an Eclipse-born, no more possessed by a netherdemon than any of them were cursed by the Shadow. And Clover was merely using this tension between witches to prop himself up in their eyes, convince them of his trustworthiness.

Kai surveyed the celebration now, spotting Clover laughing with Oleander or Asphodel—Kai could never tell them apart at first glance. The girl ducked her head shyly, hiding a pretty smile. Asphodel, then. She was the more impressionable one, always quick to blush at Clover's honeyed words and stolen glances. Like a damn flower unfurling her petals under the sun that was Clover. It hadn't taken long before the entire witch coven knew the pair was courting.

The other sister, Oleander, was stony-faced as she observed her giddy twin. Oleander's displeasure at Asphodel and Clover's courting, the wariness with which she regarded Clover, hadn't slipped Kai's notice. Nor did the way Clover's mask fell whenever Asphodel wasn't around. It was clear to Kai that Clover had no interest whatsoever in the poor girl—in any girls, for that matter. He was courting her purely to convince the witch to come find the door with them. And Kai had to give him credit: it had worked. They were leaving later tonight.

Kai took a long sip of mulled wine and made a face at the taste. He missed his flask. He missed the bitter, herbaceous taste of gin to dull out the sharp edges of his anger. He missed being in his own world, and he missed not being so affected by his magic.

He missed Baz most of all.

There it was again, that all-consuming fear he hadn't been able to shake since Baz's hand had slipped from his and the door had closed between them with a finality akin to death. *Promise me you won't go through the door,* Baz had pleaded with him, as if he'd known they'd be separated. And Kai had gone anyway, ignoring his warning. No, he'd been *forced* to go through the door while Baz was made to stay behind, both of them manipulated by Clover's Glamour magic. Right?

Kai took an even longer sip of wine, hoping to drown out the confusion in his mind. He was misremembering things. Anytime he tried to recall what happened before going through the door, it was like grasping at wisps of dreaming. Frustrating, useless, and downright maddening.

"Are you doing all right?"

Luce sat down next to him, and it was as if the churning of Kai's negative thoughts stilled at her presence.

"Fine." He handed her the wineskin. "*You* look like you could use a pick-me-up."

Luce gave him a thin smile as she reached for the wine. "I'll feel better when we leave this place."

She watched the merriment of the witches with the same wariness Kai had. She was still pale from their earlier encounter with yet another ascended hellwraith that Clover had "purged" of demonic influence–using his Tidecaller magic to calm the hellwraith girl, who like all hellwraiths had been erratic in the first moments of her ascension, lulling her to sleep long enough for her to be handed over to the hellwraith coven. Discarded of like a plague victim.

"We both know this place isn't the problem," Kai said tightly, eyes darting to Clover.

"Don't say that."

Luce's voice was an indignant whisper, her eyes wide as she glanced at Clover like she thought he might have heard them. But this was the reality of Clover putting on these great shows of power to subdue hellwraiths: it was never him who was left depleted of energy, but Kai and Luce.

When Clover used his magic in big ways, Luce's face would become ash white, as if all the blood suddenly left her body. She'd even passed out once. And Kai . . . He realized he could see darkness rippling off Clover, clinging to him when he plunged into his Tidecaller magic. Almost as if he were about to Collapse . . . but never did. Because that darkness seeped into Kai instead.

The same way Kai would absorb darkness from a nightmare. Except the darkness wasn't coming from a nightmare, but Clover himself.

At first, Clover seemed oblivious to the fact. And when Kai brought it up, he waved him off, insisting Kai and Luce must simply be vulnerable to the demonic energies roaming free in the Wychwood. Once they left, they would feel better.

But they all knew better. They all felt it, this bond between them. A triad of power. Tidecaller, Dreamer, Nightmare Weaver.

Perhaps the truth of that bond was this: that Kai and Luce were conduits for Clover, sources of power for him to feed on. Clover gained strength from Luce, the blood key, and deposited all the dark side effects of his magic onto Kai.

And now the darkness Kai kept unwittingly pulling away from Clover was weighing him down, pushing him to act out in waking, and making the nightmares worse than they'd ever been.

Maybe Clover himself is a nightmare, Kai had thought more than once. A nightmare disguised as a dream, just as the Wychwood appeared to be. Spinning pretty words and grand promises of a world that could be healed. Words like flowers in a garden bed used to hide the ugly corpse lying beneath the rotting soil.

I think you were right not to trust Clover, Baz had said. But why that was, Kai couldn't remember.

Kai gave a long, frustrated sigh. "Tell me again how we went through the door," he asked Luce, turning to her once more for a way to stay grounded to reality.

Luce gave him a worried look, as she always did, but told him what he so desperately needed to hear. Thames's Collapse. The Treasury crumbling down around them. Clover, Luce, Kai, and Baz heading down into the glowing pool that brought them into the Belly of the Beast, where Clover and Luce opened the door—the two of them now bearing a silver spiral mark on their wrists to prove it—and went through before the tide came crashing in.

Baz shoved back out, as if the door had denied him entry.

That part had always remained clear in Kai's mind. It was the details leading up to it that were hazy. Ever-changing.

"I know this has been hard on you," Luce said quietly. "But we're so close to reaching the next door, one step closer to preventing the vision Cornelius and I saw."

Kai gave a sharp laugh, motioning toward the woods. "Look around you, Luce. The supposed netherdemon possessions, the rotting, it all started when we got here. You really still believe Clover's going to save us all?"

"I do," Luce said without hesitation. But something in her tone felt forced, like she were trying to convince herself as much as Kai. "He got us this far, and if he's the answer to saving my daughter, then I'll follow him to the end."

Clover, Emory, the destruction of worlds. They had set out to change the outcome of the vision both Luce and Clover had had, but if they were trying to bring back the Tides and the Shadow to prevent the worlds from falling into chaos two hundred years from now, why then was the Wychwood rotting here and now? It seemed to Kai that whatever apocalypse they were trying to stop had already been set in motion, as if by coming here, they had set the first domino tumbling forward.

Maybe the problem was Clover. Or maybe Kai was suspicious for no reason. All he knew to be real was this darkness and anger that weighed on him, that had him questioning his own sanity.

It was almost as if the darkness was becoming too heavy for him to carry, and Kai felt like he was reaching the limit of his supposedly limitless power, tumbling toward another Collapsing.

In his mind, he saw Thames Collapsing over and over after he'd injected himself with the Tidecaller synth. As if his body could not hold that much power.

What if the same was happening to Kai now? He was taking on Clover's darkness, the dark underbelly of his Tidecaller magic. And it was stretching his own power thin. Soon it would break, collapse in on itself. And this time, Kai knew it would plunge him forever in darkness.

The Shadow's curse indeed. Perhaps there was some truth to it after all.

Mindlessly Kai traced the tattoos on his collarbone. "You know, in the Constellation Isles," he said, seeing in his mind the place of his birth and aching for it with a fierceness he hadn't thought possible, "we believe the Shadow sacrificed himself to the Deep to save the world. It's why we Luaguans tattoo the story of his sacrifice on our skin. The practice started with Eclipse-born long ago, but nearly everyone in Luagua does it now. It's meant to ward off evil of all kinds. For Eclipse-born, it's supposed to keep us safe from the dark side of Collapsing. The Shadow's curse." Kai snickered. "A bunch of bullshit, apparently. I'm going mad, and I don't know if–if I can–"

Luce put a delicate hand on his arm. "I'm right here with you. I'm not going to let you go mad."

It was true that being around Luce abated some of the darkness around Kai, clearing his mind. As if the Dreamer were a balm against the nightmares. She was only a few years older than him, but already she had the countenance of a mother. She would have been a great one to Emory. A shame they probably would never get to meet.

"We should get some sleep before we leave," Luce said. "Will you be all right?"

Kai gave her a tight smile. "I'll be fine."

The lie tasted worse than the wine did. So he kept drinking until it was true.

Later, when partygoers started to scatter for the night, Kai found himself in a quiet corridor inside the twins' manor. He sat on a windowsill overlooking the garden, with only his wine and morose thoughts for company. Footsteps echoed in the candlelit corridor, and Kai spotted Clover and Asphodel coming up the stairs. He watched from his perch in the shadows as Clover kissed Asphodel's hand demurely, and she boldly kissed him on the cheek, saying something Kai couldn't hear but knew sounded suggestive. Clover whispered something back, and then Asphodel disappeared behind her bedroom door, alone, giving him a pretty smile before it shut.

Echoing footsteps again as Clover came Kai's way.

"Moving on so quickly after Thames?" Kai asked, knife-sharp. "Didn't take you long to forget about him."

Clover's mouth tightened. For a second, Kai thought Clover might punch him for bringing Thames up. He would have welcomed the violence. But Clover hung his head and fidgeted awkwardly, as if he didn't know how to act.

"I'll have you know that I think of him often." Clover's voice was gruff, his throat bobbing with emotion. "He haunts my every step."

His eyes darted to dark corners, as if he were seeing Thames's ghost. Kai had never seen him so destabilized. Unguarded.

"Did you love him?" Kai asked.

Clover blinked at him like he'd just asked if the sky was blue. "Of course I did. Why would you ask such a thing?"

Kai merely shrugged and took a sip of wine. "Just seems to me you're rather enjoying yourself with the witch. Plus, you never talk about him."

"Asphodel is a means to an end, you know that." Clover swept the wineskin from Kai's hand and drank. "And I talk of Thames as much as you talk of Baz. Seems to me we're both mourning in quiet." He gave the skin back to Kai. "At least I'm trying to be productive."

Kai snorted. "If that's what you call manipulating that poor girl."

"Would you rather this had all been for nothing? That Thames died for us to just sit around here watching the worlds rot? That you will never see Baz again because you will die here wallowing in your self-pity?"

Now it was Kai's turn to send him a look that promised violence. Perhaps Clover knew he was itching for a fight, and he was riling him up for that very reason. Clover held Kai's gaze with his own impenetrable stare. And finally he sighed, leaning back against the windowsill Kai was sitting on.

"I apologize," Clover said, looking at his hands with something like defeat. Contrition. He traced the silver spiral on his wrist. "You're right. This place . . . with everything that's going on, I haven't let myself properly mourn Thames. I fear if I start reminiscing about him, I will think of Delia, and Polina, and all the world we've left behind. I fear I will falter and not do what's needed of me at the end." His throat bobbed. "The fears are too many. If I open the door to grief, to the memory of Thames, how deeply his death has wrecked me . . . I won't survive it."

Kai kept silent. He understood these fears more than most. Hiding behind armor. Making himself into an impenetrable fortress. It was what he'd always done. What he'd started to *undo* thanks to Baz. What he had to do again now to keep himself from crumbling.

Clover's hand on his made him look up. His turquoise eyes shone with regret. "I know it hasn't been easy," Clover said, low and raw. "For my part, I apologize. But we mustn't turn on each other, or lose hope." He leaned closer, full of determination. "We *will* make this work. And in the end, we will be reunited with those we love, I'm sure of it."

"I wish I had your optimism," Kai said. He'd meant the words to be brittle, sarcastic. Yet they came out softer, and he realized the admission was true. "But you're not the one slowly losing your mind."

"You're not losing your mind, Kai." Clover grabbed his face and turned it so their eyes locked again. "And this optimism?" he said. "It can be shared."

Kai felt warmth pour into him, a feeling of lightness he hadn't known since going through the door. His eyes fluttered closed as the feeling deepened. He realized that Clover was using magic—Soultender magic, no doubt, to alleviate this dark cloud of emotions that hung over him. And though part of him hated being manipulated in such a way, Kai had to admit it was nice to finally feel like he could *breathe*.

"You see?" Clover whispered, making Kai open his eyes to find him smiling softly. "You don't have to carry this burden alone, Kai. I'm here for you if you need me."

The Soultender magic amplified further, making Kai lean in, craving this feeling of elation. Of lightness.

It dawned on him then how close he and Clover were. Clover still had a hand on his, another cupping his cheek, long fingers snaking their way behind his neck, threading into his hair. The candlelight cast flickering shadows on Clover's face, which softened with a kind of openness Kai had never seen on him before.

The pale turquoise of his eyes darkened as they flicked to Kai's mouth, full of longing. Clover's thumb swept over Kai's cheek, his lips parting as he drew nearer, evidently taking the fact that Kai had not yet pulled away as an opening.

But Kai could see right through him. Behind the longing, the lust, there was just a boy looking to replace what he'd lost. A Nightmare Weaver for a Fear Eater. One Eclipse-born for another.

"Is this how you got Thames to worship at your feet?" Kai felt Clover stiffen as he leaned in to whisper, "Because it won't work on me."

Kai pulled back to see the hurt in Clover's eyes, the vicious storm sweeping over his features as he snatched his hands back in indignant defeat, unexpected rejection.

A swell of satisfaction washed over Kai, even as the dark cloud of emotions returned with a vengeance now that Clover was no longer using his Soultender magic on him. Because that was what Clover was: a carefully crafted illusion. A masked manipulator. And here Kai was calling him out on his bullshit, poking holes in his relationship with Thames, wondering if it had ever been real.

I just wanted you to love me! Thames had yelled at Clover at the last. *I wanted you to value me, to appreciate how far I was willing to go for your vision–our vision.*

Death. That was how far Thames had been willing to go for Clover. Kai doubted the reverse would have ever been true.

His question to Clover remained unanswered, but the fury in Clover's eyes was answer enough. They both knew Kai could not be so easily duped–not when he'd seen the truth of Clover from the start.

Kai slid off the windowsill. "Better get some sleep," he threw over his shoulder. "Sweet dreams, Cornelius."

He hoped it sounded like the threat he'd intended.

ROMIE

ROMIE BRYSDEN REMEMBERED THE MOMENT HER LIFE fractured like a tree trunk being cleaved in half, splitting into two distinct eras: before her father Collapsed, and after.

The before was full of happiness. It was bright and comfortable and warm. It was baking with her mother, the scent of pastries filling the Brysden household. It was playing outside with Baz, spending all their summers under the old willow tree behind the house. Play-acting scenes from *Song of the Drowned Gods*. Lying in the grass and watching the willow leaves dance, rustling curtains parting to reveal clear blue skies. It was the certitude that life was good, that no harm could ever be done to her or her loved ones. That nothing could ever burst this dreamy bubble of existence.

It was naive. It was rosy-hued glasses that eventually shattered, forcing her to see the reality beyond her bubble.

Her father's Collapsing made Romie notice all the cracks of darkness that had been there from the start. The frailty of her mother, who became rudderless without her husband. The fear that had always shaped her brother, which inevitably made him into a recluse, a ghost. The slippery, dangerous nature of Eclipse magic, this thing that Romie had grown up with, had always viewed as being part of her the way her family was part of her genetic makeup, the way they all shared the same blood. She had never understood why others sneered at and feared and othered Eclipse magic, until the proof of its destructiveness altered everything she'd believed.

Her father, this sweet, gentle man, turned into a killer because of it. Branded for the unstable magic in his veins. Held in the unsettling prison that was the Institute because of an accident, yes, but a crime nonetheless. (Much later, she would learn the truth about this day—that her father was not the one to blame for the rupture in all their lives, but Baz, who had Collapsed unknowingly, only for their father to take the fall.)

Back then, a part of her understood that her naive worldview was forever changed. But Romie hadn't *wanted* it to change, not when everything was already changing so much around her. Her father, gone and labeled a criminal. Her mother, fallen into a pit of depression so deep nothing seemed able to help her crawl out of it. Her brother, pulling back from Romie and everyone around him to the point where she feared she might lose him, too.

Someone had to be the glue that held them all together. Someone had to try to mend this rip between before and after. Romie wanted things to be like they used to be, joyful and loud and full of love. She wanted to silence this voice inside her that perked up whenever someone showed fear toward Eclipse-born, this dreadful, horrible voice that found itself *agreeing* with them. Because if someone as innocent and careful and steadfast as her father could do such horrible things with his magic, she'd thought, then no one was safe from the Shadow's curse, this unhallowed destruction.

Romie hadn't wanted to fear her brother's magic or let this resentment for her father take root in her heart. So she'd put those rosy-hued glasses back on. Fought to bring that innocent, naive joy of the past back into their lives by remaining bright and buoyant despite all the hardships her family was going through. Because if she didn't, everything would be plunged into irreparable darkness.

Act the part of the brave dreamer.

That was what she had done then, what she had done at every turn since.

What she was still doing now as she awaited her own death.

But death, Romie found, did not come as swiftly as she'd anticipated.

The concept of day and night did not seem to exist here in the sea of ash, where perpetual gloom reigned. Romie could only tell the passing of time by the rising and falling of daylight on the other side of the door—which was permanently open, giving them a glimpse of the mountain range beyond.

Romie and the other keys—Aspen, Tol, and Orfeyi—made a home among the dried-up fountain, which was so vast it looked more like a temple than anything. A circular base with five columns rising all around, doming over them in a trellis that joined in the middle of the fountain, where five giant statues stood, meant to represent the gods. A thick layer of ash covered their faces like dust, rendering them featureless. Unknowable. The gods all stood back-to-back against a tree emerging in the middle of the circle they formed, its branches bowing over their heads. The tree seemed made of glass, and though its crystal-like leaves were dusted with ash, Romie knew they must have once caught the light and reflected it in the most beautiful way.

As far as imprisonment at the hands of a monstrous god went, theirs wasn't so bad. They were provided food and water and blankets to fend off the numbing cold. They were not bound or gagged or restrained in any visible way, but it was clear they were prisoners all the same. Romie suspected Clover's magic kept them here, by the same persuasive power that had them all lulled into comfortable complacency at the thought of what awaited them.

Sacrifice. That was what Romie and the keys would face. In order to bring Atheia back to life, they needed to return the pieces of themselves that were Atheia's—Romie's blood and Aspen's bones and Tol's heart and Orfeyi's soul. Their human deaths for the life of a deity.

"A fair trade, wouldn't you agree?" crooned Clover.

And they did agree. Romie was no longer sure if it was because of Clover's magic or if it was her own belief. There was, of course, a large part of her that did not wish to die, to leave the world she knew behind and abandon those she loved. But then, this was the destiny she'd been barreling toward. The song she'd answered. The fate she'd been ready to die for. And the way Clover explained why it needed to be done, the picture he painted of what he'd do once he made himself into a proper god with the combined power of Atheia and Sidraeus . . . it made her *want* to believe in his vision. It made all of them believe that their deaths weren't only inevitable but justified. Glorious, even.

Once Clover made himself into a god, he told them, there would be no more divide between Atheia's creatures and Sidraeus's. Lunar mage and Eclipse-born, witch and hellwraith, draconic and eldritch, those who sang to the Celestials and the Songless who answered to the Soulless One. They would all be on a level playing field, answering to the same god. They would, all of them, know the kind of limitless power that Tidecallers had.

And wasn't that what Romie had always wanted? To know all the magics of the lunar cycle, to be more than just a Dreamer of House Waning Moon?

Her sacrifice meant she would never get to experience this

for herself. But she would die a hero, and maybe that alone was worth it.

Sudden music made Romie's ears perk up. Orfeyi was playing a melody on his lyre, and the notes reverberated within her, sharpening her focus. It was like waking from a dream, though not the kind she was used to; in fact, she could scarcely access her magic anymore, didn't even remember sleeping, thanks to whatever sorcery Clover had them under.

But as Orfeyi played his lyre, it was like the fog around her mind cleared, and she was herself again. At her side, Aspen and Tol seemed to come out of similar stupors.

Orfeyi smiled at them. "Welcome back."

All at once, the memories came rushing back to Romie. This wasn't the first time Orfeyi brought them out of their trance. He did so whenever Clover left them alone in the sea of ash—which Clover did often, claiming to be searching for the final pieces needed for the ritual. He'd recently returned from one of these outings with a terribly burnt hand and a wild, furious gleam in his eyes, raging about an instrument he could not touch but needed desperately to wield. Romie remembered him saying something about Emory, how he was waiting for her to join them before he could sacrifice the keys.

This should have set off alarm bells in Romie's mind, should have pushed her to ask questions, but this amenable lull Clover had them all under kept her quiet. Pliant.

Until Orfeyi played his lyre and made Romie and Aspen and Tol remember what Clover made them forget: that he was, in fact, the enemy.

It was a peculiarity they couldn't explain, that Orfeyi was the only one of them not affected by Clover's magic. He had told them before that it was because of the golden lyre he had with him, a gift from the Celestials, which Clover had foolishly let him hold on to.

"The Celestials," Orfeyi had explained—his world's version of the Tides, and the Sculptress, and the Forger, versions of Atheia from each world, "speak to me through the lyre, making me see the truth of Clover when you three cannot."

Romie supposed Orfeyi was calling not on the Celestials themselves, given that they were gone, but on their magic—just like lunar mages could call on the magic of the Tides, even though the Tides weren't physically there to answer them anymore.

Magic just *was*; in each world Romie had visited, it existed beyond its creator.

She caught herself marveling at the root-like scars that adorned Orfeyi's pale skin, just as she had the first time he'd snapped them out of Clover's spell, and every other time after. Lightning burns he'd gotten after attracting the Soulless One's wrath, he'd explained. "The man who's keeping us here," he'd added at their blank stares. "Clover."

"That's not who you think it is," Romie had argued. The Soulless One was his world's equivalent of the Shadow, but Clover was neither; he was something worse.

But Orfeyi had shaken his head in protest. "I know exactly who Clover is. The Celestials whisper of him through my lyre. He is the Tidecaller who will bridge the gap between worlds, the one who will bring the Celestials back into a single form so that they will be strong enough to cast away the looming dark." He'd leaned in to whisper his next words. "Except the dark is *him*. He isn't to be trusted. He will try to control the Celestials, control *everything*. We mustn't let him."

He thinks we can best the drowned gods, just like the guardian in the story, Romie had thought. She'd felt a swell of fondness for him then. Even though they'd just met, it was like she'd known him forever. They were mirrors of each other, she realized. Dreamers, both. Not by the magic they wielded, but by their intrepid natures, their willingness to go to extremes to see things through, no matter the cost to themselves.

Besting gods more cunning than them hadn't worked for the heroes of *Song of the Drowned Gods*, but could it work for them? Clover was no god. Yet.

They'd been trying to find a way to stop him from achieving that goal ever since. He was never gone for long, but it gave them enough time to scheme—and get to know one another.

There was nothing like impending doom to make people bond the way they had. It was rare, Romie thought, to know a person so completely, to trust them so implicitly, after spending so little time with them. She had already begun to feel that way with Aspen and Tol, but it was even greater now that their group was complete. Four parts of a whole waiting in death's undeniable shadow.

"How long do we have until our divine overlord comes back?" Romie asked now, glaring at the open doorway in the distance, where a few guards stood to ensure the keys wouldn't leave. *The Songless*, Orfeyi had called them.

"Not sure," Orfeyi said, "so we'd better make this quick."

The four of them lay down next to each other, ready for sleep to take them. It was a loophole that Clover seemed unaware of, that whenever Orfeyi's lyre broke whatever influence he had on them, they were able to access their magics. Romie still needed to bloodlet to call on her Dreamer ability, and did so now with a sharp wooden splinter she kept hidden in her pocket for this very purpose. A pinprick against her index finger—she couldn't afford anything bigger in case Clover noticed—and Romie dipped her hand in a cup of water.

As she drifted to sleep, she dreamed.

It was an easy thing to guide the others' sleeping consciousness into the sleepscape with her, as she had done before with Aspen and Tol in the Heartland, where they had seen a vision of Atheia. They found themselves on the path of stars and began their desperate search for answers—for Atheia's presence, her guiding hand and counsel. As it always did, the song soared around them, the harmony complete now that the four of them were here together.

That was usually the extent of it, the song bringing with it no visions of the deity who was fractured within them. But today, there was something desperate in the song, a note of urgency in the layered, feminine voices.

A hundred stars appeared all around them, dreams or visions calling for their attention. One of them burned brighter than the others, diamond-like and beautiful. Romie grabbed it, guiding the other three with her into the dream.

And there she was again. A woman with kaleidoscopes for eyes and a braided crown of iridescent hair.

Atheia.

"Please," Romie murmured, "tell us how we can save ourselves—show us how we can bring you back without dying, and without it all having been for nothing."

If the ritual worked as Clover intended, if the keys let themselves be sacrificed to bring Atheia back into a single body—then Clover would have dominion over Atheia. He would sacrifice her to the fountain and gorge himself on her power until there was nothing left of her, in true Tidethief fashion. And he would do the same to Sidraeus.

That song in Romie's soul, which was echoed in Aspen and Tol and Orfeyi, seemed to screech at the thought. From the look on Atheia's face, it was clear she didn't want this; couldn't bear to be controlled by a monster like Clover.

Atheia cupped Romie's cheek, and a strange, wordless exchange passed magically between them. The threads that bound the keys together appeared, shimmering light between the four of them. They connected to Romie's pulse points, before flowing back into Atheia like blood vessels connected to a main artery. Atheia looked at Romie with those hypnotic eyes, as if willing her to understand. But understand *what*?

The only thing that was clear to Romie was this sense of urgency emanating from Atheia. This bleak understanding that they were running out of time; that Clover would soon have what he needed, and the ritual would proceed unimpeded. Unless they could stop him.

Atheia's crystalline voice pooled into her mind. *Act the part of the brave dreamer.*

And with that, Romie was shoved out of the dream.

The four of them lay gasping in the sea of ash, staring wide-eyed at one another.

"Did you all see . . . ?" Romie began.

Orfeyi nodded fervently. "Yes."

"Atheia," Tol breathed in wonder.

Aspen's brows knitted together. "But what was she trying to tell us?"

Romie had no idea, but the urgency of it all coursed through her veins. They had to try again, had to decipher whatever this ghost of Atheia was implying.

"He's back."

Tol's defeated whisper brought their attention to the silhouette making its way through the gate. Clover had returned. It wouldn't be long now before the keys were under his spell again—or pretending to be, in Orfeyi's case—all thoughts of Atheia forgotten.

Before the lull of Clover's magic could efface all her agency, Romie shared a look with Orfeyi, knowing he understood her without words.

She needed to head back into the sleepscape—needed to dream

again so she could try, for what felt like the hundredth time, to reach Emory or Nisha or any of the others. To warn them to stay away and keep Emory out of Clover's reach, because for some reason, Clover believed the sacrifice could not happen without her.

Orfeyi needed to play his lyre as soon as he got the chance, with or without Clover gone, so they could finish what they'd started. Before the clock ran out on all their lives.

EMORY

THEY LEFT INGA AND HER COMMUNITY ACCOMPANIED by two gruff rangers who would take them to the mountains—two older men with pale complexions, reddish-gold hair, and thick beards that reminded Emory of her father. Inga had given them all horses, magnificent beasts with a hardy build, thick manes, and large hooves covered with shaggy hairs, and so they traveled by horseback through fjords and glacial valleys, the journey made daunting for those of them who had little to no experience riding horses. Which, as it turned out, was all of them except for Vera.

At the quizzical look they'd all given her when she expertly got on her very large horse while the rest of them fumbled awkwardly—Ivayne and Vivyan most of all, muttering about draconics not needing mounts, cursing the stormy skies that made it too dangerous for flying—Vera had merely shrugged, a smug smile tugging at her lips. "I grew up around horses. My mother was an equestrian."

Emory had felt a pang of longing, reminded yet again that there was this entire side of her family that she didn't know–that she would love to one day meet, if they ever got the chance to go home.

Their path coincided with the direction the compass pointed them in, which was promising. Most of them managed to get the hang of riding after a long day of it, though by the time they stopped for the night, they were all aching and sore. Virgil looked about ready to keel over, which Vera made a point to tease him about, especially after he had claimed that very morning to be familiar with riding and had spent all day showing off as he tried to measure up to Vera.

"Fine, I lied," Virgil grumbled. "Closest I've ever come to a horse is watching the races. My parents used to take me every summer we spent in Trevel."

Vera snorted. "I forget that you're from a prominent Selenic Order family. The posh sure do love their horse racing."

"Says the equestrian." Virgil contemplated her with amusement. "I wonder if our paths ever crossed."

"Doubtful. I don't make it a point to hang out with pretentious racing enthusiasts who don't actually care about the horses."

"*Pretentious?* Now I'm just insulted. And I'll have you know I care about horses *deeply*."

He recoiled in fright from the neighing horses they'd tied nearby, making Vera laugh and Emory bite back a smile, wondering if there was something brewing between the two.

Thick pine trees rose around them, sheltering them from the elements. While they ate around a fire, Emory used her healing magic to relieve everyone's aching muscles. Ghosts sprang up around her, called by her power, but she had gotten good at ignoring them. Still, she found herself wishing for Sidraeus's presence, the way his proximity always seemed to absorb the darkness of her magic.

She had to find the syrinx.

The thought had consumed her all day as they traveled. She'd kept her eyes peeled for any temple ruins lying nearby, had asked their guides about them, too, but they reiterated what Inga had already alluded to: that most ruins would be found in the mountains proper—especially any temple once dedicated to the Soulless One.

Emory did not sleep that night, afraid to face Sidraeus after she'd told him of her intentions with the syrinx. He wanted her to break it—had been adamant about it, clearly terrified of it being used. But if the instrument was like the lyre Inga believed could bring back the Celestials and earn their favor—if it might bring back the Celestials' counterpart, the *real* Soulless One, and bind him to whoever used it . . .

Then Emory had to get her hands on it. She had to be the one to use it, to bind Sidraeus to her and stop Clover once and for all.

It took two full days of riding to arrive at the foot of the great chain of craggy, snowy peaks that rose to impossible heights. From here, they would start up the base of the highest mountain, which the guides called deceptively easy; snow did not reach these tree-lined parts, and old steps were carved into the gentle incline to ease their ascent. But soon enough this path would become treacherous.

In the shadow of the mountains, everything was dark and desolate, pine trees drooping with eerie moss, not a bird or insect to be heard. There was something in the air that smelled foul, making Emory suppress a shiver.

"This used to be a place of ethereal beauty," one of their guides said, eyeing the peaks with equal parts reverence and fear, "where the winged horses roamed free. The messengers, we called them. They were the Celestials' creatures, divine messengers. Coats the pure white of fresh snow in sunlight, and wings to match. Their eyes used to glow like the sun. Nowadays . . . well. You've seen what they're like now. Tainted by the Soulless One and his followers, just like these mountains."

"This is where we leave you," the other man said skittishly. "This is no place for those who aren't Godstouched—nor is it a place for common horses, I'm afraid."

Emory was relieved to be done with the soreness of riding, but the prospect of the climb didn't seem any better. As the guides were getting the horses ready, using lead ropes to tie them together to their own mounts, one of them glanced pointedly at Vivyan, Ivayne, and Vera.

"Last chance to turn back, you three. Death lives in these mountains, the kind only the Godstouched might survive."

Ivayne merely lifted a brow at him. "When was the last time a non-Godstouched tried?"

The guides had no answer to this, and both Vera and Vivyan stood as resolute as Ivayne. None of them had a spiral mark, unlike Emory, Virgil, and Nisha, but that wouldn't stop them.

"Your funeral," the guide muttered before hopping on his horse. "Be sure to—"

His words were cut short by the whizzing of a lightning bolt that embedded itself in his chest. The man fell limply to the ground as his horse whinnied and bucked. It darted off through the trees along with the three horses it was tied to. The other guide struggled to control his own steed and the other three horses it was meant to lead. Vivyan and Ivayne already had their swords drawn and brandished, looking at the treetops where a winged horse and its rider were visible.

"GO!" the guide screamed at Emory and the others just as a horde of ash-umbrae manifested between the trees.

There was no time to consider the fallen guide, no time to see if the other one was all right as he and the horses raced off, a few ash-umbrae trailing after him. Emory and the others dashed up the mountain, an army of monsters at their backs and one of the Songless flying above them on his once-divine steed. Lightning struck a massive pine tree up ahead, making it fall on the path, blocking their way. Before any of them could think of a way to cut through it, the winged horse flew close to the fallen tree, and its rider jumped from its back, landing with unnatural grace on the path, lightning sword in hand.

They had no choice but to head off the path, into the trees. Emory used her magic to create a barrier around them, hoping it would keep the ash-umbrae and the Songless off their backs long enough for her and her friends to lose them through the foreboding brush. Fog had descended, engulfing the moss-covered trees and disorienting them until they couldn't tell which way they were going. They ran until their lungs were on fire, until there was not a sound around them, and when they finally stopped for a breather, the fog had cleared just enough that they could see nothing was chasing them. No ash-umbra, no winged horse, no Songless.

But they had veered so completely off the path, the peak they were meant to climb seemed like a distant thing now.

"We can make it back," Vera panted, looking at the compass. "There's a ridge over there, see? Connects back to our mountain."

The farther up they went, the sparser the trees became, the wind howling around them as if it wanted to knock them off the mountainside. Close to nightfall, the question of where they'd sleep weighed on them. They carried on and on, panic and dread creeping higher and higher, until at last some kind of shelter came into view.

Temple ruins built into the side of the mountain.

Emory's heart thudded wildly at the thought that the syrinx might be here. Distantly she remembered Inga's warning, but surely it was better to face whatever superstitious evil might live in these ruins than to freeze to death out in the open. They could only hope the Songless and the ash-umbrae wouldn't appear again, as they had at the last temple they'd visited.

They set up camp among the ruins and ate in silence. Thoughts of the fallen ranger and the unknown fate of his companion cut Emory's appetite, but there was nothing she could do for them now except trudge on and hope all of this had not been in vain. And so she told the others about her plan, and everyone set out to search for the syrinx. Scavenging every inch of the ruins was fruitless, but at least it kept their minds off the bleak turn the day had taken or the fact that Romie and the keys might be killed any second without their being able to stop it.

"I don't think this would have been the right temple anyway," Vera said when they gave up to sit by the fire.

She pointed to the faded carvings on the walls; they depicted peaceful scenes and clear skies. She was right. This temple must have worshipped the Celestials, not the Soulless One. If the syrinx was linked to him, then surely it would be in a temple dedicated to storms and chaos.

Emory felt defeated. The mountains were too vast; there was no way to scour every inch of them for the syrinx. But if she knew where to look, if she could learn more about it . . .

In hindsight, she really shouldn't have told Sidraeus she intended to use the syrinx. Should have let him believe she would gladly break it. Because now she needed his help—and she would likely have to grovel to get it.

When Emory fell asleep that night, it wasn't the crowned umbra she found in dreams, but a face that was achingly familiar.

"Ro?"

Romie spun to her with round eyes full of surprise. "It worked," she murmured. "It finally worked."

Emory hesitated. If this was a ghost, if this was a sick, twisted form of nightmare showing her that her best friend had died, that Emory had been too late to save her...

But Romie drew her in a tight hug, and there was no denying she was real.

"We're coming to find you," Emory whispered as she clung to her friend. "We're so close to the sea of ash, a few days at most—"

Romie pulled back, a startled, panicked edge to her voice. "No, Em, you can't come here."

"Why not?"

Darkness started to press in. Romie swore, and Emory knew the dream was slipping, though she wasn't sure on whose end it was.

Romie gripped her arms tight. "You can't come here because Clover *wants* you here."

"That can't be true. He's been throwing wrenches in our path since we got here, driving us farther and farther away from the sea of ash."

Romie shook her head. "No. We all heard him, after he burnt his hand, saying that only you could—" She was about to say something else but the darkness pressed in faster, making her dig her fingers into Emory's arms with painful desperation. "I'm serious, Em. Whatever he has planned involves you, so don't come after us. We can handle this on our own."

"Romie—"

But her friend disappeared, pulled back to a place where Emory could not reach her.

Emory didn't tell the others about the dream.

She'd mulled over Romie's words all night, trying to make sense of why Clover would want Emory if he was sending his ash-umbrae and Songless to hinder her and her friends at every step. Puzzling over what Romie said about his burnt hand, and how Emory might factor in. Clover had been a Healer once; why would he need her to tend to a burn?

In the end, whatever Clover wanted her for didn't matter. She couldn't stop now, when they were halfway up the mountain. She couldn't turn her back on Romie and Aspen and Tol and Orfeyi when she was so close to seeing them again. For them, she would risk everything.

So they kept going.

It was slow work, making their way back to where they were meant to go. The terrain here was harsh and brutal, and with no carved path to follow, they had to rely on the compass and their own wits to guide them. Whenever they found a clear enough path, something always hindered their progress: fallen trees, boulders, patches of snow too deep to tread through. It forced them to find ways around, getting farther and farther from the peak atop which sat the gate.

And at every one of these detours, they came across more temples. As if the very forces of nature were leading them there.

Some sites were ruined beyond recognition, with a single pillar remaining or nothing but the semblance of a foundation in the stone. Other sites were preserved better than the first one they'd seen, and it was a marvel they still stood at all with the force of the winds this high up.

None of them had any relics or instruments. And though no ash-umbrae appeared out of the shadows, and no Songless swooped down from the skies, Emory couldn't shake the sense that they were being watched.

She was beginning to lose hope when they set up camp for the night, this time in a cave they found high in the mountains. It was cramped and cold, but offered relief from the snow that had started to fall heavily, and when they managed to get a fire going, it heated up nicely.

As Emory looked up to the illuminated ceiling, her eye caught on the striations in the dark rock, shimmering faintly in the firelight. They looked like forked veins of lightning running through the rock, in a pattern that seemed too deliberate to be anything but. Emory followed them to the back of the cave, where the veins disappeared into the floor.

There was a gap there, between floor and wall. Emory crouched to peer through it. She could faintly see some kind of chamber beyond. The gap wasn't big enough for her to fit through. But if she used a bit of Wordsmith magic, willed the rock to chip away a bit . . .

"Look," Vera said at her side, pointing to something on the wall.

Carved in the rock was a faded depiction of a faceless god, both hands closed around a bolt of lightning. Emory ran her hand along the carving and felt grooves around it. On instinct she pushed on it—and the gap in the floor groaned open to reveal crudely carved steps that led into a dark chamber.

Emory and Vera stared at each other. Behind them, Virgil muttered, "Yeah, I'm not going into that death trap."

"Scared?" Vera shot back at him teasingly.

"Of the creepy secret chamber in the creepy caves hidden in the creepy mountains? Yes. Yes, I am."

"Inga did tell us to be careful in the ruins," Nisha said cautiously.

"Vera and I will go check it out," Emory said, "and the rest of you can stay here."

Ivayne huffed, grabbing her sword. "As if I'm letting you go down there alone."

They descended the steps into the freezing cold of the hidden chamber, Emory holding up a ball of light to guide them through the dark.

"I think we've found the Soulless One's temple," Vera said with quiet awe.

Carved pillars of obsidian stone rose all around them. The

ceiling was domed and depicted forks of silvery-blue lightning that shone in the light. In the middle of the space was an altar. And sitting atop it, covered in dust, was a glass pan flute made up of five pipes of different lengths.

The syrinx.

It looked heavy, the thick glass tubes bound by ornate silver and obsidian fixings. Emory could *feel* its power. It felt like Sidraeus, like the crowned umbra that ruled the sleepscape.

The layer of dust on it was disturbed by five fingerprints, as if someone had recently played it. And yet it was still here, pulsing with power that seemed to call to Emory, begging for her to pick it up from its altar.

An inkling crawled along Emory's skin. "Go back up," she said to the others. "Get everyone and leave."

Vera frowned at her. "What–why?"

Whatever he has planned involves you, Romie had said of Clover.

Clover, who Sidraeus said wanted the syrinx for himself. Whose hand was burned, perhaps, after he tried to take it, and whose creatures had since been pushing Emory and her friends off the path, herding them to this very place. For someone to take the syrinx for him.

"Because this is a trap," Emory said, "and we need to run like hell."

The walls around them shook. In the cave above, someone screamed. Emory heard the crashing sound of thunder, the clang of steel against steel–or perhaps steel against lightning.

Clover's creatures were already here.

Ivayne didn't wait to bound up the steps, sword at the ready. Vera followed, but Emory had to get the syrinx first. It didn't matter if that was exactly what Clover wanted her to do, didn't matter if the instrument might burn her the way it did him. She needed it–would stop at nothing now to get it.

Certainty danced at her fingertips as her hand closed around it. There was no burning, no pain. An imaginary breeze whirled around her, everything in her going still with calm.

Break the syrinx, Sidraeus had asked her to do. It would be so easy a thing to drop it and see the glass flute shatter at her feet. But there was a more powerful voice inside her telling her not to do it, that there was another way, a *better* way...

"Emory, let's go!"

Emory clutched the syrinx to her chest, feeling like she'd been pulled out of a trance by Vera's voice. Vera hadn't left. She stood at the base of the steps, gesturing at Emory to hurry as shadows filled the temple.

For a moment, Emory dared to hope she'd done something right—that just by picking the flute up, it had called Sidraeus here; that it had broken him out of his sleepscape prison, and now he would be bound to her will, and they could face Clover together.

But the shadows that engulfed her were not Sidraeus's. They felt like rotten death, and Emory knew they belonged to the ash-umbrae before they materialized around her.

Emory drew on her magic to erect a ward around her, around Vera, making it so that nothing could harm them. "Go!" she yelled at her cousin. As Vera disappeared up the stairs, Emory directed her magic to the ash-umbrae, willing them to unmake. But she stopped short as a face appeared out of their midst.

Clover.

He still wore that suit of emerald velvet, black veins peeking out of the collar, stark against his pale skin. That strange power of shimmering clouds interspersed with all the elements he'd imbibed from the previous set of keys swirled around him, making his veins flash silver and gold every few seconds. His turquoise eyes glinted eagerly as they took in the syrinx in Emory's hand. A smile lifted his mouth.

"I was waiting for you to find it," Clover said. "Only a true Tidecaller can take the syrinx off its altar." He lifted a hand that was burned. "I tried taking it myself, but I'm afraid the divine power that's in me makes me . . . no longer quite a Tidecaller."

He extended that same hand to Emory. On his wrist was a spiral scar like her own, likely from when he'd first opened the door in Dovermere in the past. But while her own mark was silver, his was black, as if whatever corrupt power coursed through his veins had tarnished the mark, too.

"Give me the syrinx," Clover said, "and I swear I will not harm your friends here with you."

Emory only clutched the syrinx tighter. "What will you do with it?"

"Complete the ritual to summon and bind Atheia and Sidraeus to me."

"And kill the keys in the process."

Clover shrugged as if that was a small matter. "They were always meant to die."

They were nearly the same words Sidraeus had told her, but Emory refused to accept them as fact.

There was a bloodcurdling scream upstairs—from who, Emory couldn't tell. It was all it took for her to make her move.

Break the syrinx, part of her mind told her.

Wield it, the other part of her countered.

Emory brought the flute to her lips. She did not know how to play, did not have a single musical bone in her body, and for a moment she feared this magic wouldn't be hers to wield, just as this world wasn't hers to be in.

But she was a Tidecaller. Straddling the line between two magics, between two realms. Able to wield the ley lines that ran through all worlds, which coursed beneath her feet, concentrated in a knot of power here in the mountains.

She *could* do this.

And so Emory blew on one of the pipes.

The sound it produced was clear and true, drowning out Clover's voice as he screamed, his mouth forming the word *No*. It was the last thing Emory saw before billowing shadows erupted around her, knocking back Clover and all the ash-umbrae. An oppressive swath of darkness rose around her, spinning like a hurricane, the wind so strong she thought she might rip apart at the seams. She was still blowing on the syrinx, the note dragging endlessly, and she could not stop, could not take the instrument away from her mouth.

All of a sudden, everything came to a halt. The music. The feeling of not being in control of her body. Emory held the syrinx away from her face, careful not to drop it. The cyclone had stilled around her. It looked like she was trapped in the eye of a storm frozen in time, in the center of a great spiral of shadowy clouds. Beyond, she could no longer see the temple—there was only impenetrable darkness with the faintest stars in the distance. It was as if she was back in the dark, empty space of her nightmares where she'd found herself with Sidraeus. Where it had felt like a thousand eyes were on her, ghostly voices whispering on a breeze.

And here they were again, calling her name.

Emory, Emory. Opener of doors, wielder of keys.

The words sounded layered, as if a thousand different voices were speaking in unison.

"Who are you?" Emory asked. Her own voice sounded odd to her ears, strangely muffled, as if she were underwater.

We are the dead. You summoned us, and so we answered.

"I . . ." Emory glanced at the syrinx in her hand. She supposed it made sense that the instrument was tied to the realm of death, if it was connected to the Soulless One—to Sidraeus.

What would you ask of us, Tidecaller?

There was warmth in that title, a note of familiarity. As if they knew her intimately, like all the ghosts her magic would call on whenever she used too much. And it didn't scare her one bit. It felt like she belonged with them, and they with her.

"It's not you I meant to summon," Emory said after a moment, "but the one who rules over the realm of death. The one who used to ferry souls."

Sidraeus.

The name was a hiss that slithered in endless echoes, spoken like a curse that grated against Emory's every sense.

She felt all the blood leech from her face at the clear animosity the souls felt toward him. "I need—I need him." She hated to admit it, but it was the truth. "He's trapped in this realm without his body, a body he can only reclaim after another deity has been revived. I thought this instrument would allow me to bring him back before that happens, but . . . Please, I need his help if I'm to stop Clover. If I'm to save the worlds of the living you all used to call home."

She was met with a heavy silence that set her on edge, the hairs on the back of her neck lifting as a ghostly breeze rushed past her.

Only those of us who were first wronged by him can grant such a request, the voices said at last. *Those of us who were sacrificed because of him. Those of us whose magic runs in your veins.*

"The first Tidecallers?" Emory breathed, eyes going wide. "Is that who you are?"

She knew now why these souls felt so familiar in such a strange way—and where she had heard their voices before.

Emory, Emory. Come find us, Emory.

These were the voices that had called her name in Dovermere all those months ago. All those times last year when she'd heard the Aldersea, the Belly of the Beast, whispering her name both in waking and dreaming, begging her to come find them . . .

She had thought it was those who'd been trapped beyond the door like Romie, at first. Then she had thought it was the keys calling to her from other worlds.

But it was *them*. The sacrificed souls of the very first Tidecallers, whose blood—whose magic and *life force*—had been used to seal shut the doors between worlds.

"Please," Emory said. "I know Sidraeus had a part to play in your deaths, but if there's any way for you to unbind him from his prison, to reunite him with his true form and secure his help . . ."

If you will it, Tidecaller, then we will make it so. But know this: his unbinding will come at a price. To no longer be tied only to the sleeping realm, he must be bound to another sort of prison. One of his own making.

"What does that mean?"

His essence will be tied to us, the souls of the sacrificed Tidecallers. Through us, he will feel the pain he has inflicted, so that when an Eclipse-born is harmed, so too will he be. The pain will be branded into his skin as a reminder of what he has done. This is the bargain we offer, and as the true last remaining Tidecaller, it is yours to make if you wish it.

Emory's stomach churned at the cruel images that flashed in her mind. She understood now why Sidraeus had wanted her to destroy the syrinx. What these souls proposed . . . they were after retribution for what Sidraeus had done to them, these first Tidecallers who'd been sacrificed to close the doors between worlds. They wanted his guilt branded into his skin. The pain of his creations forced onto him.

It was a reckoning.

And Emory had the power to decide if she allowed it or not.

She stared at the syrinx still in her hand. If this was the price to be paid for stopping Clover . . . If this was what it took to save Romie and Aspen and Tol and Orfeyi . . . she had no choice but to accept. Her stomach was in knots thinking of what this would mean for Sidraeus. *He* would pay the cost of her decision, not her, and the thought made her sick.

But she had to be willing to make tough decisions. She had to be okay with this, or her best friend would die.

Emory squared her jaw, her decision made. "Do it."

There was a beat of silence before the cyclone of shadows around her spun wildly, pulling stars into its midst as it closed in on her. It felt like death coming to claim her, and all she could do was shield her eyes from it, hugging the syrinx close to her chest.

All at once, the shadows dissipated as if they had never existed at all. Emory was back in the temple, standing in front of a bewildered-looking Clover. It was as if he hadn't moved while Emory had been with the souls of the dead, and now time had resumed.

Before either of them could react, an impossible bolt of lightning struck the ground between them, sending them both flying as the world erupted in brilliant indigo light.

BAZ

BAZ HAD NEVER FELT QUITE AS NERVOUS AS HE DID marching, invisible, into the Decrescens library next to his past self.

As promised, Kai had kept silent on everything he'd revealed to him, but Baz knew that look in the Nightmare Weaver's eyes well enough to know he had something planned.

Tonight, they were going to catch Clover on all his lies.

A look at Cordie had Baz's heart breaking for what she would soon find out about her brother. Luce, too. The sight of Clover and his past self helping each other unravel the wards to the Vault, of their friends watching them with such confidence, left a sour taste in Baz's mouth.

To think how much they'd all trusted Clover, *believed* in him . . . He wanted to wipe the hero worship off his own face, force himself to see the dark, rotten truth hidden beneath Clover's polished exterior. But he could only watch from the shadows and hope that whatever Kai had planned would achieve just that.

Once the wards were unpicked, he watched as Cordie, then Luce, disappeared down the stairs toward the Vault. As past-Baz followed the two girls, Kai hovered at the top, staring back at Clover.

"Coming?" Kai prompted, an edge to his voice.

Clover was staring at a spot close to where present-Baz stood. "Go on ahead. I'll join you shortly."

Kai's jaw tightened, his eyes darting around the empty space as if looking for invisible Baz. "We finally get past the wards and, what, you need a moment to take it all in?"

Clover's mouth lifted in a smile. "Something like that. Go with the others, Kai."

It didn't register at first, why Kai seemed to bite his tongue, why he so easily did as he was told. But as Kai went down those stairs, as Baz tried to move but found that he couldn't—he understood.

Clover had Glamoured them both.

Baz felt his hand move of its own volition, turning over so the pocket watch fell from his grasp. There was a clink of metal as it landed at Clover's feet. As Clover bent to pick it up, his turquoise eyes met Baz's, the pocket watch's invisibility having lifted the moment it slipped from his hand.

And Clover didn't look surprised in the slightest to see him.

A cruel smirk touched his lips. "I knew someone was meddling in my affairs. I didn't quite expect this, though." He tilted his head, watching Baz as if he were a puzzle to be solved. "The question is, where, or rather *when*, did you come from? Why are you here?"

The words left Baz's mouth without his permission. "From the future—the god's workshop. I'm here to stop Kai and Luce from going with you through the door."

You monster, I know what you've done, he wanted to add.

"Fascinating," Clover said, studying the pocket watch. "You won't mind if I keep this. I'd like to meet this god you speak of."

With that, Clover stepped through the arch, leaving Baz rooted in place in the dark library, unable to move or speak. Dread weighed him down as he remembered the god telling him not to lose the pocket watch or he would be unable to return to the present-day workshop.

He'd really messed things up.

How had Clover even found out about him? Baz had been so careful . . . and now there was nothing he could do except wait here until everything unfurled exactly like it had before. Clover peddling the same lies, Thames Collapsing. It wouldn't matter that Kai knew the truth of it all if Clover was Glamouring him. He'd be forced to do whatever Clover wanted him to.

Waiting was agony. Waiting was rethinking every single thing he'd done leading up to now and understanding that the god was right. Fate would always win.

There was a distant blast. Thames's Collapsing, no doubt. Everything around him shook, yet Baz still could not move. Cordie came running up the stairs moments later, her eyes going wide with confusion as she saw him, and still Baz could do nothing. He heard Cordie saying she was getting help, the panic in her voice echoing through him as she left.

And then, all of a sudden, he could move again.

Clover's compulsion must have slipped. Baz didn't wait. He willed time to stop around him as he ran down into the Vault, then the Treasury, and dove through the glowing pool that would lead him into the Belly of the Beast. Clover was here beneath the water, suspended mid-stride on his way to the bottom of the pool, trapped by Baz's hold on time.

Baz tried to pry the pocket watch from Clover's frozen hand, but the bastard held it in a death grip. By the time Baz managed to get it back, triumph singing through him at this small victory, his heart was pounding wildly, his lungs screaming for breath.

He grasped the threads of time around Clover, intending to drag him back to the surface, to stop him from ever reaching the door, because without a Tidecaller it could not open and so Kai and Luce would never go through.

Or he could leave him to drown here in this timeless, breathless state.

As if riled by Baz's murderous thought, Clover came alive, breaking free of Baz's hold on time. The waters around them swirled to life too as Baz lost his focus, pulling him and Clover down toward the Belly of the Beast. Clover shoved Baz back with a wave of power, and Baz felt himself suspended in the water, kept there by some magic or other, as Clover disappeared into the Belly of the Beast.

Baz could feel metal digging into the palm of his hand. But he was powerless to do anything with the pocket watch he'd won back, powerless to reach for the threads of time, as Clover's magic kept him frozen underwater. He felt his lungs fill with water. Felt himself slipping toward unconsciousness or death. He had failed, and now he would die here in the turquoise pool.

But then, just as darkness closed in, Baz felt in control of himself again, wondering if it meant Clover had already gone through the door. Desperately he pushed toward the bottom of the pool, hoping he wasn't too late as the swirling waters dragged him down, and he fell, gasping, into the Belly of the Beast–only to see Kai and his former self slipping through the door, Kai catching his eye as he screamed for him not to go.

His former self got shoved right back out of the Hourglass, and the tide rushed in to swallow them both, drowning them in darkness.

Baz gasped as he awoke in the god's workshop. His clothes were sopping wet. The clocks and sextants and astrolabes around him winked at him mockingly, glinting pristine in the light, unfazed by the turmoil Baz had just escaped.

The god of balance was perched on the ladder next to the loom, working out a small tangle in the threads. "I told you it wouldn't change anything," he said without even looking at Baz.

Baz's breathing came in quick, short bursts, his lungs feeling like they were full of water still, like he was drowning all over again. He wanted to cry. Wanted to rage at his failure.

Instead, he got to his feet, stormed his way to the ladder, and held out the pocket watch.

"Send me back," he said. "I want to try again."

The god finally turned, taking his goggles off to peer at him gravely. "Take a breather first. The past isn't going anywhere."

In the snap of a finger, Baz's clothes were dry again, and appearing on a table next to him was a delicate cup of tea and a plate overflowing with biscuits and scones and sandwiches. A chair grated behind him, knocking into the back of his knees so he was forced to sit. Begrudgingly, Baz took a sip of tea and a bite of biscuit. His stomach grumbled; he hadn't eaten a thing while he was attempting to change the timeline.

On the table, beneath the generous spread the god had manifested, was a canvas Baz recognized as the sketch the god had been previously engrossed in. It depicted a complex web of threads with an ornate hourglass caught in the middle. Sand swirled through both bulbs in a figure eight, a continuous loop. It had been drawn in such vivid detail that it seemed to leap off the page, and because it was easier to turn his attention to this instead of the ache inside him, Baz asked the god what the drawing was meant to represent.

"Ah, that's what I like to call fate's central core." The god sat opposite Baz, tracing the pattern of threads on the canvas. "It is what sends out the threads of fate to the loom for it to weave into the tapestry. The very heart of fate, the pillar of balance."

Baz had never hated the words *fate* and *balance* as he did now. The hourglass, the loom—these were the instruments responsible for what awaited Kai, and the unfairness of it all sat like a weight on Baz's chest.

"You know," the god said mildly, drawing Baz's attention from the sketch, "I had an apprentice before you who also believed fate could be changed. He tried to meddle with the past just as you are now, and failed every time."

Baz nearly choked on his tea. The god had never mentioned an apprentice, but he supposed it made sense that he would have had help with all these instruments he cared for.

"Where is he now?" Baz asked, wondering if this apprentice had been another Timespinner like him, or someone from another world perhaps.

The god had a distant look in his eye, as if he were remembering his apprentice, seeing him in this very workshop. "No longer with me." He finally gave Baz a sad smile, pulled back to the present. "It's the curse of being an immortal god, to see so many mortal lives come and go. I will again tell you the same thing I did him: you cannot change fate."

"Why not? What's the point of any of it if our lives are set in stone?"

The god gestured for Baz's cup. "May I?" Holding it delicately, he said, "Think of this cup as fate, holding together life and death, creation and destruction, which all swirl together to make something balanced and"—the god took a curious sip—"quite delicious. What you are trying to do is chipping away at the cup, ineffective in the grand scheme of things." Tiny chips appeared on the rim of the cup, the handle, marring its surface though never breaking the integrity of the cup or disturbing the tea inside it. "But do it often enough . . ."

The god let the cup drop—and it shattered at his feet, tea and porcelain spilling between them.

"If fate were to be broken, chaos would ensue," the god said. "You see? This is what I am working to prevent. This is why ensuring the threads of fate run smoothly is so important. And this is why you must let this go, Basil. Because what you are trying to change, if you *were* to change it, would likely lead to a more disastrous outcome than you can imagine."

Baz stared at the mess at his feet. He understood what the god was saying, but he couldn't give up—couldn't accept that this was the end and that Kai's fate was set in stone.

Maybe he didn't have to change all of fate just to change Kai's. He could keep chipping at the cup, so to speak, until the fragment he wanted gone from the pattern fell away, leaving the contents of the cup undisturbed, the larger tapestry of fate intact.

Baz lifted his chin. "You said I could attempt to change things however many times I wanted," he reminded the god. "Send me back."

The god sighed. "If you insist."

KAI

IT WAS NOT QUITE DAWN WHEN THEY SLIPPED OUT OF the estate, Asphodel guiding Kai, Clover, and Luce through the dark, quiet gardens. The remnants of the night's festivities were still there, tables laden with barely eaten food, ribbons that danced half-heartedly in the breeze, overturned goblets and crushed flower crowns and extinguished candlewicks slumbering in fat drippings of wax.

There was something foul in the air, Kai thought. As if these carcasses of a feast half-forgotten had been festering for days on end instead of a mere few hours.

They reached the garden gate that led off the estate grounds only to find it already open to the woods beyond. Clover's hand shot out to stop Asphodel in her tracks, holding the witch back as a cry escaped her lips. Luce's own hand shot to her mouth in horror. It took a moment for Kai to register what they were seeing, and when he did, he wondered for a second if this was a nightmare he had yet to wake from.

Lying in front of the gate were two witches—lovers, perhaps, who'd stayed behind after everyone else left the party—their bodies writhing as they were strangled by coils of rotten leaves and thorn-covered vines that slithered and tightened around them as if the earth sought to swallow them whole.

And hovering over them, eyes entirely black, were a group of hellwraiths.

There were a dozen of them, young and old, faces Kai recognized as recently ascended hellwraiths, and some he'd never seen before. They formed a circle around the witches' bodies, levitating a few inches from the ground, their faces blank and expressions trancelike, their hands moving in odd motions as if they were controlling the deadly, earthly coils around the witches.

"Asphodel, I swear if you leave with—"

The voice behind them gasped, cutting itself short. Oleander stood with a lantern in hand, shivering in her nightgown, having clearly followed them from the house. Her eyes were wide with horror as she beheld the scene.

Her voice must have broken the hellwraiths out of their trance. In a swift, inhuman motion, a dozen faces turned in their direction, a dozen pairs of fathomless eyes staring blankly at them. Kai stood frozen in place. There was something not right about this, something oddly familiar about the way he could not move.

He watched as Clover stepped forward, emanating a brilliant light, the same way he looked when "purging" newly ascended hellwraiths of their would-be demonic influence. The hellwraiths fell as one to the ground, and Clover managed to wrest control of the coiling vines, tearing through them with magic until the two suffocating witches were freed and, likely healed by Clover, gulping air into their lungs.

In the ensuing quiet, as the light extinguished, the hellwraiths looked around them with eyes that were clear and a confusion that skewed toward horror as they realized where they were and what had happened.

"You will answer for this," Oleander told the hellwraiths in a shaky yet authoritative voice. "Every single one of you will pay for what has happened here."

"This isn't what it looks like," said one of the hellwraiths, an older witch with graying hair. Incredulous tears gathered in her eyes as she gaped at the two would-be victims–crying now in each other's arms, with Asphodel trying to soothe them. "I swear we meant no harm."

"We have no idea how we even got here," spoke another, looking equally confused.

"Because you're all possessed!" Oleander cried out. "This is the netherdemons working through you. First they poison our woods, now they're trying to *kill us*, too. I won't tolerate another one of you near my coven. A black moon is coming. You will all be exorcized then."

Gasps and cries echoed. Asphodel gaped at her sister, uttering a low, "But exorcism is as good as a death sentence."

Oleander squared her shoulders. "We do what we must to protect our coven."

"We used to be part of your coven before you cast us aside." The older witch's voice wobbled. "We have loved ones still in your midst. You cannot mean to–"

"That was before you tried to kill two of our own. You are no one to us now."

"Oleander," Asphodel said softly, turning pleading eyes to her twin. "Can't you see this isn't their fault? They're not themselves, but we can help them instead of–of sentencing them. Cornelius has a plan to lead us all to salvation. It's why I must leave. And once we heal the rotting woods, the netherdemons will return to the underworld and the hellwraiths will be saved."

Oleander didn't look convinced, her eyes pinning Clover with a hard stare. "I don't trust him."

"I do." Asphodel gathered her twin's hands in hers. "Trust in me, if nothing else."

Clover watched this exchange with quiet anticipation, like the director of a play waiting to see the scene he'd envisioned play out exactly the way he meant it to.

This was all his doing, Kai suspected. The vines coiling around those two witches. The hellwraiths summoned to the estate in the middle of the night, their apparent possession. Netherdemons did not exist. But a Tidecaller with the power to manipulate the earth and to Glamour whoever he wanted—with magic that went beyond even that, and a penchant for theatrics . . .

As Oleander agreed to let the hellwraiths go free—too easy, too pliant—Clover caught Kai's eye, and it was all Kai needed to confirm his suspicions.

Clover had manipulated all of this. As if he'd known Oleander wouldn't have let her twin leave without this final push, this last performance where Clover got to be the hero, cementing his role as the only one capable of stopping the very real rot and the entirely fabricated netherdemons.

"It had to be done," Clover whispered to Kai as they set off toward the door at last, the first light of dawn guiding their way. Asphodel and Luce walked a few paces away, out of earshot.

"Those two witches nearly died," Kai pointed out. "And who's to say Oleander won't decide to go after the hellwraiths once we're gone? Their deaths will be on your hands, just like—"

But the names that had been on his lips vanished from memory. Clover hadn't killed anyone, had he?

Baz's words echoed in his ears. *I think you were right not to trust Clover.*

Except . . . why was that again? Misremembered thoughts swam in Kai's mind once more. Of all the disjointed pieces of dreamlike memory he couldn't make sense of, only two things had always remained clear to him: his feelings for Baz and his distrust of Clover. If this inexplicable instinct was all he had to go on, surely he had to trust it. And yet.

Kai shook away his confusion, angry at his own inability to know what was real. "All I'm saying is you'd better know what you're doing."

Clover gave him a sly smile. "I have all the powers of the moon at my fingertips, Kai, including that of Seers. I always know what I'm doing."

It was meant to be comforting, most likely. But all it did was set Kai more on edge than ever before.

"How are we meant to open the door?" Luce asked once they reached the caves. "If it required blood in our world, then here..."

"It requires a bone, yes," Clover said. He drew closer to Asphodel, stroked her face like the tender lover he was pretending to be. "Do you trust me?"

"Of course," she breathed, eyelashes fluttering against her cheeks. "I told you before, how I can feel the way our souls are connected. This song between us." She looked at Kai and Luce. "Between all of us."

"Yes." Clover kissed her hand. "We all have a part to play in what comes next. And your part, dear Asphodel, is larger than you realize."

The words set off alarm bells in Kai's mind. He tried to catch Luce's gaze, but she was focused on the door, brows scrunched up in thought.

"This will be just as we discussed," Clover said in that lover's voice, low and soft. Asphodel lay down on a flat surface created by some of the basalt columns, arms at her side and face tilted toward Clover. Like she was a sacrifice on the altar of a dark god. "It will hurt," Clover continued, "and you will feel like you're dying. But do not be afraid. I've got you."

Kai took a step forward as a dagger flashed in Clover's hand. "What are you–"

The dagger sliced into Asphodel's dress, tearing a large cut on her side. On her exposed rib cage was a spiral scar like the one Clover and Luce had on their wrists, marking her as her world's key. Asphodel met Kai's eye. "It's all right, Nightmare Weaver. If my rib bone is needed, then I trust no one more than I do Cornelius to see it done." She looked at Clover lovingly. "My healer prince."

Clover stroked her hair, then sliced the dagger along her skin.

Luce turned her face away, squeezing her eyes shut with a low swear as Asphodel screamed. Kai couldn't turn from the horror. He was transfixed by it, by the utter trust the witch was putting in Clover. More than anything, he wanted to believe that this would work–that Clover would break off one of her ribs and heal her as quickly as it happened. Kai might not like the guy, but there was no denying his power.

And Clover came through. He did exactly what he had said he'd do. He held the blood-slick rib tightly in one hand while the other cupped Asphodel's cheek as he murmured comforting words to her. Before their eyes, Asphodel's rib *regrew*, then her skin patched itself up, and all the color returned to her face. It was as if none of this had ever happened. Except for the bone in Clover's hand–which he then fitted into the groove on the door.

The door opened.

Kai and Luce were almost through it, called to it like magnets by the pull of that damn song, when Kai looked back to Clover and Asphodel expectantly. Asphodel was sitting up, still a little faint and frail, but alive, at least. Her feet dangled from the basalt columns, barely touching the ground. She braced herself on Clover's arm, trying to stand, but Clover kept her there, pressing a kiss to her temple.

"You did well," he said in a low voice, though still loud enough for Kai to hear.

Suddenly Kai doubled over, feeling that conduit between him and Clover open. Luce, too, was bent at the waist, her hand shooting out to grab Kai's arm as all the power knocked out of them like a gut punch.

"What's happening?" she breathed.

The shimmering threads linking them both to Clover crackled like live wires as they normally did, yet this was worse than any other time Clover had fed on their power. But as much as it was affecting Kai and Luce, it was nothing compared to what he was doing to Asphodel.

The witch screamed as all the bones in her body *snapped*, bending and rearranging at odd angles. For a second Kai thought it might be the Sculptress's doing, that Asphodel was somehow being reshaped the way witchlings were said to be when they were buried.

But by the look in Clover's eyes, the intensity with which he was focused on Asphodel, it was clear this was his doing.

"You were right, dear Asphodel," Clover said with a tremor in his voice, a slight note of pity or regret. "I will lead our worlds to salvation. But for that, I need to make myself into someone stronger than all the gods. Your physical bone was enough to open the door, but you still have a piece of the power I need. A piece of the Sculptress."

"I don't understand!" Asphodel cried.

"The Tides' blood, the Sculptress's bone, the Forger's heart, the Celestials' soul. I must gather all these pieces into one vessel. Into *me*. Only then will I be able to heal these worlds."

Clover shimmered in ethereal light that poured into him from

Kai and Luce, as if they were powering him up, making him strong enough to do what he did next: he lay a hand on Asphodel's cheek, holding her head as her body spasmed uncontrollably. He shut his eyes, his throat bobbing with emotion. When he opened them again, they were hard. Resolute. "Forgive me."

Asphodel went limp as he snapped her neck.

The crack resonated like thunder. A weighted silence followed, before a whoosh of power erupted from Asphodel. Kai shielded his eyes as a maelstrom of dirt and vines and leaves enveloped both Asphodel and Clover. When it dissipated, there was nothing left of Asphodel's body but the clothes she had worn.

As if she'd disintegrated into earth and greenery—the power of the Wychwood itself, which clung to Clover in swirling tendrils, until at last it seeped into him fully.

He had *imbibed* Asphodel. All her power. Everything that she was.

When Clover turned to Kai and Luce, his eyes flashed in an unnatural way. As if he really was a demon.

A god in the making.

The shimmering bonds between them fell away, leaving Kai and Luce panting, holding on to each other for strength.

"What did you do?" Luce asked in a tremulous voice.

Clover merely righted his clothes, brushing dirt from his sleeves. "What I must."

EMORY

STARS BLURRED OUT EMORY'S SIGHT, A TIDE OF PAIN threatening to pull her under. She fought back, desperate to stay afloat, to remain alert. Disorienting shadows and smoke and dust swirled around her. Her ears rang, and she couldn't tell where Clover was, couldn't hear any of her friends in the cave above.

There were scorch marks on the ground, as if the lightning bolt had burned through the very rock. In the midst of the blast, at the very origin of it, was a young man. He crouched in the thick cloud of smoke, head in his lap, holding his knees as he rocked slowly back and forth. Emory could only see his back. Bare and corded with lean muscles, skin darkened by soot.

Slowly, she approached him, ignoring the alarm bells in her head and choosing instead to follow this instinctive pull. When she was near enough to touch him, to hear what sounded like quiet sobs coming from him, she realized it was not soot that marred his skin, but wisps of shadows. They dissipated as if on a breeze, revealing pale skin smattered with copper freckles.

And a tapestry of silver spirals.

They were carved all over his back, painful-looking scars, brands that shone faintest silver. They looked new, the skin raw beneath the light pouring from the wounds. Spirals big and small ran all over his shoulders and arms and neck. He wore dark pants and nothing else, barefoot and trembling. His head was still buried in his lap, and he did not appear to hear Emory's approach, did not flinch or look up as she lay her hand gently on his shoulder.

Only when Emory crouched before him did he lift his head to meet her gaze.

She wasn't surprised at the ecliptic eyes; had known it was him in some primal way. And she knew instinctively that this was no possession as it had been with Keiran. This was Sidraeus in his true form.

For a second, Emory could only stare at him, mesmerized by his youthful splendor, his ancient beauty. Tears glistened like stars in his thick lashes before tracing lines down his full lips and chiseled jaw. The dark auburn of his hair reminded her of a setting sun or decaying leaves. He looked like the fleeting calm that came before death, the elusive light you chased in the dark.

"You." His voice came out in a raw whisper, his eyes full of an emotion she didn't understand. Then it sharpened to something vicious, anger distorting his beautiful face as he snarled, "*You* did this to me."

His hand wrapped around her throat quicker than humanly possible, but he snatched it back just as quick with a hiss of pain. Emory scrambled backward, away from him, heart thudding wildly in her chest as what just happened dawned on her.

Those spirals scarring his true form. His inability to hurt her without also hurting himself.

The pain will be branded into his skin as a reminder of what he has done.

The bargain she made with the Tidecaller souls—it had worked.

There was a blur of movement beside her as Clover appeared out of the smoke, blood running down the side of his head where he must have fallen. In his burnt hand was the syrinx. Emory had dropped it after the lightning struck, and now Clover was looking at Sidraeus with a feral sort of hunger.

"Submit to me," Clover said, magic lacing his words. "I bind you to my will."

If he knew the syrinx had already been used, that Emory had beaten him to the punch, he did not seem to care. Fear and doubt reared inside Emory as the syrinx transformed in his hand, taking on the shape of a glass collar inlaid with silver and obsidian. A delicate, shimmering chain was connected to it, and it slithered, serpentlike, from Clover's grasp, pushing the collar forward to fasten around Sidraeus's neck.

But Clover had no power over Sidraeus, who was bound now to the Tidecallers, to all Eclipse-born—and Clover was neither. Not anymore. And so the collar did not reach Sidraeus, whose face had darkened with otherworldly anger. The shadow he cast lengthened and took on the shape of the crowned umbra, towering over him like a separate entity. A clawed hand burst from the shadow without Sidraeus himself moving a muscle, and it yanked the chain away from Clover, shattering the collar on the ground.

There was a beat as Clover stared at the broken glass with indignant horror. Emory feared Sidraeus might vanish with the destroyed syrinx, but he was still here, standing in defiance of the monster who wanted to control him. He lunged for Clover, murder glinting in his ecliptic eyes.

Only Clover was quicker. And as his hand connected with Emory's arm—her wards, she realized too late, were long gone—the two of them vanished in a dark, billowing cloud of dust, leaving Sidraeus and the temple behind, his name ripped from Emory's throat in a last, desperate plea.

They appeared in a place awash in pale, dull gray light. Clover held her arm in a tight grip, ushering her toward a large hill of carved stone with stairs etched in its side in a zigzag formation. Emory couldn't move away from him or call on her magic; her feet simply followed as if of their own will. Or rather, Clover's will—there was no doubt in her mind that he was compelling her.

She was completely at his mercy. Sidraeus was not here, her hope of gaining any sort of advantage over Clover now lost. The keys would die, and her friends at the temple . . . Tides, what would happen to them now?

Out of the corner of her eye, Emory drank in every detail of her surroundings. She knew where they were, and it truly was deserving of the name they all knew it by: the sea of ash, a barren world full of nothingness that stretched as far as the eye could see.

They started up the narrow, steep stairs. Atop the hill, she could just make out a gigantic fountain, though nothing flowed from it. It was dried up, like everything else in this godsforsaken land. Used up by Clover and his greed for power.

When they reached the top, Emory's heart leapt and fell in a quick succession, and she was certain her legs would have given out from under her if she weren't under Clover's compulsion.

Because Romie was there. Romie and Aspen and Tol and a blond boy that could be none other than Orfeyi.

"Romie," Emory managed weakly, feeling tears fall silently down her cheeks as she took in the four keys standing blank-faced in a circle in the middle of the fountain, as if awaiting their sacrifice without any ounce of defiance. They looked paralyzed, turned to stone, their eyes eerily unblinking. She would have thought they were dead if it weren't for the faint, rhythmic movement of their chests as they breathed.

"What did you do to them?" Emory asked Clover, voice trembling with fury.

"Just keeping them docile until the sacrifice. Now that you're here, we can begin."

He snapped his fingers, and in unison the keys blinked, stirring even as they remained rooted in place.

Romie's head snapped to Emory as if she were a magnet drawing her gaze to her. Her face looked stricken, her mouth falling open and her eyes going wide. "No," she breathed. "Em, you can't be here, he's going to—"

"Silence," Clover commanded. He shoved Emory forward so that she was close enough to touch Romie and the others, but still unable to act of her own free will due to the compulsion. "I believe what Romie was going to say," Clover continued, "was that you, Emory, are very much needed for our ritual. You and the syrinx, that is, but I guess we'll have to do without it now." His gaze darkened. "What happened when you played it, back in the temple?"

"I—" Emory tried to fight against the compulsion, tried to lie, but couldn't. "I saw the souls of the first Tidecallers. I made a bargain with them to summon Sidraeus and bind him to me."

Clover's lip curled in contempt. "So you beat me to the punch. No matter. Once you become Atheia's vessel and your will is bound to mine, I'll have you summon him to you and then kill you both to take the deities' power." He took a deep, steadying breath, his eyes closing in bliss. "Finally, after all these years, I'm so close to being able to finish what I started."

All Emory could hear was, *Once you become Atheia's vessel . . .*

She met Romie's gaze. Her friend couldn't speak, but the anger in her eyes told Emory everything she needed to know.

Romie had warned her to stay away, had tried to prevent all of this. And Emory hadn't listened.

She'd played right into Clover's hand and doomed everyone in the process. Romie and the keys would die. The pieces of Atheia they carried, her divine essence, would be put back together inside Emory, and she would become Atheia's vessel—only to be bound to Clover to make him into a proper, evil god.

ROMIE

ROMIE WANTED TO SCREAM. IF ONLY EMORY HAD LIStened to her and stayed away. But now Romie and the keys would die, and Emory would be forever lost, her mind and body given over to Atheia. The five of them would meet their end today, and there was nothing they could do to stop it.

"It's time," Clover said, standing in the middle of the fountain with Emory at his side. He held what looked like a ceremonial knife in his good hand, twirling its pointed end against the index finger of his burnt one.

He forced the four keys to stand around him and Emory. They were marching toward their own death without protest, because he willed it so. He motioned for Romie to step up first. "We'll start with the blood."

Romie did as commanded.

To Orfeyi, Clover said, "The music, if you please."

Orfeyi fiddled over his lyre. They'd known Clover would ask him to play during the ritual. This whole thing had started with a song they'd all heard across the stars, calling them to this place, bringing them to this very moment, Clover included. It seemed only fitting to welcome Atheia back into the world with music. And the lyre, it was said, had exactly that kind of power.

Clover had tried to play it when he'd first imprisoned them in the sea of ash. He had snatched it from Orfeyi's hands and plucked at its strings as if hoping it would conjure Atheia right then and there. But the instrument had produced a sound so dissonant, a screeching so far removed from any sort of music, that it had made all their ears bleed.

Only a true musician can wield it, Orfeyi had explained. *Someone who has music embedded in their soul, life singing through them.*

And Clover, corrupt as his soul had become, was not that someone. But Orfeyi was. The lyre's chosen player. And what did it matter to Clover who played the instrument, in the end? He had control over Orfeyi anyway.

At least, that was what he believed.

Now, Orfeyi plucked at a string—a single note that perked up Romie's senses, reverberated through her soul. It seemed to say *we can do this.* Her hand did not shake when Clover passed her the ceremonial knife. It was heavier than she expected, the blade wicked sharp, the hilt wrought of some kind of metal with details of spirals and stars. Romie had a sudden flash of the night she'd gone to Dovermere with the Selenic Order initiates, where they'd all slashed their palms open to bleed on the Hourglass.

She brought the blade to her palm to do the same now, but Clover stopped her, saying, "Your wrist, please."

Romie pressed the blade against her skin. Her gaze swept desperately over Emory and the other keys. She could already imagine how the scene would play out: her blood gushing out of her open wrists until she fell limp to the floor. Clover, moving on to Aspen's bones—ripping a rib out of her much like the Shadow had, and leaving her for dead. Then Tol's heart, torn from his chest. Orfeyi's soul, taken from him as he drew his last breath.

They would all of them be dead, and the essence of the deity their disparate parts would form would rush into Emory, erasing her, too.

"Now, Dreamer," Clover snapped.

Romie sliced across her right wrist, just below the silver spiral scar she had there. And as the harsh shock of pain turned into the first drop of blood pearling onto her skin, Orfeyi began to sing. The melody was exactly the same that had called each of them here. And Orfeyi's voice . . . it was nothing short of angelic, the words in a language Romie didn't know.

She held her wrist over the center of the fountain, letting her blood spill atop the ash. Her head became thick and her knees weak, but she focused on the melody of the lyre and Orfeyi's voice, letting them soar through her as she implored the Tides, the Sculptress, the Forger, and the Celestials to come to her now, here at the end of her life, to heed her call.

In her mind, she saw Atheia in the sleepscape again, trying to make her understand something, showing her the threads of light binding the keys to Romie's pulse points, to Atheia herself.

Act the part of the brave dreamer . . .

All at once, Romie understood what Atheia wanted them to do. And it all relied on her blood.

Because Romie was a Dreamer the way Atheia had been. She had the magic of possibility, of imagination, running through her veins. And with that magic, she stood in direct opposition to Sidraeus's ruination, his power over death, the world beyond life. To Clover's own destructive power and the Tidethievery he'd inherited from the Shadow.

And blood, like water, was what connected all worlds. Connected the four of them to each other and to Atheia, too. The keys were already a part of Romie, as much as she was a part of them. And through Romie, they would be a part of Atheia, too.

If they made *Romie* into Atheia's vessel.

The keys would give back the pieces of themselves that belonged to Atheia, just as Clover intended, but only in a metaphorical sense. They didn't need to die if they bound one another's threads together, fusing their life forces to Romie, whose body would be used to house Atheia. It would be as if Atheia's bones and heart and soul lived outside her body—the vessel Romie would become—but these parts of her would still be bound to her by these threads that could not be severed.

This was the sacrifice they had to make to stay alive. Their life force bound to Atheia in this manner would mean they could never be parted from the deity, or each other, but at least they'd all get to live. Even Romie, though she would no longer be only herself, would at least not be dead.

It was the only thing they could do. Atheia needed to be brought back, there was no doubt about that. But they couldn't let her fall into the hands of Clover, who would simply take all her power until there was nothing left of her—of any of them.

Perhaps, by staying alive, by keeping Atheia's power separate even though she'd be bound to Romie as her vessel, Clover would find it harder to drain all her power. At the very least, it might give them the chance to escape him.

Darkness threatened to take Romie under, the loss of blood making her queasy. But as she looked at the other keys, she saw the same understanding in their eyes, the same hope sparking to life. She noticed the wooden splinter each of them held in one hand, just like the one she kept in her pocket for bloodletting, and the way they all held their other hand over the center of the fountain—blood dripping from their wrist to mix with hers, imbuing it with the essence of whatever part of Atheia they held. It was what Orfeyi was singing, what he was imploring the Celestials. And as their blood flowed and mixed with Romie's, the four parts would be reunited.

They had all of them been drawn to this place by the call of a deity, a song they heard across worlds. And now they would use that same song to bring that deity back to life the proper way.

Clover didn't seem to notice at first. He took the ceremonial knife from Romie and made his way over to Aspen to cut out her rib bone. Romie fought to keep her eyes open, to keep unconsciousness at bay. They couldn't let Clover get to Aspen, couldn't—

"*Romie!*"

The shout was visceral, full of anguish and desperation. It shot through Romie's nerves and made her look around her with trepidation. She expected to see Aspen's rib bone and Tol's heart in the fountain, lying in her own blood; to feel Orfeyi's soul brush past her as one might feel a breeze against their cheek. But they were still standing, Clover hovering beside Aspen, knife held aloft between them. All of them had stopped to look at her, as if *she* had been the one to scream. But the voice had belonged to Emory, who must have managed to slither out of Clover's Glamour to catch Romie just before she hit the ground.

Romie was so weak in Emory's embrace, her blood pooling beneath her into the fountain. She felt a prickle at her wrist as Emory began to heal the wound there—but Emory was yanked up with a painful yelp as Clover held her by the nape of her neck and shoved her back into the fountain. Power built at Clover's fingertips, bloodlust in his eyes as he aimed for Emory. Fear unlike anything she'd ever felt seized Romie. She couldn't let Clover kill her best friend. But she was so, so weak. Blood was pouring out of her now like a river, like the sea, like an endless night pulling her to fathomless depths.

That was when Orfeyi's song hit its crescendo.

And then there was light.

Threads of shimmering, ethereal light unspooled from the keys, mixing in with their spilt blood. These tendrils of bloody light snaked around Romie's limbs. Her right wrist. Her left forearm. Her neck.

My pulse points, she realized dimly, as her heart beat ever louder where the threads connected. She could feel Aspen's life force wrap around her wrist, imbued with her memories of Bryony and Mrs. Amberyl, of the Wychwood and all its wonders, of walking barefoot on mossy earth, and being buried beneath the yew tree for the Sculptress to reshape her bones.

She could feel Tol's life force fuse to hers as his thread wrapped around the crook of her other arm, imbued with distant recollections of his family, of the grief that followed their passing, of Tol's own painful remaking as his human heart was molded into one of solid gold.

She felt Orfeyi's life force meld to hers as his thread wrapped around her neck, and it felt like an electric wire open between them, a shock of all the things he'd been, how he heard the world in song, how it felt to pluck at the strings of his lyre, of the agony that had been the lightning strike burning through him, searing his soul anew.

Three keys. Three lives, connected to three pulse points, each one giving her more and more force. Romie watched her own blood winding itself through those threads of light and, like a live wire, travel between her and the keys. Sharing energy between them.

"What is this?"

The seething fury in Clover's voice was slow to register in Romie's mind. But of course he had noticed by now, no longer distracted by Emory. His turquoise eyes were like icy flames as he took in the blood-and-light threads binding the keys.

Romie met Orfeyi's gaze as he kept singing and plucking at the strings, the song reaching its end.

It was now or never.

Make me your vessel, Romie implored Atheia. *We are the same, you and me. Dreamers, both. My blood is your blood. The blood of Quies, the wisest of the Tides, the last in the cycle. So take me. Use me as your vessel, and let the others live.*

She felt the dawning of a presence in her mind, old and powerful and so very familiar.

Dreamer, a lovely, womanly voice said in her head. *Witch. Warrior. Guardian. Now we are but one.*

Atheia's voice.

It had worked. It had actually *worked.* Romie saw the smile blooming on Orfeyi's face as the final note left his lips. Saw the same hope and shock mirrored on Aspen and Tol, whose hands were interlaced. The threads between them grew brighter. Romie felt their hearts beating in sync in her pulse points, as if they really had become one. And Atheia was in her head, but Romie still felt like herself. Hadn't lost herself by becoming the deity's vessel.

Clover moved quicker than Romie could register, snatching the lyre out of Orfeyi's hands. There was a dissonance of chords as Clover clutched the instrument against his chest. He curled the fingers of his free hand, and Romie heard the cracking of bones, the squelching of torn flesh, the hitch of a breath. Three muffled sounds of pain rose as one. The light-and-blood threads that connected the keys to Romie *snapped,* like the chords of an instrument, and retreated into Romie.

In one swift motion, Aspen and Tol and Orfeyi fell to the fountain floor, lifeless.

Power burned through Romie. She screamed as beams of colorful light poured out of her and stars erupted behind her eyes, tearing away at all that she was and had been and could have become, until Rosemarie Brysden was no more, and there was only Atheia.

EMORY

THE WORLD SEEMED TO VANISH IN A BURST OF RADIANT color that forced Emory's eyes shut. Maybe this was death pulling her under like it had done for the keys. She hadn't been able to save them; now, she would join them.

But the light subsided. Her eyes opened, and she found that she was still alive, still herself. Not Atheia's vessel. And the keys . . .

Bodies splayed in the fountain bed. She couldn't bring herself to look at them. A sob escaped her lips, her knees buckled, but she wouldn't let herself crumble, not while the monster who had done this still lived.

Emory's eyes narrowed on Clover. Bloodlust sang in her veins. He had killed her friends, had sacrificed them without mercy, and now he was going to pay.

She called death magic to her, ready to unleash it. But all the fight winked out of her as she saw the face that appeared at Clover's side. The one ghost she'd hoped never to see.

Romie looked no different than she had before her death, and maybe that was a small mercy. A sob broke from Emory's lips as she let go of her magic, felt the crushing weight of grief settle over her. She threw her arms around Romie, hugging her close, not caring that she was a ghost or that Clover was close enough to end her own life. Perhaps it would be a mercy to join Romie in the afterlife.

"I'm sorry." Emory's voice broke on the words. "I'm so sorry, Ro."

Romie's ghost didn't hug back, but her voice breathed in Emory's ear. *"Tidethief."*

That word, the cold delivery of it, made Emory go still. Was she in a nightmare? None of her ghosts had ever spoken to her outside of nightmares. And yet, none of them had ever felt so solid—and warm.

Emory pulled back with a jerk, holding Romie at arm's length. This was Romie *in the flesh.* For a wild, hopeful second, Emory thought this meant maybe the keys *weren't* dead. That maybe Atheia hadn't come back.

She might have believed it longer if it weren't for Romie's eyes— no longer brown, but a rainbow of dancing colors, like a diamond in the light. A kaleidoscope.

"Romie?" Emory breathed.

She knew for certain it wasn't Romie by the cruel twist of her mouth. Romie's fingers dug into Emory's arms, those unnatural eyes shifting like quicksilver, glinting like a blade about to come down in a killing blow. But Romie was yanked back suddenly as Clover tugged on a chain he held. Romie wore a collar like the one Clover had sought to fasten around Sidraeus's neck, though hers was made of gold. Just like the lyre had been.

This was Atheia, Emory realized. And she was possessing Romie just as Sidraeus had possessed Keiran.

A leashed deity whose power was now in Clover's hands.

"I suppose it doesn't matter whose body you came back in, in the end," Clover mused, watching Atheia tug helplessly at her collar. "Your power will still be mine."

Atheia doubled over in pain as energy crackled at Clover's fingertips. He was calling power away from her, Emory realized, as if the collar around her neck were a conduit between deity and monster. Clover tipped his head back, breathing in deeply as magic seeped from her and swirled around him in great clouds. Magic he meant to imbibe.

But something was wrong. Clover's face scrunched up in furious concentration as he fought to draw more and more magic inside him. His breathing was coming in quick, short bursts, as if this power was too much for him to hold, even though Atheia's power was only half of what he needed to make himself into a god.

Through the pain, Atheia managed a taunting laugh. "You fool," she wheezed. "You can't possibly think you, a mere mortal, can take on all my power."

Clover's gaze cut to Emory. "Call Sidraeus here."

"What? I-I don't—"

"He is bound to your will, is he not? You used the syrinx. *So summon him.*"

There was Glamour magic laced in the command, so even though Emory didn't understand the specifics of the bargain she'd made—even though part of her wanted to fight back, to spare Sidraeus from falling into Clover's hands—she did as commanded. She spoke Sidraeus's name aloud, let it echo through her soul.

It's a trap, she thought in warning.

Please come, she thought in desperation. Because even if all seemed hopeless, even if Clover couldn't be stopped, she couldn't possibly face him alone.

She did not notice, at first, the crowned shadow that loomed behind Clover, poised to strike. Without a sound, Sidraeus's true form seemed to detach itself from this umbra-shaped shadow, stepping into the light. He had donned a jacket like the ones that the Songless wore, the navy and silver garment open to show his bare torso. The fabric was bloodstained, making Emory wonder how he'd gotten it, her mind wandering to the friends she'd left behind at the temple.

Atheia's eyes widened as she spotted Sidraeus. She growled a fuming, murderous *"You"* that tipped Clover off to Sidraeus's presence, but it was already too late. Sidraeus unleashed his magic on Clover, shadowy claws digging into skin as they wrapped around his neck and squeezed.

For a wild second, Emory dared to hope. But in that same breathless, heart-stopping second, ash-umbrae materialized all around Sidraeus, tearing him off Clover with an ease that should not have been possible. Clover whirled on him, turquoise eyes flashing hungrily as he reached for Sidraeus's power. There was no collar to act as conduit between them, but the power he was taking from Atheia still crackled at his fingertips, and maybe that was what allowed him to draw from Sidraeus, too, bringing the deity to his knees.

If the fountain was limitless power, then Sidraeus and Atheia's combined magic would be the same. And it was coursing through Clover . . . but it was burning him out. Just like the first Tidecallers who'd tried to siphon power from the fountain to give to Sidraeus.

If four of them couldn't do it, then surely a single Tidecaller could not. But Clover wasn't a Tidecaller anymore. Not entirely. Not *only*. He had the power of the previous keys—of the fountain itself—running through him. And yet here he was, burning out. Perhaps the power had festered inside him, becoming useless. Perhaps the infinite, combined power of Sidraeus and Atheia was too great for him to contain.

But Clover was nothing if not relentless, and whatever was afflicting him seemed worse for Sidraeus and Atheia. Atheia—with

Romie's features—gritted her teeth and gripped the edge of the fountain. Sidraeus grunted in pain as he knelt in the ash, held down by twisted versions of his umbrae.

And that sight was the final straw for Emory. Seeing her best friend suffering in a body that was no longer hers to control. Seeing Sidraeus, the *real* Sidraeus, hurt by an echo of his own creations.

It all came back to Clover. Emory would be damned if she let him hurt anyone else.

And here, perhaps, was her chance. Because in this moment, as he was burning out, Clover was vulnerable and not paying a single ounce of attention to her.

In him, Emory could feel the pieces of Atheia that he'd imbibed long ago. Tarnished beyond recognition, twisted into something that were no longer keys but still belonged to Atheia.

Something Emory could call on.

Sidraeus met Emory's gaze—and his voice rang clear as crystal in her mind.

Power can be taken. So take it.

Emory was too shocked to register the words at first. The spiral mark on her wrist prickled in the way it used to when she would activate it to contact another Selenic Order member. But Sidraeus's lips hadn't moved; it was like he was speaking to her in her mind just as his umbra form did, though this was not the strange, haunting voice of the crowned umbra. It was his real voice, low and level. A silky tone that spoke of quiet things, like the stillness of a lake on a winter's night, or the whisper of dead leaves as they fell to the forest floor.

When the words finally registered, Emory looked at Clover, remembering having said that to him last time she'd attempted to call on his power the way she would call on the keys. Clover had easily stopped her then. But now . . .

Now Emory didn't try to tap into Clover's own well of Tidecaller magic, nor the power he had stolen from the fountain. Understanding what Sidraeus was telling her, what he had correctly guessed that *she* had been thinking too, she did what Tidecallers did best: she called on the power of Atheia that still lived inside Clover.

Instantly Clover screamed and dropped to the ground, writhing. Those strange pulses of power that had rippled over him disappeared. There were only black veins slithering beneath his skin. His face turned ashen. His bones bent at odd angles. He clutched at his heart. And Emory had seen all this before, when she'd unwittingly taken power from Romie, Aspen, and Tol.

He seemed to be crumbling in on himself, withering away before her eyes, as if he were losing all the godly power he'd imbibed and Collapsing into something dark and unnatural. The collar around Atheia's neck unclasped and fell to the ash-covered ground, as if Clover's loss of power made it null and void. The ash-umbrae's hold on Sidraeus loosened. Clover's fury turned to Emory, sensing her interference, knowing she was the one making him weaker.

His ash-umbrae suddenly enveloped him, and Clover disappeared. The look he gave Emory before he vanished was one that promised this wasn't over. But with how weakened he'd become—how weak she'd *made* him—Emory knew he wouldn't be back for some time.

There was a moment of utter stillness, where Emory and the two deities who each had a pull on her magic stood staring at one another. And then—a thunderous noise, a tremble that had them all lurching on their feet. It took a moment for Emory to register what she was seeing. Ash spilled from the fountain like quicksand. And Emory knew the ash meant death. It meant that the worlds would keep dying, because nothing had been fixed. Clover might have disappeared, but the fountain was still depleted, the ley lines still dwindling. And now the ash of what remained of this world at the center of all worlds, this place that used to be the seat of gods, was spreading like death.

Magic would cease to exist unless they fixed it. They had to make the fountain flow again, perhaps bring the gods back to their godsworld, this place that was now a sea of ash.

Someone shouted Emory's name.

The ash in the air had cleared enough now for her to see the Godsgate far down below, an ornate thing that looked made of carved glass or ice, open onto the mountain peaks beyond. Running across the expanse of ash that separated the Godsgate from the fountain where Emory stood were Virgil, Nisha, Vera, and the two draconics.

Relief flooded through her at the sight of her friends. They'd gotten out of the temple alive, had evaded the Songless and made it here in one piece.

But the ash spilling from the fountain was like a tidal wave headed straight for them.

"Look out!" Emory yelled. She wasn't certain they'd heard her, but surely they could see the wave of ash coming their way, surely they would have the good sense to turn around and head for safety before it was too late. Emory moved toward them, desperately thinking of a way to help—but was stopped by Romie grabbing her roughly by the arms.

The look on her best friend's face was full of hatred, unlike anything Emory had ever seen on her. "This is *your* doing," Atheia hissed, nails digging into Emory's skin hard enough to draw blood. "All the power you stole . . ."

"That wasn't me!" Emory struggled to get out of Atheia's hold without hurting Romie. "It was Clover."

"You Tidethieves are all the same. And if I have to spill your blood into the fountain to restore even an ounce of magic, then mark my words—"

Emory was wrenched out of Atheia's grasp by Sidraeus. "Spill another drop of her blood, and I'll split you up into so many pieces you'll never be whole again," he said in that low, silky voice that made the threat sound all the more deadly.

Atheia's mouth curled in contempt. "Sidraeus. It pleases me to know you've come back wrong." Her shifting eyes ran down his torso at that, eyeing the spiral scars that still glimmered faintly there. "Now step away from the Tidethief. Let me sacrifice her to the fountain and fix this mess you've made."

"You and I both know her Tidecaller blood won't replenish the fountain," Sidraeus said. "Nothing will except for us—or the gods themselves. And they're not here to make that happen."

"And whose fault is that? That monster," Atheia said, pointing to where Clover had disappeared, "is a product of your unnatural magic and filthy ambition. All these problems lie with you, Sidraeus. And if the sole reason for my coming back is to wash away the stain of what you created, then I'll gladly give my life once more to see it through."

The two deities launched themselves at each other.

"No!" Emory screamed as Sidraeus sent a surge of crackling dark power flying. But Atheia easily evaded his attack, sidestepping it in a fluid motion. Beams of prismatic light erupted from her middle and pushed back against Sidraeus's shadows. Both deities braced under the impact. They seemed equally matched, neither of them gaining ground. When their magics faded, leaving them unscathed, Atheia *smiled* at Sidraeus, inviting more violence.

Emory whirled on Sidraeus with a hand to his chest. "Stop. You can't kill her—that's *Romie*."

His ecliptic eyes pinned her in place. "I don't care," he snarled at her before launching another wave of power at Romie.

Emory realized she had no control over him. She'd made a bargain to bring him back, and because of this, he was bound to her, yet she had no real power over his actions. And now he was going to kill her best friend. No. She wouldn't let that happen.

Grabbing the ceremonial dagger Clover had used to kill the keys, Emory stabbed herself in the gut.

Sidraeus *screamed*, stumbling back in pain as he searched his middle for a wound that was not there.

When an Eclipse-born is harmed, so too will he be, the souls of the Tidecallers had said.

So maybe she did have power over him after all.

Sidraeus met Emory's gaze as she twisted the dagger deeper into her gut. It hurt like hell, and she wanted so desperately to stop, to wrench the blade out and heal the pain away. But she held his gaze with a stony face, hoping he understood what this meant: that she wasn't above hurting herself if it meant keeping him from killing her best friend.

That he was at her mercy.

"Emory," he gritted out. "What she means to do is inconceivable."

"I don't care," she said with difficulty, shooting his own words back at him. Speaking brought tears to her eyes, made her breath shallow, the pain in her middle unbearable. Her fingers trembled around the blade, but she didn't falter. "If there's a chance Romie's still in there, I can't let you hurt her."

"Listen to your pet, Sidraeus," Atheia crooned. "I'll even play nice and let *you* live, for now, if only for the satisfaction of knowing you'll see me purge what you've created out of this world." She brought Romie's hand up to her face and contemplated the Waning Moon tattoo on the back of it, tracing it lovingly. "I think I'll start where it all began," she added as if speaking to herself.

It was at this very moment that Vivyan and Ivayne landed on the plateau the fountain was built on, their draconic wings unfurled and beating wildly. They were carrying Virgil, Nisha, and Vera–having picked them up, Emory supposed, to avoid the avalanche of ash–and set the three of them down now on shaky legs.

"Romie!" A thousand different emotions danced on Nisha's face. The lines of her body went slack in relief as she lurched toward Romie.

"Don't!" Emory wheezed in warning.

But Nisha had already stopped short, the smile slipping from her face the second those kaleidoscope eyes met hers, and she realized this wasn't Romie at all.

With that unnerving smile, Atheia vanished—dissolving into a great swirl of shimmering air that gusted out of the sea of ash quicker than Emory could make sense of. Sidraeus raged, moving as if to follow her, but stopped as Emory gave another twist of the dagger.

Only when Atheia had fully disappeared and Sidraeus was on his knees looking defeated did Emory pull the dagger out of her stomach. She fell to her own knees, blood spilling in the ash. Dizziness threatened to pull her under, but she stayed lucid enough to call on her healing magic, tending to her wound until the pain subsided to a faint numbness.

Distantly she was aware of Virgil and Vera fussing over her, asking if she was all right. Of Vivyan and Ivayne holding their swords a breath from Sidraeus's neck. Of Nisha staring, aghast, at the spot Romie had vanished. But Emory tuned them all out, her eyes glued to the three bodies lying in the fountain bed, almost entirely buried beneath the ash.

Aspen and Tol and Orfeyi, the three keys whose lives had ended for Atheia to live. Emory hadn't wanted to look at them before, but she forced herself to do so now. She sent a wave of healing toward them, desperate to find a trace of life, something to fix.

But they were dead.

And as what little could be seen of their faces disappeared beneath the ash, Emory wept.

BAZ

IT ALWAYS STARTED OUT THE SAME WAY: BAZ STANDING on Dovermere Cove, watching his past self heading to Cadence with Kai, before making his way up to the Eclipse commons.

It always ended the same, too: Kai going through the door, and Baz ending up in the god's workshop, having failed once more.

The timeline always reset to the original one, and so each time, Baz tried a different method of stopping the outcome. His first attempt had been fueled by desperation. His second, he left all subtlety behind and confronted Kai from the start, hoping that honesty would wield the best results and that together they could come up with a plan. If anything, it felt good not to be alone in this as Kai vowed to do everything in his power to stop Clover.

The chaos that ensued in this timeline still haunted Baz so much that by the third attempt, all he did was observe from the shadows as a ghost–he'd always been good at that–unwilling to change anything at all until the very last second.

In this fourth attempt, Baz strove for balance. He wouldn't

outright show himself to Kai, but couldn't remain entirely a ghost, either. So he left clues. Wrote Kai letters that he slipped in his room. *Don't trust Clover. Don't go through the door. Don't, don't, don't.* He left some for his past self, too, hoping to sow seeds of doubt in both their minds, enough to make them ask the right questions, enough to change the outcome.

But it was as if they never even saw any of his messages. As if someone were destroying them before they could.

Baz thought it might be Clover himself, given how he'd been onto him in the first and second timelines. So he watched Clover closely. Watched Thames, too, since they were both joined at the hip, and Thames, being Eclipse-born, could have easily found the clues Baz left around Obscura Hall. But neither Clover nor Thames seemed to be meddling in Baz's scheming.

The longer he observed them, the more it pained Baz to see how much of Thames was wrapped up in Clover. Their love was obsessive, unhealthy. And more one-sided than Thames believed, because surely Clover did not love him if he was so willing to let him go in the end, watching him Collapse to his untimely death.

Suddenly the answer smacked Baz in the face.

This all started with Clover—and Thames, who did his bidding.

It starts at the root, not the leaf, Baz remembered telling Emory once, when they were in Romie's greenhouse practicing Emory's Sower magic. The root of the problem here had always been Clover. Clover manipulating Thames to Collapse; Clover making Thames take all the blame; Clover replacing Thames with Kai as his Fear Eater slash Nightmare Weaver.

Perhaps this was how Baz could dupe fate. Not by trying to rewrite history entirely, but by replacing one with the other. Not by chipping away wildly at the cup until it might fracture, but by taking out the fragment he was so desperate to erase from the pattern and patching it up with something else to keep the cup intact.

If someone with nightmare magic was needed to go through the door with Clover and Luce, it would not be Kai. This time, it would be Thames.

Guilt churned in Baz's gut at the thought, but he reminded himself that he was doing this to save Kai, and Thames was meant to die anyway. It left the question of Luce, and for that, he felt sorry, thinking he might leave Emory's mother to her grim end. But if fate was irrevocable, and Baz could only save one of them . . .

Who knows—maybe Thames would exert some influence on Clover as they traveled through worlds together, and neither he nor Luce would perish. Maybe it was a small kindness, however twisted, to give Thames more time, to stay a while longer at Clover's side, before meeting his end.

For this to work, Baz needed Thames not to Collapse—to never get any ideas about making a Tidecaller synth that he would inject himself with and succumb to.

Clover and Thames would never have found out the truth about Collapsing if they hadn't realized both Kai and Baz had already Collapsed and now had limitless power. And so Baz tried to alter this one event, turning the knobs on the pocket watch to fast-forward to that day Kai brought a horde of umbrae into the secret library room. Activating the invisibility feature on the pocket watch, Baz watched his past self sitting in the Decrescens library with Clover. Thames came by, asking where Kai and Luce were, before he headed toward the secret room, where he would find them coming out of dreaming with a tempest of darkness all around them.

Baz pulled at the threads of time around Thames and made him pause, freezing him where he stood a few feet from the painting that led into the secret room. His heart pounded furiously as the seconds ticked by, and then the library shuddered under the weight of an explosion of darkness that spilled from the now cracked painting. Baz saw his past self rush toward the room along with Clover. He froze them, too, before remembering that past-Baz had helped Kai and Luce fight back the darkness. If he didn't go into that room to help Kai now . . .

Shit. Baz started to run toward the secret room, but a hand grabbed the back of his shirt, yanking him to a stop. Baz whirled around and shoved his assailant away in panic, wondering distantly if he'd dropped the pocket watch, if the invisibility had stopped working. If his own time magic had slipped.

He'd frozen everyone in the library, and no one was supposed to see him. Yet staring right at him stood a student with blond curls and blue eyes, and for a second, Baz thought it was Clover–that the Tidecaller had somehow evaded Baz's magic. But it wasn't Clover, as evidenced by the House Waning Moon sigil on the boy's hand. Baz had never seen him before, but the boy looked at *him* with recognition–and a sharp, frantic sort of anger.

"You're only making things worse," the boy seethed.

There was a flash of metal from around the boy's neck as he moved toward Baz as if to lunge at him again.

Another explosion of darkness from the secret room–and Kai's voice, screaming–had them both turning their heads at the sound. Baz took off again toward Kai, but something hit his head.

He fell limply to the floor, and darkness took him.

Baz gasped as he came to. He was in the god's workshop again. His head throbbed from whatever had hit him, and he winced as he brought a hand to the tender flesh.

That boy . . .

You're only making things worse.

Had he been the one to hit Baz? How had it made him come

back here, when the timeline hadn't even come to its end yet?

The god was nowhere in sight. Baz tried to get up, but a spell of dizziness kept him down. The pocket watch was still in his hand. He looked it over, fearing it might have gotten damaged somehow, which might explain why the invisibility feature had stopped working. It was the only explanation for that boy seeing him. Unless . . .

Baz froze as he saw the piece of paper tucked into the pocket watch. He flicked the magnifying glass open, and the piece of paper slipped free from its grooves. He unfolded it to find looping handwriting he didn't recognize.

Next time, meet me in Decrescens library. Reaper section.
Don't tell the god.

"Well? Any luck?"

Baz quickly crumpled the piece of paper in his fist. The god was making his way toward him, dabbing his forehead with a cloth.

"I . . ." Baz's thoughts ran wild. He wanted to tell the god what had happened, but the note sowed doubt in his mind. He had a suspicion as to who the boy was, remembering the flash of metal that had glinted around the boy's neck. He cleared his throat, getting up on his feet. "I'm ready to go back now, please."

The god chuckled darkly. "I swear you have a stubborner head than anyone I've ever met. Well, nearly everyone." His eyes pierced through Baz. "Are you sure you wish to go back again so soon?"

"Yes. I'm sure."

The god sighed, snapped his fingers.

And when Baz found himself on Dovermere Cove for the fifth time, he headed not for Obscura Hall, but for the library.

To meet the boy he suspected had been the god's apprentice before him.

EMORY

THE GODSWORLD TREMBLED AGAIN AS ANOTHER WAVE of ash spilled through the door; on the other side, the skies had darkened to an impossible black, giant forks of neon lightning threatening to bring the entire mountain chain down. Emory could make out a horde of white spots in the sky–the Songless astride their winged horses, she was sure of it, heading their way as if called here by the disappearance of their master.

"What happened here?" Nisha's question cut through the silence like a knife. She stared at the three body-shaped mounds of ash in the fountain, then at the spot where Atheia had disappeared. "What happened to–to Romie?"

Emory's throat closed up. "I couldn't stop the keys from being sacrificed." She struggled to get the words past her lips. "And Romie became Atheia's vessel."

Nisha's shoulders dragged low, a strangled sob torn from her lips. There was no real surprise in her reaction, as if she'd already pieced as much together but had not wanted to believe it.

There was a weighted silence, heavy with grief, as the horror of it all settled over them. Emory pushed to her feet, Virgil and Vera helping her up.

"Are you sure you're all right?" Virgil asked.

His face was drawn tight as he eyed Emory's bloodied middle. Emory couldn't help but notice the trembling of his hands, the gauntness of his expression.

"Are *you*?" she asked, glancing between him and Vera. They both looked utterly spent, just as the others did. "What happened at the temple? How did you all get here?"

"Not with *his* help, that's for certain." Ivayne spat, eyes narrowed on Sidraeus, who glared right back at her. She and her mother still held their blades to his throat. "The Night Bringer left us there to fend for ourselves against an army of Songless, not even deigning to tell us what had happened to you."

The Night Bringer. So they knew who he was, despite him wearing a different face.

Emory could picture the scene that must have played out at the temple after Clover had whisked her away: Sidraeus climbing up to the cave where her friends had been facing the Songless; the Songless attacking him, perhaps not recognizing his power as that of the true Soulless One; Sidraeus unleashing himself on them, reminding them exactly where their magic had once come from; and then vanishing from thin air as Emory summoned him to her side.

"There were so many of them," Vera said, face pale. "The Songless would have killed us if it weren't for Ivayne and Vivyan and well, let's just say we almost didn't make it."

Emory didn't miss Vera's furtive glance at Virgil, nor the way his eyes remained downcast. Blood dripped from a wound in the palm of his hand, a telltale sign that he'd bloodlet. Bleak understanding dawned on her: he must have used his Reaper magic.

Had likely taken a life in order to save his own, and their friends'.

"What about him—should I cut him down where he kneels or are you able to control him now that he's bound to your will?" Vivyan asked, propping the tip of her blade under Sidraeus's chin.

His attention had been on the Godsgate, as if he were planning to disappear as Atheia had and follow her to the end of all worlds if he must. Now he looked at the draconics with cold calculation, the lines of his body tensing like he was about to disarm them. But then, as if feeling Emory's eyes on him, his gaze caught on the bloody dagger still in her hand. She gripped it tighter in warning.

"I can't exactly control him," Emory said without letting her focus waver from Sidraeus, "but he's not a threat, and he can still be of help."

Yet the draconics didn't put their swords down as Sidraeus rose to his feet with a scowl, and neither did Emory's grip loosen from her dagger.

"How did Atheia do it?" she asked Sidraeus. "Vanish like that?"

It looked like it took everything out of him to give her a response. "A power of hers, to take the shape of the elements of whatever world she's in. I expect she's heading to the previous world's door. She won't stop until she reaches your world."

To wash away the stain of what you created . . .

Understanding hit Emory. That was what Atheia meant when she said she'd start where it all began.

"She means to eradicate Eclipse magic." Emory breathed the words out in disbelief. It was the only explanation for Atheia's threat, except . . . "I thought Atheia couldn't travel between worlds without you to guide her through the sleepscape."

Sidraeus gave her a hard stare. "I suppose she's unbound from the previous conditions that tethered her to the living realms, just as I seem to be untethered from mine."

Emory hadn't even thought of it. Before, when Sidraeus was still roaming these worlds with Atheia, he'd never once done so in his true form. Atheia had found a way to bring him into the living realms, yes, but only as his shadow self–as an umbra. He'd wanted to experience the realms of the living as his true self. And now he could, thanks to the bargain Emory had made through the syrinx.

She didn't expect him to see it that way. The hatred in his glare, the hint of betrayal behind it, burned through her core.

The world shook again, sending everyone tumbling.

"We need to get out of here," Vivyan said. "Get somewhere safe."

"Where?" Ivayne huffed. "Nowhere feels safe now."

"With Inga and her people?" Vera suggested. "Just to regroup. Figure out our next move."

"Hold on," Virgil said, turning to Emory, "what did you mean about Atheia *eradicating* Eclipse magic? What would that mean for you, Em? And Baz, and Kai? If Atheia gets rid of Eclipse magic somehow, do you all just . . . die?"

Emory looked at Sidraeus for an answer, but he evaded her gaze. "I don't know," she said. "But she'll stop at nothing, not even the end of the worlds, to see it done."

"Then we need to go home," Nisha said. She'd been quiet until now, the mix of devastation and grief and determination on her face an echo of how Emory felt. "We need to stop her."

A look passed between Nisha and Emory. Neither of them said aloud the too-big, too-hopeful thought that popped into their minds. That perhaps they could find a way to save Romie. To exorcize Atheia out of her, the way Sidraeus had eventually left Keiran's body.

Only this time, the vessel couldn't die.

"I'm all for that idea," Virgil said as the ground lurched beneath them again, "but how in the Deep do we get out of here?"

The ash below them was still a veritable sea, a riptide they would get lost in if on foot. Vivyan and Ivayne couldn't carry all of them to the door. And besides, the other side didn't look any more inviting than in here, with the awaiting Songless ready to attack them.

Emory turned to Sidraeus. "Is there nothing you can do?"

Sidraeus only stared at her—then laughed, a short, cruel huff. "You bargain away my soul, use whatever *this* is"—he motioned to his spiral scars—"to bring me to my knees, and now you want my help?"

Emory ignored the twisting guilt in her gut. "We're in this together now whether you like it or not. If Atheia's headed to our world, if she's going after Eclipse-born . . . That pain you felt from me earlier? It will be *nothing* compared to the pain you'll feel from *all of us* who have a trace of your magic. You want to take your revenge on Atheia? Then help us stop her."

A confusing mix of emotions shone on Sidraeus's face before he seemed to catch himself and fight for neutrality. For a second, Emory thought he might kill her here and now, consequences be damned. But he only extended a hand to her.

"Grab on to me," he said. "All of you."

At Emory's hesitation, Sidraeus's voice rang in her mind. *Don't you trust me, Tidecaller?*

There was an edge of challenge there as he held her gaze. She didn't trust him—*couldn't*. But she trusted that his thirst for revenge would outweigh everything else. And so she grabbed his hand.

His skin was pleasantly warm, and she found herself looking at him, still trying to make sense of the *real* him. For a moment, she got lost in his ecliptic eyes. She used to find them unnatural, haunting. But perhaps that was just because of the face he had been wearing then.

In this face, his true face, his eyes were nothing short of breathtaking.

Emory looked away, trying to chase away such thoughts. Vivyan was the first of the group to relent, moving to Sidraeus's other side and laying a hand on his forearm. Her other hand, Emory noticed, remained on her sword. Everyone else followed suit.

Sidraeus never looked away from Emory. She locked eyes with him again.

"Hold on," he said.

His shadow lengthened over him, appearing again like this separate entity, as if the crowned umbra was always by Sidraeus's side. It swallowed them all up like the dark maw of some great beast, and the sea of ash around them vanished.

Emory held on to Sidraeus for dear life, feeling like she were being squeezed through a tunnel of oppressive dark. Stars rushed past them at dizzying speed, a maelstrom of swirling black interspersed with glittering spots. This felt nothing like when Clover had whisked her away from the temple; that had felt like she'd dissolved into nothing before coming back to herself in an entirely different place. This . . . it was as if Sidraeus had become the darkness—the shadow he had embodied in the sleeping realm—to travel from one place to another, just as Atheia had become the elements.

Emory's eardrums popped as the darkness suddenly abated. They now stood on the mossy banks of a familiar hot spring—the place where they'd first arrived in the fourth world. In the distance, Emory could see the storms raging over the mountains they'd just left behind.

She blinked up at Sidraeus, trying to work out what just happened. Her friends looked just as confused and queasy from the experience. Virgil doubled over to spill his guts on the snow-covered ground.

The runes on Sidraeus's skin were bright with ethereal light. "I can only travel this way within each world," he said. "We'll need to cross through the space between worlds by foot."

Emory searched their surroundings. "But—how do we find the

door back to the previous world? I thought it was impossible to go back through the doors."

At least, that's what they'd assumed. Never backward, always forward. It was why Emory and Romie had never been able to find the door they'd first come through in the Wychwood to return home. Why they'd been forced to find the next door instead.

"There is a way to travel backward," Sidraeus said. "If you have an instrument Atheia and I created. A compass we gifted to our disciples in case they ever got trapped between worlds or separated from the Tidecallers who had the power to move freely between worlds."

The Veiled Atlas compass.

Vera clasped it where it hung around her neck. Sidraeus eyed it with a flicker of unreadable emotion. "That compass would reveal the way back to you," he said, then turned to Emory. "But a Tidecaller can find the door without it."

"How?"

Sidraeus had Emory stand on the ley line and listen to it as she once had. It felt corrupted beyond measure, but she managed to find the point where its magic converged in a nexus of power. *Now call on it,* Sidraeus's voice said in her mind, nearly making her lose focus. *Make it manifest itself. Like a secret you're coaxing into the light.*

Emory let the allure of his voice wash over her. Everything in her seemed to go calm. She called on a blend of Unraveler and Wordsmith magics, willing the door to appear, the same door they had stepped through to enter this fourth world. It did, shimmering into existence before their very eyes—an ice-covered basalt door, much like the one Elín had guided them through to bring them to the hidden community in the grotto.

Emory pressed a hand to the door and jerked back in surprise as it opened, already unlocked.

As if Atheia's passing through here had unlocked it for her, eliminating the need for keys. Because she *was* the keys, and they were her.

For a second, Emory let herself hope that the doors being open might mean the worlds would stop dying, the power from the fountain able to flow freely through worlds again. But the image of the empty fountain flashed in her mind, and the ley lines beneath her feet still felt wrong, rotten. The fountain was dead. It didn't matter if the doors were unlocked; there was no flow of energy feeding into the ley lines, and so the worlds would keep dying.

There had to be a way to replenish the fountain.

But first: stopping Atheia from destroying the Eclipse-born.

With one last look over her shoulder, Emory left the stormy world behind and stepped into the sleepscape. They walked up and up the spiraling path of stars until they reached the already-open door that led into the Heartland's Sunforge–the door Emory had blasted open. Here, they said goodbye to Vivyan and Ivayne, who understandably felt the need to go back to their own world to deal with the rot spreading there, too.

"I trust you'll give him hell if he steps out of line," Ivayne said as she hugged Emory, clearly meaning Sidraeus. He hung a few steps back, the lines of his body taut while he scanned the sleepscape, as if he couldn't wait to get out of here.

"I will," Emory said, certain he could hear them. "Say hi to Gwenhael for us, will you?"

Ivayne squeezed Emory's arm like a promise before joining her mother at the threshold to their world.

"Be safe, all of you," Vivyan said with a doleful smile.

And just like that, the two draconics were gone. They hadn't been with them for very long, but parting ways felt like another gutting loss that Emory couldn't bear.

The rest of them kept going through the sleepscape. With

Sidraeus walking alongside them, they didn't need to go through each individual world again. He would lead them directly to their own.

And so they bypassed the marble door with the knotted knob that would lead to the Wychwood. Kept going along the path, feeling the darkness pressing in, making breathing harder and harder the farther they went, the longer they stayed in this realm they were not meant to exist in. Only Emory was fine. And Sidraeus, too, who belonged to this realm despite not wanting to be confined to it.

Finally, they came upon the silver door adorned with etchings of waves.

Emory nearly burst into tears upon seeing it, remembering the last time she'd been here, finally reunited with Romie. And now she was returning without her, but with a tiny hope that she might still save her.

Emory pushed against the door, the silver cool against her skin, a feeling of rightness singing in her blood.

They were going home.

ROMIE

ATHEIA BLEW THROUGH THIS WORLD SHE ONCE KNEW so well, her heart breaking at the storm-wrought destruction. She could feel the ley lines beneath the earth, these rivers of power that the fountain fed into. Except the fountain was dried up, and the power that trickled here was foul, spoiling the magic she had created.

Everything had changed, yet Atheia still knew where to find the way to the previous world. The door that stood there–locked by the gods to seal the way between realms–angered her. She still remembered when the doors had been open, when the ley lines flowed freely between realms, the divine power of the fountain running like healthy bloodstreams. That was no longer the case.

Atheia blasted through the door with a scream that sounded like a howling of wind, calling on all the elements of this world to unlock the door. She was not going to be kept out. She was the keys, after all. And while, before, she would have needed Sidraeus to help her cross through the sleeping realm on an eclipse, she found she did not need him now. As if being brought back together again had shattered whatever limitations had existed on her before.

Atheia forced herself to go through each world the same way. In the Heartland, she moved through the unnaturally cold lands as embers on a breeze, lamenting the absence of dragons in the sunless skies. In the Wychwood, she ran through the root systems beneath the earth, despairing at the rot that festered there. And finally, she flowed into the world she had always loved best, where the moon and tides had always welcomed her home.

She fell to her knees in the wet sand, a sob slipping from her vessel's lips as icy waves lapped over her legs, washing the blood from her hands. The blood her vessel had spilled to allow her to come back.

It was strange, being in a body not her own. But the girl—*Romie*—had been right: the similarities between them coursed through Atheia as she let the girl's memories, her very essence, wash over her. Dreamers, both. Resentful, both, of those who carried Sidraeus's magic—though the girl was trying very hard to pretend otherwise.

And most of all, both were grieving the loss of the others who had carried a piece of Atheia. The others she had sung to, calling them to each other, to the sea of ash that was once the godsworld, so that she could return to the realms of the living she so dearly cared for.

Aspen, Tol, Orfeyi, her mind supplied as Romie's memories of them rose to the surface.

Atheia listened more closely to the faint trace of her vessel's essence that still remained. At the forefront of her emotions was a great, endless grief for these friends she had made. The sense of loss was harrowing. Romie had felt such a strong sense of kinship to Aspen, Tol, and Orfeyi, and now they were gone. Killed.

If only Emory had listened to me. If only she hadn't shown up.

A tangled web of emotions sprung up at the thought of her Tidecaller friend. On the one hand, Romie was relieved Emory had not been harmed. On the other, she couldn't help but place part of the blame for the keys' deaths on her. Emory hadn't trusted her, and everything had gone wrong because of it.

The brunt of Romie's rage, though, was reserved for Clover. *He* had been the one to kill the keys. He was the Tidethief Romie wanted to see destroyed.

Just as Atheia wanted to destroy Sidraeus—to eradicate the stain of his magic.

A millennia's worth of feelings overcame Atheia at the thought of him. Her opposite. Her perfect match. Her lover.

Her betrayer and enemy.

Sidraeus had looked no different than when she had last seen him centuries ago, except for those spiral runes burned on his skin. She had no clue what they were or how he'd obtained them, but one thing was for certain: they'd been hurting him. And Atheia took no small amount of pleasure at the idea, even as her own heart twisted painfully with old, resurging feelings.

There was too much history between them. So much Atheia wished to take back, to forget, to burn from her heart. Her heart, which he had broken. Her trust, which he had shattered.

As the waves lapped around her, her vessel's body shivering, Atheia was possessed with the sudden need to make Romie understand—to wash away the girl's trepidation at the thought of what Atheia was setting out to do. Atheia didn't want to feel alone, didn't want to fight for room with her vessel's conflicting feelings. They could inhabit this body together. Seek revenge against Sidraeus and ensure the preservation of her own creations *together.*

But first Romie needed to see things as Atheia did. And so,

with the Memorist magic of the Waning Moon, Atheia shared her memories.

Atheia had always embodied the human's ability to dream. As the hand of the four gods she served, a conduit for their power, she was able to dream up magic in different ways and mold it as a true visionary.

Her life revolved around creation, imagination. She took pride in what she built in these worlds that were like a blank canvas, the magic she shared with these humans who worshipped her. She was the divine breath that blew through them at their behest, and she *thrived* on the love they gave back to her. It was her whole reason for existing–to be seen as benevolent and beautiful, loved by these people who saw her as their god and whom she loved so deeply in return.

She had never gotten that love from anyone else.

The gods she answered to had all but cast her out, leaving her to do their bidding on her own. They never cared enough about her to love her; they only wished for her to carry out their will. Atheia was a god in her people's eyes, yet she was still doomed to be *her* gods' puppet while they languished in the divine gardens they called home, barely sparing a glance for the worlds they'd created.

At least Atheia had her people's love, and for a time this was all she needed.

Yet nothing could ever quite sate this loneliness she felt.

Until Sidraeus.

A mirror soul to hers, as lonely as she was, as abandoned as she felt by the god he answered to. In those early days of their courtship, when Atheia first brought Sidraeus into the lunar world as his shadow self and his presence created a new brand of magic, she saw it as the missing piece to her own creations. A balance that she alone could not conjure. It completed the work of art she'd started and made a masterpiece of it.

They had created such beauty together, with these two magics. And when Sidraeus spoke of wanting more—of wanting to see the other worlds, create other magics; of wanting to come into the realms of the living freely and in his true form, not this bodiless, nightmare version of him that he had to settle for—Atheia found herself wanting the same things. She yearned to be with him fully, body and soul, and keep creating masterpieces together without the limitations set by their gods.

She had never wanted anything more in her life, until the jealousy and resentment crept in.

Atheia had always been alone, but now she found herself sharing the limelight—her people's devotion split between her and Sidraeus. She *wanted* to share all of it with him. But these worlds, these people, this magic . . . they had been hers and hers alone for so long that sharing them now proved difficult. Especially as Sidraeus gained more and more favor, and the natural divide between their powers began to create divides between their people.

Especially as she started to feel the toll of *his* creations on *her*.

The magic born of Sidraeus's presence could not survive in this world without Atheia's own magic. They were intrinsically entwined. Eclipse magic was its own thing, but it fed on lunar magic—on *her*.

She didn't mind at first. Sidraeus always said she was the answer to all his prayers, the answer to his call for help, for freedom, for the chance at creating something of his own. *You called, and I answered,* Atheia would say fondly. It had given them the idea to call his creations Tidecallers. These people born of the eclipse, who called on the Tides to sustain the magic of both the moon and the eclipse inside them.

Atheia was fond of them as she was fond of Sidraeus. They were hers as much as his, and she loved them as deeply as she did her lunar mages, none more so than a girl she could have called sister for how close they'd become.

Until that resentment set in. Until ugly thoughts wormed their way into her mind, making her see these creations as cheap copies of her own, copies that twisted the pure magic she had spent so long building in this world, made it darker, impure. That resentment grew until she viewed Sidraeus as a thief. Someone who took what she graciously offered and tried to make it all his, to make it *better* than hers.

Still, Atheia stomped away that jealousy. She and Sidraeus had a dream, a shared vision: to elevate themselves to the godly status they were always meant to have. To be gods in their own right, ruling over every realm the way they saw fit and sharing their power widely and without limits. To rule over the realms of life and death, together.

But all these desires would be their downfall. She knew this for certain when her gods began to whisper of the chaos that loomed over the worlds. They said the god of balance had seen it in the tapestry of fate, this havoc that would spread across the realms of the living until there was nothing of them left.

Atheia knew it for what it was: divine retribution.

She had gone against the gods' wishes to keep her and Sidraeus separate, confined to their respective realms. She had taken Sidraeus out of the sleeping realm and brought him into the realms of the living, and by allowing him to create these new magics, by letting the Veiled Atlas travel between worlds, it would create an imbalance in the very fabric of the universe.

She was devastated. To know that all her dreams and ambitions might fall away to nothing... She couldn't bear it. Had to protect her creations—the humans she loved, the magic they shared—no matter the cost. Even if it meant losing the Tidecallers she still cared for despite everything, the sister she might have had. Even if it meant losing her one true love, being apart from him except on eclipses, the way it had initially been. The way it was always meant to be.

Atheia was willing to sacrifice it all for the preservation of her creations.

Sidraeus was not.

He would not hear of it. Only grew bitter and angry at her reasoning. *If the realms fall, it will be our doing,* she told him. *We never should have gone against the way of things.*

To which he scoffed, saying, *It's the way of things that is wrong. And this idea that what we created here will lead to some great, worlds-breaking imbalance . . . I reject it. Look around you, Atheia: all I see are worlds that are flourishing.*

Atheia could not reason with him. She felt his desperation, the despair that darkened his face at the thought of going back to the grim existence he'd known. And Atheia could not help but think that he cared more about losing this freedom than he did about losing her.

It stung. She loved him, but evidently that love was not enough for him. So she, too, would choose these worlds and their magic over him.

If the worlds were bound to crumble because of Sidraeus's presence in the living realms—because of these *Tidethieves* that kept leeching power away from Atheia, from the worlds themselves—then they all had to go. And Atheia would do anything to make that happen.

So she betrayed him. While he moved forward with his plan to wrest magic from the fountain, she appeared before the gods themselves and confessed to them what she and Sidraeus had done. What Sidraeus was trying to do now. She pleaded with them for mercy on both their parts.

Send him back to the sleeping realm, she begged, *and his Tidecallers with him. Do what you must with me, for I know I was wrong and must be punished. But please. Restore the balance between our realms, and I swear neither I nor Sidraeus will ever again go beyond our borders. Your will is ours, forevermore.*

But the gods merely sneered at her in anger. She was too late, they told her, because Sidraeus had already come this way with his most faithful Tidecallers, weaseling his way past the Godsgate to try to steal power from the gods.

Atheia couldn't believe it. *Did it work?* she asked in equal parts horror and admiration, dread and hope. Jealousy and love.

A thousand emotions rushed through her as the gods told her of Sidraeus's failure. How he tried to siphon the fountain's power through the four Tidecallers at his side, only to see those Tidecallers burn out entirely from the overload of power, like dying stars collapsing in on themselves. The blast that echoed through them passed through all worlds, all realms, ushering their destruction faster.

Atheia had felt it. Her power had waned to naught for a terrible, heart-stopping moment. She had thought she was dying, pulled from the loveliest dream into a terrible nightmare. But when she'd opened her eyes, it had been over. Her power left intact.

Now she knew what had caused this brief impuissance. His Tidecallers must have reached out to her magic—unwittingly or not, it did not matter—as they tried to take the power from the gods' fountain. But they failed, and threw the worlds into deeper horror as a result.

What will happen now? Atheia asked the gods.

Fate has already been set in motion, they replied. *The balance of the universe is forever undone. There is no fixing what is broken beyond repair, other than to wipe clean the board and start anew.*

But why not just get rid of the Tidecallers? Atheia pled. *If they are the cause of this impending destruction, if they are the source of this problem, then surely you can get rid of them before the damage is done. Spill their blood and seal the doors between realms with it.*

The four living gods seemed to consider it. But the fifth, the god of balance, shook his head at the last, his word reigning supreme over the others. *It would not be enough.*

Fury swept through Atheia. She clenched her fists, trembling with the force of her barely leashed rage. This was Sidraeus's fault. Her creations, all her hard work, would be *wiped clean*, destroyed forever, because of *him*. Because of his thirst for power and freedom and inability to compromise. Because she had let him into her realms, into her heart, and he chose power over her.

The gods trapped Sidraeus in his prison between the stars. They told Atheia she would be confined furthermore to the godsworld. That, once they wiped clean the board and started anew, she would never be allowed to set foot in the realms of the living. Never be allowed to create as she once did, to share magic with these people she loved and who loved her.

She would be nothing more than a handmaiden to the gods, who would pull her strings like puppeteers as they remade the worlds in the blandest way possible. Without magic, they said, for they couldn't risk history repeating itself.

But a life without magic, without *imagination*, was no life at all.

Atheia raged and cried and despaired. She prayed.

One god answered.

The moon goddess had always had a soft spot for Atheia. She was far from loving by any means, for Atheia did not think gods knew what love was. But she had always taken an interest in Atheia's creation, made her feel valuable for it. It was probably why Atheia favored the lunar world. And now the moon goddess came to her under cover of secrecy, at her most dire hour of need, and helped set her free.

A creator cannot die if their creations survive, the goddess whispered to Atheia, *just as a board cannot be wiped clean if its key pieces remain fused to it.*

Atheia had stared at her in confusion. *I don't understand....*

We cannot go against his word, the goddess whispered, *but you can. Scatter yourself across our realms—your realms—and you might just save us all.*

At once Atheia understood. She never doubted the goddess's intent, saw the fear well enough in her quicksilver eyes. The goddess did not wish for the destruction of worlds, no more than Atheia did. Perhaps the other living gods felt the same, it was just that none of them could go against the god of balance.

But Atheia might.

So Atheia escaped the godsworld with a plan.

She would not let the god of balance wipe clean the fruit of her efforts, the masterpiece she had created. Understanding the moon goddess's cryptic words, Atheia fragmented herself, leaving a part of her in every world she had called home.

Her blood poured into the seas of the lunar world, the Tides forever flowing into the veins of its mages. Her bones burrowed deep into the soil of the Wychwood, so the Sculptress could shape magic into the flesh and bones of its witches. Her heart burned eternal in the fires of great volcanoes and the dragons they spawned, the Forger's strength melded into the hearts of its faithful knights. And her soul remained adrift on the winds of the final world, taking as many shapes as there were Celestials, breathing their magic to those who kept music alive.

Each part a key. A failsafe to prevent the total destruction of worlds.

And it worked—the worlds had not been reset, and Atheia's

creations had been kept alive, her magic preserved.

But then this Clover person—this *Tidethief*—had imbibed that magic. He had stolen the previous incarnations of Atheia, gorging himself on the power of their bearers to make himself into this monstrous imitation of divinity. He had chased away the gods from their godsworld, had taken every last drop of the fountain for himself, and reduced the divine garden into a wasteland. So many lives slain for nothing, because now that stolen power was festering inside him, and he needed more.

The realms would fall to ruin because of him. At least Atheia could take comfort in the fact that he had failed at imbibing her own divine power, and Sidraeus's, to make himself into a proper god. But she knew he would stop at nothing to try again. And if he succeeded, he would destroy all of Atheia's magic to rebuild the worlds in his image. In *Sidraeus's* image.

The reign of the eclipse.

Atheia would have liked Clover to destroy Sidraeus in that damned fountain. Would have liked to do it herself, so she could be rid of the thorn in her side that was her former lover. And perhaps his destruction would have brought about the destruction of his creations.

A creator cannot die if their creations survive.

No. It wouldn't be so easy. But she could damn well try.

The waves grew stronger around her. The tide was coming in at frightening speed. Atheia pushed up to her feet, shivering from the cold in her sopping clothes. There was a wrongness to the sea, a dark hunger that frightened her.

I cannot let this world fall, Atheia thought pleadingly to Romie's sliver of consciousness. *If the price of saving it is culling Eclipse magic from it, then I'm sorry, but I have to see it done. Please understand.*

A thrum of empathy met her words. Still hesitant, there was no doubt about it, but it was perhaps the best Atheia could hope for. She could feel Romie's anger and disappointment at her Tidethief friend, feel her rage against the Tidethief god, two sides tugging on the rope of her grief. Atheia could use those feelings to further sour her against the Eclipse-born.

I don't want your person to be erased by my presence in your body, Atheia told Romie, meaning every word. *I want us to do this as one. Take my hand and let me pull you up from the depths your consciousness went to. Let us share this body and face this darkness together.*

She felt Romie's consciousness reach out to the metaphorical hand she extended, and Atheia pulled her up. Atheia had experience being split into multiple identities, so it wasn't all that unfamiliar to share consciousness with Romie now. And they were so alike, she didn't mind it at all.

"Welcome back, daughter of Quies," Atheia murmured, the words swallowed by the tide.

Let's save this world, Romie replied with resolve. *Together.*

BAZ

BAZ WASN'T SURE HOW LONG HE WAITED IN THE REAPER section of the Decrescens library. Students came and went, and he remained, invisible, a ghost watching the living go by. Until one of those students sat across from him and looked directly at him, smiling.

"You got my message."

Baz looked him over, wondering how he could have mistaken him for Clover before. There was the House Waning Moon sigil tattoo, for one thing. Plus, the boy's hair wasn't quite as pale or as long as Clover's; his eyes were a deep blue, not the ghostly turquoise that haunted Baz's every thought. And where Clover's features were delicate and finely chiseled, like a god sculpted out of marble, this boy's were sharper, like they were hewn from stone. Strong jaw. Strong nose. Rugged good looks. Younger than Clover, yet timeless, somehow. And his clothes . . .

Slacks and a sweater that were too modern for these times.

And around his neck, hanging from a chain, was a pocket watch identical to the one in Baz's own pocket.

"You're him, aren't you?" Baz blurted out. "The god of balance's apprentice. The one that came before me."

The boy gave himself a half-hearted flourish. "In the flesh."

Baz frowned, remembering how the god had made it seem like his apprentice had died. "But if you came before me . . . how am I seeing you now?"

"Haven't you learned by now that time isn't linear?" He tapped the pocket watch around his neck. "Working for the god means existing out of time, being able to travel between moments at will." He shrugged. "So two time travelers meeting in a time that holds significance for us both? Sounds pretty normal to me."

"What significance does this hold for you?"

"From the looks of it, I've been at this far longer than you have," the boy said, ignoring Baz's question. "Being fate's overseer . . . that's my job. I'm here to ensure everything happens as it should."

"That's why you've been destroying my notes to Kai," Baz said accusingly. "You don't want me to change the outcome."

At Kai's name, the boy's face dropped. "That's not . . ." He looked guilty. Torn. "I'm mostly here for Thames."

"Thames?"

A nod. "The way he dies is important. And you trying to mess with that could make everything worse."

The way he dies . . . "You mean how he Collapses?"

"Taking that Tidecaller synth. Collapsing because of it."

"But . . . why?"

"Because I wouldn't be here otherwise." Seeing Baz open his mouth to press him further, the boy added, "But that's not why I wanted to meet with you. You're trying to change Kai's fate, right?"

"A fate worse than death, according to the god," Baz said grimly. "The kind of oblivion that's entirely irreversible."

"Yes, well. Oblivion is what awaits *all* of us if we don't save Kai from his fate."

"What?"

The boy shushed him as a few students looked their way, frowning as they likely couldn't see the two invisible time travelers talking to each other.

"All I know," the boy said in a low murmur, "is that Kai ends up in the deepest recesses of the abyss, what we in this world call the Deep—but not as a soul, not as someone who died. And because that's never happened before . . . Well, let's just say his fate isn't something that's fixed into the larger design of things. As such, it remains changeable."

Baz's mind raced, trying to imagine Kai in what was essentially *hell*.

"But what you're attempting to do here, in this time, is futile," the boy continued. "Kai *has* to go through the door. You're never going to be able to change this simple fact." Before Baz could argue, the boy held up a hand. "Think of it this way: there are crucial points in the tapestry of fate, like sections of pattern that can never be undone. But the threads around those fixed patterns? Some are more fragile than others. Some are still waiting to be woven into the tapestry. Which means those are the threads you need to try and change. Kai going through the door, that's an undoable pattern. But what comes after . . ."

"A loose thread," Baz murmured, and the boy nodded. "But how do I get to Kai if I can't follow him to where he is now? Does it mean I can't save him from his fate at all? And what did you mean when you said we'll all face oblivion if I can't—"

"One thing at a time," the boy interrupted with the ghost of a smile. "What you need to focus on is Kai, who you *can* save . . . but not now. Not here in the past."

He took out a neatly folded paper from his pocket and unfolded it on the table between them. It looked like a school document that was typed up on a typewriter, but the paper was old and thinning. In between the faded block letters was tiny, handwritten script. And in the middle of the page, someone had drawn a tree. The top part of it was flourishing, while below, the roots twined in a way that could make a second tree, this one bare and dead looking, if the page were flipped.

In the middle of the tree was a spiral with a lock at its innermost point.

"What is this?" Baz asked.

"A ritual that might undo one of those undoable patterns. That might disrupt the entire fabric of fate."

That might save Kai, was all Baz heard.

He studied the page closer, trying to decipher what the script said. "Wait—this is in another language!" he exclaimed. "Can you read it?"

"No. It's the language of gods, a language very few know."

"How is this helpful to me then?" Baz wasn't daft enough to ask the god of balance to translate a ritual that might undo the very thing he lived for. "If no one can decipher it . . ." He stopped short as the answer came to him: *Selandyn.* The Eclipse professor was an Omnilinguist, able to understand all languages.

The boy was looking at him knowingly, as if he'd expected Baz to come to this very conclusion.

"Who are you?" Baz asked, trying to puzzle the boy out. His gut told him he could trust him, but there was something about him, about this whole situation, that set him on edge.

The boy gave him a sad smile. "I'm someone who wants the same thing you do. Which is why you can't say any of this to the god. He can't know you're trying to undermine fate."

"That ship's already sailed, I'm afraid."

"No, not like this. What you're doing here? This time traveling?

The god knows you won't end up changing anything. Otherwise he wouldn't have sent you. But this"–he tapped the paper–"*this*, he can't find out about. Because this is your one shot at *actually* changing fate. Not just for Kai, but for all of us."

"If you have this ritual, why haven't you tried it yourself?"

"It's hard to explain, but where I am now . . . rather, where I will be . . . I have a different part to play. This one's yours." He got up, his chair grating loudly on the floorboards. He studied Baz for a second, chewing on the inside of his cheek. There was something wistful in his eyes, something like regret, when he finally said, "I hope we see each other again."

Baz stared at the drawing of the tree intensely. A question on his lips, he looked up–only to find the boy had disappeared.

Baz did not know how to make himself go back to the god's workshop besides coming to the end of the time loop, so he sped up time until it was the night before his past self and the others would set out to undo the wards. He wanted a moment to himself to think all this through before he had to return to the god, and so he sat in the Eclipse commons, invisible, and studied the ritual the apprentice had given him well into the night.

Eventually he must have fallen asleep.

He realized he hadn't gotten any rest while going through these time loops, save for once after his second attempt; the trauma of that one had made him reticent to jump back in, so he'd heeded the god's advice and took some time to rest before jumping back in for the third attempt.

Now sleep pulled him into a familiar nightmare. He couldn't remember the last time he'd been haunted by the printing press. It didn't feel as nightmarish to him now, as Baz sat down in the wreckage, hugging his legs to his chest. Maybe he'd seen too much of actual fear to be fearful of this memory anymore.

He felt a familiar presence at his side. Kai sat next to him, watching the printing press with something close to fondness.

"Been a while since we've been here," he said wistfully.

"Yeah," Baz breathed. He realized with sudden horror that this might be the last time he spoke to Kai here in the past. That it might be the last time he saw him *ever* if he couldn't work out the ritual.

Kai gave him a quizzical look. "You all right?"

A storm of feelings rose up inside Baz. How powerless he felt against the unconquerable beast that was fate. The sliver of hope he would hold on to now that he had this senseless ritual. This unending dread at the thought of losing Kai for good.

Without thinking, Baz leaned in to kiss him. It was soft and lingering as he tried to etch the memory of Kai's lips in his mind. Of the supple feel of his hair against his fingers, and his scent like crisp midnight air. Not wanting to break the kiss, he rested his forehead against Kai's, closing his eyes.

He wanted to tell Kai he'd find a way to save him. Wanted to tell him how scared he was of losing him forever once he went through the door. But he'd tried this all before, and nothing had changed. So instead, Baz said, "Whatever happens, promise me you'll remember that . . . that I love you."

I love you.

Three words neither of them had ever said to the other, neither in dreaming nor waking.

Kai pulled back to look into Baz's eyes with such depth and love echoed back, it made Baz want to cry. The words felt momentous. They were truer than anything Baz had ever spoken. And for a moment, he hoped those words would somehow survive the end of the time loop. That future-Kai would remember them, wherever he was. That he would hold on to them until Baz found a way to bring him back to him.

Kai opened his mouth to say something, but Baz pressed the tip of his fingers to his lips. "Don't say anything back," he whispered. "Not until all this is over."

Not until I fix this. Not until we see each other again.

Because if Kai *were* to say it back, Baz wanted it to be real.

Kai pulled Baz's hand away from his mouth and pressed a kiss into the palm before lacing his fingers through his. His smile was answer enough, and as Baz woke, he swore he could still feel Kai's lips on his skin.

For the last time, Baz watched Kai go through the door without him. Then, when he appeared once more in the god's workshop, he looked the god straight in the eye and said, "You were right. I can't change the outcome."

The god blinked at him a few times, clearly taken aback. "Well," he bumbled. "I'm glad you've finally come to your senses. I know it can be a hard truth to accept, but there are still things you *can* change, Basil. Out there, in your own time."

"I know." The folded-up ritual burned in his pocket. He handed the god the pocket watch. "I'm ready to go now, if we're done here, that is."

The god looked delighted. And though Baz yearned to ask him about his old apprentice, to poke and prod about all the things the god was clearly hiding from him, he did not.

He had to trust that the apprentice was right.

And if the god of balance wanted Baz at present-day Aldryn, then that's where Baz would go. Because there he would find a way to change Kai's fate, even if it was the last thing he ever did.

KAI

KAI STARED IN SHOCKED SILENCE AT THE EMPTY PILE OF clothes where Asphodel had been. In truth, he shouldn't have been so surprised by the act; he'd always known there was something vile inside Clover.

The image made Kai remember Clover's recurring nightmare, the one where Clover was bent over Cordie, cradling her body as she died. Clover had no tears to shed for Asphodel now. And perhaps that was the truth of him: outside of his love for his sister, this was a man who was cold to the bone, heartless to his core. He only cared for people so long as they were useful to him, but once they served their purpose, they were expendable.

And now Clover had *imbibed* the witch's life force. He'd taken her power, down to the very last drop, because that's what he felt he had to do to achieve this vision of his as the world's savior.

What he said about Emory bringing about the destruction of the worlds . . . It's not true.

The pieces came together in Kai's mind with sudden clarity, a memory he could barely remember having, but there nonetheless. Before Clover could stop him, Kai threw himself at him, grabbing him by the collar and shoving him hard against the basalt columns.

"Baz was right," Kai said with a bitter laugh as Clover tried unsuccessfully to slip from his grasp. "You're going to lead these worlds to their doom."

Anger pulsed through Kai with such ferocity, a voice in his mind telling him to end it all right here, to stop Clover before it was too late. Before he could give in to that violence, he was blasted back by a surge of white-hot light emanating from Clover. Kai hit the ground painfully. Stars danced in his eyes as he tried to push up on his elbows, a sharp pain in his side. Luce was suddenly crouching over him, helping him into a sitting position. He wiped at the trickle of blood running down his chin, glowering up at Clover.

"I'm not going to break the worlds." Clover's hands glowed bright, his eyes flashing an unnatural shade of turquoise. He looked almost holy. "I'm going to rebuild them anew. Make them better."

Kai laughed darkly, wincing at the pain. Had he cracked a rib? "You're a fucking liar."

"Kai," Luce said in a placating tone.

"Come on, Luce. You have to see him for what he is. He means to kill those he swore to protect, all to make himself into a god. Your vision—it was never Emory who was going to plunge the worlds into oblivion. It's him. It was always going to be him."

Luce frowned at Clover, still shining with that unnatural light. Something shifted in her eyes, as if she were finally starting to see the truth of him. Clover stepped toward her, her name slipping from his mouth like a plea, but she moved out of his reach. Clover flinched as if she'd slapped him.

"Is it true?" Luce breathed.

"You don't understand," Clover started. "What I did—"

"*You killed her like it was nothing!*" Kai shouted, gesturing toward the empty pile of clothes. "How the hell do you justify that?"

Clover's face darkened into a scowl, his mask dropping at last. "Someone has to bear the weight of this task. I said I'd do what was needed of me even if it broke me. This is what I have to do for the greater good."

It was all but an admission to what he'd become. A monster with no remorse who would do it all over again.

"Now come." Clover extended a hand to Luce. "We have another world to get to."

Kai half expected Luce to accept this explanation, to side with Clover even after seeing what he did to Asphodel, too enticed by Clover's lies and the promise of saving her daughter. But she had heard the admission as plainly as Kai, and it was betrayal that shone in her eyes as she stared at Clover.

"I trusted you to help me save my daughter from her fate," she said in a tremulous voice. "We were supposed to be heroes, meant to stand by your side as you led us to a *solution*."

"And that is exactly what I'm doing. There are different ways to be heroes, dear Luce, and this sacrifice was Asphodel's one act of heroism. A small piece fitted into a larger pattern."

Luce shook her head, tears falling down her cheeks. "You're a monster." Her chin wobbled, but she lifted it in defiance. "Are you going to take all our power until there's nothing left of us, too? Are you going to bleed me to death—your own kin?"

This at last seemed to get through to Clover, this reminder that Luce was a distant descendant of his. The light around him vanished. For a second, he seemed to reconsider, to *doubt* himself—something he never did. He looked at Luce as if seeing someone else in her features, another girl who shared his blood, one who had stayed behind in their world. Someone, Kai realized, who could very much keep the Clover bloodline going should her brother never return.

"I would never hurt you, Luce," Clover said, and though it was her name he spoke, it was Cordelia's that echoed in the softness of his voice. That mask of his went back up as he looked to the darkness beyond the door. "What I did to Asphodel . . . the same won't be needed from you two. I need you both with me. And I'd much rather we keep going the way we've been, as a united front working toward a common goal, rather than with me forcing you."

Kai spat blood on the ground between them. "Screw you."

Again there was a chip in Clover's mask, something waning behind his eyes. "So be it, then," he said with a brokenness he couldn't quite hide.

A flick of his hand had power tugging on Kai's limbs, forcing him to stand. It was the same for Luce, who gasped as she lurched to her feet. Clover turned toward the door, forcing them to follow him against their will.

"You're going to the Deep for this, Cornelius Clover," Luce said, and it was spoken like a curse. If she hadn't been a Dreamer, Kai might have thought she was a Wordsmith, speaking these words into existence.

"Perhaps." Clover didn't look back at them before he disappeared through the door, so sure was he that they would follow. "But at least I'll go there knowing I fixed our worlds and left behind a better place."

He truly believed it. That he was doing everyone a favor by going to these lengths. That he was going to make the worlds a better place, even if it required bloody murder, three times over.

Kai felt utterly defeated. Like for once, he knew all the fight he had inside him would be for nothing, so what was the point of even trying? Clover could Glamour them without speaking a single word, make him and Luce do whatever he needed them to.

If either of them rose a finger against him, he would have already seen them coming. Would stop them as if it were child's play. If this were a game of chess, Clover would be a grand master, and they were nothing but amateurs. No matter what move they made, he would know fifteen different ways to counter them or use them to his own advantage.

They were stuck with him, no matter what they tried. Because he *needed* them.

Yet Kai couldn't stand idly by while Clover did this same thing to the warrior and guardian next. Couldn't watch as Clover manipulated them, gaining their trust, giving them empty promises of bravery and heroism before plunging a knife through their backs, erasing all that they were to make himself into this monstrous semblance of a god.

He met Luce's gaze as they walked through the door after him and knew she thought the same.

He thought about shoving Clover off the path of stars. Imagined the dark nothingness beyond swallowing Clover up, dragging him into oblivion. Maybe, if he opened himself up to the dark tug of his magic, he could call the umbrae somehow, use them against Clover . . .

Clover slowed to keep pace with Kai, and for a second, Kai feared he'd heard all his murderous thoughts. But he seemed oblivious to them as he said, "I need you to know I didn't do what I did lightly."

"Yes, I'm sure you're completely broken up about it," Kai deadpanned.

Clover's mouth thinned at the sarcasm. "I told you I feared I would falter in the end if I opened myself up to grief. That's why I have to close myself off to it. To all this pain I have caused and will cause still. I hate it as much as you do, believe me. But it's the only way to make it right. The only way to make all this hurt and loss count."

"Whatever you need to tell yourself."

A shove. A push. That's all it would take.

Clover stepped in front of him, hand alighting on Kai's chest. Kai sucked in a breath as a wave of healing washed through him, mending whatever had broken at his earlier fall. Clover wiped blood off the corner of Kai's mouth.

"I tell myself what I need to hold the nightmares at bay," Clover said. "Surely you of all people must understand."

Kai frowned at Clover's hand still on his chest. Then looked him in the eye. So very human—that's how Clover appeared in this moment. A boy trying to hold on to his humanity. Pleading with the only people who might understand.

But there was no understanding this. No sympathizing with such monstrous acts.

Tentatively, Kai tested the agency of his own limbs. It seemed Clover's compulsion didn't go beyond a command to follow him, and so Kai was able to wrap his fingers around Clover's wrist, ever so gently. Kai scrunched up his brows as he leaned closer to Clover, making it appear as if he were finally changing his mind, finally accepting that this darkness between the two of them was the same.

It wasn't. Would never be.

"The thing about keeping nightmares at bay," Kai said, "is that eventually, they always catch up."

With all his might, Kai twisted them around so that Clover toppled at the edge of the path. And then he *shoved*.

Swirling shadows joined the momentum of his push, swallowing Clover whole. The umbrae called here by Kai's presence.

And just when he thought he'd done it—that he'd gotten rid of Clover, sent him to the void beyond the stars—the shadows withdrew, umbrae screeching in pain and fear as glaring light cast them back. Kai shielded his eyes. When the light dissipated, when the screams of the umbrae faded, Clover was still standing on the path of stars, light rippling off him, tendrils and vines keeping him rooted in place. His face was stony and cold. He didn't look surprised at Kai's attempt at ending him; had likely seen his intent before Kai shoved him.

But now he was *pissed*.

A maelstrom of vines and dirt and leaves, of knotted tendrils of light and dark, shot from Clover's hands to wrap around Kai like a vise. Somewhere, Luce was shouting. Then she was similarly bound. Clover's eyes shone bright turquoise, his hair fluttering on an inexistent breeze. Power crackled around him. He looked like a vengeful demon, like a spectral god. The magic squeezed around Kai, making him gasp for breath.

Kai was going to die here, he was sure of it.

"Go on, kill us, then," he said on a breathy laugh, which only seemed to piss Clover off even more. Good. He wanted Clover to be driven to a rage, if only to prove to them both what kind of monster he was. To prove to *himself* that he wasn't the only one defined by anger.

If Kai could never know peace, then he would make damn sure Clover was denied it too.

"DO IT!" he screamed with all the air left in his lungs.

Darkness pressed in at the edges of his vision. Perhaps this was always how it was meant to be: that he should die here in the dark among the stars, still clutching that anger he'd been carrying all his life, the same anger he'd always used as armor and weapon both. He wasn't afraid of death. There was no peace for him either way.

Fear Eater, Nightmare Weaver.

The familiar voice slithered along Kai's bones. It came from all the umbrae lingering around him, all the dark places they hid in, speaking through all of them so that it was layered and many. But it was a singular voice in a guttural tongue that Kai understood intuitively. Judging from the unchanged look on Clover's face, he didn't hear it. Only Kai did.

The voice of the crowned umbra.

But it was different from when he'd heard it before, when his nightmares had often been haunted by the crowned umbra in the wake of Emory slipping through the Hourglass. It was strained and croaking now, as if it hadn't been used in a millennium. As if speaking through the umbrae took every single ounce of his power.

I will help you, the voice said, *if you promise to free me.*

The words jostled a memory. A long-forgotten dream that Kai remembered with sudden clarity. He knew it was a dream—a nightmare, back at the printing press he'd visited so often in sleep—but it felt too real, too vivid in his mind. How Baz had kissed him as if they'd never see each other again. The weighted look in his eyes, like he was trying to tell Kai something beyond the words that spilled from his mouth.

Whatever happens, promise me you'll remember that . . . that I love you.

Kai choked on a sob as all the air was squeezed from his lungs.

Promise me, and live, the crowned umbra's voice said.

Baz's face stark in his mind. *Promise me you'll remember . . .*

"I promise," Kai managed to grit out, unsure which voice he was replying to. It didn't matter. He was dead anyway.

But then—a tidal wave of darkness. Not death, but the umbrae, charging over to them like soldiers on a battlefield. They passed right through Kai and Luce and swarmed around Clover. Whatever power he'd wrapped around Kai and Luce loosened, enough for Kai to gasp for air, to catch his bearings. His hand shot out to Luce. Together they ran from Clover as he *screamed*, as the umbrae kept swarming and swarming until he was buried beneath a heap of nightmares.

Kai and Luce did not stop running. There was no knowing

which door they were running toward. Back to the Wychwood or onward to the Wastes. It didn't matter; all that mattered was getting away from Clover while they had the chance.

Free me, that voice boomed in Kai's mind. *Promise you will pull me from this nightmare and into the realms of the living.*

Kai could see a door in the dark, glistening gold. They were so close. . . .

Silver light erupted at their backs, drowning out the sleepscape like a negative photograph showing stars as dark spots in an ocean of white. Kai knew it was Clover's power blasting away the umbrae, because of course the bastard would survive this place, a god in the making whom nightmares could not stop.

Kai had only a second to pull Luce into the shield of his arms before the blast hit them. The force of it shoved them forward in a rush of searing light and screeching umbrae desperate to evade it, and there was nothing they could do as this riptide of power swept them over the edge of the path of stars.

They were falling.

No one was ever meant to veer from the path. It was like diving at too great a depth under the sea, where everything became a crushing weight, a space no one could exist in. It was an abyss, empty and unknowable.

It was death.

Kai wanted to rage at the cruel irony of it all. He, a Nightmare Weaver. Luce, a Dreamer. Both were well-versed in the ways of the sleepscape. Both had survived so much of its strange horrors, and this, despite constantly pushing the boundaries of what was safe here, venturing further than any other adept of the sleepscape, save perhaps Romie.

All for it to end in this final daring moment.

Anger and Luce was all Kai had to hold on to as they plummeted to their deaths. An endless sort of fall, the space around them becoming more and more oppressive the further they fell. Their hearts would likely give out before the end. Or maybe this was to be their hell: an eternal fall, a constant state of powerless fear.

But then . . . Kai's feet struck something solid. The breath was knocked right out of him as he and Luce came tumbling in a heap on the floor—because those were *floorboards* beneath them, the wood splintered with age, its dark polish flaking from scuff marks and years of use.

Kai felt his stomach plummet as the floor *lifted*, swooping upward in the dark. It was like being in the Obscura Hall elevator, though the stomach-dropping feeling was ten times worse here with the oppressive weight of the world around him. And now the floor was *tilting*, and Kai found himself sliding down the near vertical slant, Luce screaming at his side as she was flung down. He grabbed on to something—a post of some kind—and snatched Luce's hand with his free one. She held on to him for dear life as they climbed up through the dark at impossible speed. Kai shut his eyes to fight off the vertigo.

And then his ears suddenly popped as the floor righted itself and the world became less oppressive. Still oddly weighted, but manageable; he didn't feel like his limbs were being crushed, like his skull was about to cave in and his eyes pop out of their sockets.

Kai met Luce's equally perplexed and relieved gaze. "Kai." She jerked her chin up, eyes going wide. "Look."

The post Kai had been holding on to—it was a mast. A great billowing sail, dark and moving like liquid silk, was attached to it.

They were on a ship. Sailing through the dark between stars, for those *were* stars around them. Yet they seemed distant, sparse. Not like the multitude of them that made up the path between worlds.

Kai and Luce helped each other to their feet. They were unsteady on the moving ship, but at least it didn't seem like it was going to topple over again anytime soon, its sail calm and steady. They came to stand at the side of the ship, peering at the dark.

"What is this?" Luce murmured.

But they both knew. The breezeless dark, the strange, distant stars . . . They were sailing through the space beyond the path. Just like the girl of dreams and the boy of nightmares from the epilogue.

This ship, whatever it was, had saved them from plummeting to their deaths. Or maybe this *was* death. A vessel carrying them to the afterlife, if there was one at all.

"Praise the Deep, am I ever glad to see you."

The voice crept along Kai's bones, lifted the hairs off the back of his neck. Slowly, he turned to its owner and knew then that surely he and Luce *must* be dead, because the face that smiled at him with such pained sorrow was that of a ghost.

And it was not one he was pleased to see at the end of all things.

"What the fuck is this?" Kai breathed roughly. "Why are *you* here?"

If he took offense to Kai's brusqueness, the boy did not show it. "The gods of the living have been waiting for you two," said Farran Caine. "And I'm here to bring you to them."

PART II

THE GODS OF THE LIVING

THE GODS OF THE LIVING SANK TO THE BOTTOM OF the abyss with a dissonant thud.

This was no place for such beings as them. It was the antithesis of their godsworld, barren instead of flourishing, a graveyard of souls too dark for their once luminous divinity to touch. They were supposed to be vitality incarnate, effervescent and enduring, forming together an ineffable harmony. But not in these hellish depths.

The living did not belong with the dead. Yet here they were in death's domain, forced to cower in the cold and the dark to preserve what little divinity they had left. It had waned to near extinction, stolen by the monster who had cut them off from their source of power and sought to make himself a god in their place.

They would make him pay.

Centuries may pass before they clawed their way out of here, but what were centuries to gods, even diminished ones? It gave them time to orchestrate their return to the living, to formulate a plan that, ironically, rested so much on death and those touched by it.

It was only a matter of time now before they escaped this prison. And once they did, they would bring the false god to his knees and save the realms of the living that he was bound to destroy in their absence.

KAI

EITHER FARRAN CAINE WAS ALIVE, OR KAI WAS DEAD. Neither option made any sense, but here they were, on a silk-sailed ship floating across the cosmos.

Luce looked between them quizzically. "You two know each other?"

A trace of Farran's dimpled smile, tinged with sadness. "We have . . . a history."

"Yeah. A history of you screwing me over." Kai wanted to laugh at the absurdity of the situation. "But that's two hundred years from now. Clearly, hell doesn't account for time, otherwise death would have spared me your ghost."

"This isn't quite hell," Farran said. "And you're not exactly dead."

"No? But *you* are. You died years ago. Centuries from now." Fucking time travel logistics. "You're *dead*."

What did that make of Kai and Luce if not dead too?

"I did experience death, yes," Farran said. "But I was brought back. I guess you could say I was never really mortal to begin with."

"Then what the fuck are you?"

"Immortal, obviously," Farran said with a weak smile at his bad attempt at a joke. "I was brought back to life to become an apprentice to the god of balance."

"You mean that bastard crowned umbra?" Maybe it was some kind of death god, looking to claim souls, and Farran was a wraith doing his bidding.

But Farran shook his head. "Not him. He's no god."

"Did this god of yours send you to save us, then?" Luce asked. "I thought we were plummeting to certain death before you showed up."

"The god of balance doesn't know our paths are crossing. Or maybe he does, I don't know. Anyway, my allegiance is no longer to him. I've jumped ship, pardon the pun, and I serve other gods now. The only ones who might help stop what's coming."

Kai and Luce exchanged a wary glance.

"I know this is all confusing," Farran said. He looked toward the horizon, as if mapping out their progress through these sparse stars. "There'll be time for all your questions. We've got a long journey ahead."

"Where are we even going?" Kai bit out.

"To hell," Farran said. "To seek the gods who are trapped there."

"I take it this *history* between you two didn't end well?"

Luce's question snapped Kai out of staring daggers at Farran, who was busying himself around the ship, making sure it stayed the course. The course to fucking *hell* itself, apparently.

Kai breathed heavily through his nose, trying to tamp down all his anger. "What gave it away?"

"The glaring, for one. The venomous animosity, for two. All the makings of a lover spurned, if I had to guess."

"Has anyone told you you're too observant for your own good? It's annoying."

"That doesn't answer my question."

Kai sighed. "It was a long time ago."

Luce hummed in thought. "And yet you're still glaring."

Kai gave *her* his most menacing glare. She held up her hands in a show of innocence, dropping the subject. Kai brooded on the matter. He didn't care about Farran or what happened back then. He was more so interested in figuring out why the hell he was *here*–and how.

When Farran finally came back to sit with them, Kai crossed his arms and said, "Talk."

"Where should I start?"

"Oh, I don't know, what about explaining how it is that my back-stabbing asshole of an ex managed to escape death, meet a god, travel back in time, and suddenly decide to give a shit enough about me to save me from plummeting into the unknown."

Farran gave him a dimpled smile. "Funny, I don't remember you being so cynical."

"That tracks. You're the reason for it."

The smile slipped at that. Farran cleared his throat. "I owe you an apology for that. Both of you."

"Me?" Luce exclaimed with surprise.

"It's not just Kai I have a history with. Except you would have known a different version of me."

"I don't understand . . ."

"The thing about being apprentice to a god who rules over time and fate is that I know things about my past that no mortal ever should. And by *past*, I mean, well, past *life*."

Kai huffed a laugh. This all had to be some great cosmic joke.

Farran ignored him as he went on: "My first death was . . . unnatural. Through some kind of loophole, the god of balance took notice and called my soul back from the afterlife. He shaped me into someone he could eventually use at his side, molding me to fit the pattern of fate in a certain way. And then he sent my soul back to the realms of the living through means of reincarnation. Thus Farran Caine was born. I had no knowledge then of past lives or gods or what my soul was created to do. Everything I did, I believed was by choice, but turns out it was always fate's design. Every decision I made was predetermined by the god's tinkering of my soul, his way of ensuring everything played into fate's design. Because certain things needed to happen in a specific way."

"What *things*?"

"Sowing the seed in the minds of Keiran, Lizaveta, and Artem about waking the Tides. My death in Dovermere to spur them on."

"And me?"

Farran couldn't look Kai in the eye. "Yes, you. Dating you fueled the others' disdain of Eclipse-born and their desire to wake the Tides. Breaking your heart sent you toward another."

Old anger and hurt surfaced in Kai until he wanted to smash something. "So it was never real between us."

At this, Farran's head jerked up. "It was. If nothing else, you have to believe that. I didn't know at the time that my actions were predetermined to serve the god. It's only when I died and ended up back at the god's side that I remembered what purpose he'd driven into my soul. It was only then that I remembered who I'd been before, in my previous life."

"Who were you?" Luce asked, frowning at him as if to see who else might be hiding beneath his features.

"You knew me as Thames."

Luce's hand shot to her mouth, covering a bewildered gasp. Kai was too numb to react—didn't know how many more absurd revelations he could take.

"Something about Thames's death caught the attention of the

god," Farran continued. "The way Thames injected himself with a Tidecaller synth to make himself limitless, only for it to corrupt him from the inside and ultimately kill him . . . I guess this left a mark on his soul—on *my* soul—and the god thought to use that to his advantage, a loophole he could explore. He thought I'd be an ally because I'd want to get justice after what Cornelius did to me. And I was, for a time. Before I found out what fate has in store for us—what the god has been working toward."

"Which is what?"

"To wipe clean the slate and start the worlds anew. I saw it myself in the tapestry of fate. What Cornelius is going to do is meant to be so disastrous that the god thinks the only way to prevent it is to throw away the fabric of our universe and start a new tapestry from scratch. Everything we've been, everything we are, everything we could still become . . . just wiped completely forever. No reincarnation in sight. Not even an afterlife. Every soul, every particle dead and alive that makes up our universe, gone and forgotten for something new to take shape."

Kai fisted his hands at his sides, feeling angry at the world, at this god who thought he could treat them like chess pieces on a board. What was the point of going forward if that was the fate that awaited them?

"But why does the god want that?" Luce asked, her voice pitched high with mounting frenzy.

"He says that, before the universe tips toward the kind of chaos there can be no coming back from—before the gods themselves are all killed by Cornelius and the worlds fall under his dark reign—the only way to preserve balance is to start anew. Think of it as a scale. On one side, balance and peace. On the other, chaos and ruin. If the scale were to tip fully toward the side of chaos, the side that awaits us if Clover manages to make himself into the one true god, there would be no coming back from it. The gods would be dead, and under Clover's monstrous rule, darkness and suffering and hate would destroy all that is good in our worlds."

"So this is some bullshit self-preservation thing," Kai seethed. "This asshole of a god is willing to let us all fall into oblivion for the sake of saving his own neck."

Farran nodded. "That's why I left him. Everything I was doing, ensuring the cogs of fate worked as they were meant to, was playing into the very destiny the god of balance wanted us heading toward: total oblivion for us, a fresh start for the gods."

"Is there no way to change things?" Luce looked horrified, and Kai knew she was thinking of what this meant for Emory. "Instead of wiping us all from the map to preserve balance, why doesn't the god help us stop Clover?"

"Because that's just it: he's the god of *balance*. He can't meddle with fate directly even if he wanted to, because he's meant to be an impartial surveyor."

"He meddled with your fate, didn't he?" Kai noted.

"Like I said: loophole. I was a loose thread in an unchangeable pattern, and he took advantage of it. But something as big as Clover becoming this supreme god who brings about the end of the universe as we know it . . . Even the god of balance can't stop such a fate in its course. The only thing he *can* actively do is wipe clean the slate if things get out of hand. It's what his very nature is set to resort to, a last recourse to preserve balance in the face of utter chaos. Only, the thing is . . . there are others whose hands are not so tied by fate, who are willing to do what must be done to prevent such an end."

"The four gods of the living realms," Luce breathed.

Farran nodded. "They're who I set out to find when I left the god of balance because they're our best chance at thwarting fate and surviving. And they're who we're sailing toward now because I need your help getting them out of the abyss."

ROMIE

MEMORIES OF THE COLLEGE THAT ROMIE KNEW SO intimately overlapped with Atheia's own recollection of what this place used to be, so very long ago. There had always been power here, on this spot that sat above the door to this world. Dovermere, it was called then and still now.

Before it was a college, before it was the temple that had preceded it, it had been the place Atheia and Sidraeus would gather with their faithful Veiled Atlas, these like-minded individuals who had wanted to open the boundaries between worlds. Tidecallers whose magic was key to this expansion of limits.

The last time Atheia was here was to beg Sidraeus to return to his realm and take his Tidecallers with him. The breaking that happened that day—the love and trust between them shattered by their unwavering opposing stances—was an echo that had carried, traveling over centuries to this very moment. The divide between lunar and eclipse a result of it.

Atheia could feel it beneath her bare feet, the history of this place that was enmeshed in her very being, everything she had experienced here before her splintering, and everything that had come after in her absence.

If she closed her eyes and let the sea breeze brush against her skin, if she breathed the briny air deep into these lungs that were another's but also hers, she could almost imagine she had gone back in time to that place that had held so much significance to her. But everything was different. There was a desperation in the air, a threatening, rumbling force driving the sea, a visceral *feeling* that clawed inside her, letting her know this was not the world she had left behind.

There was a wrongness here, an emptiness where lunar magic had once overflowed. Her life's work, swept away like a flimsy castle in the sand. Teetering now on a delicate edge that could see it obliterated for good.

The motto on the college's iron gates greeted her mockingly. *Post tenebras lux; iterum atque iterum.* After darkness, light; again and again. That's what the lunar cycle was meant to be. What the nature of all the magics she'd created was. But now they faced infinite darkness, an everlasting end brought upon by the stain of Eclipse magic.

Unless we put an end to it first.

Romie's thought echoed in the chambers of Atheia's mind, brimming with a righteous anger that Atheia herself felt.

"Who goes there?"

A man in a charcoal uniform appeared at the gates, peering at her with an air of authority. *A Regulator,* Romie's mind supplied. A figure of magical authority meant to regulate the use of magic. The thought inflamed Atheia at first—magic should be accessed *freely*—but then, their allegiance did skew in favor of lunar magic, not eclipse.

The man rubbed at his eyes as Atheia drew closer to the gates, as if trying to make sense of what he was seeing. She knew what she must look like: unseasonable clothes still dripping wet from the beach, walking barefoot on gravel in the late winter cold, eyes dancing in all the colors of a divine rainbow. She gripped the bars and pressed her face between them. They smelled like iron; like blood. Like magic.

She smiled at the man. "Open the gate. I wish you no harm."

The words, laced with a Glamour, tasted divine. She was the mother of all lunar magics, and it was a comfort to know that it flowed out of her unencumbered after so long.

The man fumbled over himself to open the gate for her. He had a silvery full moon tattooed on the back of his hand. Atheia glanced at the waning crescent on her own hand, reminded, thanks to Romie's memories, that lunar mages now could only access a single tidal alignment, depending on when they were born. A travesty she hoped to rectify.

The college was magnificent. There was symmetry in the cloisters and columns and towering elms that surrounded the central quad, in the middle of which was a statue representing the Tides of Fate, this multi-deity that Atheia had embodied. Young Bruma of the New Moon, beautiful Anima of the Waxing Moon, motherly Aestas of the Full Moon, and wise Quies of the Waning Moon.

A swell of pride and love rose within her as she stood close to the fountain, admiring every detail of those four faces. Not exactly done in her likeness, but she supposed it did not matter; it was a lovely testimony of the devotion lunar mages had for the Tides even long after Atheia had left their shores.

Everyone is staring at us.

Romie's voice had Atheia snapping out of admiring the statues. Indeed, students were peering at her from the cloisters, whispering among themselves with wide eyes and quizzical brows.

"Hey, are you all right?" someone called out to her.

And then, another voice: "Isn't that Romie Brysden?"

Recognition swept over the gathered students. There was a hum of confusion and disbelief and fear, mixed with something else Atheia couldn't quite put her finger on.

"She was dead!" someone shouted. "She was one of the drowned students last year."

"Isn't she a friend of the Ainsleif girl?"

More people gathered in the quad now, voices repeating Romie's name like it was an accusation.

Suddenly another one of those charcoal-clad Regulators marched toward her, beady little eyes taking her in like she was prey. Two more Regulators were at his heel.

"Rosemarie Brysden," the beady-eyed one said. "My name is Captain Drutten. I'm going to ask you to come with us."

Atheia raised a brow. "To what end?"

"It's my hope you might help us locate your family members, for one thing." He gave her an oily smile. "And I'm very curious to know where a supposed drowned girl has been all this time, especially one who was friends with the Shadow reborn."

He means Emory, said Romie. Her feelings were all over the place at the mention of her family, anger rising at the thought that her association with Emory might cause her and her loved ones harm.

"I assure you I am no friend of the Shadow," Atheia told the Regulator. "And I can answer any questions you have right here in front of all these faithful lunar mages."

"There's no need for that. Now come along, Ms. Brysden."

"I will do no such thing."

The Regulator's ears reddened, his eyes darting to the whispering crowd as if Atheia's disobedience were an affront to his authority, an embarrassment he refused to allow. He squared his shoulders, voice low as he said, "Then you leave me no choice."

Before she knew what he was doing, the man reached for her arm, and the cold sting of metal brushed her skin.

Atheia wrenched free of his grasp before the restraint could close. "Get your hands off my vessel."

This seemed only to inflame him more. She felt magic slither toward her, as if this man were trying to compel her. Using *her* magic against her—the magic *she* had created as the Tides.

"Stop," she commanded in a booming voice.

His eyes went wide as he froze. Power thrummed around Atheia as she stepped closer to him. She felt like a giant even though he stood a good head taller than she.

"Lift a hand to me again, lunar mage," she said, "and I will not be so benevolent."

"Who are you?" the man asked on a shaky breath.

"I am the Tides you worship. I am Bruma and Anima and Aestas and Quies wrapped in a single vessel."

Murmurs again rippled through the crowd.

"That's not possible," the man said. "The Tides are gone. They're in the Deep, put there by the Shadow . . ."

"That might have been true." Somewhat. Atheia laid a gentle hand on the man's face. "But Romie Brysden brought me back."

Eyes went wide with fear and wonder, and she delighted in it, this feeling of divinity among mortals that she hadn't felt for a millennium. Atheia swept a gaze over these lunar mage students who would have once been her loyal followers, her devoted worshippers. Who could be once more now that she'd returned.

"If the Tides are back, why is our magic still lacking?" a student spoke up, expression pinched with skepticism. "Isn't their return supposed to restore it to what it once was, accessible to all, no matter our ruling house or tidal alignment?"

Murmurs of assent ran through the crowd, making an unpleasant feeling slither up Atheia's spine. She did not have that power, could not give them what they wanted from her, and whose fault was that?

"I know you wish to regain the full might of your magic," she addressed the crowd. "To see it flow freely once more, without any limitations. You wish to have the culprit of your dwindling powers gone. To wash away the Shadow's stain from this world. Believe me, I am here to help you fulfill this wish. But there is an obstacle that stands in the way: the Shadow and his followers.

"I have it on good authority that the Shadow himself will be setting foot on your shores soon. Help me capture him, and I will deal with him myself. His death will mean the death of his magic." At least, that was the hope; Atheia would see it done one way or the other. "And then," she continued, "I will give back to you what was once yours. I will bless those faithful to me with all the lunar magics at my disposal. You will once more know magic without limits. This I promise you."

There was a commotion as a woman with salt-and-pepper hair trimmed short and wearing a tweed suit cut her way through the gathered students. *The dean of Aldryn,* Romie's memories provided.

"Dean Fulton," Drutten greeted the woman. "Ms. Brysden here— she says—"

"I heard." Dean Fulton's dark eyes never left Atheia's face. "Thank you, Captain Drutten, I'll take it from here." To the students, she said in a raised voice, "Back to your classes, everyone. *Now.*"

The students eventually scattered, eyes lingering on Atheia. They did not know what to make of her, and she couldn't exactly fault them for it. She wore the skin of a dead girl who had been friends with the public enemy that was Emory, the Tidethief, the Shadow reborn. Of course they wouldn't believe her outright that she was the Tides returned.

The dean watched Atheia carefully. "There are people who will be wanting to talk to you." It sounded like she wanted to add *Ms. Brysden* at the end of her sentence but thought the better of it.

Behind the dean were two boys, students who did not leave with the rest of their peers. Atheia knew their faces through Romie's memories, recognizing them as members of the current Selenic Order cohort at the college: Louis Clairmont, a Healer with brown curls, and Javier Oritze Belesa, a Wardcrafter with long dark hair and fine features.

Recognition was stark on both their faces–and more importantly, *belief*. They were part of the Selenic Order; their entire life goal had been to bring back the Tides. And here she was, returned in the body of one of their initiates. If anyone would believe her, it was them.

Romie's thoughts quickly formulated a plan, and Atheia couldn't help but be grateful for her vessel's wits and knowledge. If there was an ally to be found in this world, people who would not only believe her outright but also help her achieve her goal of eradicating Eclipse magic, it was the Selenic Order. Particularly the Tidal Council, the leaders of this secret society who were named in honor of the four Tides, in honor of *her*.

Atheia smiled at Louis and Javier, turning her wrist out to show the silver spiral there that she knew was mirrored on their own wrists. "Shall I call on the Tidal Council, or will you?"

BAZ

ALDRYN COLLEGE LOOKED GRIM AGAINST THE BLEAK winter sky.

Baz emerged from the caves surprised to find he could do so by simply walking out instead of treading water; the low tide was pulled farther back than what was normal, making the entire cove a stretch of dark, wet sand as far as the eye could see. The unveiled shoreline was in a state of erosion like Baz had never seen before, hinting at powerful tidal bulges.

Indeed, from his low vantage point on the beach, he could see parts of Aldryn College had been worn away by the ravaging tides. The secret staircase that led to the Eclipse commons was still intact, though it was missing some steps, large gaps where rock had broken off. The old lighthouse had toppled over, lying on the uncovered seabed amidst a pile of dark gray rock that Baz had to wind his way around. If it had fallen a bit closer to the cave mouth, it might have blocked the entrance completely. Destroyed Dovermere altogether.

Baz felt like he'd appeared in another world. The feeling was stranger—bleaker—than when he and Kai had fallen through time to an older Aldryn. If this was the physical state of the world, if the tides were already acting out of sorts like Clover had anticipated they would, what did that mean for them all?

He didn't know what to do next, didn't even know where everyone was. Would his father and Jae and Selandyn be in the Eclipse commons, relying on the wards to keep them safe from the Regulators? Would they have taken refuge elsewhere, like at Alya's Veiled Atlas tavern?

A great roaring split the silence, followed by the sound of a hundred seagulls taking flight, crying in what sounded like alarm.

Baz scanned the coastline and froze as he saw the horizon.

The tide was coming in. Not gradually, as it should have, but all at once. The wave unfurling toward him was gaining momentum and height, until it was a great, impenetrable wall of dark blue steel. A tsunami that would no doubt be higher than the cliff itself once it reached him.

A wave like that would take down the cliff, and the whole school with it.

Before Baz could call on his magic to stop it, another kind of magic crackled overhead. He saw a shimmer of something at the top of the cliff, which trickled like water down to the seabed. He realized what it was: a ward being put up, a shield stretched over the cliffside to protect Aldryn from the incoming tide.

A face appeared in the window of the Eclipse commons, but it was not one Baz knew. It wasn't even an Eclipse-born. The person spotted him on the sand and shouted something Baz couldn't hear.

And then a second face appeared in the window, one he knew well.

Drutten. The Regulator who'd made Baz's life a living hell.

A predatory sort of smile touched Drutten's face. More people appeared in the window, pointing at Baz and shouting things he couldn't hear from down here, and he realized by their charcoal uniforms that they were all Regulators.

They sent a wave of magic toward Baz. He knew it was magic by the unnatural way the dozen of arrows came at him, precise and in sync, ethereally translucent as if they were made of air. Some kind of mixture of Wordsmith and Reaper magic, perhaps? Funny how his brain went into scholarly mode trying to decipher what magic this was when death was coming straight at him.

Baz tried to get out of their way, but the arrows changed course, following him. He flung out his magic at the very last second, stopping them midair, and unraveled their threads backward so they never existed at all.

His heart pounded in his chest as he stared wide-eyed at Drutten and his companions. They were trying to *kill* him. They had taken his *home*, and now they were out for his blood. And the tide was ever rising. Soon Baz would be annihilated, trapped between a wall of sea and one of rock.

Baz tore toward Cadence, away from the caves and the Regulators. He flung his magic out toward the giant wave on his left, trying to halt its progress, but it was like trying to stop the entire sea, the world itself. And half his mind was on the magical assault that was happening still, another volley of enchanted arrows shooting his way.

And then Baz heard his name.

Emerging from the path in the tall grass that led to Cadence were two people running toward him, waving their hands wildly to get his attention. Baz squinted, adjusting his glasses on his nose to better see who it was. One of the girls had dark brown skin, with long, tight braids swinging behind her as she ran. Ife Nuru. One of the Selenic Order members.

Baz tensed, not knowing if he could trust her. But then, why would she risk running *toward* deadly arrows and the monstrous incoming tide?

And that's when he recognized the other woman. Alya Kazan, her white-blond curls so similar to Luce's that Baz felt a pang of grief like a punch to the gut. Alya, he knew he could trust. And when both women stopped at the edge of the grass, beckoning him over with increasing urgency, Baz knew they would get him to safety.

He ran as quick as he could, lungs burning as he drew in cold air and breathed out magic to stop the arrows behind him and slow the tsunami coming in. When he finally reached them, he nearly crashed into Alya, panting loudly.

"What are you–" he tried, "how did you know–"

Alya was bent at the waist, fighting for breath. "We've been monitoring the coast in case any of you returned from the other worlds," she explained.

"And I saw you coming," Ife said. "In a vision, I mean."

She was a Seer, Baz recalled, catching a glimpse of the House New Moon sigil on the back of her hand.

Alya eyed the wave warily. "There's a train that'll take us to Threnody–"

"Threnody?" Baz echoed, confused.

"That's where everyone is. We needed a safe house away from the Regulators. Jae's got a place there."

Of course–the safe house where Jae had been training Collapsed Eclipse-born in secret.

"Are the others not with you?" Ife asked, searching the coastline behind Baz.

"Others?" Baz repeated.

"Vera, Kai, Nisha, Virgil . . ."

Right. The last thing people here would remember was Baz going through the door with all of them. They didn't know about their group being separated, about the time travel, about Clover.

"It's just me," Baz said softly. "Is my dad . . ."

"He's fine," Alya cut in. "In Threnody. But there will be time for all that later. We need to get behind the wards around Cadence before that wave hits and–"

Ife drew a sharp breath. "What in the Tides' name is *that*?"

She was pointing to the mouth of Dovermere, where shadows spilled from the cave, slowly crawling over the silt and sand and lighthouse ruins. Drutten and his people had also spotted the disturbance and were now turning their magic on the cave mouth rather than Baz.

Baz had half a mind to let go of his magic so that the incoming tidal wave would drown whatever was trying to seep out of the cave and maybe break against the cliffside so hard that it would take Drutten with it. He was already straining against the force of the Aldersea, wouldn't be able to hold it much longer.

But then–shapes emerged from the shadows. Baz's first thought was that the umbrae might have slipped through the cracks when he emerged from the door, but these were *people*. Three faces Baz recognized as Virgil, Nisha, and Vera, dressed in clothes that belonged to another time, another world. One he did not recognize at all, a boy with dark auburn hair, his features timeless and his eyes flashing oddly in the daylight. And the last . . .

Mousy blond hair that was longer than he remembered. Messy fringe no longer kissing her brows but curling around her chin. Eyes like the Aldersea rising to meet them.

Emory.

She was *here*.

And she was walking straight toward Drutten's arrows.

"No!" Baz shouted, reaching desperately for the threads of time that would stop the arrows from hitting their new target. But the arrows *exploded* before they reached Emory or the others, crackling with dark energy that was then shot back toward the Eclipse commons, making Drutten and his people scramble for safety.

Baz's grasp on the tidal wave slipped, and there was a horrible sound as the wave picked up speed, momentarily freed from time's hold. Alya clutched her neck, Vera's name on her lips. Ife was shouting Virgil and Nisha's names, but they didn't seem to hear her. More magic shot from the Eclipse commons toward the beach, but it never reached the newcomers, as if some sort of protective ward enveloped them. A ward no doubt erected by Emory.

But even she wouldn't be able to stop the Aldersea coming for them. Baz ground his teeth and with all his might pulled on as many threads as he could grasp. He couldn't control the entire Aldersea at once, but he erected a perimeter around the cove that stood outside of time, frozen to the elements outside of it, so that the wave would break against it, and not *them*.

He wasn't prepared for the sheer force of the tide as it hit. It beat relentlessly against his magic, wave after wave breaking against his time shield, quickly eroding it despite his best efforts. Miraculously, he managed to keep the shield up until at last the tide was drawing back out toward the horizon, leaving those on the beach unscathed.

Baz fell to his knees, out of breath, out of strength. But Emory and the others were still in the line of danger, not from the Aldersea but from Drutten and his Regulators.

With the tide receding, it was safe for them to climb down the secret stairs from the Eclipse commons. Half of them were heading for Emory and the others, and the rest toward Baz, Ife, and Alya.

Suddenly a thick blanket of darkness unfolded across the cove, attacking the Regulators. They retreated toward the Eclipse commons, shouting in terror at whatever they saw in the shadows chasing after them—shadows that were coming from Emory.

Baz heard Drutten yelling at his people to get behind the school's wards as Emory advanced calmly through the chaos, sand and sea and shadows swirling around her in a lethal dance.

This was not the same Emory he knew. If Baz had thought her different at the beginning of the school year, in the wake of Romie's drowning, that was nothing compared to what he saw now. There was a hardness to her. As if all the sharp edges that perhaps had always been there were filed to barbs now. As if the storm clouds in her eyes had turned into a hurricane, promising a flood. An all-consuming destruction of those around her—and perhaps herself, too.

Baz stepped in front of her. "Emory."

Those stormy eyes met his. For a second it felt like she didn't see him. That she didn't remember who he was and would doom them both, letting the hurricane of her power drown them to ruin.

But then the clouds lifted.

A glimmer of light. A flash of something soft and tender and hopeful.

"Baz?" Her voice came out in an awed whisper. Her brows scrunched up in confusion as the power around her flickered in and out. Like she didn't fully trust what she saw. "Is it really you?"

Baz approached her with his palms up. "Of course it's me."

She swayed on her feet, a sound somewhere between a laugh and a sob spilling from her lips. And then her arms were around Baz, her face buried in his neck, and he was holding her tightly, so tightly, if only just to prove to himself that she was real. That this was real.

"I'm sorry," she cried into his shoulder. "I tried everything, but she's—Romie's gone, Baz."

Baz held her at arm's length, her tearstained face breaking his heart as much as her words. "What do you mean, gone?"

"She's Atheia's vessel. The Tides, I mean. They have her now, and they've come here to—they're here because—"

Baz could barely understand. All he heard in what Emory said was that Romie was alive, and *here*, in this world.

"I can sense her near."

This came from the auburn-haired boy hovering behind Emory. His head was tilted toward the cliffside, and his nostrils flared as he inhaled the brine of the sea. He took a step, face darkening with something hungry and dangerous—until a cry of pain slipped from him as he stumbled back, clutching his side.

He glowered at Emory, face contorted in pain and rage. "I was promised vengeance."

"Not yet," she gritted out.

Baz caught her as she lurched on her feet. It took a moment for the bloodied dagger in her hand to register. Blood seeped through her clothes where she—

"Did you *stab* yourself?"

Emory waved off the high-pitched concern in his voice with a watery smile. "I'll be fine. Is there somewhere safe we can go and—"

"This is ridiculous," the boy cut her off. "We can end this all right now if you just let me go after Atheia."

"I said *no*." Emory's steely tone sent a shiver up Baz's spine.

The dark power that emanated from the strange boy was unsettling. "Who is he?" Baz asked, fighting the urge to pull Emory away from him.

"This is Sidraeus," Emory said. Then, haltingly, "Otherwise known as the Shadow."

Baz's eyes went wide as he took in the Tides-damned *deity* standing before him—as the Shadow himself looked back at him with familiar ecliptic eyes, reminding Baz of the darkness that had spilled into Keiran's revived corpse.

Behind him, Alya swore. "The Tidelore cultists are going to have a field day with this."

It couldn't possibly be the Shadow. He looked nothing like the hundreds of images Baz had seen of the supposedly evil Eclipse deity, but then again, those might have been overly influenced by the Tidelore faith's hatred for Eclipse-born over time. He noticed then the spiral marks etched on his skin that peaked out from beneath the embroidered navy jacket he had on. They were like replicas of the spiral Emory had on her wrist, but multiplied, some small and some large, looping together in a great pattern. All of them glowed faintly.

"We need to get to safety before the tide comes back," Ife said. "Or worse—Drutten and his Regulators."

She was holding on to Nisha, who smiled faintly at Baz. Virgil gave him a jerk of his chin, looking graver than Baz had ever seen him. Whatever they'd gone through to get here, it was bleak.

Baz turned to Alya, who was fussing over a tired-looking Vera. "You mentioned a train to Threnody?"

Alya gave a tight-lipped nod. "But the Regulators will probably be there waiting for us by now . . ."

"Why Threnody?" Vera asked.

"There's a safe house there," Baz said. "For Eclipse-born."

Emory frowned. "Do you know where exactly in Threnody it is?"

"Near the old prep school is all I've been told," said Alya.

"Can you get us there?" Emory asked the boy—the *Shadow*. They exchanged a weighted glance, a silent conversation seeming to pass between them as time ticked on. Baz didn't miss the way Emory gripped the dagger tighter, a threat that had the Shadow squaring his jaw and narrowing his eyes at her.

"Fine," he said at last. "I'll help. But you owe me, Tidecaller."

"No." Emory leveled him with a stony glare. "I *own* you."

The Shadow looked like he was going to throttle her, yet all he did was proffer his arm. She rested her hand on it, smug satisfaction tugging at her lips, leaving Baz to wonder what in the Tides' name was going on here.

Emory instructed everyone to grab on to the Shadow. Baz was last to do so, hesitantly resting his hand next to Emory's. The Shadow's ecliptic eyes snapped to him the moment Baz touched him, as if seared by the contact.

And then darkness swallowed them all whole, and Dovermere Cove disappeared around them.

It felt oddly like when the threads of time in the sleepscape had dragged Baz and Kai back into the past, a maelstrom of swirling darkness pulling him at vast speed somewhere he did not know. But these were not threads of time, nor any magic Baz knew or understood.

When the world finally stopped spinning, he found himself standing on a familiar beach. Tall grass sang on the sloped dunes behind him. Seagulls flew overhead. If he strained his ear, he could almost hear the sound of Romie's laughter as she ran into the waves.

He met Emory's gaze, and it was like that precious shared memory flitted between them.

And then the Shadow had his hands wrapped around Baz's neck, his eyes flaring unnaturally, mouth curled on a snarl. "I can smell him on you," he hissed. "Did he send you here to return me to my prison?"

Baz sputtered, legs kicking wildly beneath him as the Shadow lifted him from the ground. He was distantly aware of Emory shouting at the Shadow, grasping at his arms to make him let go of Baz. Darkness gathered around him as if he were an umbra, tendrils of it wrapping around Baz's torso and neck to squeeze the breath out of him.

Then, just as quickly as it started, his feet hit the ground, and the darkness receded. The Shadow seemed taken aback, gasping for breath just as Baz was, the silver spirals on his skin flaring bright.

"You have the stench of time on you," he snarled at Baz, rubbing at his own neck as if *he'd* been the one being choked. "What did the *almighty*"–he spat the word like it was a curse– "promise you?"

"Who are you talking about?"

But even as Baz cried out the question, he knew the answer. And when the Shadow spoke his name, there was not a doubt in Baz's mind who he meant.

"Equilibris."

The god of balance.

"Look," Nisha cried out, pointing farther up the beach, where the air seemed to shimmer and part like a curtain. Out of it appeared someone walking toward them with purpose. Beneath their open wool coat, they wore slacks and a billowing shirt with ample sleeves and layered necklaces.

Baz's heart leapt at the familiar short hair, jet-black and streaked with more silver than he remembered. "Jae?"

Jae Ahn broke into a wide grin. "Thank the Tides, it is you!"

Baz was engulfed in Jae's embrace, holding on to them tightly, heart swelling to know they were okay. It was in this moment that he finally allowed himself to breathe deep and think to himself that perhaps everything was going to be okay.

EMORY

JAE AHN PARTED THE AIR LIKE A CURTAIN AGAIN, WAVing them through. Emory remembered Baz talking about the Illusionist, and seeing them now, the kind of magic they wielded, she understood Baz's quiet reverence for them.

When the group stepped through, they were still on the beach, but Emory could feel magic crackling around her. Not just Illusionist magic, but Wardcrafter, too.

"We've shielded the perimeters with all sorts of magic," Jae explained as they led the group up the dunes. "Wards against the tide and prying eyes. Illusions to keep folks away. Helps that most people in these parts have evacuated farther inland because of the tides. It's a wasteland. Perfect for our safe house."

"How long have the tides been acting like this?" Emory asked, thinking about her father, alone in his lighthouse in the remote Harebell Cove. She hoped he was all right, that the Aldersea hadn't damaged their home.

"Since last fall."

"Which was how long ago, exactly?" For all she knew, more than a year could have gone by since she'd gone through the door, because time, as they'd found out, did not run the same in each world.

"It's early March now, so I reckon about six months ago." Jae gave her a sidelong glance. "Your father, Henry, is with us. He'll be so happy to see you."

Emory blinked at them. "You know who I am?"

"Of course. You're the famous Emory that Basil here's told me all about." Baz blushed at that, muttering something under his breath that had Jae smiling slyly. "Everyone knows who you are. I'm afraid you've left quite the mark, and when people find out you've returned . . . the Shadow reborn!"

Behind Emory, Sidraeus gave a gruff snort. Emory bit her lip, not wanting to correct Jae and reveal Sidraeus's identity just yet.

"Oh, this is going to be fun," Virgil muttered.

Ife asked him something, and he replied in a voice too low for Emory to understand, presumably filling her in on who Sidraeus was. Emory was dying for a chance to ask Ife about the rest of the Selenic Order members—Louis and Javier—and how she'd found herself here to begin with. She didn't recognize the other woman who was with them at first, but seeing the familiarity between her and Vera, she had to assume this was one of the Kazans.

One of her *aunts*.

Emory found herself stealing a glance at Baz again. She couldn't believe it was really him. It was like her mind was trying to make sure he was real and not a ghost or a figment of her imagination. But this was *Baz*. Though he did look different—there was a confidence to him she'd rarely seen, an assurance in his skin that made him seem taller, older, wiser. Whatever he'd gone through had changed him.

She wondered how *she* must appear to him. Broken. Full of

darkness. Something to fear, or perhaps to take pity on. Especially after seeing what she'd done on the cove.

She thought of her father again with trepidation now, uncertain how *he* would react to the new her. If he might take one look at her and know all the things she'd done. If he would accept the darkness that enveloped her now.

Her silent exchange with Sidraeus earlier came back to mind. When she'd asked him if he could take them here the same way he'd gotten them out of the sea of ash, his voice had echoed in her mind.

I might be willing to help, if you'd stop threatening me with that dagger and asked nicely.

Emory had fought to keep the surprise off her face; she hadn't expected this mind connection to last. *So you're invading my mind now?* she'd thought, wondering if he would even hear her.

He'd huffed in reply. *Invading? Please. Your mind is laid bare to me. A consequence of this bargain you've made, I presume.* His eyes had turned violent. *Don't think I won't kill you for what you've done to me.*

Emory had gripped the dagger tighter in response. *So try it. I'd love to see just how far this connection between us goes.*

She knew she'd won this battle of wills the moment he'd narrowed his eyes at her. Of course he wouldn't try to kill her; not if there was a chance it might kill him, too.

"I *own* you," she'd said aloud, the words tumbling out more confidently than she felt. But those silver spiral runes were proof that Sidraeus's fate was tied to her–to all Eclipse-born–thanks to the bargain she'd made. And she would use that as leverage against him as long as it served her, if it kept him from killing Romie.

Emory cut him a glance now, wondering if he could hear *all* of her thoughts. She'd have to be careful, learn how to ward her mind.

They came upon an old building that used to be an orphanage long ago, then had been converted into dormitories for the prep school for a time, before falling into disuse and disrepair. It was a bit dilapidated, all crumbling brick and loose roof shingles.

The front door opened, revealing a familiar bearded face—and every worry Emory had was gone in an instant. She ran ahead of the others and threw herself into her father's arms.

"My sweet girl," he whispered, cheek resting on the top of her head. "I thought I'd lost you forever."

"So did I." Emory wanted to break down crying, feeling her throat close with all the emotions overwhelming her. He smelled like home, and she breathed him in, pretending for a moment that they were at the lighthouse in Harebell Cove, that she had never left, that everything was still the same.

She wanted to ask how he'd gotten mixed up into all of this and why he was here, but she let him go and held her tongue, conscious of all the people behind her—and those inside the old orphanage who craned their necks to see the new arrivals. Emory recognized none of them except for Baz's parents, who burst into tears as they engulfed their son in a tight embrace. Most people, Emory realized, had Eclipse sigils on their hands. There must have been more than two dozen of them, all gawking at her and the others as they stepped inside.

"Basil, my dear boy, come and give an old woman a hand."

This came from an aging woman Emory recognized as Professor Selandyn. She pushed her way to the front of the group, walking slowly with the help of a cane, which Emory didn't remember her using before. Baz extricated himself from his parents' embrace and swallowed the professor in his arms. She seemed tiny compared to him. Emory had never seen the Eclipse professor so frail, and it hit her how much the woman had aged in such a short time. Professor Selandyn patted Baz's cheek with a fond smile. Her eyes flitted over to Emory, and that smile grew.

"I knew you'd find her," she told Baz. "You brought the Shadow reborn back to us."

"Actually . . ." Baz met Emory's gaze. He swallowed thickly. "We only just found each other. I was . . . A lot has happened since we left."

Professor Selandyn scanned their group, doing a double take as she saw Sidraeus. "Clearly." She frowned. "Where's Kai?"

Emory's heart sank. She'd been so focused on Romie, Atheia, Sidraeus, and every little thing in between, that she hadn't clocked Kai's absence until now. Her gaze snapped to Baz. The devastation on his face was brief before he schooled his features into stiff tenacity.

"We lost each other. But I . . . I'll find him again."

Emory knew there was more to the story. Could see it plainly in his eyes, in the way his throat undulated as he swallowed back whatever emotion he was suppressing.

"And Romie?"

This came from Baz's mother, Anise. She was looking at Baz with such hope, but when Baz turned to Emory, so did everyone else.

Emory closed her eyes to keep the tears from falling. *Romie's gone because of me,* she thought. *Again.*

Familiar guilt threatened to choke her. But then a hand brushed hers, and she opened her eyes to see Nisha at her side, giving her a nod of encouragement. Emory took in a steadying breath. "Romie became the vessel to the Tides. And she's come back here . . ." She peered at all the Eclipse-born staring back at her. "To eradicate Eclipse magic."

People spoke all at once, their shocked murmurs rising ever louder. Emory could feel Sidraeus hovering behind her, watching with careful awareness as if ready to disappear if he sensed any sort of hostility toward him.

Jae managed to get everyone to quiet down. "Seems we have a lot to catch up on," they said, looking between Baz and Emory, "but if what you say is true . . . if the Tides have truly returned . . ."

"It is true," Emory asserted.

Jae blanched. "Surely they wouldn't want to *eradicate* Eclipse magic."

"Rosemarie would never want that," said Anise. She clung so tightly to her husband's arm, her knuckles were white.

"She won't have a choice," Nisha said in the gentlest way possible. "She's the Tides' vessel now, forced to do their bidding." She met Emory's gaze. "Unless we stop her."

"How?" Baz's father asked. "How can we stop a deity?"

Tell them.

Sidraeus's voice in her mind.

Emory faced the Eclipse-born. "Because we have a deity of our own on our side."

"The Shadow reborn," Jae said, looking at Emory.

She shook her head. "I'm not the Shadow reborn. I'm just a Tide-caller." She locked eyes with Sidraeus as he stepped at her side, tilting her head up to look at him. "*He* is the Shadow. And he's here to help us."

Silence swept the commons.

"But . . . he's only a *boy*," said a woman with tattoos like Kai's peeking from the collar of her blouse. "And he looks so young . . ."

"I assure you, I am he," Sidraeus said in that low, level voice.

Shadows gathered around him, slithering along his limbs. They reminded Emory of when she'd first found him in the sleepscape, when he was still in his umbra form and had taunted her with his shadows. The way her breath had hitched as they slithered around *her* limbs. She chased the memory away, watching the awed faces around her as the shadows lengthened, as they took the shape of an obsidian crown atop Sidraeus's head. His eyes flashed silver and gold, the light swirling and dipping around his pupils, the very embodiment of the eclipse.

"Forgive me," breathed the woman who'd said he looked young. "Mighty Phoebus."

Your people did not always know me as the Shadow, Emory remembered him telling her. *They called me Phoebus, once. The bright one. Associated with the sun because I appeared to them on an eclipse.* The name seemed to draw the slightest smile from him now.

"We are at your mercy," a man said with a hand to his heart. "We are yours entirely."

He and the Luaguan woman bowed their heads in reverence. A few other people quickly followed suit, holding their tattooed hands to their hearts, the Eclipse sigils turned to Sidraeus in recognition of this deity they owed their magic to. But most, Emory noticed, kept their heads high and their hands at their sides, staring at Sidraeus with looks ranging from careful skepticism to outright distrust.

A young man, pale-faced and wearing a teal blazer embroidered with what looked like the emblem of one of the Trevelyan colleges, scowled at Sidraeus.

"I'll believe you are who you claim to be once all threats to Eclipse-born vanish." His words were infused with a dark thread of anger. "Until then, why should we bow to a deity who abandoned us? How are you going to set all of this right?" Nods of assent fueled him to go on. "Most of us haven't seen our family for months and can't go home for fear of being caught. We have friends imprisoned at Institutes all over the world, loved ones who've had their magic ripped away from them. And let's not forget about the people we've lost to Collapsing incidents or those who we might have hurt during our own Collapsing. So much death and harm caused by the Shadow's curse–*your* supposed curse. Can you undo that?"

Emory half expected Sidraeus to lash out at him, but all he said was a stiff, "No, I can't."

"Then why should we follow you, if you can do nothing for us that we can't do ourselves?"

The question was met with silence. As Emory studied Sidraeus's expression–the tightness around his mouth, the barest furrow between his brows, the sudden dullness in his eyes–she saw it for what it was.

Guilt.

Etched on his skin was the memory of the first Eclipse-born–of the Tidecallers he'd led to the godsworld and watched die as they burnt out trying to take the power from the fountain, and those he'd sacrificed to appease the god of balance. But the runes must be nothing compared to the hard stares of the Eclipse-born who stood before him now, a stark reminder that they had survived in spite of him, fending for themselves in a world that had not been made for them, suffering the vitriol and hatred of lunar mages that wanted them gone.

Not everyone here saw Sidraeus as a savior. And maybe he wasn't. But Emory knew they needed him, one way or the other.

"You don't have to trust him," she said to the displeased Eclipse-born. "All I ask is that you trust *me*. I know most of you don't know me, but I want the same things you do. I want to save Eclipse magic and stop our world from being destroyed. I've come face-to-face with all the monsters who are trying to ruin us, and even though I–I've failed to stop them, I think we can do so together. But we need the Shadow on our side."

She wasn't sure where the confidence came from. It felt false, a mask slapped on to hide all her insecurities, but an encouraging nod from her father had her believing otherwise. Those who had challenged Sidraeus kept quiet, maybe not entirely convinced but willing to listen, at least.

Emory wanted to prove herself to them. She would find a way out of this mess.

This time, she would not fail.

BAZ

BAZ CAME OUT OF THE SHOWER FEELING BETTER THAN he had in a long time. When he was in the god's workshop, whatever magic lived there seemed to keep him clean and fresh in perpetuity, but there was nothing quite like a warm shower and a change of clothes that weren't from two centuries ago. Bless his parents for anticipating his return and bringing some of his things with them; Baz hadn't expected to find such comfort in wearing one of his favorite knit sweaters.

He ran a towel through his wet hair–he'd have to ask his mother to give it a trim later–and put on his glasses, staring at himself in the old mirror above the rickety dresser. They'd all been assigned a room. Thankfully, there were plenty to go around, what with this having been the old boarding facility. Someone must have spruced the space up a bit, because the bed was surprisingly comfortable, with sheets that smelled freshly laundered.

Baz let himself sink on the pillow he propped up against the headboard, releasing a long sigh as the events of the day replayed in his mind. After the reveal that the Shadow now walked among them, Jae had filled them all in on what had happened during their absence from this world.

As Baz had seen with his own eyes, the tides had grown wild and destructive, affecting not only their infrastructures, but their magics, too. Lunar mages could only access their magic with bloodletting now, even on their moon phase. Some reported being less powerful than before, feeling like they were depleting their magic every time they bloodlet, without it regenerating the way it should have.

It was as if magic were slowly becoming extinct—except for the Eclipse-born, most of whom had all deliberately forced their Collapsing after realizing how it would expand their limits. They did so under the watchful eye of Jae and with help from Baz's own father, whose Nullifying magic helped attenuate the force of their Collapsing.

It came as no surprise that this power imbalance had fueled hatred toward the Eclipse-born, feeding into the Regulators' narrative of them being the cause of all this madness. The Tidelore faith had made a resurgence as a result, with more people than ever believing in the myth that portrayed the Tides as good and the Shadow as evil.

"It's become a bit of a widespread cult," Jae had explained bitterly. "A perverse movement spearheaded by the Regulators."

"And the Selenic Order," Ife Nuru had added with a glimmer of guilt in her dark eyes. "Which is why I left them."

The Selenic Order was riding this wave of hysteria too, using it as a blanket excuse to take silver blood from Eclipse-born held at Institutes without threat of repercussion, all so they could make more synthetic magic.

"The Order distributes it widely within the Tidelore cult," Ife had said, "and sells it to whoever else can get their hands on it. With lunar magic dwindling, you can see how valuable it's become."

"The synths are a weapon," Baz's father had gravely pointed out. "They're meant to level the playing field between lunar mages and Eclipse-born."

Baz was sick to his stomach knowing where those synths came from. It was especially vile and twisted on the Selenic Order's part to be taking Eclipse blood to make weapons to use *against* those whose blood was taken.

Kai would have ripped them all to shreds if he knew. He would also have loved to see this band of Eclipse rebels hiding from the law, forcing their Collapsing here under Jae's watchful eye. Baz could imagine it so plainly, the pride Kai would have felt at being here with Eclipse-born from all corners of the world, old and young, fighting to enact real change.

Baz had been introduced to most of them earlier. There were the dozens of Collapsed Eclipse-born that Jae had been training in secret before all this, as well as students who'd come to Aldryn for the Quadricentennial, like Rusli, the Luaguan student Baz had met briefly before going through the door. Rusli had been reunited with the Luaguan friend of his that had Collapsed and whom Jae had been training. Her name was Sana, her magic akin to Nullification, like Baz's father, though it was an odd variation of it that nullified not magic, but *senses* like sight and smell and hearing, which she could negate for a time or suppress entirely.

Most others were Illusionists like Jae, though some had the kind of magic Baz hoped wouldn't be needed, like a Poisoner who could turn any liquid fatal, and someone who called himself a Festerer, able to make sickness take root inside someone.

There were non-Eclipse-born, too. Some were familiar faces—Alya, Ife, Emory's father, Baz's mother—but others Baz had never seen, like the powerful Wardcrafter who was responsible for keeping the safe house untouched by the destructive tides.

A pit of sadness opened in Baz as he stared at his empty room. Kai should be here. And all Baz could do now was hope with all his being that the god's apprentice was right; that there was something here in the present that would help Baz bring Kai back.

Baz reached for the paper folded up in his pants pocket. He unfolded it carefully, studying the odd-looking tree and the words in that strange language. It was the first time he'd done so since the god's ex-apprentice had given it to him.

"So you met a god."

Baz startled, hiding the sheet of paper from view on instinct alone. Emory stood in his doorway, leaning on the frame. She'd clearly also just gotten out of the shower, her damp hair drying in soft waves, her cheeks rosy, looking comfortable in loose pants and a too-big sweater that might have belonged to her father. Seeing she'd startled him, she gave Baz an apologetic smile.

"What was that like?" she asked.

Baz rubbed at his neck where the Shadow had grabbed him. "Well, he didn't try to kill me, for one."

Emory grimaced. "Sorry about that. He has . . . issues . . . with this god of yours."

"He's not *my* god," Baz said weakly. His eyes flicked to her. "Though you and the Shadow seem . . ."

"What?"

Baz flushed. "I don't know."

Part of him felt uneasy that some people here suddenly decided to worship at the Shadow's feet. The other part of him . . . well, it hadn't slipped his notice that a lot of people remained wary of the Shadow's return. Maybe they'd all internalized the myth that painted the Shadow as evil and the Tides as good, something they would need to unlearn if they were to work with him.

"Can we trust him?" Baz asked.

"He's saved me more times than I can count." Emory crossed her arms. There was an edge of defensiveness to her voice. But then she seemed to consider the question, and she admitted, "But he's a deity with an agenda of his own. He wants revenge on Atheia. The Tides, I mean. And your god, too, I suppose."

Equilibris, the Shadow had called him. A fitting name, Baz thought.

"Why does he want revenge?" he asked, all the different versions of the myth of the Tides and the Shadow converging in his mind. He needed the truth.

Emory sighed, uncrossing her arms and stepping into his room. "It's a long story." She eyed the bed uncertainly.

Baz motioned for her to sit. And as Emory launched into the story of Atheia, Sidraeus, and the gods, and how Sidraeus came into her life by way of possessing Keiran, Baz thought how strange it was to be here with her. On one hand, it felt completely normal to be discussing deities and magic the way they had before. As if no time had elapsed at all. But on the other . . . there was no denying how different they'd become. The things they'd gone through had molded them into different versions of themselves, unrecognizable from the people they'd been before she'd gone through the door.

"I can't help but feel like it's my fault again," Emory admitted when she was done recounting her tale. "If I had listened to Romie and stayed away . . ."

"Don't go down that path. Trust me, dwelling on all the things you could have done differently helps no one. You trusted your gut, managed to keep the Shadow out of Clover's hands and wrangle him to our side. I have no doubt we'll figure out a way to fix things and bring Romie back."

Emory gave a half-hearted nod, her gaze drifting as if she were already planning ways to do just that. Baz had seen the way she carried remorse before, but this was different. Like she was taking responsibility instead of wallowing in shame. Swimming with purpose in the ocean of guilt that had tried to drown her for so long.

"What happened to Kai?"

The question came out quiet, hesitant, like Emory knew there was something Baz wasn't saying. Something that hurt too much to talk about.

Baz heaved a long, shuddering sigh. "It's a long story too."

"I'm all ears if you want to tell it."

And Baz did. He told her how he and Kai had ended up in the past, how they'd befriended Clover and been burned by him. How Baz had found himself in the god's workshop, and what he'd done to try to reverse Kai's fate.

Tears welled in Emory's eyes as he recounted Luce's story. He answered all the burning questions she had about her mother, told her, too, of the real Clover ancestor the Kazans hailed from—not Cornelius, as they'd been led to believe, but Cordelia. By the end, he couldn't tell what Emory felt. She wiped at her cheeks and stared off into the middle distance, a crease forming between her brows.

"All this time," she breathed, "I thought my mother didn't want me."

Baz's heart lurched. "She wanted to save you."

The truth should have been a comfort, he thought, but Emory looked shaken, her whole life put into a new perspective, one she didn't know how to make sense of.

"Do you think we can save them?" she asked quietly. "Romie and Kai and . . . Luce."

Baz wanted to laugh at the irony of the situation. It felt like they'd gone back to the start, with him and Emory against the world, Romie gone, and Kai trapped somewhere horrible.

"We have to try," he said.

He couldn't bring himself to broach the subject of him and Kai. How close they'd gotten, and what had happened between them. Baz wasn't sure why he felt *guilty* over it now that Emory was here. The way he saw it, the possibility of anything happening between him and Emory had left with her the day she'd gone through the door. But that was how he saw it *now*. He was reminded of the time shortly after she left, when he'd still held out hope. When the door of possibility had been left ajar, pending her return.

And he'd turned to Kai instead. Fallen for someone else. Slammed that door in Emory's face.

A ridiculous thought to have if she never even felt the same way about him to begin with—especially after she'd taken advantage of his feelings for her. But that didn't matter anymore.

He would tell her about Kai later. For now, it was his secret to hold close to his heart. If there was one thing he was certain of, it was that she was keeping things from him, too. The smaller, more personal details that he had no right to demand from her. She looked haunted, perhaps by what had happened with Keiran. Being betrayed by him, losing him, being taunted by a deity wearing his skin, losing him again. It must have taken its toll on her, especially with everything else going on.

Emory reached for his hand, giving him a watery smile. "You have no idea how good it is to see you again."

"You too." Baz glanced down at their joined hands. Her New Moon tattoo over his Eclipse one. "You should get that fixed."

"What?"

"Your sigil. You're one of us now. Tides, you brought the Shadow himself back to our shores! Seems to me you should have an Eclipse sigil."

Something flashed in the depths of her eyes, like longing for this chance to fully be part of House Eclipse.

Footsteps echoed in the hall. Through the open door, Baz glimpsed Professor Selandyn walking by.

"Professor!" he called out, hand slipping from Emory's to reach for the folded-up ritual. "If it's no bother, I've been meaning to ask for your help with something . . ."

"No bother at all, Basil."

The professor sat down in a rickety chair that had been tucked in a corner of the room. She pored over the paper for some time, her mouth thinning as she worked to decipher the language.

"I've seen this language before," she said, "in Clover's journal, remember? This is some kind of ritual, if I'm to understand. It speaks of divine symmetry, the correspondence between all things. This line here . . ."

She spoke words that slithered up Baz's spine. From the way Emory's face blanched, she'd also heard this old, strange tongue before.

"What is above is reflected below," Professor Selandyn translated. "Fitting, given the imagery of the tree."

She was right. Trees were curious because they experienced a sort of mirrored growth, with their roots pushing deeper into darkness while their branches extended toward the light. It reminded Baz of a line in Clover's work—well, *Baz's* work—about the Wychwood:

Trees have roots planted firmly in the underworld and hands that graze the heavens.

Underworld. Like the abyss where Kai was fated to go.

"The wording is strange, though," Professor Selandyn said with a frown. "The above and below could also be read as *sideways*, or *across*."

She tilted the page on its side so that the tree was laid out horizontally, flourishing branches on the left, roots on the right. Baz was struck by the thought that it looked, almost, like lungs.

Perhaps it would have been a more fitting metaphor to call him the lungs...

His own lungs felt like they were burning as he fought to keep his breathing steady, a wild inkling taking root inside him.

"There are phrasings I can't quite decipher," Selandyn said. "If I'm to make sense of this ritual, I'll have to study it further."

"We can ask Sidraeus about it," Emory suggested. "Not sure how willing he'll be to help, but I've heard him speak this language before."

"A language of gods," the professor mused. She peered at Baz. "This ritual, what are you hoping it might do?"

Disrupt fate. Change everything.

Baz gulped. "It's how I might save Kai."

Whatever the ritual might entail, there was no doubt Baz had a role to play. The lungs imagery only solidified this. It couldn't be a coincidence that he considered himself the lungs of the story—the writer who had breathed life into the tale that set all of this in motion—and that this drawing of a tree clearly also portrayed lungs.

What is above is reflected below. What is on one side is mirrored on the other. Baz didn't know what it meant in regard to Kai, but he was ready to find out and do what he must to see him again.

ROMIE

ATHEIA COULD FEEL HIS PRESENCE LIKE A SPLINTER under her skin.

She had known the moment Sidraeus had appeared in this world, not long after she had. Like a note of brimstone in the air, a pestilence on the horizon. She felt sickened to her core, and yet she hungered for him all the more for it, desperate to sink her teeth in him and destroy him. Make him pay for the damage he'd done to her beloved world.

From her window, Atheia watched the unbridled sea below. She had been set up in the empty quarters of a professor who'd recently been dismissed for his outspokenness in support of Eclipse-born students. An office space on the top floor of the palatial Pleniluna Hall, dressed in white marble and gold filigree, velvet curtains, a plush light blue settee, and a soft carpet beneath her feet.

Atheia had opened the window to let in the night breeze. She'd been given new clothes to wear but found she did not particularly care for the fashion of the century, yearning for the flowing, diaphanous gowns she had worn during her time here. So she'd shucked out of her earlier attire—a silky white shirt with a velvet pinafore dress over it that hugged her vessel's curves and was scandalously short as far as she was concerned—and had slipped into what she understood to be a nightgown, the loose muslin falling to her knees. The cold nipped at her skin despite the shawl wrapped loosely over her shoulders, but she didn't mind it one bit. It made her feel alive.

A knock came at the door. "Come in," Atheia said.

Entering the room were four people she took to be the Tidal Council, the leaders of the Selenic Order, followed closely by Louis and Javier, the last remaining members of the Order's current cohort at school; the rest of them were either dead or traitors that had flocked to the Eclipse-born's side.

"So this is her," said the oldest woman here, small in stature with a cloud of silver hair and a face lined with history. Her eyes shone with an excited glimmer as they took in Atheia. She had the sigil of House Waxing Moon on her veiny hand.

"She looks well for a dead girl," a tall, reedy man noted gruffly, leering at Atheia in a way that made her conscious of the thin nightgown. His hand bore the sigil of House New Moon.

"I was never dead," Atheia said, tightening the shawl around her.

The old woman smacked the man aside, seeming to humble him a bit. "I'm Leonie Thornby," she introduced herself. "It's an honor to be standing before the Tides of Fate in the flesh."

"Hold your horses, Leonie," said another man whose Full Moon sigil flashed as he crossed his arms over his heavy chest. "We still haven't confirmed this vessel nonsense to be true." He narrowed his eyes at Atheia. "There's only one way to know you're who you say you are. Viv?"

This he called to the fourth Tidal Council member, a statuesque woman with a haughty expression and the sigil of House Waning

Moon on her hand. She advanced toward Atheia looking almost bored, her mouth pinched in contempt. "Vivianne Delaune." She spoke her name like it was something to revere, or fear. "I'll be sifting through your memories to confirm what you have claimed. If you try to block me . . ."

"I won't, Memorist." Atheia made an inviting motion. "I have nothing to hide."

The woman cut herself and bled in a shallow bowl of water to access her magic. Atheia felt her rummaging through her mind. When she was done, Vivianne pulled back with wonder.

"She's telling the truth." Her whisper was low and tremulous. "She's the Tides. All four of them combined."

Atheia jutted her chin out. "Call me Atheia."

The woman immediately bowed her head in a show of respect, with Leonie and the reedy man following suit. The heavyset man of House Full Moon hesitated, still not fully convinced, it seemed.

Atheia tilted her head as she rummaged through his mind with magic of her own. "You mistrust me," she noted. "And even if I am the Tides, you do not wish to bow to a girl half your age who failed her initiation. Well. I'll have you know Rosemarie Brysden survived much more than any of you ever did or ever could. She achieved what all of you Selenics have failed to do since the Tides left your shores: she brought them back. Brought *me* back. So I believe the proper response here is to *bow*."

The man bent at the waist, influenced by the Glamour in her voice. When she let him go, he remained there, quivering. "Apologies," he said, "I should never have doubted."

"No, you shouldn't have." Atheia lifted his face up to look at her, delighting at the mix of fear and begrudging respect she saw in him. "But I am benevolent. So let's start over, shall we? There is work to be done."

The Tidal Council proceeded to tell her about the decline of lunar magic and how they'd been taking steps to overcome it. When Atheia found out about the origin of the synthetic magics they injected themselves with–made with the silver blood of Eclipse-born–she felt a rage inside her at the thought of lunar mages forced to debase themselves in such a way. Forced to resort to tainting themselves with the very magic she wanted to eradicate.

It was sickening.

But in another way, it was only fitting that these Eclipse-born gave back what they had stolen. Their magic was derived from the first Tidecallers, and so they were as much thieves as their predecessors had been.

"I want to see this Institute where the synths are made," Atheia declared. An idea was dawning, and she needed to see the process done with her own eyes to be sure it would work.

They made plans to go the very next day. And as Atheia watched the Order members bowing once more before retreating from her quarters, she couldn't help the swarm of memories that washed over her. How similar this all was to the Veiled Atlas she had known, before they'd sided with Sidraeus.

The difference was, *these* people were *her* people. They wielded the lunar magic she had bestowed upon them, and she knew they would not turn their backs on her as Sidraeus's creatures had. They would not break her heart as the original members of the Veiled Atlas had. Because, despite everything, she had loved them, those Tidecallers. She had believed they added depth to this world, that they were the missing color to her tapestry of magic. But they had made their allegiance clear.

They had chosen wrong. And she would never be fooled again.

A heart-shaped face appeared unbidden in her mind, narrow dark eyes full of bright hope and laughter, a curtain of silky black hair blowing in the wind. It was a face Atheia would have liked to forget.

Atheia shook away the memories and snuffed out her vessel's curiosity like a candle. A sudden noise made her turn from the window's vista to the door. A cat approached her from the shadows. Where it had come from, she did not know, but her vessel recognized it immediately, a wave of fond love pouring out of her. *Dusk*, it was called. It seemed well fed, which meant it hadn't been abandoned what with Romie's brother being gone. Likely it had found another student to take care of it. Atheia reached a hand to it. The cat sniffed at it–and hissed, its hackles rising, before it scurried away through the door left ajar.

Atheia felt Romie's gutting sadness seeping through. This feeling of being alone, of wanting companionship, struck a chord of compassion within Atheia.

Take heart, she told Romie. *We have each other now.*

EMORY

OUT OF HABIT, EMORY SEARCHED FOR ROMIE IN DREAMS, but her friend's sleeping consciousness wasn't there. Perhaps Atheia had no use for sleep.

The dreaming mind she did encounter was Virgil's. She expected to find him in the thralls of the worst sort of nightmare for how haunted he'd been since they'd left the sea of ash–since he'd used his magic to kill–but his dream was surprisingly peaceful.

Virgil was in the quad at Aldryn, sprawled on the grass, his face turned up to the sun. A schoolbook lay open beside him. Laughter had him open his eyes. Lizaveta was sitting down next to him, and it was a version of Lizaveta that Emory scarcely recognized. Light and airy, without the coldness she'd known her by. It was Lizaveta the way Virgil saw her.

The scene changed, and Virgil now stood in front of an old, yellow-leafed tree. For a second Emory thought they were still in the courtyard, but a quick glance around showed they were inside.

The Decrescens classroom was just as Virgil had once described it to her: full of vines growing along the walls and ceiling, and delicate flowers, roses and poppies for the most part, preserved beneath glass domes or growing in clusters along the stone paths carved on the floor. It was a great garden that felt like something that belonged to House Waxing Moon, not House Waning Moon. Except for the tree that grew at the center of it.

The tree's branches grazed the glass dome above their heads. The soft light from outside hit the yellow leaves just so, making everything golden. As Emory came to stand beside Virgil, she watched the leaves go from that rich gold to crisp brown. In the silence, the dead leaves fell at their feet, and she understood that this dream-Virgil was using his Reaper magic to make the seasons turn, just like he'd told her, long ago, that Reapers did to this tree. Practicing their Reaper magic on it in the way it was meant to be used. Not to kill, not to end life, but to see the beauty in endings, how they paved the way for new beginnings.

Emory studied Virgil's pained expression, the tears running down his cheeks. She was worried about him. There was a heaviness to him that even the promise of wine earlier at dinner hadn't been able to alleviate, and now this.

Virgil met her gaze. Whether or not he recognized that she was the real Emory visiting him in dreams, she couldn't tell.

"I've never taken a life, you know," he said. "All this time, I took pride in being a Reaper because I saw the peaceful side of it. But now . . . now . . ." He hiccuped, halfway between a laugh and a sob. "It's tainted now, isn't it?"

"It's not." Emory slid her hand in his and rested her head against his shoulder.

He broke down at her side and finally told her what had happened. How the Songless had attacked the cave as Emory was taken away by Clover. How the draconics had fought them with everything they had, ordering Virgil, Nisha, and Vera to run. How one Songless had slipped past, charging at them on his winged horse, lightning lance aimed at Nisha or Vera, Virgil couldn't remember. He hadn't thought twice about sending a wave of Reaper magic to save them. The Songless had fallen, and the now riderless horse had bucked wildly before taking to the skies, as if it had sensed the death magic and wanted to get as far away from it as possible. It had given the other Songless pause as their own horses became skittish, and between that and Sidraeus's sudden appearance and subsequent vanishing into thin air, it gave the others the chance to escape.

Virgil swept a hand over his face. "I can't shake the image of the light leaving that man's eyes. I took his *life*."

"You saved lives, too." Emory understood his pain, the guilt he must feel. "This might mean nothing," she murmured, "and I don't know how to take the pain away. But you have to know it wasn't your fault. You did what you had to."

Virgil didn't look too convinced, but he composed himself, sighing deeply. With a half-hearted smile, he pulled her in close, and together they stood in the shadow of the Reaper tree, trying to keep the beauty of death magic alive between them.

Emory frowned at the tree. Where before, all its leaves had fallen, leaving only bare branches that cast eerie shadows, the tree was now lush and green; more alive than what it had first been when she'd walked in. "How does it do that?"

"Do what?"

"Grow back. Is there Sower magic imbued in it or something?" It would be the only explanation for the tree becoming full again after Reaper magic was used on it. Unless this was just the dream working its nonsensical magic, and the reality was different.

Virgil watched the tree contemplatively, as if he'd never wondered before. "Must be." He looked at Emory with an attempt at a crooked smile, at his chipper self. "I told you I'd bring you here and give you lessons one day. We have time—want to try your hand at using your Reaper magic on it?"

Emory had only ever let herself lean in to this darker strand of magic as a last resort, a knee-jerk reaction. Like when she'd killed one of the eldritch creatures that had attacked them at the Chasm. She wasn't even sure she could use other magics while dreaming in the sleepscape. And maybe it was because of this that she let herself try.

She sent a wave of Reaper magic toward the tree and watched its leaves turn golden once more. There was something vast and depthless about the tree. It was marked by death right down to its core, as if all the years of Reaper magic being used on it had left scars, lending it power that was at once ancient and dark, calm and serene.

Emory withdrew her magic, cold licking up her spine, as the first brown leaf fell from the tree, dancing a slow, arcing death through the air. The tree was turning dark and rotten, until suddenly it dissolved into black sand and swirling shadows.

Whispers grew in her ears. Darkness pressed in at the edges of the dream. A nightmare looking to devour it. Emory needed to leave lest she put Virgil's consciousness in danger.

She stepped out of his dreaming and into a familiar scene. Trapped inside the hourglass was the very same tree that had been in the Reaper classroom. It had rematerialized, black sand and shadows becoming wood and leaves once more.

And she recognized this tree, had seen it earlier, drawn on the ritual Baz was trying to decipher.

What is above is reflected below. What is on one side is mirrored on the other.

A chill went through her as she realized she was no longer alone. Those words were spoken in the same strange tongue

Professor Selandyn had used, though it was not her voice that said them now, nor even Sidraeus in his umbra form. The voices were many and layered. They whispered the words over and over, swirling around Emory until she was dizzy from the overlapping sounds.

There was sudden silence—before the hourglass shattered.

Emory shielded herself from the shards of glass and sand and shadows. Pain tore through her, sending her falling to her hands and knees as she coughed up oozing black water and silvery blood. She felt *something* move inside her, pushing against her lungs, climbing up her throat. A vine emerged from her mouth. Barely able to breathe, she pulled at it and found narcissus and hollyhocks and orchids and poppies growing along it, the lunar flowers slowly turning to glass. She pulled and pulled but felt her bloodied hands slipping and the glass flowers breaking inside her, a thousand tiny shards cutting her up from the inside until she wanted to *die*.

She curled up on her side to do just that. Flowers sprouted all around her, as if growing from the shards of glass, multiplying and crawling along her skin, digging their roots in her. She would be buried under a mound of them, here in this nightmare version of Dovermere. And just when she couldn't handle any more pain, she *screamed*—glass shards cutting along the columns of her throat—as names were branded in bright silver on the skin of her bare arms. Travers. Lia. Jordyn. All the other initiates who'd lost their lives in Dovermere because of her. Lizaveta. Keiran.

Aspen. Tol. Orfeyi.

Romie.

"How does it feel," a voice behind her said, "to wear your guilt on your skin?"

Sidraeus had appeared in the nightmare, not as his umbra self but in his true form. His features were cast in shadows, his outline limned in the soft light that emanated from the stars beyond. And his eyes held a hard cruelty that had Emory understanding this was *his* doing.

Retribution for the pain she'd been putting him through thanks to the bargain she'd made.

"I may not be able to hurt you out there without hurting myself," Sidraeus said, "but in the dark confines of your mind, you alone feel this pain." The shadows around him seemed to spread toward her, climbing over her, twining with the lunar flowers to wrap around her limbs, to keep her rooted here. "I own the realm of nightmares, Tidecaller, and so in here, *I* own *you*. Remember that the next time you mean to threaten me."

"Please," she heard herself whimper as Sidraeus began to fade against the darkness.

A sardonic smile was the last thing she saw before he disappeared, his voice echoing inside her mind with grim finality. *Sleep well.*

She was being buried beneath lunar flowers and shards of glass and tendrils of darkness, and there was no way to stop it. Part of her knew none of this was real, that this was just another nightmare. But it wasn't. This was Sidraeus in all his divine power, giving her a taste of just how strong he was, showing her exactly the kind of deity she was dealing with.

Emory closed her eyes, willing herself not to be afraid, trying to breathe through the pain so she could break free of it. This was *her* mind, and she was in control of it, not him.

Light poured out of her, tearing through every dark thing, healing all the pain.

She woke with a gasp, drenched in sweat. Patting herself down, she found no shards of glass piercing her skin, no flowers embedded in her limbs, no names carved in silver on her arms.

None of it had been real. But the memory of the pain lingered like a bad taste in her mouth. For a second she felt small, weak, put in her place by this deity she had dared to mess with. She couldn't fall back asleep and risk suffering the same pain all over again—and yet she refused to cower like this.

Before she knew what she was doing, she tore out of her bed and stormed out into the quiet corridor, shaking with righteous anger.

Deity or not, bargain or not, she would not let Sidraeus threaten her like that.

Emory tried not to panic as she searched the boardinghouse and couldn't find him. What if it had all been a distraction, keeping her trapped in the worst nightmare imaginable while he set off to hunt down Atheia?

So quick to jump to conclusions. His smooth voice rang in her mind. *I have to say, I'm impressed at how quickly you escaped that pleasant little nightmare.*

Emory gritted her teeth. *Get out of my head.*

Stop inviting me in, then.

I did not—Where are you? I swear, if you've gone after her . . .

I haven't gone anywhere.

She heard a soft sound coming from a room down the hall, the door left ajar so that a sliver of light fell on the corridor floor. She marched over to find an old office, by the looks of it, with a library full of dusty books. A lamp on the desk was turned on, dimly illuminating the room.

Sidraeus stood staring out a window toward the sea. Emory couldn't help but take him in. The shock of thick, dark auburn curls that framed his face perfectly. The lean build of his body, and how the dark dress shirt he'd thrown on, rolled up at the sleeves, revealed muscled forearms. In the half-light, the runes on his arms and neck glimmered silver. They looked less raw than they did before, yet if he felt the pain of every single Eclipse-born, surely he must be suffering at all times to some degree.

He looked like someone who was trapped, longing to get out. Emotions played on his face that Emory didn't understand. He must not have realized she was there, and seeing him so vulnerable reminded her of when he'd first appeared at the temple, such devastating pain on his youthful face. It doused some of her fury, leaving her uncertain.

"Contemplating leaving us behind?" she asked.

Sidraeus schooled his features but kept fixing the horizon. "You know I could find Atheia and end this all before the sun rises."

"So why don't you?"

"You mean aside from your constant threats of bodily harm?"

"After the hell you just put me through, I'd say we're even."

Sidraeus smirked at her before looking out the window again. "Maybe I've come to realize that if I go after her in a temper, all it will do is confirm what the people of this world already believe of me. I'll have stepped into the role of villain they've cast me in, and they'll turn on the Eclipse-born with more ferocity than they already have." His tone was surprisingly contemplative, until his next words shot at Emory like icy daggers. "And since my fate is tied to them and their pain, I'd rather not be made a victim."

Emory gulped down the rising guilt in her throat. "I had no choice," she said in a low voice. Not an apology—she would not apologize for the bargain she'd made.

"There's always a choice." Sidraeus gave her an appraising look, as if he could appreciate the viciousness of what she'd done. "You said to me once there was no world that existed in which we could be anything but rivals. Do you feel such hatred toward me still?"

"Hatred would mean I felt anything for you at all."

"So it's indifference you claim."

"Yes."

That tastes like a lie.

The words spoken in Emory's mind sent a shiver up her spine, a prickling on her wrist. She felt her cheeks heat at the intensity in his gaze, anger rising in her throat.

"I unbound you from your prison before Clover could bind you to him," she said defensively. "I'm the reason you're here in your true form instead of just a nightmare version of yourself."

A thoughtful hum. "I suppose none of it matters, in the end, if the world is doomed to fall regardless."

"Not if we find a way to replenish the fountain and stop Clover," Emory said without any real conviction. That task felt impossible now. And with Clover in the wind, who knew what he was up to.

"Clover is not the one I'm worried about," Sidraeus said.

"Then who?" Surely not Atheia; he wanted revenge on her, but didn't seem to view her like a threat. More like a thorn in his side. The answer came to Emory all at once: "The god of balance."

The god Sidraeus had once answered to, the one who had sentenced him to his prison among the stars. The same god whom Baz had met, and whom Sidraeus believed had sent Baz to retrieve him.

Shadows appeared around Sidraeus as he stepped away from the window. He was taller than Keiran had been, and the effect as he came to tower over her was all the more terrifying. Quiet fury was written across his face.

"Equilibris," he seethed, "is a tyrannical god who serves one thing and one thing only: the preservation of balance. He will not bend for anything or anyone, and if your time-wielding friend thinks he can get away with whatever he's playing at—"

"Baz is the smartest person I know, and the most careful. He knows what he's doing."

"Neither of you knows Equilibris like I do. As the master of fate, he's always one step ahead. There's no undermining him. I'd be careful around the time-wielder. He might be playing right into Equilibris's hands, whether he knows it or not."

Emory shook her head, unwilling to entertain this idea for a second. "I trust Baz with my life. I can't say the same about you."

The shadows around Sidraeus seemed to spread toward her slowly. His ecliptic eyes had her hypnotized. "I have lied to you, and you to me," he said, voice low and silky. "To pretend otherwise would be a disservice to us both. But it seems we need each other now, so I'm willing to put all that unpleasantness behind us if you are."

Sidraeus held out his hand to her, a delicate hope shining on his face, mixed with a sliver of uncertainty. It was there and gone in a flash before he seemed to catch himself and fight for neutrality. But Emory did not move to grab his hand. She wanted to trust him, but the taste of blood and the sharpness of glass in her mouth lingered.

Sidraeus's mouth lifted as he sensed her reticence. "I promise not to torture you in nightmares again if you promise to stop stabbing yourself."

Tides damn her. "Cross me and I'll gut you."

"I'd expect nothing less."

And so Emory gripped his hand. She swore there was a flash of relief on Sidraeus's face, as if this simple gesture of trust, tentative as it may be, meant more to him than she knew. She glanced at their clasped hands, mesmerized by the warmth of his skin, the feel of him. The silver spiral on the inside of her wrist matched the ones that ran all along his arm and the back of his hand, a perfect fit. This close, she could breathe him in. His scent was warm and woody. Like vetiver. It reminded her of the sleepscape, as if the sleeping realm clung to him even here in waking, embedded in his true form.

When she looked into his eyes again, they reflected a rawness she felt within herself. The same fear and darkness and guilt—the same hope that this was something that could work. That they truly could trust each other.

It was like staring into a mirror.

What is above is reflected below. What is on one side is mirrored on the other.

What Sidraeus had said about Equilibris, how the god cared only for the preservation of balance, played in her mind again, along with those whispers she'd heard in her dream. Baz's image of the tree. The same tree trapped in the hourglass. The same tree that existed in the Reaper room in Decrescens Hall.

Emory pulled back sharply, staring at Sidraeus with a sudden idea. "I need to show you something."

BAZ

A PERSISTENT KNOCKING AT HIS DOOR WOKE HIM FROM a deep, dreamless sleep.

Judging by the dim light coming through his window, it was barely dawn. Baz groggily reached for his glasses and hurried to pull the door open. Emory stood on the other side along with a sleepy-looking Virgil. The Shadow hovered a few steps behind them, looking sullen at being dragged into whatever this was.

Baz palmed the back of his head. "Um. Hi?"

"Sorry to wake you," Emory said, "but this couldn't wait."

"It very well could have," Virgil lamented, rubbing at his eyes.

Emory ignored him, shoving him inside Baz's room.

"Is everything all right?" Baz asked.

Emory was rummaging through the small desk tucked between the bed and the wall. "I'm assuming Professor Selandyn still has the ritual?"

"Yes . . ." Baz eyed the Shadow, who trailed quietly into the room and shut the door behind him, looking about as pleased to be here as Baz was to have him in his space after he tried to strangle him. "What's this about?"

"No idea." Virgil plopped down on the bed. "These two barged into my room and dragged me here. And I was having the loveliest dream, too . . ."

Emory looked pleased with herself when she found a blank piece of paper and a pencil. She held them out to Baz. "You still good at drawing?"

"Well, I—"

Emory all but shoved the paper and pencil in his hands. "Could you draw the tree that's on the ritual? I need to show Virgil and Sidraeus."

Sidraeus. It sounded so . . . personal . . . coming from her mouth. "Why?"

"Because I think I know what the ritual might entail. And I need these two to confirm it."

Virgil put the pillow over his head. "It's too early to require my help."

Baz laid the paper on the desk and leaned over it, pencil at the ready. He blinked the sleep out of his eyes and carefully sketched the tree as he remembered it. Emory hovered over his shoulder, nodding fervently.

"May I?" she asked, snatching the drawing from Baz before he'd even finished and holding it up to Virgil, who still had his head buried under the pillow and might very well have fallen asleep. "Virgil, tell me what this looks like."

A grumble of protest as the pillow came flying. Virgil sat up and peered at the drawing. The death glare he gave Emory was nothing short of spectacular. "You woke me up to look at a drawing of a tree?"

"Not just any tree. You *just* dreamed of this."

"How do you know what I was dreaming about?"

"I was there with you, remember?"

"Oh. I thought I was dreaming you up." He grinned at her. "Emory Ainsleif, you sentimental thing, you. What an honor to have you checking on me in my sleep."

Emory swatted him. "Focus. Doesn't this remind you of the Reaper tree?"

Virgil squinted at the drawing again. "I mean, I guess? No offense to your talents, Brysden, but this could be any old tree."

"What's the Reaper tree?" Baz asked, feeling confused.

"Just this tree that's in Decrescens Hall that we Reapers practice magic on."

"I felt something when I used magic on it," Emory said. "Granted, it was in a dream, so maybe that's all it was . . . But what if there's more to it?"

"Like what?"

Emory grabbed the pencil from Baz. He refrained from protesting as she traced lines around the tree he'd drawn. At first, he didn't understand what he was staring at. Then it hit him.

"An hourglass?"

It was like the tree was trapped inside one, the branches in the top bulb and the roots in the bottom one. Emory looked over her shoulder at the Shadow—Sidraeus—who peered down at the drawing with a frown.

"You were there when I dreamed of this," Emory told him. "It's not the first time I've dreamed of the Dovermere door being an actual hourglass. Even before, when Romie was trapped in the sleepscape . . . Every time I saw this, the glass would shatter and something would come out. One time, there was an opening at the bottom. Like a portal. And now recently there's been this tree trapped inside. Glass shattering. And you appearing."

"So what does it mean?" Virgil asked, taking the question right out of Baz's mouth.

"We have a tree connected to a portal in my dreams," Emory said, "a tree connected to a ritual meant to save Kai, and a tree back at Aldryn that's been killed by Reaper magic countless times over." She looked at Virgil. "Don't you think it's odd that it keeps coming back to life without any of you making it regrow? You told me no Sower ever comes in to nurse it back to health after you've used Reaper magic on it. So what makes it come back to life?"

"It couldn't possibly be . . ."

This came from Sidraeus in a hushed whisper.

"What?" Emory pried.

"There used to be trees like this in the godsworld. They connected it to the realms of the living, the sleepscape, and even the underworld."

"Like that glass-looking tree that towers over the fountain?" Emory asked.

"That was always the main one, yes, but there used to be many more before the godsworld became the sea of ash. The way Equilibris described it was that the flourishing top of the tree represented the heavenly godsworld. The middle of the tree where you see that spiral, that was meant to represent the sleeping realm as well as the four realms of the living. And the roots below, those represented the underworld."

"Trees have roots planted firmly in the underworld and hands that graze the heavens . . . ," Baz recited.

"I thought the underworld *was* the sleepscape," Virgil said, frowning. "Or the Deep. The sea of ash. Whatever the hell it's called, no pun intended."

Sidraeus shook his head. "What you might consider the afterlife is divided into parts. Death brings all souls to the sleeping realm, yes, but they must be ferried in one direction or the other. The godsworld is the heavens where souls go to find eternal peace—or where they seep into the fountain so that their souls can be resurrected into new life. But the underworld . . . the underworld is the place no soul wishes to go. Only the most corrupted of souls get sent to what we call the abyss, the first layer of this underworld. Here they are tortured for eternity, denied a chance at eternal rest or new life."

Baz blanched. This was where Kai and Luce had gone, but . . . "What does this have to do with the tree?"

"When we founded the Veiled Atlas, Atheia managed to smuggle seeds from these trees out of the godsworld. We gave them to members of the Veiled Atlas to plant in each of their worlds, for them to tend to this piece of godhood and shape it into something that might feed into the ley line and become a source of magic all its own. I thought Equilibris had destroyed them all, just like he did the Tidecallers. But I suppose that if a Tidecaller survived, they could have found a way to get this past him too. Because by the sound of it, this could be one of those trees."

A seed taken from the garden of the gods that had grown into this tree—a tree that had likely stood at Aldryn when the college was a temple to the gods, and long before even that. A tree that had since been brought back to life and died a thousand times by the magic of Reapers.

"Sorry, am I the only one who fails to see how a tree is gonna save your nightmare-weaving boyfriend?" Virgil asked in a dubious tone.

Baz blushed, avoiding everyone's gaze. Was it that obvious?

"This Nightmare Weaver." Sidraeus was staring at Baz. "I remember him. He first passed through the sleeping realm centuries ago, while I was still in my prison. I recognized him when you and he passed through the sleeping realm again more recently, that day I escaped." The day he'd taken possession of Keiran, he meant. "He and I had made a bargain during his first passage. He and the Dreamer woman he was with . . ."

"Luce?" Emory interjected, her eyes going wide at the mention of her mother.

"They'd been trying to escape Clover. I sent them help in the form of a thousand umbrae, asking the Nightmare Weaver to free me in return once he left the sleeping realm. But he never made it out. He and the Dreamer fell into the abyss beyond the stars. I could no longer feel them then. No mortal soul has ever set foot in hell, to my knowledge. They must be as good as dead, I'm afraid."

His gaze had shifted ever so slightly to Emory. There had been nothing soft in his voice or his words, but seeing the devastation on her face seemed to give him pause.

"Kai and Luce can survive it," Baz said, both for Emory and for himself, as those severed threads flashed in his mind. This was what the ritual was for. The fate he had to undo.

Emory gave him a small, grateful smile that vanished as Sidraeus spoke again.

"The abyss, they might survive," he said. "So long as they haven't fallen into the void beyond it."

"Sounds lovely," Virgil quipped. "Dare we ask what this void is?"

"No one really knows. No soul that has ever gone into it has ever returned. It is a great, black nothing. Some say it's a place where souls go to be unmade. Others believe it to be a way out of this universe. A door that might open onto infinite shores beyond this one."

A grim silence settled over the room. A place where souls went to be unmade—was *that* the fate Equilibris had seen for Kai and Luce, what the god's old apprentice believed awaited *everyone* if Kai couldn't be saved? An unmaking. *Oblivion.*

Baz refused to see it become reality. He studied the drawing again. "I think this tree is depicting a portal to the underworld. And if it's the same as the Reaper tree . . . then we need to go back to Aldryn."

When he brought it up to Jae later that morning as the two of them sat at the top of the dunes, Baz expected the Illusionist to push back, tell him getting into Aldryn was impossible, what with it swarming with Regulators. To his surprise, though, Jae considered it in earnest.

"We've been talking about pushing back against the Regulators," they said, "trying to find ways to get more people outside of our little resistance here to join our cause. Having a presence on campus again—say, by reclaiming Obscura Hall and using it as a base—would help us organize with the students and professors there who might be sympathetic. They could help us get the word out easier."

"But how?" Baz asked. "Drutten's out for blood. And as for the Tides . . . No one's going to let us just walk into Aldryn and take over Obscura Hall."

"Which is exactly why we haven't done it. We were waiting for the right moment, the right leverage, the right support . . . I suppose with the Shadow at our side now, we have just that. But you saw how some of the others reacted to him yesterday. They don't trust him, and they won't trust Emory so easily, either."

"Do you?"

"Wholeheartedly. But what we're trying to do isn't about breaking through to one or two people. It's an entire movement. And if the Tides have truly returned to our shores intent on eradicating Eclipse-born, we need to act now more than ever, before the Selenic Order and Tidelore cultists use that as a reason to come at us with more viciousness than before."

"Any ideas?"

Jae stared at the boardinghouse in the distance, a glimmer of mischief in their eyes. "A few."

Baz wanted to feel reassured by this, but it seemed like the clock was ticking ever on, and he wasn't any closer to saving Kai. He told Jae more about the ritual, the Reaper tree, and his own half-baked theories about his connection to this tree that, when tipped sideways, looked like lungs.

"I still can't believe you're the one who wrote *Song of the Drowned Gods*," Jae huffed. "To think I've dedicated my life to scholarly research on this book, and all this time the author's been growing up in front of me!"

Baz gave them a bashful smile. He didn't know how to feel about this yet, his opinion of Clover all the more tarnished now that he knew what became of him. What he did to Emory, to Romie, the keys.

"The ideas still originated with Clover, though," Baz said forlornly, thinking of the journal he'd seen Clover bent over so many times, writing snippets of his visions and dreams, which would go on to inspire the book Baz had always been fated to pen. "In a way, it's like I stole them from him."

"It's not stealing if his name's the one slapped on the cover," Jae argued. "And the story is all you."

"You're wrong there," Baz said. "I might have written it, but the story's always been yours."

Jae's brows shot up. "Mine?"

"You're the one who introduced me to it. Who sparked my love of stories to begin with. And you're arguably the person who knows the story best. You see nuances in it that no one else does. If you hadn't gifted me a copy when I was younger, if you hadn't told me the book was a portal to other worlds, I might not have become so obsessed with it. And if that were the case, then I could never have written it when I traveled to the past. Maybe the book would never have existed at all. So you see? If anyone should take credit for its existence, it's you."

"Well," Jae said, clearing their throat. Their eyes shone with emotion. They reached for Baz's hand and patted it affectionately. "Thank you, Basil. I'm sure you of all people understand how much that means to me." They cleared their throat again as they shot to their feet. "Now, I'm going to need you to repeat all that in front of Alya, because she's been giving me grief about never returning Clover's journal to her, and I think this might earn me a few points back in my favor."

Baz grimaced at the thought of the journal he'd left behind in the past. He hadn't taken it with him when he was pulled through the portal on a page to the god's workshop. He supposed it was now lost forever.

"How's that going with Alya?" he asked Jae. "Trying to mend your relationship with her?"

Jae shrugged, failing to hide their smile. "Well, now that we're both here, I figured it wouldn't hurt . . ." They stared off at the horizon where waves were picking up speed, the high tide coming in again. "To think you found Alya's sister two hundred years in the past, of all places," Jae mused with a bewildered shake of their head. "Alya never fully believed Adriana was dead, you know. At least back then, when we were together. I hope for her sake—and Vera's, and Emory's—that we don't lose her all over again."

The words stuck with Baz, weighing on his soul. This was the downside of hope: the prospect of failure. There was a way to save Kai and Luce, and that ignited a blazing optimism inside them all. But if they failed, it would destroy them.

EMORY

IF SOMEONE HAD TOLD EMORY, NOT SO LONG AGO, THAT she'd one day be sitting with her father, her aunt, and her cousin, casually having tea and discussing the possibility of saving her mother from hell, she would have thought it was the start of a terrible joke. But here the four of them were, and it felt like the strangest, most beautiful dream to see how easily Vera could make Henry laugh, to know that every time Alya's eyes lingered on Emory, a fond smile on her lips, it was because she was seeing Adriana in her features.

If this was what family felt like, Emory was sorry to have missed so much of it. She soaked it in now as they talked of her mother, who was beginning to feel less like a myth and more like a real flesh and blood person. A person she had gotten all wrong, it seemed.

All these years, she'd thought her mother had abandoned her because she didn't want her. But according to Baz, everything Luce had done had been to *save* Emory—and she had ended up in the Deep for it.

Her gaze drifted across the busy dining hall to where Sidraeus, Baz, and Professor Selandyn sat discussing the ritual. The stiff, awkward way Sidraeus held himself was almost comical next to the other two, with Professor Selandyn's overt friendliness and Baz's usual anxious state.

Sidraeus clearly didn't want to be here, surrounded by Eclipse-born who were still giving him a wide berth and dirty looks. He'd been mostly keeping his distance from everyone, no doubt sensing the fear he instilled in some. Yet he was still here, Emory had to give him that. He seemed to have let go of his vendetta against Atheia for now, shifting his focus to the ritual–if only to ensure they weren't doing exactly what Equilibris wanted them to do, he'd told her.

Emory couldn't say she cared, so long as her mother was spared the oblivion she was destined for.

She was too absorbed watching Sidraeus to realize the room had suddenly gone silent. Everyone had turned to Jae, who stood with a grave-looking Ife.

"We've received word from a trusted source," Jae announced, "that Romie–or rather, Atheia–is at the Institute, taking a special interest in synth-making."

Emory noticed the absent-minded way Ife traced the spiral mark on her wrist. An inkling of who this trusted source might be formed in her mind.

"Apparently," Jae continued, "she's even encouraged the Regulators to force Eclipse-born prisoners to Collapse if they haven't already so that they can get more silver blood. And that's not all. There's talk of the Selenic Order hosting some big event at Aldryn. They've invited important names from all over, from Regulators and Tidelore leaders to major donors and political figures invested in the college. Our source says this is when the Selenic Order plans to officially declare the Tides' return. They want to make a big show out of it and take all the credit."

"When is this happening?" Baz asked.

"In two days."

Emory's thoughts raced. If the Order publicized the Tides' return, news of it would spread like wildfire, and Atheia's agenda against the Eclipse-born would only give more credibility to those already out to get them. "We need to get ahead of this," she said. "Make our own grand reveal about the Shadow's return before they can spin the story however they want."

Jae nodded in agreement. "We need a way to appeal to everyone, get them on our side. It might be dangerous, a little reckless even, but if we were to disrupt their evening in protest..."

"Screw this." The pale-faced scholar who'd been so confrontational with Sidraeus yesterday—an Illusionist from Ilsker College, Emory had learned—rose to his feet, chair grating loudly on the floor as he did. "What we need to do is break into the Cadence Institute and set all the Eclipse-born free. We can't just sit idly by while they're left to suffer there."

"We've been over this before." Jae spoke over the mutters of assent that followed the scholar's statement. "The Institute's security is not as lax as it once was. That place has become a fortress. There's no way we can get in, much less break anyone out."

"What about him?" someone asked, pointing to Sidraeus. "If he's really the almighty Shadow, then breaking past a few Regulators and wards should be nothing to him."

Sidraeus remained as stoic as ever, though there was an eagerness to him that made Emory think he might be inclined to agree, if only to get his hands on Atheia.

"It's not just Regulators and wards we'd have to get through," Emory argued, "but Atheia, too, and she's out for blood. You think she won't expect him to come, that she won't have some kind of trap laid out for him?" This she spoke directly to Sidraeus. A warning and a plea to stay put and remember what he'd said to her just last night. "If we barge in there laying waste to the place and attacking everyone that stands in our way, they'll villainize us even more than they already have. We need to play this smart, consider other avenues before going after them guns blazing."

It was what she should have done back in the fourth world—listened to Romie's warning and thought things through instead of forging ahead anyway and leading the keys to their deaths. Emory had been driven by desperation, and desperation could only ever lead to mistakes. The keys had paid for hers; she couldn't afford to let history repeat itself now.

The Ilsker scholar crossed his arms. "So what do you suggest, Tidecaller?"

"We get our message out before Atheia does. Write the first line before the Selenic Order dictates how the rest of our story goes. And if we have to march on Aldryn to stop them, so be it."

Emory met Baz's gaze, knowing he would be thinking the same thing she was. If the Selenic Order were planning to unveil Atheia at Aldryn—the very place they needed to be to perform the ritual—then this was their chance to bring down two birds with one stone.

"I might have an idea," Vera piped in. She'd propped her feet up on the long communal table, and as everyone turned to look at her, she nodded toward a pile of dusty radio equipment tucked away in a corner. "You want to get your message out to the world, that's how we do it."

"You sure you know what you're doing there?"

Virgil voiced the skepticism everyone felt as they watched Vera tinkering with the radio.

"You all might have your fancy magic," Vera said, catching her tongue between her lips in concentration, "but this is where I shine."

Radios, much like telephones, were a relatively new invention that had originated in Trevel and made their way across the world, becoming a source of information to rival the humble newspaper. The island of Elegy was behind the times when it came to radios, and so long-range transmission of voice messages was nearly impossible, restricting broadcasts to the island alone. But they needed to go wider than Elegy. They needed to reach potential allies in the Constellation Isles and Trevel, all the way to the far reaches of the Outerlands.

If they could broadcast their message out to the world, they might get people from all over to join their cause, or at the very least to hear them out and challenge their own perceptions of Eclipse-born. The hope was to have it spark real change for Eclipse-born—and make Atheia's task of destroying them harder, if there were fewer people believing her lies.

Vera, thankfully, had studied engineering at Trevelyan University and knew just how to tinker with their transmission to allow it to reach the biggest radio broadcast companies in Trevel and Luagua. She walked Emory through the inner workings of what she was doing so that Emory could lace Amplifying magic into the transmission to help the message reach even wider.

The radio crackled to life, emitting a static noise that had Vera giving Virgil a cocky smile. "Told you I'd make it work." She motioned for Emory to sit across from her at the desk. "Ready, cousin?"

Emory felt self-conscious with everyone's attention on her. There was Jae, Baz, Theodore, and Henry in one corner of the office they had all crammed into; Virgil, Nisha, and Ife hovering behind Emory; a few Eclipse-born she had yet to learn the names of watching her with varying degrees of skepticism and hope; and Sidraeus by the window, hanging back from the group, sticking to the shadows like he was one himself.

Emory found herself marveling at the way the sunset blazing outside brought out the coppers and reds in his hair. The spirals climbing up his neck seemed gold in the light, making him look like the burnished sun itself. As if sensing her eyes on him, he met her gaze. She didn't know what he might be thinking—if he thought all of this was a waste of time. But he was here at least. If not in solidarity, then maybe out of curiosity.

Nerves gathered in her stomach as she stared blankly at the metal microphone Vera pushed in front of her. Beside it was the script that she, Baz, and Jae had worked all day to write. Well, Baz had written most of it with Emory and Jae throwing ideas while looking over his shoulder. He was technically an *author*, after all—and they needed this speech to pack a punch.

Vera pressed a button and nodded at Emory. Silence fell heavy in the room. Emory met Baz's eye, and his nod of encouragement was all she needed to gather her courage and start talking into the microphone:

"My name is Emory Ainsleif. You might know me as one of the Aldryn College students who drowned in the Dovermere sea caves last fall. And you may have heard rumors that I am a Tidecaller. I'm here today to address these rumors." She paused, swallowing past the dryness in her mouth. "I am indeed a Tidecaller—the Shadow reborn."

The lie had her finding Sidraeus's gaze, feeling her cheeks warm at the intensity of it. They didn't want to incite more fear by stating outright that the *actual* Shadow had returned—not when some of their own were still mistrusting of him. And so, for now, they would play into the narrative that the Regulators had already put in place: that as a Tidecaller, Emory was in a way the Shadow reborn.

"And while I did not drown at Dovermere," she continued, "I did journey into the Deep to find a way to restore magic to what it once was." Another twisting of the story. "Unlike what the Regulators would have you believe, neither I nor my fellow Eclipseborn are the cause of the problems our world is facing. As

Tidecaller, I am the link between both sides, the bridge between lunar magic and Eclipse magic. And I'm here to tell you that it's only by coming together that we can restore magic and fix our drowning world.

"Yes, I'm a Tidecaller, and my blood runs Eclipse. But I was born a Healer of House New Moon. My allegiance has always been to Bruma, and when I became a Tidecaller after experiencing a brush with death, that didn't change. If anything, I grew closer to Bruma—to all four Tides—because suddenly I was of all four houses. Think of me as a mirror, reflecting the magics around me and making them my own. But I do not *steal* that magic from lunar mages. The same cannot be said for those in power who steal magic from Eclipse-born."

Emory paused, feeling anger build in her veins at the words on the page. The thought that Keiran had been the one to start this, the synthetic magics made from the blood of Eclipse-born. The thought that *she* had taken synths before, not knowing where they came from, how they were made. It was sickening to think his legacy lived on in such a gruesome way. She wanted to bring down everyone who partook in the making of synths.

"With the dwindling of lunar magic, synthetics are being sold to whoever can afford them. But these are not a solution. They are *extortion*, made by forcefully and illicitly taking the blood of Eclipse-born who are being held at Institutes. The silver blood of those who have Collapsed and were given the Unhallowed Seal. This is why Regulators want to keep Eclipse-born in their Institutes: to profit off our blood. This is why they criminalize Collapsing, why they tell cautionary tales about the Shadow's curse. But here is the truth: the Shadow's curse is not real. Those of us who've Collapsed haven't fallen prey to some imaginary darkness. We are in control of our power. The curse is a lie invented by Tidelore cultists and Regulators to make you fear us—to justify the hatred thrown our way and make Eclipse magic the scapegoat for everything bad happening in the world.

"But Eclipse-born are not the problem. We don't want to hurt anyone. We don't want to sow more division. We simply want justice for our own, and for the world to be in balance again. So instead of blaming what's happening on *us*—on our very existence—ask yourselves who exactly is profiting off this imbalance and who is suffering for it. Ask yourselves why professors and students from prominent colleges like Aldryn, Karunang, Ilsker, Sevstar, Awansi, and Fröns have disappeared after voicing their support for Eclipse-born. Ask yourselves why the Eclipse-born in your lives, be it neighbor, friend, family, acquaintance, have all been forced into the shadows, when the only other option they face is imprisonment. Ask yourselves which side of history you wish to be on: compassion or hate."

Emory met Baz's gaze as she prepared to utter the conclusion he'd been so adamant to write—words Clover had spoken once, he told her, that they would use again now, spoken by another Tidecaller, one who was a distant descendant of the Clover line. Another reclaiming of the words of a man the whole world had once idolized.

"All magic is born equal," Emory read. "There is no lunar magic without Eclipse magic, no sea without a shore, no Tides without a Shadow. So let us stand together, united against the tyranny of those who would tell you otherwise. Stand with us, and let's heal our world together."

A weighted silence—and then Vera clicked a button, and static drowned everything out once more.

"Right," Virgil exclaimed, clapping his hands. "Enough doom and gloom and serious speeches for the night. I think this deserves a bit of celebrating, yes?"

Jae smiled. "There's a few jars of moonbrew down in the kitchen cellars."

Virgil's eyes went wide. "Tides and Shadow bless you, Jae Ahn." He looked at Sidraeus still hovering by the window. "What do you say, Sid?" The nickname earned him a murderous glare. "Sidraeus," Virgil rectified with a nervous chuckle. "Your shadowy divineness?"

A muscle feathered in Sidraeus's jaw, almost as if he wanted to laugh at the ridiculous form of address. But his mouth kept that disdainful curl as he turned back to the window, muttering something about mortals under his breath.

"Come on, cheery," Vera said to an affronted-looking Virgil, leading him away as he moaned about no one ever turning him down for a drink before.

As others started filing out of the room, giving Emory encouraging nods and smiles, Jae clasped her shoulder gently. "You did good."

"We all did," Emory said, feeling a sense of belonging and pride flutter inside her.

All they could hope for now was that their message had been heard loud and wide—and that, like a small ripple forming in the sea, it would grow into a powerful, undeniable wave.

ROMIE

THE INSTITUTE WAS A FAR CRY FROM THE DANK DUN-geons Atheia remembered from her day, where criminals of all stripes had been left to rot in the cold and the dark. But the essence remained the same.

There was a peculiar energy to the place, especially when blood was drawn from an Eclipse-born. The lights flickered in and out, as if shying from the surge of unlimited power contained in that silvery substance. Liquid magic. The *wrong* kind of magic, until it was mixed with the blood of a lunar mage to create a synthetic version of whatever tidal alignment they were born with. A synthetic that could then be used by anyone to wield such magic.

It wasn't exactly the eradication of Eclipse magic that Atheia had first envisioned, but it was ultimately what was happening here. Draining Eclipse-born of every morsel of power contained in their blood to give back to those who were always meant to carry magic in this world.

Atheia had been coming to the Institute for the last couple of days now, watching how the synthetics were made, taking inventory of all the Eclipse-born who were contained here, encouraging Regulators to round up more and more Eclipse-born and force their Collapsing upon them in order to access their silver blood.

The Tidal Council was a near permanent presence at the Institute, overseeing all of this. Even the two boys, Louis and Javier, spent most of their time here instead of at the college, being groomed to take leadership roles within the Order once they graduated. Javier, she learned, was a legacy who bore the name of one of the Order's founding members, though none of his Belesa relatives who'd been Selenics before him were alive today to see him carry that legacy. Louis, on the other hand, had no familial ties to the Order whatsoever.

Atheia was intrigued by them. According to Romie, the other Order member who should have been with them was Ife Nuru, yet the girl had abandoned the other Selenics to side with the Eclipse-born, just like Virgil and Nisha had sided with Emory. It was odd, then, that these two boys had remained. Was it loyalty to the Order that kept them here, or something else?

When Atheia looked into their minds, no memory raised suspicions. And yet there was something there that caught her attention. She'd been showering them with attention ever since, interested to know everything there was about them and their time spent with Emory. With Keiran, too, this boy who had led the Order's quest to wake the Tides.

Atheia would have very much liked to meet him.

She stood with Louis, Javier, and the Tidal Council in the clinical room where Eclipse-born had their silver blood taken. Two Regulators brought in a woman who was fighting with everything she had, screaming at the top of her lungs in another language. They managed to strap her to the gurney, but the young woman did not stop fighting even then.

Atheia's heart nearly dropped at the sight of her. She looked so much like someone she had known. Jet-black hair, narrow dark eyes . . . and two distinct beauty marks on her cheek, one pale and smooth, the other dark and raised, overlapping the edge of the first one. Like a moon creeping over the sun to eclipse it.

The resemblance was almost uncanny, and yet the differences were there the more Atheia looked. This was not the same woman. Of course it wasn't, because the person Atheia was thinking of was long since dead.

"This one was a new professor at Karunang College," the Memorist from the Council, Vivianne, said as she sifted through the woman's memories. "She was at Aldryn for the Quadricentennial and was found helping other foreign Eclipse students escape the Regulators. That's when she was brought here and made to Collapse."

The woman spat at Vivianne's feet. "May you all go to the Deep for this."

Atheia stepped closer, eyes trailing the woman's collarbone, where fine lines and geometric symbols were tattooed on her skin. "What are those?"

The woman only glared at her.

"They're traditional to Luaguan culture," Vivianne said, sounding bored. "A way to ward off the evil of Collapsing. Baseless superstition, clearly."

A Regulator burst into the room then, his face pinched with concern. He carried an odd-looking device. *A radio*, Romie called it. "I—excuse the interruption," the Regulator panted, "but I think you'll want to hear this."

The crackle of the radio gave way to a voice both Atheia and Romie recognized. It was Emory, going on and on about the power of unity and Eclipse magic and healing the world together. The message came to its end and started over, as if on a loop.

Atheia saw the flicker of doubt on the faces around her, the

Regulators and the Council members. It was there and gone, but it was clear they were taking Emory's message seriously. Atheia couldn't let them start to doubt what they were doing, couldn't let Emory's words corrupt them from the path they walked.

The Eclipse-born strapped to the gurney laughed. "You're all going to pay for this. The Shadow reborn will not let what you're doing here stand."

"Silence," barked Leonie, the elderly Council member. To the Regulators, she said, "Someone get a syringe and take her blood already."

"Wait," Atheia said. "I have other plans for this one."

An idea was forming. She watched Louis and Javier closely. "How long have you had those shields up in your minds?"

They blinked at her. "Wh-what?" Louis stammered.

"It's a well-constructed ward, I'll give you that," she said to Javier. "It speaks to your talent as Wardcrafter that no one else noticed. Small enough to pass undetected from, say, a Memorist, and iron-clad enough that no Unraveler would even know how to look past it." Atheia tilted her head, smiling. "But of course, as a deity, I see through it plainly enough."

Javier narrowed his eyes at her. "I don't know what you're talking about."

She laughed. "The ruse is up, and the wards are down. If Vivianne were to look in your memories just now, she would see the truth: that you are here to act as spies, feeding information to your friend Ife in the Eclipse-born resistance through the Selenic Mark you bear."

Vivianne's mouth fell, her shock mirrored on the other Council members. Atheia could sense her rifling, now unencumbered, through the boys' memories.

"It's all true," Vivianne breathed.

Louis reached for Javier's hand, the two of them fitting together in grim solidarity, recognizing they had been made and there was nothing they could do to refute the word of a deity.

"Lock them up," the New Moon leader of the Council said to the Regulators, his face red with anger. "Get them out of our sight."

Atheia stopped the Regulators with a gentle hand. "That won't be necessary. I have a better use for these two."

Her eyes went to the Eclipse-born watching this exchange with a puzzled yet guarded look. It might have been Emory who'd sent that radio message out, but she spoke for all Eclipse-born, for Sidraeus, too. And Atheia had a message of her own to send.

You might want to look away for this, she told Romie as she lifted a surgical knife from a tray and got to work.

EMORY

WHAT JAE HAD SAID WERE *A FEW JARS* OF MOONBREW ended up being a whole cellar full of them.

"Can you believe it?" Virgil exclaimed, grabbing as many jars as his arms could hold. "Barely any wine in this place, but moonbrew they've got enough of to last us through the coming apocalypse."

Jars of the cloudy liquid were passed along to everyone in the safe house, and even the disagreeable scholar and his friends joined in this moment of levity. Even *Baz*, whom Emory had never seen drink before. It was a delight to see the pink tinge to his cheeks, the easy smile he wore, the way his voice grew louder as he talked and laughed with family and friends, so very carefree.

Only Sidraeus kept to himself, sticking to the shadows and watching the merriment with an unreadable expression. But Emory could tell there was something like longing there, a desire to be a part of such mundane behavior. What kept him from joining in, she didn't know.

The night went on and thoughts of Sidraeus vanished from

her mind just as he seemed to vanish from the party. Emory found herself listening to her father, Alya, and Vera exchange memories of her mother; found herself laughing until her sides hurt at the stories Jae and Theodore told as they reminisced on the early years of their printing press, as Professor Selandyn poked fun at them by telling her own stories of them as students back in the day.

Emory hadn't felt this light in ages. Being here felt oddly like home. Maybe it had to do with the fact that her father was here, a piece of the home she'd always known. And Baz, too; the home she'd come to find in all the mornings spent with him hunched over books in the Decrescens library, in all the tiny moments where familiarity had breathed in their silences. Or even the family she had found in Vera and Alya, a different kind of home she was still getting used to.

But it was more than that. Here she was surrounded by people who were ready to fight, and she'd never felt such a sense of belonging before. Of community.

When she'd first learned of her Tidecaller abilities, she'd balked at the idea of belonging to House Eclipse, had fought desperately to hold on to her identity as a Healer. She'd wanted to be accepted by the Selenic Order, to be seen as valuable by people she believed would protect her and the truth of her magic. But that mindset had shifted over time, until lying about her identity had seemed more daunting to her than anything else.

And now that she was finally back here, nothing had ever felt more right than being part of House Eclipse. Fighting for justice alongside them.

Emory found herself looking at her New Moon tattoo. In this moment, she wanted desperately to have an Eclipse one.

Maybe there was someone here who had experience with tattoos. If anything, Baz had talent with drawing—though, remembering how queasy he'd been the first time he'd stuck a needle in her arm to draw her blood and test it in the selenograph, he was maybe not the best person to ask.

She searched for Baz now but couldn't find him. As Virgil plopped down on a chair next to her, Vera, and Nisha, a sudden solemnity fell over the four of them. They hadn't been alone together since coming back from the sea of ash, and it struck Emory that no one here could understand what they'd gone through—the worlds they'd traveled, the people they'd met and lost along the way.

As if the same thought crossed his mind, Virgil lifted his glass of moonbrew. "To the keys."

"May their souls find the rest they deserve," Nisha whispered with tears in her eyes.

The four of them drank as one. Emory felt hollow. She could scarcely believe they were gone. Aspen, whom she'd grown so close to, whose own mother and sister—the latter likely still in a coma—didn't even know she was gone. Tol, whom she hadn't known for long but admired all the same. And Orfeyi, whom she'd been robbed of knowing at all.

She'd failed them. Hadn't been able to save them from sacrifice. And though Romie wasn't among them, she may as well be, if Emory didn't find a way to separate her from Atheia.

Nisha's gaze found hers. "Tell me we can save her," she said in such a broken voice it made Emory want to curl up and cry.

"I don't know," Emory said in earnest. "But I'm not giving up on her."

Nisha gave her a wobbly smile. "Me neither."

Later, when the celebration had mostly died down, Emory found Baz outside sitting in the tall grass, watching the nighttime waves. She plopped down next to him, realizing with a giggle how unsteady she was after all the moonbrew.

"Careful," Baz said with a laugh of his own. The moonlight reflected in his glasses, outlining him in silver.

"I can't believe we're back on this beach," Emory said.

"Feels like this is where it all started."

Baz leaned back on his elbows, long legs splayed out before him. He gazed at the sky with such longing, Emory couldn't help but do the same, reminded of the time they'd been in Romie's greenhouse watching shooting stars together. Romie's absence had been as stark then as it was now.

For a time, they were silent, with only the rhythmic crashing of waves between them.

"You know what I miss?" Emory said. "The Noviluna Hall coffee cart."

Baz made a sound of disgust in the back of his throat. "That coffee tasted like cardboard."

"I don't care. I loved it. And it was always funny seeing you pretend to drink it when I brought you a cup."

Baz grinned. "I miss the Decrescens library."

"Of course you'd miss the *library* of all things."

"What? I miss the quiet. The early mornings when there was no one but you and me." He glanced back at the safe house. "There are so many people here. I'd give anything for a good library to escape into."

Emory smiled. At least some things about him hadn't changed. "I miss the Eclipse commons," she said, keeping this little game going. "I didn't get to spend enough time there."

"I miss Dusk," Baz sighed. "I hope he's being taken care of."

"Yeah, poor thing."

"I thought you hated him."

"I don't *hate* him. It's not my fault I kicked him in my sleep *one time* and the damn cat never forgave me."

They laughed together, the moonbrew perhaps making this

funnier than it was. But it felt so normal that Emory forgot everything else as they kept reminiscing about their time at Aldryn. She suddenly had an image of them in Obscura Hall, sitting on the sofa after she'd ventured into the sleepscape for the first time. How close they'd been. The way she'd touched his hair, wondered at how different he looked without his glasses.

He looked no different to her now. He was Baz, steady and sure and real and *here*. He smelled of coffee and citrus and home. She was reminded of what he'd said to her that time in the Eclipse commons. How he'd shared with her that he wanted to become a professor at Aldryn to make it into a sanctuary for Eclipse-born. A place where they could feel safe.

You're good at this, Baz, she'd told him then, and still thought so now.

And as their eyes locked and the laughter faded from their lips, she was struck with the same thought she'd had back then, imagining what it might be like to kiss him. Without knowing what she was doing, she leaned in to find out.

"I'm with Kai," Baz blurted out, dodging her advance.

Emory pulled away sharply, the words slow to register in her moonbrew-addled mind. She covered her mouth in horror as the weight of what she'd tried to do hit her. "Tides, I'm such a fool. I should have known you two were—"

"I meant to tell you earlier." Baz's cheeks had turned pink. "Sorry."

"Why are you sorry? That's—I'm the one who's sorry." She should have seen it before. The signs were there, after all. Baz's desperation to find Kai, the look in his eyes when he spoke about him. Virgil joking about Kai being Baz's nightmare-weaving boyfriend. And hadn't part of Emory always suspected there was more to their friendship?

She covered her face with both hands, wanting to disappear.

"Can we please pretend I didn't do that and just blame it on the moonbrew?"

A breathy chuckle from Baz. "Sure." He sat up and drew his legs against his chest. He looked at her over his shoulder, searching her gaze. "Can I ask . . . was it ever real between us?"

"Of course it was." The words left her mouth before she could think.

There had been nothing accusatory about his question, no anger or pressure. But it laid bare a truth that not even her answer could deny.

This—her foolish attempt to kiss him—was her using him all over again, seeking comfort in a moment of turmoil, familiarity at a time where the world seemed to be ending.

Baz must know it. It was why he'd asked such a question, his way of calling her out on it, his gentle prying into her mind to see if she had ever truly wanted this, or if she had only ever used him with another end in sight.

But it *had* been real, there was no doubt in her mind about this fact. She could have seen herself with him. She imagined it now, how life would have been if she'd given him a chance instead of falling prey to Keiran's calculated charm. If she'd stuck by Baz when they were still at prep school instead of retreating from him the way everyone else had, letting their friendship turn to dust before it could flourish into something more.

If she hadn't been so consumed by this perfect image of what she'd thought she wanted her life to look like, she could have been happy with Baz. He would have made her a better person. That was the impact he had on people. He made them want to grow and improve and become people worthy of his love.

She regretted it, never giving him a proper chance. Manipulating him the way she had.

But there was no taking it back. She couldn't rewind time the way Baz might. And she wouldn't want to, especially not if it meant taking away what he had found with Kai.

Kai, who was infinitely better to Baz than Emory ever was. Who'd always seen his worth and never shied away from it.

Maybe this was her punishment. To be too late in seeing Baz the way she saw him now. To have lost him before realizing what they might have been.

Emory sat up and laid a hand on Baz's arm. "It *was* real," she repeated, swallowing past the lump in her throat. "But it's over now, isn't it?" She gave him a weak smile. "You and Kai were always meant for each other. I just hope I haven't ruined everything between us. I don't want to lose you again."

"You won't." Baz pulled her in against him. "What we have can never be ruined."

And here at last was the final truth between them, the final card laid out on the table. The could-haves and what-ifs, and the friendship that remained. That would always remain.

Even as her heart hurt for the version of them that might have existed in another life, Emory was grateful for this.

This time, she wouldn't be so careless with his friendship. She would hold on to it and never let go.

BAZ

BAZ WENT TO SLEEP THAT NIGHT FEELING ODDLY peaceful.

Another version of him might have tossed and turned agonizing over what had happened with Emory on the beach. Wondering if he'd done the right thing, said the right words.

For the tiniest of moments, it was as if he'd been transported back to *before*, when a kiss from her would have meant everything to him. Where he would have gladly lost himself in her, forgiven everything she'd done to him and ignored how different she was now–how different they both were–if only so that he could stay in this perfect bubble of contentment, in this moment he had once dreamed of making reality.

It was real, she'd said. *But it's over now, isn't it?*

That was the nature of dreams. They shifted as clouds did, taking on different shapes over time or disappearing entirely to make room for something else. Something better.

The old Baz might have dreamed of having Emory finally see

him and *want* him. But that dream had reshaped itself so that it was not Emory he saw in it, but Kai. The Nightmare Weaver who had always seen him, the most terrible parts of him, *all of him*, and had never abandoned him. The boy he chose to give his whole heart to, without ever questioning if he was enough for him.

Baz would always love Emory. But that love had softened to something else. It was companionship. Kinship. A bond he would always be grateful for and never take for granted. It was as if, when he'd watched Emory go through the door in Dovermere, the feelings he'd had for her had gone with her. And when she reemerged, they had changed just like she had.

A part of Baz did wonder how different things might have been if Emory had given him a chance back when they were younger. But dwelling on the past, on all the what-ifs, helped no one. Especially when his mind was fixed on saving the one who made up all of his new dreams.

So they'd shut the door on the what-ifs. Agreed that what they *did* have—this friendship that was more profound than any Baz had ever known—was enough for both of them.

A loud crashing sound pulled him from his slumber.

Baz reached immediately for his glasses. The room was suffused in the faint gray light of dawn. His mouth was dry from drinking all that moonbrew, and his mind struggled to wake, to process the scream he heard coming from somewhere in the safe house.

Footsteps and voices echoed in the hallway as people drowsily inquired about what was going on. Baz tore down the stairs with the rest of them, heart hammering, head throbbing, to find a panicked Emory kneeling over someone writhing in pain on the floor.

Sidraeus, his face distorted in anguish. The runes on his skin seemed to be *burning* him, flashing bright silver.

"What is it?" Emory asked him, eyes wide with shock. "Whose pain do you feel?"

"Someone"–Sidraeus bit back a sob–"close."

Emory looked desperately around to find the source of the Shadow's misery. Just then, Virgil and Vera burst through the safe house's front door, flushed and out of breath. Sand clung to their clothes as if they'd been lying on the beach, and Baz couldn't help but notice that Vera was wearing Virgil's sweater.

"There are people out there," Virgil wheezed. "Just outside the wards. I think they're badly hurt."

"Who?" Jae asked with a worried expression.

"No clue. They were screaming for help." Vera jerked her chin at Emory. "So we rushed back here to get it."

Emory hesitated, still kneeling over Sidraeus. "Go," he gritted out. They seemed to have some mental exchange before Emory pushed to her feet.

"Hold on." Jae blocked her way with an outstretched arm. "This could be a trap."

"If he's in this much pain," Emory said, pointing to Sidraeus, "then whoever's out there is Eclipse-born."

Jae swore, letting her through. Everyone rushed out of the safe house, Virgil and Vera leading the way with Emory close at their heel. The late winter skies were gray, the air thick with mist, the Aldersea a steely presence in the background. Three people were sprawled on the beach. Two of them seemed to be bent over the third, eerie dark shapes cutting through the mist.

Virgil stopped dead in his tracks when he was close enough to see their faces. "It's Javier and Louis!"

Jae tore away from their group, running toward the two boys who couldn't see or hear them through the wards, and parted the air like a curtain to lift the illusion. Javier and Louis turned toward them as everyone stepped past the wards. Both of them looked like they'd seen better days: Javier had a busted lip, and Louis's pale brown curls were matted with blood. There was also a gash on Louis's palm, and he was bleeding into a shallow pool of water. Bloodletting, Baz realized, to access his Healer magic. Because the third person was badly hurt, skin pale and emaciated.

For a moment Baz had a sense of déjà vu. Travers. Lia. Was this another body washed ashore? But no, not a body. There was life left in the young woman's dark, glassy eyes. Her long black hair was sticking wetly to her skin, thin lips parted as she writhed in pain. She wore the plain, colorless clothes of those held at the Institute, Baz realized, and on her collarbone were traditional Luaguan tattoos like Kai's. On her left hand was the Eclipse sigil, with the jagged *U* of the Unhallowed Seal marring its surface.

And her skin, mangled and slick with silver blood, looked *wrong* somehow . . .

"Help her!" Louis yelled as tears ran down his face.

Emory was already at his side, working her own healing magic over the woman. But the woman's limbs went still with a final spasm, her eyes fixed on the dawn skies above, and Baz knew it was too late.

"She's gone," Emory breathed, shoulders slumping. "I'm so sorry."

Louis covered his face, breaking down in tears. To Javier, Baz asked, "Who was she?"

"That's Professor Sao." The answer came from Rusli, who stood with an arm around his Luaguan friend Sana, the two of them grief-stricken. "From Karunang College."

One of the professors who had gone missing.

"*She* did this," Javier seethed. "Romie. The Tides."

Nisha's face went bloodless, her hand covering her mouth.

"What happened?" Ife asked in a horrified whisper.

"She knew we were spies," Louis said grimly, wiping the tears from his face. "She looked into our minds to find out where the safe house was and brought us here with her magic. She's already gone," he added quickly as everyone tensed, glancing nervously around them. "Said she only wanted to deliver a message. To the Shadow."

As if conjured by the name alone, Sidraeus appeared behind Emory, clearly no longer affected by the pain he'd felt now that the woman was dead. His face was tight with some unreadable expression as he looked at the body.

And that's when Baz realized why he'd thought the woman's skin looked wrong: spirals had been carved all over her, the lines raw and caked with dried blood. As if to make a mockery of the silver spirals on Sidraeus.

Sidraeus's ecliptic eyes swirled angrily at what Atheia had done—at what Romie had been forced to do with her own hands, the Tides acting through her.

A heavy silence settled over the beach. The wind howled around them, the waves crashing silently in the distance. And then Baz noticed the shadows gathering around Sidraeus. He seemed to be trembling with fury. He took a step away from the body and began to disappear, but Emory yelled a desperate "Don't!" before launching herself at Sidraeus.

And the two of them vanished.

EMORY

EMORY CLUNG TO SIDRAEUS'S ARM FOR DEAR LIFE AS stars rushed past them at dizzying speed. The moment she'd seen the rage on his face, she'd known he would go after Atheia, his desire for revenge rekindled with a passion. But he must not have expected her to grab on to him. She heard him swear as her grip loosened around him and she nearly let go. Then his hands were around her wrists, a viselike grip to keep her from being swallowed by the soaring emptiness around them.

Emory's ears popped as the darkness abated and bright light made her squint. There were cobblestones beneath her feet, a familiar street bordered with quaint stone cottages and shops. In the distance, she could just make out the outline of Aldryn College sitting atop its hill.

They were in Cadence.

Sidraeus shoved away from her. "Why did you do that?"

Emory gaped at him. "Why did *you* go off like that?"

The streets seemed completely empty–no doubt Cadence had

been evacuated, given the intensity of the tides and its proximity to the shoreline. Still, at the sudden shriek of gulls nearby, both Emory and Sidraeus tensed, expecting their raised voices to have sounded some alarm. Sidraeus invaded her space and all but dragged her into the dark alley behind them. He towered over her as he cornered her against the wall, shadows swirling around him.

"What Atheia did crossed a line," he said in a low voice that was more terrifying than the shouting. "And she needs to pay."

"You promised me you wouldn't go after her. That you wouldn't hurt Romie while she's her vessel."

"I made no such promise."

"Going after Atheia will only spark more hatred against us Eclipse-born, you said so yourself. We have a plan—"

Sidraeus huffed a bitter laugh. "If you can even call it that."

"Please. We need to do this right."

The sound of approaching footsteps had Sidraeus pressing in close, hands resting on the wall on either side of Emory's head to trap her there. A thick swath of shadows enveloped them both just as a Regulator appeared at the mouth of the alley. He stopped and glanced their way with a frown. But he couldn't see them—not as they blended with the shadows and were rendered further undetectable by the Wardcrafter magic Emory called on.

When the Regulator finally moved on, Emory kept her ward up even as the shadows around her and Sidraeus dissipated. Her mouth went dry as she realized just how close they stood, with her still pinned between him and the wall.

Her gaze dropped involuntarily to his mouth, farther down still to the spirals on his neck as his throat bobbed. The image of the Luaguan professor, those horrible scars like a mockery of Sidraeus's, flashed in her mind. The way Sidraeus had doubled over in pain before they'd found her . . .

"How badly did it hurt?" Emory asked in a small voice, all too conscious that this was her doing–that she had allowed this bond between him and other Eclipse-born to exist.

The same thought seemed to flash in his eyes. For a second, fear spiked inside her. His hands on either side of her, so close to her neck . . . she was putting her life in the hands of a deity who could easily kill her. But Sidraeus shoved off her, his back hitting the opposite wall. It still didn't leave much space between them in this cramped alley, but Emory found herself releasing a breath all the same, especially as Sidraeus slid down into a crouch.

"The pain, I can handle," he said gruffly as he rested his head back against the wall and closed his eyes. "I've *been* handling it these past few days."

That must be why he'd kept to himself, Emory thought. Suffering in silence at all the pain, however small, that Eclipse-born from all over were experiencing.

"Distance makes the pain bearable, like a constant scratching that's easily tuned out," Sidraeus continued. "But this . . . mutilating that poor woman to mirror my own scars . . . Atheia knew exactly what she was doing. Reminding me just how much my people have suffered because of me." He opened his eyes to look up at Emory, full of anguish. "I failed them back then, and these runes won't let me forget it."

The admission, as well as the position they found themselves in, made Emory remember how vulnerable he'd looked when he'd first appeared in his true form. She wanted to reach out to him like she had then, lay a hand on him to provide comfort.

She wanted to apologize for her part in his torture. For this bargain she'd made against his will.

"You can't carry this guilt forever," she found herself saying, thinking of what he'd told her not so long ago, about her own guilt over Keiran's death. *The longer you let it weigh on you, the harder it will be to set it down.*

Sidraeus huffed a cold laugh. "But I have to carry it, don't I? Their memory is carved on my skin. And what Atheia did . . . the person she chose to do it to, the similarities between her and—" He clamped his mouth shut, as if realizing he'd said too much.

"Who?"

Sidraeus looked away from her, his gaze settling deeper into the alley, as if he could see someone else there, a memory taking shape. "Her name was Tala," he said, a wistful note in his tone. "She was one of the first Tidecallers, a pioneer of the Veiled Atlas. Luaguan, just like that woman, with such similar beauty marks on her cheek. Tala was like what I imagine a sister to be, like family, faithful and kind and . . . and my actions led to her sacrifice all the same, just like it did the rest of the Tidecallers whose deaths are on me."

The full weight of the bargain she'd made hit Emory like a brick. To never be able to forget this . . . was she any better than Atheia, who had used this to draw up Sidraeus's suffering? A twist of the knife to inflict such pain on a person Atheia knew would remind Sidraeus of someone he had cared about. Someone whose death had probably tormented him all these centuries.

"So you see," Sidraeus said, "you're not the only one haunted by the ghosts of your past."

His gaze fell to her throat, as if he could picture Keiran's ghost wrapping his fingers around it. As if he remembered doing the same to her when he was in Keiran's body, and again in his umbra form. Was that regret in the depths of his eyes? There was a rawness to his features that made him look younger, sitting here in a dark alley. Not a god, but a boy tortured by the thousand things he might have done differently if he'd known where his choices would lead. Someone who, against all odds, wanted to right the wrongs of the past, even if that meant diving deeper into his darkness and resorting to murderous revenge.

Emory felt exposed, like she was staring into a mirror that reflected all the ugliest parts of herself, and yet she couldn't turn away from him. She slid down the wall opposite him so that they were eye level again. "The sacrifice you felt you had to make at the time," she said, "I see now that you chose what you thought was the lesser of two evils. And if I, a Tidecaller, can see that . . . then you need to forgive yourself already."

When Sidraeus spoke, his voice was softer than she'd ever heard it. "You speak of forgiveness, yet you still carry the weight of your own guilt."

Emory swallowed hard, tearing her gaze from him. It was too much, to be seen the way he saw her. Funny how it had been all she'd wanted once. But that had been a softer Emory, an Emory who wasn't a killer, who didn't have a closet full of demons and ghosts. This Emory, the girl she was now . . . There was such darkness inside her, she was scared anyone who saw it would turn away. Like Romie had at one point.

But Sidraeus didn't turn away.

"I told you, we're more alike than you think," he said in a low murmur. "And if I am worthy of your forgiveness, then you are worthy of mine."

His words eased something in her chest. It was as if she could finally breathe. She'd already decided that she had the power to forgive herself for what she'd done, but to hear it from someone who saw all of her, darkness and all, and accepted it all the same—not only accepted it, but offered to share it . . .

"Forgiven, then," Emory breathed.

"Forgiven," he agreed.

Whatever tentative truce they had come to before seemed to shift into something bigger now. An understanding. A sense that they could finally trust each other—that they were in this together.

Somewhere close was Atheia, either still at the Institute or back at Aldryn. For a second, Emory could imagine Sidraeus bringing them there with his traveling magic. Demanding retribution for what had been done to the Eclipse-born.

But they would do this the right way. And for the first time, she trusted that Sidraeus would agree.

Emory got back on her feet and extended a hand to him. "Come on then, Sid. Let's go plan our revenge."

He narrowed his eyes at the nickname Virgil had used for him. But his annoyance felt false, betrayed by the barest tug of his lips. He didn't correct her, either, as he grabbed her hand and dragged himself up.

They stood a hairsbreadth apart, the air between them charged with something new and terrifying and profound. He didn't let go of her hand, didn't put distance between them, only held her gaze as stars sped past them, until they were standing on the beach once more.

There were more people now gathered outside the wards, most of them too absorbed by an unfolding disagreement to notice Emory and Sidraeus had returned. Jae and the Ilsker scholar were at the center of a shouting match, the latter threatening to march on the Institute right this moment, to hell with the risk.

Sidraeus pulled away from Emory to crouch over Professor Sao's body like a somber vigil, whispering words too quiet for anyone to hear. Emory's heart lurched at the sight. Her hand was still warm from Sidraeus's grip, her New Moon sigil stark against her skin. A reminder of where she'd started and what she'd done since.

There was no erasing who they were, as she and Sidraeus had concluded. But maybe they could choose who they wanted to become going forward.

And Emory didn't want to be someone who kept acting out of a place of fear and desperation.

She stomped over to the Ilsker scholar, ignoring the looks thrown her way. "If you're serious about breaking into the Institute, then I might have an idea."

"Anything to avoid more of this." There was no hesitation in his voice, only pain as he pointed to Professor Sao. "She didn't deserve this. And we can't leave our own behind to suffer the same horrors."

"I agree." Emory met the eye of everyone gathered on the beach. "What the Tides did . . . this wasn't just a message to the Shadow, but to all of us. They want to scare us away from stepping into the light. Let's not let them."

"What do you suggest we do?"

The initial plan had been to show up at Aldryn, unannounced and en masse, to disrupt the Selenic Order event happening tomorrow night. They had already sent out the call for others to do the same, Jae reaching out via underground networks to anyone and everyone who might have heard their initial radio message and wanted to voice their support of Eclipse-born. The idea was to take Atheia and the Order by surprise—and to use this protest as a cover for Emory, Baz, and Sidraeus to slip undetected into the Reaper room, while others reclaimed Obscura Hall.

But maybe there was a better way to go about it, all while getting justice for Professor Sao and everyone else held at the Institute in the process.

"We send out another radio message," Emory said. Certainty soared through her as a plan formed in her mind. "We tell the world exactly where to find us, so that when the Regulators are looking away from the Institute, they won't see us coming."

ROMIE

ATHEIA STARED AT THE SILVER BLOOD SCRUBBED FROM her hands as it washed down the drain, hypnotized by the way it swirled and shimmered in the water. It was *almost* pretty. Just like the Eclipse woman had *almost* looked like Tala, the Tidecaller who had been like a sister to Sidraeus. To Atheia, too.

She hoped the sight of her had hurt him just as badly as each spiral carved into her skin had.

Atheia still heard the Eclipse woman's screams. Somewhere in the recesses of her mind, she could feel Romie's revulsion, hear the fading echo of her own screams of protest at the horror Atheia had wrought. But it had been a necessary evil. A message sent to Sidraeus. A lure for what came next.

And yet Tala's face haunted her, drawing something like guilt from deep within her.

Atheia scrubbed her hands harder, washing away any lingering trace of remorse even as memories flooded her mind. The early days of the Veiled Atlas, when she and Sidraeus and Tala had spent countless hours talking about ways to reach other worlds, then the godsworld. The time the three of them had spent traveling through realms. Tala had been a leading figure among the first Tidecallers, so full of potential and life and charm that Atheia herself had been swept away by her, just as Sidraeus had. She had loved her, just as she had loved all the lunar mages she shared her magic with, perhaps more so because of how warm and human and kind Tala had been.

She was a light that drew everyone to her. The one Tidecaller Atheia had been utterly swept away by, and the one Tidecaller whose betrayal hurt more than all the others combined.

Yet another thing Sidraeus had stolen from her.

She was done letting him destroy all the things she would have loved to call her own.

Whenever Atheia slept, Romie was alone in her own mind.

Though not entirely. She was no longer ever truly alone, be it in waking where she shared her own body with Atheia, their mind split down the middle and coexisting in one vessel, or in sleep, where Romie found herself surrounded by the other keys.

She knew they were dead, yet here they were in her dreams, Aspen and Tol and Orfeyi, as seemingly alive as they used to be. The threads that had briefly connected them in the fountain were still there, wrapped around Romie's pulse points. Wrist. Forearm. Neck. She could still feel that crackling energy coursing between them as if the threads were *alive*, even though her friends were dead, and this was only a dream.

Perhaps they were a part of her now, just as they were all part of Atheia.

Dreamer. Witch. Warrior. Guardian. Now we are but one.

But they did not seem to be of one mind.

Ever since the sea of ash, Romie had realized that, as Atheia, she was tapping into other magics the way she'd envied Emory doing for so long. This had always been what she'd wanted out of her time with the Selenic Order—to be more than a Dreamer of House Waning Moon. To know every facet of power that the moon and tides had to offer, not just the magic she'd been born with. Now she was the vessel of the Tides, and she had gotten her wish.

She should have reveled in it. Should have found some semblance of peace or contentment at knowing that all her dreams had come true. She had reached the song at the end of the world, had brought the Tides back to these shores, had all their magics now running through her veins.

And yet.

"Maybe we were wrong to trust Atheia," Aspen and Tol and Orfeyi would say to her in dreaming. "Her goal, her methods . . . Can't you see it's all wrong?"

Their comments began to fray at Romie's resolve, a voice of conscience in her head that grew louder every time she was with them. She knew firsthand how ruthless Atheia planned to be to eradicate Eclipse magic, had tasted her anger, her thirst for revenge.

But Atheia was convincing. *Seductive.* As soon as Romie woke, as soon as she found herself sharing consciousness with Atheia again, any unease she'd felt disappeared.

"Once we get rid of the Shadow, the stain of him will be washed from all Eclipse-borns' souls," Atheia promised her. "They'll be saved, redeemed. Washed clean of their sins, in a way. Is that not what you want?"

Romie did want that. She wanted to save Emory and her brother and her father. Even though a part of her realized this made her exactly like Keiran, following the path he had started down.

And after what Atheia had done to the Luaguan professor . . . what she'd pried out of Louis and Javier . . .

What she meant to do next...

The haunting image of silver blood, of spirals carved into skin, followed Romie in sleep. She had not looked away as Atheia had told her. She had borne witness to the horror of the scene—had felt the blood on her own two hands—and in the process had become more disjointed from her own body and this deity who shared it.

A necessity, Atheia had told her gently, sensing her trepidation.

A necessity, Romie told Aspen and Tol and Orfeyi's ghosts now, feeling the judgment of their gazes.

The words were becoming harder to believe, but she would keep saying them until they rang true once more, if only to absolve her part in Atheia's sins.

EMORY

TONIGHT WAS THE NIGHT THE ECLIPSE-BORN TOOK FATE into their own hands.

Emory glanced at herself in the mirror once more, nerves bunching up in her stomach. She was dressed in shades of argent: high-waisted, steel-colored dress pants, a silky silver blouse, and a light gray blazer rummaged from the few garments of hers that her father had brought with him here in the hopes that she would return from her journey through worlds. She looked like any other student might, except for the way Nisha had done her hair, braided up in an elaborate crown atop her head, interspersed with the four lunar flowers and a golden sunflower—and the porcelain mask covering the top half of her face.

According to Javier and Louis, who'd been privy to the final details of this grand soirée, those in attendance would be wearing porcelain masks depicting the Tides, just like they had the night Emory was first introduced to the Selenic Order in the lighthouse. And so, to flip this practice on its head, those who showed up in protest would storm Aldryn with masks of their own—masks that represented their solidarity with or belonging to House Eclipse. It was Nisha who'd had the idea.

Emory's mask was a thing of beauty, made to stand out from the rest and pin her as the Tidecaller. It was a far cry from the cherub-faced mask representing Bruma, Tide of the New Moon, that she'd worn that night at the lighthouse last year. The porcelain of this mask was cracked down the middle, the delicate seam filled in with shining silver. The right half was painted white and turquoise to mimic frothing waves, which faded to the deep black of the left side of the mask, full of swirling shadows and stars.

Half lunar, half eclipse. The Tides and the Shadow living in her veins.

As she came downstairs, Emory was filled with an emotion she couldn't quite name as dozens of Shadow masks stared back at her. They looked nothing like the actual Shadow who walked among them, but they were terrifyingly beautiful, primed to make an impact. Sculpted porcelain made to look like a skull crowned in the eclipse itself: a moon and sun carved over the face, the sun's rays spiked and lethal, but also slightly rounded to look like a sunflower. The whole mask was painted gold, silver, and black to resemble an eclipse.

Everyone was dressed in dark, somber tones in contrast to Emory's silver-inspired look. Paired with their terrifying masks, the effect was a bit ominous—which might seem counterproductive while wanting to prove a point that the Eclipse-born were nothing to fear, but they looked all the more resplendent for it.

Emory spotted Baz right away, his mask looking slightly less terrifying, what with his glasses worn awkwardly over it. He'd donned a charcoal dress shirt and a black cardigan, and was fiddling nervously with his crooked tie.

He spotted her and stilled, lips parting. "You look . . . ," he started, seemingly at a loss for words. "Wow."

Emory fussed with a flower in her hair, feeling self-conscious with so many people watching. "You too."

"The glasses are a nuisance," Baz muttered. "And this damn tie–"

"Here." Emory fixed it for him, fighting a smile. She met his eye, sudden worry curdling in her stomach. "Are you sure about this?"

"As sure as I can be."

"One word from you, and we can–"

"Emory." Baz trapped her wrists between his hands. "We're in this together now."

"I know."

She felt that kinship between them soaring to new heights, especially as Baz's eyes caught on her right hand and a sense of pride radiated from him. He held her hand between them, admiring the tattoo that graced the back of it.

It was new but not. Emory had talked to him about it, sharing how she wanted to mark herself as belonging to House Eclipse for good, but didn't want to fully erase the fact that she'd started out as a Healer of House New Moon. So instead of getting the Eclipse sigil tattooed on her left hand or erasing the New Moon sigil that was on her right, she had combined the two. Behind the black disc crowned in a wreath of silver narcissus, there now was a golden sunflower. It looked almost exactly like the Eclipse sigil; though where the black disc on Baz's hand was bare, hers was the silver narcissus-crowned new moon.

When she'd brought the idea to Baz, he'd sketched the blended sigils for her, and then she'd gotten someone with experience to tattoo the design on her. This turned out to be Jae, of all people, who smiled slyly at the shock on Baz's face, mysteriously hinting at the dozens of tattoos they'd given themself over the years, all conveniently hidden beneath their clothes.

"It suits you," Baz said to Emory now, giving her tattooed hand a squeeze before dropping it. "You're where you belong."

Her heart swelled to hear it. She'd fought back against her Eclipse identity so much at first. And now here she was, fully leaning in to the image of the Tidecaller, the picture of the Shadow reborn people believed her to be. The sense of belonging was overwhelming as she looked around at everyone here ready to put themselves on the line to fight for the Eclipse-born.

Only a few people would stay behind tonight: Louis, in case a Healer was needed once everyone returned; Alya; Baz's mother; and Emory's father. The rest of them had been divided into two groups. The first had already left, taken by Sidraeus to a spot near the Institute, where they would do a bit of reconnaissance. Their group consisted of Jae and Vera, who were both familiar with the place, as well as the Ilsker scholar, a few other Illusionists, the Poisoner, and the Festerer.

Everyone else, Eclipse-born and lunar mage alike, was going to Aldryn—even frail Professor Selandyn held her masked head high, a proud smile on her lips as if she'd been waiting for this day all her life.

"Remember you're only there to observe," Emory had reminded Vera before her cousin left with the first group. "Sidraeus will take us to you the second we're done with the ritual, and that's when we go in."

Vera had made a mock salute. "Don't go into the Institute without Shadow and Tidecaller backup. Got it."

"You sound like Virgil. Don't think I've forgotten about *that*, by the way."

"What?"

"You and Virgil. What exactly were you two doing outside yesterday before you spotted Louis and Javier beyond the wards?" Even with everything else going on that morning, Emory hadn't failed to notice the state of them, all swollen-lipped and covered in sand.

"Ah, well. I'm not one to kiss and tell." Vera's smile had told Emory enough. Her cousin had pulled her into a tight hug. "Tell Aunt Adriana hi for me."

Emory had squeezed her back, not wanting this to be goodbye. "You can tell her yourself once she's home."

She could only hope this would work.

The room went quiet as Sidraeus appeared out of thin air. Emory's breath caught in her throat. He really did look the part of the Shadow, wearing a suit of black that fit him like a glove, those spiral runes peeking out of the collar on his neck. His mask was cracked just like her own, the seams filled in with gold, contrasting beautifully with the black of the skeletal-shaped mask. A wicked crown of obsidian rested atop his dark auburn curls.

And as those ecliptic eyes found hers across a sea of people, as all the tension seemed to lift from his shoulders, Emory knew that the conversation they'd had yesterday in the alley . . . It had changed something between them. They *were* mirrors, in so many ways. And this time, Emory *wanted* to keep looking at her reflection. At the way she was reflected in his eyes, even as he peered into the dark truth of her.

And Tides. He was beautiful.

But she couldn't focus on that now.

Sidraeus came to stand beside her, sparing a solemn nod for Baz while his eyes still held Emory's, taking her breath away all over again. "Are we ready?"

She knew he meant it as a collective *we*, but when he spoke, it sounded like he did so only to her, as if they were the only two people here.

"Ready," Emory breathed, grabbing the hand he extended toward her.

The Tidecaller and the deity who favored her. They looked the part. Mirrored opposites, lunar and ecliptic, light and dark.

Now they just needed to convince people that there was nothing unhallowed or evil about them and their magic, and hope that Atheia and the Tidelore faith hadn't already corrupted everyone's minds against them.

Sidraeus transported everyone to the iron gates of Aldryn, where the silver-wrought motto glistened in the moonlight: *Post tenebras lux; iterum atque iterum.* After darkness, light; again and again.

A crowd was already gathered here, all of them wearing dark clothes and Shadow masks of their own, a veritable sea of supporters chanting in unison to be let in. Directly on the other side of the gates stood men in Regulator uniforms, their faces set in stoic annoyance.

The gates of Aldryn had never been closed or guarded this way. They'd been expecting this, but Emory still felt anger rising inside her. She pushed to the front of the crowd to *make* the Regulators open the gates if she had to.

She noticed then the dozens of students on the other side of the gate who were shouting things behind the line of Regulators. The idea of former classmates screaming obscenities at those who supported Eclipse-born made Emory want to strike them. Until she heard what they were shouting.

"Open the gates!"

Their anger wasn't directed at the protesters—it was directed at the Regulators.

Emory's gaze fell on a familiar face among the lunar students. It took her a beat to recognize Penelope West. Gone was the doe-eyed girl with the bubbly nature; in her place stood a girl molded of fierce tenacity, her dark hair cut in a severe slant just below the chin, her mouth running a mile a minute as she shouted at a burly Regulator two heads taller than her. She looked fearless, confident, and the makeshift Shadow mask in her hand—which all the students gathered behind the gate had, either in their hands or on their face—made Emory's heart swell.

"Nel?"

Penelope's head whipped toward her at the sound of her nickname. There was a moment of confusion as Penelope took her in, making Emory remember she had on her mask. She grabbed hold of the iron bars, the newly combined sigil on the back of her hand facing out. Penelope's eyes went wide with recognition as she took in the tattoo.

"Em?" Penelope tried to get past the Regulator, but he blocked the way.

"Step back from the gates, please," barked another Regulator at Emory.

Emory gave him a hard stare. *"Open the gates,"* she said, lacing Glamour magic in her words. She addressed all of the Regulators at once, extending her magic to them. *"Let us all through, and do not come after us."*

A glazed look passed over their eyes, and they all complied with her command, the gates screeching open to cheers and applause. Emory stepped through with everyone else. Hands pulled her to the side, and she found herself face to face with Penelope.

"Tides, it really is you," Penelope breathed.

Emory felt a thousand emotions choking her up. Last time she'd seen Penelope, Emory had been led to believe that her friend had ousted her as a Tidecaller to the dean of Aldryn—before Penelope had been doomed to have her memory wiped by the Selenic Order. Guilt spiked through Emory thinking how bad of a friend she'd been to Penelope.

"I'm sorry for everything, Nel," she said. Maybe this wasn't the time with everything going on around them, but she had to get the words out. "I'm sorry I wasn't there for you, and I'm—I just—thank you for being here."

Penelope squeezed her hand. "A bunch of us heard your message on the radio. You have our support, whatever you need."

Emory looked around to find Baz and the others in the crowd. "Do you know where this party is taking place?" Where were all the Selenic Order members and the Tidelore leaders and Regulators who'd been invited?

"No idea. They've been guarding the gates since this afternoon, so if anyone came in, it wasn't from here."

Could they have all come in through the Eclipse commons? Where was Atheia?

Baz caught her eye and motioned for her and Penelope to follow the rest of the protesters up to the quad. Emory's heart raced as she climbed those eight steps, one for each of the moon's phases. There were a few students out and about, walking across the frozen lawn or through the cloisters, probably on their way from their last classes or heading to the dinner hall. The apparent normalcy of their lives set a fire in Emory.

While Eclipse-born were forced into hiding, when one of their own had been killed while at the Institute, lunar students were going about their day without a care for anything that was happening to their Eclipse counterparts.

Part of her wondered if she would have been one of them had she never become a Tidecaller. Would she be ignoring the suffering of others if that suffering did not affect her? She hoped she wouldn't. She was glad she'd never have to find out.

Students had noticed their large, masked group by now, some giving them odd, quizzical looks, some stopping completely in their tracks to murmur among themselves, some scattering off, unease written all over their faces. But others immediately joined in, whipping out Shadow masks of their own and growing the number of protesters gathered in the middle of the quad.

At Baz's nod of encouragement, Emory stepped onto the ledge

of the Fountain of Fate, standing right next to the statue of Bruma. Murmurs spread through the quad like a rising tide, speculating about her identity.

"Is that Emory Ainsleif?" someone gasped.

Emory had a sudden sense of déjà vu.

That's the girl who came back from the caves.

The student who survived the Beast.

The one the tide did not claim.

Except these murmurs now were twisted into something else, half excitement from the protesters, and half viciousness from the students keeping their distance, who whispered *Tidethief* and *heretic* and *revenant* and *unhallowed*.

Loudly, a student spat, "Get the Regulators! She's the Shadow reborn!"

At this, Emory drew herself taller. "I'm not the Shadow reborn," she said, hoping her voice carried and did not tremble. "But I am the girl who brought the Shadow back from the Deep."

She extended a hand to Sidraeus, and when he took it, it was not only his flesh she felt against her skin, but the cold whisper of his umbra self. As he stood on the ledge of the fountain with her, his shadow detached itself from him like it was a being all its own, and it grew until it was higher than the fountain, until it towered over the entire quad, drawing gasps from the crowd. Before fear could mount, the giant crowned umbra was unmade before their eyes, dissolving into dark swaths full of twinkling stars that unfurled into the crowd like a blanket.

Some students still cowered in the cloisters, but others stepped forward in curiosity, gaping at the hundreds of stars hanging in the darkness that filled the spaces between protesters. Emory infused each star with magic that would make the beholder see fragments of truth in its glow: memories she had taken from Baz and Theodore and other Eclipse-born about the realities of

Collapsing and the bleak horrors experienced at the Institute; the truth of where synths came from, taken from the minds of Virgil, Nisha, Ife, Javier, and Louis; Emory's own perilous journey from unlocking her Tidecaller abilities to learning to control the darker side of such gifts; Professor Sao's gruesome, senseless death.

But for every hard truth, she made sure moments of beauty shone through as well, imbuing each star with memories full of joy and companionship and belonging that she'd shared with Baz and the other Eclipse-born. With memories of Sidraeus's, too.

He had opened his mind to her, letting his memories pass through her so that the truth of who he was became evident to those around them. They left out the details of the role he'd played in the Tidecallers' demise, sharing only the love he'd had for them, the pain of their loss that had sat with him through his centuries-long imprisonment in the sleepscape. The hope he'd always had of making the world better—not just for his own creations, but for everyone.

Emory hadn't let herself use this much power since the sea of ash, but with Sidraeus at her side drawing the darkness from her, she felt invincible. There was power in the kind of magic she was wielding. It was like the fall equinox festival when lunar mages of all houses used their abilities to put on a show, only it wasn't just awe she hoped to inspire here, but a spark of change. She saw it take hold in the faces of all those who looked at the stars, their heads lowered in shame and their eyes shining with horrified acceptance, as if they finally understood the kind of unjust world they lived in and the part they all played in it, consciously or not.

But as Emory and Sidraeus let go of their combined magic, as the darkness abated and all those stars faded, it became clear that some people were still unconvinced.

"Go back to the Deep," someone yelled, eliciting murmurs of assent.

"You're the reason our magic is fading!" another student intoned.

"The world is ending because of all you Eclipse-born. That's what the Tidelore faith says!"

"That's not true," Emory yelled over the rising voices. "Yes, magic is dwindling and the world is in shambles, but that's what we're trying to fix. The Tidelore cult wants you to believe magic can only be restored by destroying Eclipse-born. Yet we're the ones fighting to save *everyone* from the doom that—"

Something whirred past her ear and shattered against the statue of Bruma behind her. Had someone thrown a *rock* at her? No. It was an arrow, exactly like the ones the Regulators had shot at her and her friends when they'd emerged from Dovermere.

"Shit," Baz swore, his face drained of color. "We need to get out of here. *Now.*"

Dozens of armed Regulators had appeared in the cloisters, trying to get through the protesters. Damper cuffs shone at their belts, and power surged from them, clearly the result of some synth or other. They shouted at students to get back, some of them all too happy to comply.

Emory's blood boiled as magic was flung their way, the Regulators clearly trying to get to the Eclipse-born. But she erected a protective ward over their group, keeping the Regulators from reaching anyone in the quad.

"Come on." Baz tugged at Emory's sleeve. "We've said our piece, sowed the seeds. Now we need to move forward with the plan or this will all have been for nothing."

Emory stepped down from the fountain, Sidraeus following suit. Baz was right. They couldn't make people jump to their side, could only hope the magic they'd worked here tonight would lead some of them to see the truth. The ritual had to take precedence over everything else.

Sidraeus froze at her side, his ecliptic eyes flaring. "She's coming."

He didn't have to say her name. Emory knew Atheia would show up eventually, drawn by the promise of ending her enemies and unveiling herself as the Tides. She couldn't see Romie's face in the crowded quad, but she could sense her near, Atheia's power calling to her.

They had to leave now before Atheia stopped them from reaching the tree.

"What do you need from us?" Penelope asked, that fierceness of hers surprising Emory once more.

"A distraction," Emory said. "Some of us need to get to Decrescens Hall, others to Obscura Hall. Don't let the Regulators or *anyone else* follow us there."

Penelope nodded. "Got it."

As she and other protesters began to shout at the Regulators, a sea of Shadow-masked people pushing back against a wall of charcoal uniforms, Emory and her friends acted according to plan. There was no time for goodbyes as their group split up, the majority heading to Obscura Hall to reclaim it with help from the Wardcrafter, who would erect the wards around it once more so that only Eclipse-born and their allies would be able to go in. It would be their base in Aldryn College. Or at the very least, a way to keep out the Regulators. If Eclipse-born couldn't have Obscura Hall for themselves, then no one else should either. It was their home, their safe haven. It would be once more.

The rest of them—Emory, Sidraeus, Baz, Virgil, Nisha, Ife, and Javier—headed for Decrescens Hall to find the Reaper room and the strange, deathless tree that grew there.

If the ritual worked as it should, Emory would meet her mother for the first time—and perhaps change all of fate in the process.

KAI

H‌ELL, AS IT TURNED OUT, LOOKED EXACTLY LIKE THE Deep most lunar mages believed souls went to after death.

If Kai had thought the starry expanse they'd been sailing through was strange and cold and dark, it was nothing compared to the abyss. It was like the bottom of a depthless ocean, with deep crevices and jagged ridges and peaks; forests of algae in hues of dark purple and green and blue that rippled slightly on imaginary currents; flat plains that seemed to stretch on for eternity, littered with odd-looking bones and shells; and everywhere, a darkness so impenetrable, it would have been impossible to see anything if not for the lanterns that Farran lit up all around the ship.

For a second, Kai wondered if they *were* underwater. The small particles all around him looked like floating sediment or air bubbles. But it was *ash*, falling around them in slow motion, coating this strange world in a sheet of lifeless gray.

There was an unpleasant smell of sulfur in the air, foul and pungent.

Amid the forlorn landscape were statues of people, dull stone covered in lichen and barnacles and that foreboding ash. There were hundreds of them, so lifelike that Kai got the unsettling impression they were tracking the ship's movement as it glided by.

"Don't," Farran hissed at Luce as she reached out to touch the statue of a woman with what looked like dragon wings sprouting from her back.

Luce snatched her hand back, alarmed by the panic in Farran's voice. "What–*who* are they?"

"They're the souls of those who've been condemned to the abyss. They're trapped in stone down here, their minds forced to live through suffering worse than the darkest of nightmares, over and over again without reprieve. Unless they find a way to accept what they've done."

Luce raised a brow. "How do they do that?"

"Process their mortal failings, let go of all their baggage. Forgive themselves, basically, for a chance at moving on." Farran's eyes shone with a strange, wistful quality. "A chance at a new life."

"I'm guessing," Kai muttered, glaring at the sheer number of statues, "that most of them don't get that?"

"You'd be guessing correctly." Farran pointed out a statue swallowed so completely by the elements that it was rendered featureless, with clumps of strange, yellow crystals growing on its surface. "That's brimstone–sulfur. It feeds on despair and guilt, looking to crystalize souls and keep them down here forever. The souls who've been here the longest, those who've been completely swallowed by brimstone . . . there's no leaving for them. Not ever."

"That's horrible," Luce murmured with a pained expression. "All these souls . . ."

Trapped in stone, doomed to suffer torture for eternity in a hell of their own making.

Kai shivered at the thought. Was this what would await him, when all was said and done? A nightmare world for a nightmare boy. He'd seen so much of pain and fear already, had let it seep in through the cracks of his armor and fester inside him. He didn't want to end up here where they would remain embedded in his soul, fossilized anger and darkness that would weigh on him forever.

He studied Farran's face—the tightness around his mouth, the haunted bruises beneath his eyes, the taut lines of his body, as if every inch of him revolted against being down here. This was not the bright, buoyant boy Kai remembered, but someone well acquainted with the kind of pain and suffering hell encompassed.

"How do you know all this?" Kai asked, if only to confirm his suspicion.

Farran shied away from his knowing gaze. "Because Thames's soul—*my* soul—spent some time here after he died. Before the god of balance reincarnated me."

His hands gripped the railing, white-knuckled around this one flimsy safeguard keeping him separate from the tortured statues he'd once been part of. Seeing the ashen quality of his face, Kai *almost* felt sorry for him. But maybe Thames had deserved being sent here; he'd done horrible things alongside Clover, after all. Or was that another misremembered memory?

"I don't remember all of it, Thames's suffering," Farran continued. "It comes to me in bits and pieces, like fragments of a nightmare you're eager to forget upon waking. But being down here always draws it up to the surface."

"And when you're not down here?" Luce asked. "Where do you go?"

"I stay on the ship, sail as far as it'll let me. And when I need even more of an escape, I have this." He tugged on a chain around his neck, revealing a curious pocket watch. "Stole it from the god of balance's workshop. It lets me travel to any point in time, to live in the past for a while until the magic wears out and it deposits me right back here." A wan smile ghosted his lips. "I guess it's the price I paid for leaving the god's side. To be trapped here with no real way out except this temporary reprieve."

The ship skewed with sudden violence, sending Kai tumbling straight into Farran. The boy tried to hold him steady even as Kai shoved off him with a glare.

"Guys." Luce's voice was high-pitched, her face pale as she held on to the ship's rail. "What is that?"

Before them was what looked like a rip current or jet stream made of swirling ash and white-hot flames. And the ship was heading straight toward it.

Farran swore as he hurried to grab hold of the mast. "Brace yourselves," he called over his shoulder. "It's about to get ugly as we pass through the hellfire stream."

"The *what*?" Luce echoed.

"It's nothing. It's fine." Farran had always been a shit liar.

"Can't you steer the ship away?"

Farran shook his head. "This is the path we have to take. Just hold on, and whatever you see, whatever torture you experience, stay on the—"

His words were drowned out as the ship glided into the hellfire stream. Screaming filled Kai's ears as faces appeared in the gusts of brimstone and fire and ash that swirled around him, like translucent ghosts, wayward souls clawing at him to pull him overboard. Kai couldn't see or hear Luce and Farran in the chaos. The smell of sulfur was cloying, and every ghostly form that grazed his skin *burned.*

These spirits were desperate, angry, and as they engulfed him, they drew up Kai's own anger to the surface.

He felt every wicked shard of it tearing at his insides, this anger that had shaped his life and stayed with him like splinters stuck beneath the skin. Anger at his parents for always leaving him, forcing him to adapt to new environments and grow faster than perhaps a child should. Anger at the world for how he was treated simply for being Eclipse-born. Anger at the Institute who'd put his magic to sleep and the Selenic Order who'd lined their pockets with his blood. Clover for turning out to be such a pathetically evil piece of shit. Farran for breaking his trust and his heart all those years ago. The universe itself for ripping Baz away from him.

The spirits recognized that anger. They fed on it, eager to make Kai one of their own, to turn these individual splinters into one implacable weapon, an unstoppable force they might wield to hurt and maim everything around him and put an end to his own torment in the same breath.

The temptation to go with them was undeniable, this *need* to jump off the ship stronger than anything Kai had ever felt. He took a step forward, those ghostly arms pulling him toward the rails. The part of him that wanted to fight back kicking and screaming was trapped in his own mind, powerless to do so. His hands gripped the rail against his will. A foot lifted as if meaning to hook over the rail so he could jump off.

Into the Deep he would go, bound to remain with things worse than nightmares. Just where he belonged.

Arms wrapped around his middle and pulled him back. The spirits screeched louder in his ears, their translucent mouths elongated and their eye sockets hollow and dark as their fingers sunk into him, shedding his skin–

With a grunt, Kai fell back against the floorboards. Hands were still on him, and he shrugged them off, scurried back, only to realize it was Farran. Farran, who'd fallen to the floor with him when he pulled him back from the guardrail. The spirits were gone, their screams with them, and the ship was sailing unencumbered now through the abyss, the hellfire stream behind them.

Luce sat on the floor a few feet away, clutching the mast, tears running down her cheeks, looking as hollow and shaken as Kai felt. "Is it over?" she asked in a small voice. "Someone tell me it's over."

"It's over. We're safe." Farran got to his feet and offered Kai a hand.

Kai ignored him, damn well able to stand on his own. "What the hell were those things? I thought you said souls here were trapped in stone."

"The ones that were sent here, yes—the souls that have been judged and condemned to an existence in hell. But *those* souls . . ." Farran's face was tinged green as he glanced over his shoulder. "They are wayward souls that don't necessarily belong, who've been finding themselves trapped here for some time now, ever since the fountain of gods was depleted. They're trying to find a way out. To seek the eternal rest they were robbed of." Under his breath, he added, "I've never seen so many of them, though. Never felt them so . . ."

"Hungry?" Kai suggested.

Farran's gaze met his, full of understanding.

Luce was hugging herself tightly. "The things they made me feel, all the guilt they drew up about leaving my infant child . . ." She trailed off, her skin white as the ash that had resumed falling slowly, almost peacefully, around them.

Kai knew how she felt. The taste of anger was still in his mouth, like blood drawn from all the splinters embedded in his soul. If it hadn't been for Farran, he would have jumped off the ship, and what then? Those spirits were hungering for power, for a way out, and Kai never wanted to find out what happened if they got their way.

"You're welcome, by the way," Farran said as if reading Kai's mind. "I know it doesn't make up for everything I did to you, but maybe—"

"I'd say go to hell," Kai interrupted, "but seeing as we're already in it, how about you just shut up about the past?"

"Ignoring it never helps."

"Says the guy who's lived not one but two lousy, hateful lives." Kai snickered. "The nerve of you, to think you can swoop in and, what, earn my forgiveness? Atone for your sins?" He stepped into Farran's space, lip curling in disdain. "Here's the thing: I don't give a shit about you or your past. So call us even if that's what you need. I couldn't care less."

Farran looked like he wanted to snap back, and part of Kai wanted him to. He wanted this anger the ghosts had touched on to be drawn up further, wanted to drown in it only to feel something, to remind himself that he was alive despite being in the pits of death itself. His hands fisted at his sides; Farran's eyes tracked the motion. His face hardened–then slackened as his gaze caught on something behind Kai.

"We're here," Farran said. "Time to meet the gods."

Their ship docked at the base of a crude obsidian hill. Pillars dark as pitch rose out of the jagged black stone, appearing to gobble all the light from the ship's lanterns. Some kind of ancient temple ruins, from the looks of it. A hellish throne fit for the ruler of hell, if such a being existed.

The skin on the back of Kai's neck prickled as he followed Farran up the steps carved in the hillside. He felt watched. Thought he heard something whispering in his ear, a chilling breeze brushing against his cheek. Turning to glance at Luce, he was met with an unsettled expression that mimicked his own.

"You feel it too?" she whispered.

A sharp nod was all he gave in reply, not trusting his voice in the thick quiet. There was something expectant in the air, a thrum of jubilation that grated against Kai's nerves. Like their presence here was an anticipated thing, and any second now something or someone would pounce on them–to do what to them, that was the unnerving mystery of it all.

But when they reached the top, no one and nothing was waiting for them. They were alone in the middle of the obsidian temple, where five columns rose along a circular base, doming into a trellis overhead that seemed made of gnarled tree roots. Kai ran a tentative hand over a spindly root, feeling an odd power coming off it. The bark was not wood, he found, but obsidian. The roots ran all over the temple floor, winding around columns and pieces of jagged obsidian. When Kai tipped his head back, he could just barely make out the base of the tree trunk that rose, seemingly suspended in midair, over the trellis of gnarled roots. He couldn't see its branches or leaves, the impenetrable dark gobbling everything up past the base of the trunk. It gave the distinct impression of this being a tree cleaved in half, leaving only a stump and fossilized roots behind.

"This is meant to be a replica of the divine fountain in the godsworld," Farran explained in a low timbre. "This entire place, really, is a mirror to the godsworld, a nightmarish reflection. Or, well, nightmarish before the godsworld became the sea of ash that Clover made it into." He patted a thick root, some distant memory playing behind his eyes. "This tree connects abyss and godsworld. When someone dies, their soul either climbs up to the godsworld, emerging from the tree's flourishing branches, or it descends into the abyss through these roots."

"A harrowing experience to have lived through, I'm sure."

The voice made Kai spin around, heart caught in his throat. A woman stood at the top of the stairs, her bare feet soundless against the obsidian stone.

Farran bowed his head. "Goddess of the moon. You're a vision as always."

The goddess of the moon.

Kai couldn't help but stare at her. Part of him hadn't thought these gods real at all, but here she stood, in the flesh. And she truly was a vision, a tall, willowy beauty with pale, pink-tinged skin and long hair that went from black at the roots to silver at the tips. She was clad in a dress that seemed spun of moonlight. Her cunning expression was like quicksilver, ever shifting. There was a mercurial quality to her, something cruel yet sweet hiding beneath the surface, as if she were a wolf who might tear you up in one vicious snap of teeth or adopt you as one of her pups to fiercely protect.

Her long fingers tipped Farran's chin up. He seemed mesmerized by her, a supplicant at an altar.

"I see you've brought us our salvation," the goddess said, her quicksilver eyes shifting to Kai and Luce. "The boy of nightmares and the girl of dreams."

Kai thought of the *Song of the Drowned Gods* epilogue—of these same characters who had sailed to the rescue of the four heroes of the story. Only the four heroes, in this case, were four gods who'd been banished to hell by a fifth one with the power to annihilate the universe.

"Is this the part where you tell us what, exactly, you need us for?" Kai said more sharply than he'd intended, still feeling on edge, especially under the goddess's scrutiny. Did he imagine the narrowing of her eyes as they lowered to his chest, where his tattoos, he realized, peeked out of his shirt collar?

"It is proper to bow before gods," the goddess said, voice as cold as the deepest oceans.

Before Kai could utter a retort he might regret, he heard the sharp inhale of Luce's breath.

He saw them too: the other three gods who appeared at the top of the stairs.

The first was a woman with a soothing, motherly aura about her, all round and soft where the moon goddess was sharp and slender. Her lips were stretched in an inviting smile. She had deep brown skin and salt-and-pepper coils that grazed her shoulders. The fabric of her high-necked dress seemed to be made of delicate leaves a thousand shades of rust and green and gold, the same colors echoed in her irises. The goddess of the earth, no doubt.

Then, a man who could only be the god of the sun. He appeared to be strength incarnate, a living weapon, well over six feet tall–perhaps closer to seven–and wearing nothing but some type of leather war skirt, with a rich red cape draped over one shoulder, revealing a sculpted torso and powerful arms. He had long, supple black hair and a golden brown complexion like the light of a setting sun, and his dark eyes were as piercing and calculating as a hawk.

The third had an androgynous appearance. Their white hair fell in lustrous waves down to their slim waist. They wore a draping pearl-colored robe that revealed part of a leanly muscled torso, pale skin smattered with freckles, an arm adorned with delicate silver and gold bangles. They had the air of a trickster, their cornflower-blue eyes full of mischievous laughter.

"Bow before my siblings," the goddess of the moon commanded.

And Kai, despite everything inside him rebelling for some reason he couldn't understand, bowed. He heard one of them laugh, a crystalline, almost childlike sound, and when he lifted his head, it was to see the god of the air gleaming at him and Luce.

"How delightful it is," they said, "to be in the presence of mortals. Such life inside you."

The goddess of the earth breathed in deep. "It's delectable, after spending so long in this lifeless prison."

The four of them had magnitude, a presence that couldn't be denied. Kai felt Luce step closer to him, and he knew she felt it too–their otherworldliness, this ancient power they possessed. And yet, despite all of this, they seemed . . . human. Plain. Not exactly powerless, but perhaps not as powerful as Kai would have expected of gods.

As if reading his thoughts, the goddess of the moon said, "When the false god who calls himself Clover took all the power from the fountain in our godsworld, we were left without our godly might. Only a morsel of our divine power remains."

Kai frowned. "Clover can't have possibly made it to the godsworld yet. We were *just* with him, and he was only leaving the Wychwood."

"The abyss is timeless," said Farran. "It doesn't work in the same linear way as it does out there."

"For us," added the goddess of the earth, "it's been centuries since Clover showed up in the godsworld and all but forced us to hide down here."

"Since Equilibris sent us down here to rot, you mean," growled the god of the sun, flexing his impressive muscles as if aching for a fight.

The god of the air laid a placating hand on the sun god's bicep. "You know the alternative would have been Clover finishing us off. At least here, we're safe."

"I grow tired of *safe*. We were not meant for such a tedious existence." The sun god spat on the floor. "Especially when Equilibris remains free to roam *his* realm, while ours have been plundered by a thief."

"The thief will pay."

The goddess of the moon spoke the words low and cutting, like a blade arcing through water. It was a promise, and by the look in the other gods' eyes, they all were in agreement.

They meant to kill Clover.

Kai didn't miss the complicated emotions that crossed Farran's face. He didn't look shocked; probably knew, or at the very least suspected, that the gods would want revenge on the man who'd taken their power. But there was something in Farran's expression—bleak resignation, or maybe reluctance—that made Kai wonder how much space Thames's old feelings took up inside him, despite everything Clover had done to him.

"Thought it was Equilibris you wanted to stop," Kai said. "Isn't he the one who's threatening to reset the worlds?"

The goddess of the moon waved a nonchalant hand. "Nothing he hasn't threatened before. Besides, he won't need to resort to such measures if Clover is eliminated and our worlds are restored to their former glory."

"But we can't do that from the abyss," said the god of the air, their eyes scintillating. "Which is why we've been seeking a way out, biding our time here until we could step into the worlds of the living. And here you are at last."

Kai's skin prickled unpleasantly at the way the gods looked at him and Luce. He tried to catch Luce's eye to see if she felt the same. There was a crease between her brows as she seemed to consider what they'd been told.

"Why the worlds of the living?" she asked. "Clover would be in the godsworld. If you mean to stop him—"

"We cannot go back to the godsworld and risk Clover finishing us off," the goddess of the moon said sharply.

"He is too powerful for us now," explained the goddess of the earth, a sad smile tugging at her full lips. "But by setting foot in the realms we've created, we have a chance to shore up our power, gather our strength."

"And force the thief to give us back what is ours," the god of the sun gritted out, pounding a fist in his hand.

Luce looked entirely convinced. It shouldn't have come as a surprise to Kai—she'd do anything to save her daughter, and if it meant trusting these gods to stop Clover, so be it. But he couldn't shake the nagging sense that they were pawns on a board, and the gods the game masters willing to win at all costs.

"How exactly do we get out of here?" Luce asked, full of hope. "Can we sail the ship back to the path of stars and make our way through one of the doors?"

The gods laughed like it was the funniest thing anyone had ever said. "If it were that easy," the goddess of the earth said, "our emissary here would have carried us from the abyss a long time ago."

Farran shifted uncomfortably at the title. *Emissary.* He met Luce's questioning gaze and said, "The ship is bound to the abyss and the deepest depths of the sleepscape. It won't go beyond where I rescued you from, and that was already pushing the boundaries. There's no going back up to the path of stars."

Luce's face blanched. "But then, how do we leave?"

The goddess of the moon gave Farran a weighted look. "Did you deliver what we asked of you? To the boy?"

Farran nodded. "The ritual is in his hands."

"And you think he'll be able to decipher it?"

"I've known him to make sense of more complex rituals in the past. I have faith he can do so again."

Farran's eyes shifted to Kai as he spoke, as if he were nervous about his reaction.

"Then it shouldn't be long now," whispered the goddess of the moon, tipping her head up to the gnarled roots above them. The other gods did the same, their smiles expectant, hopeful, *ravenous*.

That unnerving feeling Kai couldn't shake only amplified. He glanced at Farran again, but the boy wouldn't meet his gaze. "Care to explain what the hell's going on?" Kai growled.

"Did he not tell you?" the god of the air quipped. "You mortals and your secrets. Always so delightful."

Kai grabbed Farran by the collar of his shirt. "What. Are. They. Talking. About?"

At last, Farran met his gaze. "We needed someone in the living realms to open a portal into hell. Someone who'd have a reason to take such a risk."

"*Who?*" Kai demanded.

The answer set all his nerves aflame.

"Baz."

BAZ

BAZ COULDN'T HELP BUT GO OVER THE RITUAL STEPS IN his mind as they hurried toward Decrescens Hall, thinking of all the ways it could go wrong.

But if it went *right*, he could be seeing Kai this very night.

The Reaper room was thankfully empty when Virgil led them inside. It was just as he'd described, like a vibrant greenhouse plucked from Crescens Hall and transplanted here in a corner of Decrescens Hall, completely out of place in this house meant to represent sleep and endings and death. The golden-leafed tree in the center seemed to engulf the room, its branches grazing the domed glass ceiling beyond which stars glimmered in a dark sky.

Baz couldn't breathe. He loosened his tie, a far cry from the satin neckcloth he'd worn two hundred years ago, yet the memory of Kai's fingers at his neck as he did it up for him came to mind nonetheless.

Please let this work, Baz thought, aching for the moment he might hold Kai in his arms again.

With Professor Selandyn's help deciphering the ritual—and Sidraeus lending a hand with nuances in the translation—they knew the ritual was a way to access the path between godsworld and abyss, heaven and hell. The tree was a portal, albeit nothing like the doors they had known so far. Once open, it would allow them to walk the path between godsworld and abyss—the same path that Sidraeus used to ferry stray souls to.

"Think of it as the inside of a tree trunk," Sidraeus had explained. "Those of you who've been to the godsworld have seen the crystal-leafed tree that flourishes there. It connects to the abyss, where its dark roots emerge. The path that ties both realms together lies in the space between, on the inside of this massive trunk, spiraling like tree rings. Once we open up the portal, we'll follow the path downward to the abyss . . . and hope we can easily climb back up once we've pulled your friends out."

Baz took a steadying breath. *One worry at a time.*

"Found it." Emory had been circling the trunk, searching for any indication of a portal opening. The same spiral mark that was found on all other doors was carved into the bark, so faded with age it was no wonder it had remained unnoticed all this time.

She looked up at Baz as he stepped to her side. "Ready?"

"Let's hope this works," he said shakily.

He was the one who had been given the ritual, the one so desperate to save Kai that he was willing to face the unknown bowels of hell itself. Here was his part in the story, the heroic stakes to claim as his own, and he was terrified. But he had to do this.

It was his turn to be a key—the fifth part that never quite fit with the others, that never belonged to Atheia like the blood and bones and heart and soul did. He was the lungs that answered to time alone. And as the Tidecaller, representing both life and death, above and below, Emory was the hand that would fit this fifth key into its lock, so to speak.

Baz pressed a hand against the trunk, right next to the carved spiral. He couldn't exactly give up a lung, but he could give his breath.

A breath in, a breath out.

He could feel each thread of the portal, this ancient power hiding beneath the surface. He pulled on every one of them, coercing the portal to reveal itself, to open how it might have once in the past or would again in the future.

Baz wrenched his hand away from the bark as it burned. There was a crack of thunder as the tree was split open by a thread of lightning that ran up from its roots and all along the trunk. The air felt *alive* with the sizzle of this fork of lightning, pulsing with the kind of magic Baz had only felt in Dovermere and in the god of balance's workshop, the kind of otherworldly power that was unknowable, dangerous if it were ever to fall into the wrong hands. The lightning itself felt alive, carving paths along the trunk, spirals and jagged lines and symbols Baz did not know, until the design created an arch–a doorway.

Emory pressed a hand to the sizzling keyhole in its middle, and it opened onto a familiar darkness. She turned to Baz, wide-eyed. "We did it."

Baz's face split into a smile as relief flooded through him. He hadn't *wanted* to doubt that the ritual would work, but that doubt had very much still been in the back of his mind.

The others peered into the darkness visible through the portal. "I wouldn't celebrate quite yet if I were you," said Virgil. "Not when you're the ones going in *there*."

At the trepidation in his voice, Baz forced himself to look at the darkness more closely. At first glance, he'd thought it looked exactly like the starry expanse beyond the Hourglass in Dovermere. But this darkness was complete and impenetrable.

"You're sure you want us to stay behind?" Nisha asked, glancing between Emory and Baz. "We can come with you—"

"Speak for yourself," muttered Virgil. Ife and Javier seemed as eager to go through the portal as he was, which was to say not at all.

"The four of you are needed here to guard the portal," Sidraeus said. "You're our tether back to the living worlds."

There was a heavy, tense silence as they all looked at one another. Emory met Baz's gaze, waiting for him to be ready. He moved closer to her, to Sidraeus, to the dark maw of the portal that opened between them.

"Be careful," Nisha said. "All of you."

Emory squeezed her hand in a silent goodbye, a promise they'd see each other soon. She made to step through the portal, but Sidraeus stopped her with a grave expression.

"Remember what I said." He spoke the words to her, but clearly meant them for Baz, too. "This is *nothing* like the sleepscape you have come to know. Traveling between worlds is one thing. Traveling the path between godsworld and abyss . . . there is no knowing what you might see or which direction it might push you."

Baz tamped down the fear rising inside him. Such was the purpose of this path: for souls to choose between what was essentially two very different afterlives. As ferrier of souls, Sidraeus's role had been to lead stray ones to this very path for them to move on to the next phase of death. Here, the souls of the dead who traveled the path were plagued by hallucinations, the worst parts of their psyche drawn up to torment them. These visions and how they dealt with them—what they chose to do with this mortal baggage they carried—were meant to lure them one way or the other. Either to the godsworld where they would be reincarnated through the fountain, or to the abyss where they would suffer damnation.

The souls judge themselves, Sidraeus had said. *The choice is theirs alone.*

To Sidraeus's knowledge, no living mortal had ever walked the path, so there was no knowing how these visions would affect Baz and Emory now.

Sidraeus stepped through the portal ahead of them, as if to ensure the way was clear, or perhaps to appease this realm of death by presenting a familiar face first.

Emory gave Baz a final glance, and for a moment Baz was brought back to the last time he'd seen her go through a door. Only that time, it was a door he could not follow her through. Now that they were doing this together, whatever awaited them on the other side suddenly felt less daunting. The same thought seemed to cross her mind, a fond little smile tugging at the corner of her lips. The steel blue of her eyes was steady and sure, an ocean that would not let anything stop it, not even death. They seemed to hold a promise. That everything would be all right.

She stepped into the dark, and Baz followed.

Sidraeus was right; this was not the same star-lined path they'd all come to know.

The dark that swallowed them seemed infinite, oppressive; the very path beneath their feet made of the blackest obsidian. The only reason Baz could tell there even *was* a path and he wasn't simply floating in a void-like space was due to the odd, silvery flames lining the way at wide intervals, hanging between columns of obsidian that bordered the path.

Directly in front of them was an altar, also made of obsidian, above which an ornate hourglass hovered a few inches in the air, laid on its side. Inside, a stardust-like material swirled in a perfect infinity loop, continuous and unbroken.

When a life ends, one's soul is repurposed. Returned to the fabric of the universe. Think of an hourglass being flipped over, sand filling a previously empty bulb. An end becoming a beginning.

The god of balance's words pounded in Baz's ears as he took in the hourglass. Its iron frame was wrought with the finest of detail, the glass bulbs pristine and polished. It seemed to pulse with a great, unfathomable power. And Baz had seen it before, sketched on a canvas by the god's own hand.

Fate's central core, the god had called it.

Here was the heart of fate, hanging between heaven and hell. The very instrument responsible for producing the threads that the loom wove into fate's tapestry.

Indeed, Baz could see these threads shimmering ever so faintly out of the hourglass. There seemed to be thousands of them, *billions* of them, expanding out of the hourglass, crisscrossing like an elaborate web just like the god of balance had drawn.

Baz knew, with sudden clarity, that this was why he was here. Fate's central core . . . it called to him, pulled on his soul. As if it had been waiting for him, the Timespinner, to step into his true role.

Mouth suddenly dry, Baz turned to Emory and Sidraeus–and found he was alone.

Panic seized him. He couldn't tell up from down anymore, as if the path had turned sideways, a tree tipped on its side so that there was no distinguishing abyss from godsworld. He did not know which direction to move, or if he should stay here with the hourglass marking the way out, waiting for the others to reappear.

That's when he saw her.

"Romie?"

His sister looked almost as shocked and elated as he felt. Her face split into a smile he had sorely missed, the kind of wide grin that brought him back to better days, to summers spent beneath the willow tree as kids, careless and free.

"Baz!" She threw her arms around his neck. "You're here."

He fought back tears, a laugh, a sob. She felt so real, so solid.

They pulled apart, and Baz couldn't even recall the last time he'd seen her. It felt like it was yesterday; it felt like a lifetime ago. She looked the same, other than her hair being a bit longer. Her brown eyes shone with starlight, with mischief and dreaming.

"This can't be real," Baz murmured. He looked around, suddenly reminded who he'd come here with. "Emory . . ."

"Don't worry about her," Romie said pleasantly. "She got what was coming."

Baz frowned. "What do you mean?"

He saw it then—the body sprawled on the path, blond hair unmade from her braided crown, lunar flower petals tangled in the golden strands. Emory's eyes were glassy, fixed unseeing on a point above. Blood pooled out of her, and it was *silver*, before it became black and oozing.

Baz ran to her side. "No, this can't be . . ." He turned to Romie with horror. "What happened?"

"She's Eclipse-born, Baz. A Tidethief at that. Her blood must be returned where it belongs. Just like all the others."

As if conjured by her words, countless bodies appeared around them, their spilt silver blood pooling onto the path. Faces Baz recognized: Jae, Selandyn, Rusli, and all the others he'd come to know at the safe house. His own father.

Kai.

"No . . ."

"I'm sorry I had to do it," said Romie. She held a dagger that dripped silver blood. Her mouth was downturned. "I'm even sorrier that I have to do it to you next. But it's the only way you'll be free of the Shadow's taint."

Baz shook his head, stumbling away from her, until he tripped and went sprawling. This couldn't be happening. "You're not my sister," he breathed, crawling backward. "You're Atheia. Romie would never do this."

Romie's eyes shifted colors like a prism as she knelt and leaned over him, holding the dagger to his throat. "Wouldn't she?" The curve of her mouth was imbued with a cruelness that was never Romie's. "She has always resented Eclipse magic, a secret in her heart that took root and festered until resentment became fear became *survival*. She understands this world cannot survive with the taint of Eclipse magic present, and she, like any survivor, is willing to do what must be done to save it."

The edge of the dagger dug into Baz's neck.

"Romie," he breathed, "please . . ."

Her eyes went brown again. That cruelness gone, leaving behind a pained expression. Tears ran down her cheeks. "I'm sorry, Baz. But she's right—I have to do this to save the world."

She slashed the dagger across Baz's neck.

Silver blood gushed out of him. Pain and agony unlike any he'd known tore through him. Romie held him as he died, whispering tearful sorrys even as she still held the dagger to his throat. As he looked at her, Baz couldn't find it in himself to hate her or even blame her. This wasn't his sister. This wasn't real. And even if it *were*, he did not believe for a second that her mind had not been poisoned by Atheia.

With his last breath, he said, "It's all right. I forgive you."

Romie stopped crying. She looked at him for a moment that seemed suspended in time before her features contorted, her face elongating into something born of nightmares. She seemed *furious* with his forgiveness, enraged at being denied something. She screamed a horrible sound and lunged at Baz as if she were a monster about to devour him—

Baz held his hands up to his face, but the pain he expected never came. He opened his eyes to find he was alone on the obsidian path. No bodies. No possessed sister. His hand flew to his throat where there was no wound, no blood.

It had all been in his head.

A soft sound made him turn around. He was no longer alone: Sidraeus was a bit farther down the path from where Baz stood next to the hourglass. And Emory . . .

Baz's heart faltered as he spotted her farther still down the path, in the direction he knew in his gut to be the abyss, even though the path still appeared like a linear, vertical thing rather than the spiraling staircase it had first appeared as. A way to confuse souls, Baz assumed, so that they would unconsciously choose whether they went to the godsworld or the abyss, drawn blindly in whatever direction called to them.

Did that mean, on some level, that Emory thought she belonged in the abyss? She moved slowly as if sleepwalking, her back to them so they couldn't see her face. And though the abyss *was* where they were headed, an inexplicable fear gripped Baz.

"Emory—"

But Sidraeus was already at her side, pulling her gently back. She blinked up at him, coming out of her trance. Baz didn't hear the words Sidraeus whispered to her, only saw the slight nod Emory gave him, her face so, so pale, as if she'd actually been drained of blood like Baz had seen in his own hallucination.

The path that led toward the abyss felt so oppressive. Baz had the unshakable thought that if Emory had reached the abyss while still in thrall to whatever strange forces were at work here, she would have never returned. By the looks of it, Emory could feel it too. She kept glancing toward the abyss, as if sensing a presence there, something that might be calling to her. Baz, who still stood next to the hourglass, wanted desperately to drag her back up the path, far away from the allure of hell. Sidraeus seemed to have the same thought as he reached for Emory's wrist, eyeing her warily.

"I'm fine," she said to his wordless inquiry, shaking him off. "Really, I am." She looked at Baz, calling out, "Are you?"

He nodded, swallowing thickly.

"We should keep moving," Sidraeus said. "Before another vision takes hold of you two, and your will is no longer your own."

Emory seemed to steel herself, her hands balling into fists at her side. "Let's go to hell, then."

But as she and Sidraeus started down the path, Baz found himself glancing at the hourglass again.

Above, below, side to side, something whispered in his ear, the language of the ritual dancing behind his eyes. *A mirror, an hourglass, a scale onto which balance must be kept. A breath in, a breath out. Divine symmetry.*

"Baz?" Emory was looking back at him expectantly. "Are you coming?"

The obvious answer would have been yes. This was why they'd come: to retrieve Kai and Luce from the abyss. Baz wanted nothing more than to save the boy he loved, to pull him out of the dark. And yet, instinct kept him rooted in place beside the hourglass.

"I think—I think I need to stay here," Baz said, voice tinged with disbelief at his own words. "I can't shake the feeling that my part in this lies here. That this is where I need to be."

Emory's shock mirrored how Baz felt. How could he stay here when Kai needed him? But this felt bigger than Kai, bigger than Baz, bigger than all the forces that had conspired to keep them apart and brought them so close again. Hadn't the god of balance told him that he'd know what his role entailed when he came to it? Well, this was it. He had never been so sure of anything.

And if there was anyone he trusted to save Kai in his place, it was Emory—and the Shadow at her side.

"Come on," Sidraeus urged her. "We need to keep moving."

"But Baz—"

"I think he's right. And it wouldn't hurt to have someone stay behind in case we need him." Sidraeus eyed the hourglass, then

Baz, as if trying to puzzle something out that he couldn't quite grasp. Neither he nor Emory appeared to see the threads connected to the hourglass, only Baz, which only solidified his certainty that whatever his role was, it lay here.

Emory at last seemed to understand, or at least accept that he wouldn't change his mind. "Be careful," she told Baz, and with one more worried look back at him, she and Sidraeus disappeared down the path.

Leaving Baz alone at the heart of fate.

EMORY

"DO YOU WANT TO TALK ABOUT IT?" SIDRAEUS ASKED. "What you saw while in the path's thrall."

Emory kept walking down the spiraling path, avoiding his insistent gaze. "Not particularly."

The first face she'd seen when stepping onto the path was her own. Or rather, a face that looked eerily similar to hers, despite being older. She had known right away who it was: her mother in the flesh. Adriana Kazan. Luce Meraude. Mother, sailor, standing before her daughter at last.

"My sweet girl," she had said, breaking into a smile. Her blue eyes were full of unshed tears as she opened her arms wide. "How you've grown."

Emory hadn't been able to stop herself from running into her embrace. But the comfort she should have found there soured in her heart, making Emory step away from her.

"Why did you leave me?" Emory breathed.

Her mother's smile fell. "I was trying to protect you."

"All you did was *break* me." Emotions she didn't know she'd had burst out of her like a swollen river bursting past a dam. "You abandoned me, lied about my birth, when all this time you *knew* what I'd become, what I'd have to endure. How could you?"

The pain on her mother's face turned sharp and vicious. Her next words left her mouth in a snarl. "What about all the people *you* abandoned? Like mother, like daughter, they say. And you, daughter of mine, have been so quick to hurt the people around you if only so they don't hurt you first. You have no right to reproach me for doing the same. Yes, I knew what you'd become. A leech of light. A girl of shadows. A harbinger of death. In the end, maybe you did your friends a favor by abandoning them. They will be better off without you."

That was when Emory was assaulted by visions of all the people she'd hurt and abandoned and let down at one point or another. It seemed like everyone in her life surrounded her, adding to her mother's voice.

"All these people who fight for you, protect you," her mother kept going, "and still you blame them for your troubles. Still you want more, and more, and more. It's never enough, is it? You'll become like him–Clover, whose blood runs in your veins, whose power you share. You *are* him. And everyone you've ever loved will die for your desires."

Emory saw herself using power, pulling power from others. Saw herself taking hold of Sidraeus's hand as they rose on dark thrones overlooking a sea of ash, all the power of the gods coursing through them, Clover dead at their feet, Romie too, everyone else bowing before them. She saw herself killing Clover; saw Clover killing her; saw Sidraeus running a blade through her heart, and she repaying the favor. Saw Romie and Baz flying off as birds in a sky that she could not follow. Saw herself clipping their wings and taking their power of flight for herself, leaving them behind so that she would not be the one abandoned.

She saw herself alone.

Alone, alone, alone, because her mother was right: this desperate need for acceptance, this desire to be valued, had only ever pushed people away. One day she would truly be alone, and there would be no one to blame but herself.

Maybe she preferred to torture herself with this guilt and fear of abandonment that was still dragging her down rather than shed it for good and show up for the people in her life, no matter how hard it might be.

Maybe hell was what she deserved.

Her mother had smiled at her like she knew what she was thinking. She reached a hand to Emory in quiet invitation. Perhaps hell would not be so bad if her mother was there too.

A step—and before Emory's fingers could graze her mother's, someone gripped her arm tight, breathing her name. Reality came crashing in like an ice bucket dropped over her head. Her mother was not there. And when Emory turned, it was to see Sidraeus looking at her with consternation, his fingers digging into her arm. Baz was several feet behind him, and she realized she'd been walking toward the abyss without even knowing.

"Whatever it is you saw," Sidraeus had said, "it isn't real. Understand?"

She'd nodded. But oh, it had felt real, the pull of hell calling her forth.

And now here she was, her mind her own again, yet still willingly heading toward it.

Emory and Sidraeus kept walking down the path in silence, and she was glad he didn't push her to admit what she'd seen. Still, she had so many questions about this place, about where they were headed. Curiosity finally got the better of her.

"The souls who choose to go down to the abyss," she said slowly. "Do they ever get to . . . move on?"

Or was eternal damnation what her own soul had nearly chosen?

Sidraeus seemed to consider his answer. "Most souls remain there forever, too caught up in their own personal hell to earn a chance at new life. They are trapped in stone, weighed down by torment of their own making. But if they break free of it, shed their past . . . It is said a freed soul transforms into a bird, taking flight from the bowels of the abyss to climb back up this path through the roots of the tree. And make their way up to the godsworld fountain to be reincarnated."

The image should have been beautiful—calling to mind the gulls Emory, Baz, and Romie had chased on the beach of their youth. But all Emory saw was the gulls from the vision the path had subjected her to. The taste of being left behind, and leaving others behind.

She wanted out of this place.

"We're almost there," Sidraeus said quietly, as if sensing her unease.

Emory latched onto the calmness of his voice. For someone who'd yearned so long to escape the sleeping realm, the death and dark he was born to, it must be a strange homecoming to find himself here again. And yet, looking at him, the sureness of his steps, the way he seemed to *belong* to the dark, she couldn't help but wonder if part of him had missed his realm. Or at least, the freedom he'd had to roam within its vast borders before he was imprisoned by the god of balance.

"Have you ever been this far down the path?" She wanted desperately to understand him, if only to escape her own mind.

"Never had a reason to. The stray souls I ferried here chose their own way. I might have walked alongside a few of them for a time, when they needed it, but never far."

There are no souls on the path now, he added in her mind. *Yet I feel them waiting in the abyss, restless and angry. It's as if, with the fountain in the godsworld all dried up, they had nowhere to go but hell, forced down there even if they might not belong. I fear what they might do once we get there.*

An unpleasant shiver ran up Emory's spine at the thought of encountering an angry mob of ghosts. She had experience with ghosts, had been plagued by them for so long, she shouldn't fear them so much anymore. But Sidraeus's concern worried her. The deity she'd come to know was nothing if not sure of himself. Until now.

The path seemed narrower here; their arms brushed as they walked side by side. Emory let the warmth of him anchor her. Soothe her. It cleared her worries enough that a thin, tentative courage clawed its way to the surface. In her mind, she said, *Whatever awaits us, we can face it together.*

She felt Sidraeus's eyes on her and tilted her head up to meet his gaze. She wanted him to know she trusted him at her side. There was no one else she'd rather have with her to face the hell they were walking into.

His lips parted, eyes trailing down to her mouth, and she realized how close they stood; realized they'd stopped walking, too. She was about to step away when Sidraeus's head snapped to attention.

Emory barely had time to register what was happening. Suddenly she was pinned against one of the obsidian columns bordering the path, with Sidraeus's body pressed against hers. He was enveloping her like a shield, she realized, as a howling, raging wind blew past them, like a tempest of power. The sound of it assaulted her ears. She thought she heard distant screaming voices, all of it an unhinged melody.

Peeking under Sidraeus's arm, she glimpsed a face in the strange rush of power. Someone was moving past them, heading up the path. Their features seemed distorted within the gust of power, shifting between multiple faces, giving the impression it was not one person but many.

One of them, she thought she recognized. The ghost of a boy she couldn't place but was certain she'd seen before. He seemed to feel her eyes on him and began to turn his head toward her. Sidraeus pressed closer against her, blocking her view entirely. She could only hear the wind that kept rushing past, raging, unending.

Until at last it stopped.

Sidraeus didn't move for a time. And when he did pull back, it was slow and tentative, keeping her trapped within the frame of his arms. His face was so close to her own, she could feel his breath on her skin, panting in sync with her own labored breathing, laced with the same fear she felt. As if reluctantly, Sidraeus pulled farther away to glance over his shoulder, making sure the path was clear before letting her go.

Whatever that had been was gone.

"Were those—was that a soul?" Emory asked breathily.

"No." Sidraeus's voice cracked. "Those were gods."

Before the words could register, screams echoed from farther down the path. Sidraeus grabbed her hand and tugged her toward it with renewed urgency. The path became so narrow she had to trail behind him, though his hand never left hers.

The ground suddenly disappeared beneath their feet, and they were falling through a tangle of obsidian roots, Sidraeus pulling her against him, and she holding on to him for dear life, bracing for impact.

It never came. They landed softly on their feet thanks to the thick swath of shadows Sidraeus had conjured around them. For a second Emory could see only darkness, Sidraeus holding her steady like an anchor. Then the shadows dissipated, and details came into focus. They stood in the middle of what looked like the fountain in the sea of ash, but a dark twin of it.

They'd made it to hell.

And standing in front of them, half turned to stone, were Kai and Luce.

KAI

BAZ. OPENING A PORTAL INTO HELL.

It was all Kai could think, all he could hear as Farran struggled against his grip. Farran had kept this from him. The slimy bastard had somehow reached through the recesses of time to find Baz and manipulate him into getting these gods out of the hell they were desperate to escape.

The pieces of the puzzle all fell into place in Kai's mind. "You knew Luce and I would be falling off the path, didn't you? You meant to bring us to the abyss so that Baz would have a reason to open this damn portal."

"Kai," Farran sputtered as Kai's hands squeezed his windpipe. "Please–"

"I swear, if anything happens to Baz, I'll make you regret ever being reincarnated."

"Nothing's going to happen to him." Farran's face was red as he fought for breath. "He doesn't–he won't have to–"

"Let him go, Kai."

Luce was tugging at his arm, but Kai didn't care, rage overtaking him, darkness pulling him under, as if exacerbated by this dark place they were in. As if hell wanted him angry, wanted him feral, all so it could feed on those negative emotions and keep him down here forever.

"Enough."

Kai was ripped away from Farran by the sun god's mighty grip. It only enraged Kai even more. *"Don't touch me,"* he snarled.

The god let him go as if burned, a yelp slipping from his lips. He stared at his hands with confusion that quickly turned to anger. "What did you do to me, boy?"

"Kai."

Luce was looking at him with wide eyes. Staring, like everyone else, at Kai's collarbones—where his Luaguan tattoos shone faint silver.

Before Kai could make sense of things, the floor beneath his feet rattled, the roots above his head shaking as if under the impact of some great, terrible force. A thunderous sound filled his ears, like a boulder being pushed down a cliff. Or a heavy door being opened.

The goddess of the moon smiled, her head tilted back to stare at the roots above. "The way lies open, my siblings."

Baz had opened the doorway to the living realms.

"See?" Farran spat at Kai, rubbing at his sore neck. "I knew he could do it. I would never have made myself or you or him suffer through the ripples of time and hell otherwise. Now we can *all* leave here and save the worlds we call home."

The god of the air laughed, mischief dancing in their eyes. "Such a hopeful way to look at things. If only it were that easy."

Confusion knit Farran's brows. "What do you mean? I thought—"

"You played your part well, Reaper," the goddess of the earth praised him. "You told us about the tree we knew would open a portal. Delivered our ritual to the Timespinner at the proper moment in time, thanks to that pocket watch of yours. And brought the Dreamer and Nightmare Weaver to us so that both the Tidecaller and Timespinner would have the proper motivation to save us. Now we can leave, you're right about that. But not all of us. The abyss, as you know, does not relinquish mortal souls freely."

"Lucky for you," the god of the air said with a mischievous smile, "we only need one of you to act as our vessel and emissary in the living realms. One whose soul has already been touched by the divine."

A strangled, bitter laugh tumbled out of Kai's mouth. The gods had never meant for him or Luce to leave this place. Only Farran, who seemed to come to the same horrible conclusion, eyes going wide as they met Kai's. They had all been manipulated, all been used. And it was too late now to stop the gods from doing what they'd always intended.

It happened at dizzying speed: the four gods dissolving before their eyes, turning into specks of colorful dust that swirled around Farran in a maelstrom of power. Farran screamed, his eyes shifting to quicksilver to rust to fiery coals to lightning blue. Roots reached down to him, curling around his torso and pulling him up into the depths of the tree.

And just like that, the four gods of the living realms vanished with their emissary.

Desperate not to be left behind in the abyss, Kai made to follow them but found that he could not move, his feet rooted to the floor beneath him.

"What's happening?" Luce cried out.

She was also frozen in place, kept there by obsidian roots that crawled up her ankles, same as Kai. Unimaginable pain shot through the base of his feet and spread to his ankles. He heard himself scream, the sound mixing with Luce's own helpless cries.

They were turning to stone, like all the souls of the dead sentenced to the abyss. As if hell was claiming their souls, too, even if they weren't dead. They might as well be, if there was no way out of here.

But something fell out of the canopy of roots above, landing before them. Two people, one of whom Kai recognized with painful awareness.

"Emory?"

The name spilled out of Luce's mouth on a shaky, terrified breath, as if she didn't trust her own eyes, didn't trust this to be real. Maybe she thought this was the start of her eternal damnation, a vision of the daughter she had abandoned and set out to save against all odds and would never see again outside of her own tortured mind. But Kai knew this wasn't a torment of hell; there was no reason for him to be seeing Emory if it was. And Emory's expression as she took in her mother was too raw, too complex, to be anything but real.

That expression steeled itself, becoming stony determination, as she erupted into light. Warmth spread through Kai, and the pain in his legs began to subside.

She was healing them, he realized. Casting back hell itself to prevent it from claiming their souls. The light emanating from her, enveloping them in its warmth, flared brighter and brighter. Emory screamed at the strain, this big a feat of magic surely taking a toll on her. The boy at her side hovered close, an obscure figure amid the dazzling light, as if he were Emory's own shadow, the darkness around him growing thicker as she flared all the brighter.

But hell was fighting back with everything it had, unwilling to let them go. Because while Kai's limbs were flesh and bone once more, while the roots keeping him in place receded, a ring of white-hot flames suddenly erupted around the temple, trapping them in.

Distant, familiar screeches sounded through the hiss of flames. The smell of sulfur that hit Kai was overwhelming, and he knew it meant the wayward souls of the dead were coming—that they were no longer contained to the hellfire stream their ship had sailed through, perhaps called here by the opening of the portal into the living realms or even Emory's magic.

Or perhaps they still hungered for Kai's and Luce's souls, as unwilling to see them leave as the abyss seemed to be.

"We need to get out of here." The light around Emory had extinguished. She was glancing at the network of roots above their heads, assessing how they might reach it. "Can you get us back up there?" she asked the stranger with her.

Kai wanted to tell them both not to bother—that according to the gods, the abyss wouldn't relinquish mortal souls, which meant they were trapped here. But just then, the wayward souls of the dead came rushing through the ring of flames around the temple, faces distorted on horrifying screams. And they were all aiming for Emory.

The boy at her side stepped in front of her, shadows swirling around him until he was no longer a boy but a towering umbra with clawed hands and depthless eyes and a wicked crown of obsidian that Kai had seen before, *held* before.

The crowned umbra pounded its foot on the ground. A crack echoed loudly, full of reverberating power, as dark waves shot the spirits back and created a protective layer of shadows all around the temple, keeping the souls on the other side of the ring of flames.

There was a sound like splitting wood above Kai's head as tendrils of shadow shot from the umbra to pull at the obsidian roots, tearing an opening in the tangled mass of them. The dislodged roots rearranged themselves to create a ladder they could climb.

Go, the umbra's voice rang in the sudden quiet. *I can't hold them for long.*

Kai wasted no time. He tugged Luce out of her transfixed state, ushering her toward the ladder. But Luce only gripped her daughter's arm, her face a tapestry of unspoken emotions reflected on Emory's own face.

"I'm right behind you," Emory said.

Kai went first, helping Luce over the lip of the opening once he'd made it up. They were on a path of obsidian, in darkness more oppressive than that of the abyss. Kai could feel *life* farther up, like a gentle breeze rushing down, and knew it was the portal into the living realms somewhere near.

Maybe they were getting out of here after all.

Luce screamed as dark, spindly roots reached out of the abyss to wrap around her wrist. Kai felt them grab hold of his ankle, trying to drag him back down to hell. Light emerged from the opening as Emory appeared at the top of the ladder and cast her magic at the roots, which shrank back as if singed. Kai scrambled up the path, heart pounding wildly.

A horrible screeching made Emory lower herself back down the ladder. "Sid?" she called out to the crowned umbra below.

There was no answer save for a chorus of ghastly screams. Whatever Emory saw had her going white with terror. Hands still gripping the top rung of the ladder, she turned to Kai and Luce. "Climb up the path until you find Baz. He'll get you both out of here."

Kai knew what she meant to do before she did. Luce seemed to guess at it too, for she reached for her daughter with a desperate cry, fingers grazing her wrists just as Emory let go of the ladder and disappeared in the chaos below.

Roots burst through the opening once more, a thousand of them now reaching for Kai and Luce like the tentacles of a great and terrible beast looking to plunge them back into the abyss.

With hell at their heels, they ran.

BAZ

ALONE ON THE PATH BETWEEN GODSWORLD AND ABYSS, Baz went to work analyzing the complex tapestry of threads coming out of the floating hourglass. He ran delicate fingers through the ethereal, immaterial strands, getting faint impressions of different people through time. He let instinct guide him until his magic found the threads that connected to Kai and Luce, both of them intertwined.

Baz tugged on these threads with his magic, following the now familiar course they took through time. The Wychwood they'd gone through with Clover. The sleepscape swallowing them up. The dark depths of what had to be the abyss. An obsidian path spiraling up, bringing them ever so closer to where Baz stood . . .

Those threads cleaved again. Fated oblivion. The end.

But the ritual, rescuing Kai and Luce from the abyss . . . wasn't it all supposed to *avoid* this fate? Baz wanted desperately to let go of his magic and go tearing down the path to pull Kai out of hell himself, to see him one last time before oblivion could come. But those whispers were in his ear again, making him reach out to another thread, one that was connected to Kai and Luce but ran back up the path in the opposite direction—in the godsworld. Here, it connected to another's fate. Someone else Baz was familiar with.

Clover.

Their fates were tied. Kai and Luce in the abyss, Clover in the godsworld. A triad of power, connected by threads that Kai himself had noticed when dreaming, this bond they shared that could never quite be explained.

Curiosity had Baz exploring Clover's thread further. When he'd done so before, in the god's workshop, Clover's thread had been too far out of his reach for him to see. But perhaps being at fate's central core made it easier to follow.

And Baz could see *everything* in it. Clover's past—how he'd watched Kai and Luce fall off the bridge of stars between the Wychwood and the Wastes; how he'd journeyed through the other worlds alone, killing the warrior and then the guardian, taking their power, before going after the gods, too. His present—how he sat in the godsworld, recovering from his last encounter with Emory, raging against his failed attempt to gorge himself on Atheia's and Sidraeus's power and make himself into a proper god.

And his future—the threads of Clover's life fraying into a hundred different possibilities. Baz followed the brightest and thickest one, assuming it was the thread with the likeliest outcome. What he saw made his stomach drop:

Clover, now a god in full, stood triumphant over Emory's slain body in a world reduced to ash. Then—nothing. The thread of Clover's life ended, but not because he was dead. It was the same way Kai's and Luce's threads ended. But this oblivion wasn't reserved for a single person. *Everything* came to an abrupt end. As if the universe itself ceased to exist, and from the ashes emerged a new one.

As if someone had wiped the board clean and started everything anew.

Heart pounding, Baz backtracked and followed the other fraying threads of Clover's future. In one possibility, Clover died at the hands of Emory, though it wasn't the Emory that Baz knew; it was an Emory who had made herself into a dark god like Clover, her power corrupted beyond recognition.

In another, Clover killed Emory, Sidraeus, and Atheia in one fell swoop, spilling their blood into a great fountain, before turning on the boy who'd given Baz the Reaper tree ritual–Equilibris's old apprentice–whose face shifted between his own and four others who Baz understood to be the gods of the living realms.

In yet another, Clover stood over those same four gods, though they were in their own bodies here, hollowed-out husks that Clover had bled of every morsel of power. Wiping ichor from his mouth, he smiled tauntingly at Equilibris. *So you've come to stop me at last*, Clover said, before this thread ended in oblivion, just like everyone else's.

Every possibility spelled death, and every one of these threads ended the same way: with the worlds resetting, and everyone Baz had ever known ceasing to exist forever.

Baz pulled back from the hourglass. An overpowering dread rose inside him. No matter how he looked at it, the outcome remained the same: obliteration. A complete erasure of life as they knew it.

A sudden gust of wind knocked him back as it rushed past him. Before Baz could make sense of what he was seeing–the ghostly outline of a boy in the midst of a strangely shifting whirl of ethereal power–it slipped through the portal, disappearing beyond.

Baz stood transfixed. It had happened so fast, but the face he'd seen, those rugged features and deep blue eyes that had stared right at him before disappearing through the portal . . . He knew this boy. It was Equilibris's old apprentice.

A horrible inkling seized him moments before the screaming began. It came from far down the path in the direction of the abyss. Like a howling wind passing through a tunnel. Cries of agony. A name—Baz's name—called in a voice that should have been midnight smooth but was sharpened now by desperation.

Baz tore down the path. He didn't question if this was another hallucination. Nothing else mattered now but reaching Kai, because he knew in his gut that this was him, really him, and something was terribly wrong.

And he was right. He'd made it only a few steps from the hourglass when they came into view: Kai and Luce running toward him, looking exactly as he remembered.

For a second, the breath was knocked right out of Baz at the sight of Kai. He wore clothes that hailed from a different era, a loose-fitting ecru shirt tucked into dark breeches, the shirt laces at the top undone at his chest so that the tattoos around his collarbone were visible. Baz imagined closing the distance between them and embracing in some sweeping, romantic reunion. Imagined stepping out of the portal together and putting this all too real nightmare behind them.

But it was as if hell itself were pulling on Kai and Luce. Spindly black roots were wrapped around their limbs, making every step an impossible torment. Panicking, Baz wound the threads of time back on these roots, trying to send them back to where they came from. Some of them let go for a second before they shot forward again with renewed force, completely out of Baz's control.

"Brysden." Kai's voice was hoarse. The roots were encircling his chest, tendrils of them wrapping around his neck as if to entomb him. "There's no point. The abyss won't let us go."

Those dark, midnight eyes that Baz loved so much, usually so full of starlight, were dull now. Haunted. These were the eyes of someone resigned to the idea that salvation was completely out of reach.

"No." Baz refused for this to be the end. He closed the distance between them and tried to pull at the roots with his bare hands. "This was my purpose. To bring you out of hell. The god's apprentice said—"

"Baz." Kai weakly grabbed his wrist. "The only reason you were sent here was to open a doorway for the gods to escape through. That piece of shit lied to you—to all of us. It's too late now."

Baz gazed down at Kai's fingers around his wrist, realizing why they felt so off. The tip of them was black obsidian. A whimper from Luce had him glancing at her. She wore the same look of defeat on her tearstained face as roots and obsidian slowly overtook her.

Kai and Luce were turning to stone before his eyes, as if becoming part of the very path beneath their feet.

Baz realized then what they had already pieced together: it had all been for nothing. Opening the Reaper tree portal, setting foot on this path, pulling Kai and Luce from the abyss . . . None of it mattered because Kai and Luce couldn't return to the world of the living. The abyss had claimed them, and now they belonged to the realm of death.

Baz shouldn't have been surprised. The god of balance did warn him that there was no changing fate. Pulling at loose threads, trying to create snags in the tapestry, attempting to dupe fate however he could . . . All pointless, in the end.

And yet . . .

In his fourth attempt at changing the past, he'd sought to replace Kai with Thames as the one who would follow Clover through the door. A reversal of fates, so to speak, that he never did see the outcome of because he'd been interrupted by the god's apprentice.

What if it was the answer now?

"Baz." Kai's voice was faint. "I know you made me promise not to say anything back until all this was over, but I need you to know before it's too late. I love you too."

For a moment, Baz didn't understand—until he remembered the nightmare they'd shared the last time he'd gone back in time.

Whatever happens, promise me you'll remember that . . . that I love you.

His last, desperate attempt to try to change fate. In some small way, it had worked—Kai had actually remembered what Baz had said to him in dreaming.

This couldn't be the end of their story. Not after everything they'd gone through to get back to each other.

The hourglass called to Baz again. Purpose sang in his veins as in his mind he saw again how Kai's and Luce's fates were tied to Clover's through whatever bond they shared. A triad of power, two points of a triangle condemned to hell, while the other was confined to the godsworld.

Above, below, side to side. A mirror, an hourglass, a scale onto which balance must be kept. A breath in, a breath out. Divine symmetry.

Baz sprang toward the hourglass with sudden clarity. This was the price of taking Kai and Luce out of the abyss: there needed to be someone to take their place, to balance the scales. A Tidecaller in the godsworld in exchange for a Nightmare Weaver and Dreamer in the abyss.

A reversal of fates.

If Clover were the one bound to the abyss, it would rid them of him for good, trapping his corrupt soul where it belonged. Maybe it would prevent the future Baz had seen, the bleak fate that awaited the worlds.

And if Kai and Luce were bound to the godsworld, Baz was willing to bet they could walk right through this portal—that the rules of heaven weren't as cruel as those of hell, and it would let them return to the realms of the living without resistance. Even if they couldn't, they would still be better off ending up in the sea of ash rather than the abyss. From there, they could make their way through the doors back to their own world—back to Baz and Emory and everyone who wished to see them safely returned.

Baz's hand touched the hourglass. A sense of rightness spread through him as he held those three fates quite literally in his hands, Kai's and Luce's connected to one side of the hourglass, Clover's to the other. All the other threads within the crisscrossing pattern disappeared, retracting into the glass bulbs, until there were only these three shimmering lines unspooling from the hourglass. All Baz had to do was to *turn it*, and their positions would be reversed.

A turn of the glass, a reversal of fate, until Kai and Luce were above, and Clover deep down below where he had always belonged.

"Brysden," Kai called out weakly. His legs were entirely turned to stone, and only his face was visible now beneath the roots.

"If this doesn't work," Baz breathed, "I'll find you in godsworld."

The ground beneath him tilted as he flipped the hourglass over.

EMORY

THERE WAS NO ESCAPING THE WAVE OF HUNGRY SOULS that swept over the dark temple. They had made it past the ring of fire and raged so furiously against the protective dome of shadows Sidraeus had erected that it was barely holding, a flimsy defense around him. From the strain on his face, he wouldn't last much longer.

Emory lowered herself down the ladder and fell with a thud at his side. She unleashed her own magic, weaving light through his shadows to reinforce the ward around them. She could only hope they'd buy enough time for Kai and her mother to find Baz and make it out of the portal.

Her mother. She still couldn't believe it. There had been such recognition on Luce's face, a mirror image of the hallucination Emory had been subjected to on the path, but there was no denying she was real here. It was odd to see her in the flesh, this person who had existed only in Emory's imagination. Luce was younger than expected, given the time travel; she couldn't be much older than

Emory herself, in her mid-twenties at most. But her eyes–her eyes held years and years of anguish, aging her into someone who'd been through too much in too short a lifetime.

Seeing her so close, Emory had realized she *had* seen her before, when Kai had found her in the sleepscape once. And now she was here again, not in dream form, not a hellish vision, but real. So many hopes had risen inside her, hopes for a future in which she might get to know her mother, process all her tumultuous feelings with her.

But only if they got out of hell first–something these ghosts did not seem to want, their assault taking everything out of Emory.

She spoke to Sidraeus in her mind. *What do we do? What is it that they're after?*

Magic, came his answer. *Life itself. They must sense that a portal's been opened, like the gods we felt rushing past us on the path. If they escape into the living worlds . . . I've never seen souls so restless, so hungry for chaos. We can't let them escape.*

The souls trying to claw their way through their magic were like wisps of stardust or ash, mostly immaterial, though translucent faces flashed in their midst. So many faces, young and old and unfamiliar to her, their mouths open wide in bone-chilling screams.

Tidecaller, some seemed to whisper. *Use our power as your own, then set us free.*

Emory realized what the souls of the dead wanted. They were a source of power, much like those that used to fuel the fountain and run through worlds to power the ley lines. To feed magic itself.

And if a Tidecaller were to call on them, they might harness the souls' power. Just like Emory could harness the power of the ley lines.

With that kind of strength, she might be able to defeat Clover. Perhaps even to restore the broken worlds. The divine fountain itself.

Yes yes yes yes yes, the souls whispered, hungrier now, fighting more desperately to get to her. They were looking to escape this place through her. *Use us, then free us.* Another bargain with ghosts.

But their taunting whispers and inhuman howls had Emory wanting to claw her ears off and scurry as far away from them as possible. She didn't *want* their power; it felt rotten to the core, twisted with a desperate anger she knew would twist her own soul, corrupt her beyond recognition. Like Clover.

Familiar features within the chaotic swirl of souls caught her attention.

His features.

Keiran Dunhall Thornby, his boyish face distorted by whatever purgatory-like hell he was held in. What choice had he made on the path, she wondered? Had he decided he was worthy of forgiveness for every vile thing he did, worthy of a chance at a new start, a clean slate–but had been denied eternal rest like all these other wayward souls now eager to feed into Emory's power?

She would be *damned* if she let him anywhere near her again.

Recognition seemed to flare in his hollow, ghostly eyes. He redoubled his assault against the shadowy dome, the souls around him doing the same, and suddenly they burst through, rushing toward Emory, as if they were giving her no choice in the matter. She screamed as they whirled around her, seeking a way in. They would *make* her draw their power inside her, if only just for a chance to feel magic–*life*–again as they tore through her.

They felt like the umbrae, growing stronger with her fear. Maybe it was best to give in to this dark force. To use it however she could to bring an end to the one who'd started this.

Even if she knew with utter certainty that there would be no coming back for her if she did, no healing the stain they would leave on her.

Keiran's ghost smiled at her as it drew closer. It was a twisted lover's smile, tauntingly seductive, as if he'd been waiting for death to reunite them.

"Emory." Sidraeus was holding her face in his hands, snatching her attention away from Keiran. He was in his true form again, no longer the crowned umbra. They stood together in the middle of this hurricane of souls, nearly all his shadows gone, nearly all her light faded. The runes on his skin were bright with pain—an echo of her own?—but his face was calm, like the eye of a storm that soothed everything inside her. "You have to go. The nature of your magic should let you walk freely out of the abyss. I'll hold the souls back while you—"

"No." She wouldn't leave him, and she was fairly certain that if they let their barrier down, the souls would rush right up the path and wreak havoc on the world. An idea suddenly crossed her mind. "What if we ferry them up the path?"

The souls were doomed to feed on pain and fear and guilt and chaos because the cycle of life and death was broken. That was why they were here. With the fountain depleted of its magic, souls weren't being reincarnated. They were trapped here in the only part of the afterlife that could host them. But if they could ferry the souls up the path to the godsworld, if they could put them in the empty fountain and find a way to replenish it with magic—to make divine power flow through it again—maybe they could be laid to rest.

She shared this with Sidraeus through the bond in their mind. As ferrier of souls, he had the ability to lead them up the path. But they were both depleted, outnumbered by these tortured souls. That didn't seem to deter Sidraeus in the slightest as the language of gods spilled from his mouth. Whatever words he spoke made the souls perk up and flock to him.

Sidraeus tugged on Emory's hand with a sense of urgency. *We have to move quickly.*

They went up the roots and began to run for their lives up the path, the souls at their backs. There were too many for Sidraeus to ferry properly, and these souls were wilder now that they were on the path, as if the prospect of heading to the godsworld—or perhaps escaping into the realms of the living—sent them into a total frenzy.

The moment Emory spotted Baz, Kai, and her mother farther up the path, she shouted at them to move, to get out of here before the onslaught of ghosts could reach them.

So why weren't they *moving*?

Her gut sank as she noticed her mother's limbs. Kai's, too. They were turning to stone just like before. But hell had no such hold on Baz. In a swift motion, he grabbed the hourglass that hovered above the obsidian altar, and time stood frozen.

Three threads of ethereal light shot out of the hourglass. Kai and Luce looked down at their chests, where two of these threads connected. The third thread disappeared down the path toward the godsworld.

Emory had no idea what was happening or how Baz was keeping time frozen for everyone on the path and all these ghosts at her back. She was struck again by how powerful he was—and more so, how unafraid he appeared to be wielding this strange power.

She watched, mystified, as Baz turned the hourglass over, ever so slowly, gritting his teeth as if it were the heaviest of objects. Wind tore at his hair, tore through the path. It felt like the darkness and stars of the sleepscape; it felt like the sooty desolation of the sea of ash. And when it lifted, it revealed a new figure on the godsworld side of the path.

Clover, black veins stark beneath his ashen skin, turquoise eyes lit with that unnatural glow.

Baz finished turning the hourglass over and set it back down on the altar with a grunt. There was a soundless, breathless pause before the world seemed to flip on its head. Where Kai and Luce had stood next to Baz on the left of the altar—on the abyss side—they now stood on the opposite side. Hell no longer had its roots in them, and their limbs were flesh once more.

And standing where they had stood was Clover, face etched in surprise, then in fury, as the roots of hell wound around him, keeping him in place.

Something like smug satisfaction played on Baz's face. But whatever hold he'd had on time seemed to have vanished, and the souls at Emory's back were on the move again, their wailing loud and visceral.

Clover's head whipped toward the sound. His eyes rounded as he beheld the souls that erupted past Emory and Sidraeus. Before she could stop them from engulfing everyone on the path, their words sounded in her mind again.

Tidecaller. Use our power as your own.

Clover met Emory's gaze a second before she realized he must have heard it too.

The path started to tremble, crumbling at the edges, obsidian columns disintegrating before their eyes. There were faces in the chaos, a thousand souls taking shape within. Emory caught the slightest motion from Clover, standing with his arms open as if to accept death itself.

He was calling the souls to him.

Desperation sang through Emory. If he took control of these souls, he would become unstoppable. So Emory called to them too, now desperate to grab hold of them before Clover did. But around her, her friends were screaming in pain, and she had to protect them. Power tore through her, the veins under her skin glowing bright silver as she reached her limit. Maybe this place made her not as limitless as she thought—maybe she actually would Collapse this time, and doom everyone to this purgatory.

It happened too fast for her to make sense of, even as time seemed frozen. Clover wrested the ghosts to him. They were like stardust seeping into him. His eyes glowed with otherworldly power. And this was what these souls had become: a power source all their own, something dark and angry and chaotic ready to be harnessed. Something powerful enough to turn someone into a god.

As Clover looked at Emory from the middle of a silken hurricane of souls that swirled around his limbs, she knew that was what he had become.

A god with the power to put an end to her and everyone here—and all the worlds if that's what he wanted.

BAZ

VEINS RAN BLACK ALONG CLOVER'S SKIN, A GHOSTLY sheen lighting his eyes, his hair flowing around him as if on some invisible breeze. The threads that had bound him to Kai and Luce turned black, dissolving entirely before Baz's eyes.

Baz understood then that turning the hourglass–switching fates–had solved nothing. Because Clover was no longer a Tidecaller, nor even a man.

He had risen as a god, and now he would destroy them all, just like Baz had seen in all his futures.

Fate running its course. Inevitable, no matter how hard they tried to change it, no matter how many snags they created in the tapestry.

A broken teacup flashed in Baz's mind, and as his eyes fell on the hourglass, he was suddenly reminded of Emory's dreams. How the glass would shatter and something or someone would always come spilling out of it.

What if it wasn't about releasing anything trapped inside the hourglass–but breaking fate entirely?

Out of the corner of his eye, he saw Clover advancing toward Emory and Sidraeus, power singing at his fingertips. Saw Luce hurling herself in front of her daughter, yelling at Clover through angry tears that he'd become the very thing they'd set out to stop. Felt Kai hovering at his own shoulder, as if ready to pull Baz away from danger at any second.

Power shot out of Clover, leaving Baz no time to think, to study the problem that lay before him with a cool, level head.

He smashed the hourglass against its altar.

Pain in his hands, shards of glass embedded in his skin—and all hell broke loose. Threads snapped, unraveling in the dark. Glass exploded and turned into dust that swept up and down the path, swirling into great gusts. The path itself trembled beneath their feet, starting to crumble at the edges, obsidian disintegrating and fading into the darkness around them, suspended between the unmoored threads of fate.

The air was thick with potential. As if, now that fate was broken, anything was possible.

Clover must have sensed it too. He paused his attack, turning to Baz, to the shattered hourglass. The frenzy of souls around him became agitated, ravenous with the same hunger reflected in his eyes. Before anyone could react, he disappeared within a maelstrom of power that rushed past them all, shooting toward the godsworld.

"You foolish boy."

Baz spun around. Equilibris stood on the other side of the altar, staring wide-eyed at the broken hourglass, then at the snapped threads, the crumbling path. His voice was calm, but there was a tremor of something beneath it that betrayed the god's emotional state. "I told you not to mess with fate, and you go ahead and *break* it?"

"I did what I had to," Baz gritted out. "I saw the outcome—what fate had in store for all of us. It didn't matter what anyone did. It would always have ended up with the worlds being reset. With *you* wiping us all from the board and starting anew."

Something flashed in the god's eyes, before a snarl had his attention snapping to Sidraeus. The Shadow was hurling himself at the god, his face etched in fury, a thirst for revenge. The god held his hand out and Sidraeus froze, held in place by whatever power the god wielded.

"You bastard," Sidraeus growled. "I let you sacrifice all my Tidecallers back then so you wouldn't need to reset the worlds. And you were going to do it anyway?"

The god shrugged. "So I lied. I couldn't do what I was meant to while your creations lived."

"Then why didn't you go through with it?"

The god narrowed his eyes at him, before shifting to Emory. "Not all Tidecallers were sacrificed, were they?"

Bleak understanding shot through Baz. In all the visions where he'd seen the worlds come to an end, Emory and Clover always died or became twisted versions of themselves, no longer Tidecallers but something beyond that.

The worlds couldn't be reset so long as a Tidecaller existed. Someone to embody the delicate balance between life and death, creation and destruction. A power the gods had never intended to exist.

It was why Equilibris hadn't been able to reset the worlds back then. Because a single Tidecaller had survived, and since then, there had been more of them over time. Perhaps there had always been one, a last failsafe against utter obliteration.

Now Clover was a god, no longer a Tidecaller. But Emory still was. She was all that stood between Equilibris and that bleak fate.

But I broke that fate, Baz thought. *It no longer has to end that way.*

Equilibris looked at him as if he'd heard the thoughts in his mind. "You've doomed us all."

KAI

THE PATH EXPLODED. THEY WERE DOOMED INDEED AS IT lurched dangerously, like a spiral staircase whose tethers had been blown out and would send them all falling back into the abyss.

The god of balance moved toward Baz fast as lightning.

Kai was faster.

He had already let Clover slip away despite the pent-up rage that had made him want to wring his neck, to force him to experience even a tiny fraction of all the hurt he'd caused. He would not let this god take Baz—wouldn't let Baz slip through his fingers so soon after they'd been reunited.

He latched onto Baz's arm just as the god reached him too, and the three of them were swept up by a vortex of threads that felt entirely too familiar.

For a second, Kai thought they would end up in the past like last time. Instead, they were in what looked like a workshop that was in a state of total disarray. It was as if the chaos they'd left behind had followed them here. The glass panes of grandfather clocks were shattering before his eyes, instruments were falling off their shelves and crashing to the floor, strident whistles were making a cacophony of sound, needles whirring as they spun uncontrollably.

And in the very center of it all was a giant loom that had fallen off its perch, the threads it had been spinning all tangled up as plumes of smoke rose from it. The god of balance stared at the broken loom, gripping his hair tightly and muttering a string of unintelligible curses.

This was his workshop, Kai realized. The very same one Farran had described to him.

While the god had his back turned to them, Baz bent to pick something up and pocketed it quicker than Kai could see what it was. Baz met his gaze. Kai still held his arm tightly, afraid he'd lose him if he let go. As if thinking the same, Baz grabbed his hand, interlacing his fingers through his.

"Is this real?" Kai whispered. *Are you real?*

He'd been wondering ever since Baz had appeared on the path. Too afraid to ask in case it was hell's way of torturing him, or his own mind playing tricks on him again.

Baz's answer now wiped away that fear. "Yes, it's real."

Kai let out a long exhale, leaning his forehead against Baz's. "I never thought I'd see you again."

"Neither did I," Baz breathed.

"This would all be very touching if you hadn't just obliterated fate."

Beside the toppled loom now sat the god of balance, shoulders slumped, beads of sweat pearling on his forehead. Kai couldn't help but be underwhelmed by the sight of him. He'd thought the four gods of the living seemed plainer than expected, but at least they'd had a commanding presence. The god of balance just looked hopeless, defeated.

Voice shaking slightly, Baz asked, "Why did you bring me back here?"

The god took four pocket watches out of his ugly patterned vest and studied them morosely. His face grew graver by the second. "Do you understand what it is you've done?"

"I did what I had to," Baz said, gripping Kai's hand tighter, "to save those I love."

The god peered at Kai. "By switching his fate with Clover's, yes, only for Clover to evade that fate once you broke the hourglass. And now he's made himself into a god, drawing on the souls of the dead to power himself."

"He was going to destroy us all," Baz argued. "And once he did that, *you* were going to reset the worlds."

The god shook his head. "It doesn't matter now. Chaos has won. The tapestry of fate is destroyed. *You* did so by breaking the hourglass. I can't see the outcome now. I don't know what will happen next. And I certainly cannot fix what Clover has done with his newfound godhood."

Kai felt Baz's hand go slack in his. "What did he do?"

"He has remade the worlds. You threw balance off its axis by breaking fate, and now everything has descended into pure chaos. Clover seized the opportunity to harness power like no other. The power of us true gods will dwindle until there is nothing of us left. Our magic, our *universe*, is in Clover's hands now, and he will do with it as he pleases." A sharp, nearly hysterical laugh. "It's all over."

Baz shook his head in defiance. "No. There's always hope."

"Hope?" The god rose to his feet, looking angry now. "What is hope in the face of a tyrant god? What is hope against the kind of destruction there is no coming back from? What Clover has done is irreversible. He has fueled himself with death itself, and so death will keep eating away at this new universe of his like termites until there is nothing left of the realms."

"And you resetting the worlds would have been better?" Kai snapped.

"Yes. It would have been a fresh start, a spark of new life. You won't get that now. Clover's destruction will be absolute, and no one can stop him, not I nor the four gods, not–"

"Emory could." The conviction in Baz's voice was unwavering. "I've seen her defeat him."

Equilibris gave him a pitiful look. "You broke that fate, Timespinner. Your Tidecaller will never have the kind of power Clover imbibed. She will never be strong enough to stop him. It's only a matter of time before she dies, and by then, you'll be begging me to reset the worlds. Only it will be too late, because my power will be spent, and the universe as we all knew it will end forever."

Hopeless, hopeless, hopeless.

The words resounded in the silence that followed. Kai didn't want to believe the god; he wanted to rage at this exhausting outcome. At his side, Baz was shaking his head in denial, tears welling in his eyes.

"If you don't believe me," the god said, "why don't you see for yourself what Clover has done."

He gave a snap of his fingers, and suddenly Kai and Baz were seized by those damn threads again, pulled into darkness and stars, their hands clasped tightly together, neither of them daring to let go.

EMORY

CLOVER AND THE SOULS WERE GONE. BAZ AND KAI, too—taken away by the god of balance to Tides knew where. There was Emory and Sidraeus and her mother, left on this path that was nearly gone too.

Sidraeus found her in the chaos, holding her steady. "We need to go through the door, quick."

"I can't leave without Baz and Kai."

"Then I'll stay. I can find them, bring them back."

Emory saw the lie on his gaunt face. He was as drained of power as she was. Silver still danced faintly beneath her skin. She didn't trust herself to use another drop of magic. Her eyes caught on her mother, trying to hold herself steady against the altar as the path came crumbling around them. If they didn't get out now, all of them, they would die here.

So Emory made a decision. She grasped Sidraeus's wrists tight. "I'm not leaving you, either."

He looked almost relieved. And it broke her heart to realize that he'd been willing to stay behind for her even knowing he might never come back out. This might be his domain, but it was crumbling before their eyes. There was no knowing if he'd survive it.

She pulled him toward the portal, let him go only to take hold of her mother's hand instead. The three of them ran through the gust of glass and dust and wind and stepped through the doorway, unimpeded, as if hell no longer had a hold on any of them, as if this place that was falling apart was glad to see them go.

Emory fell on the floor of the Reaper room, wrists smarting as she hit the ground. Her mother lay on one side of her, Sidraeus on the other. She sat up and spun back to the tree, where the doorway was still open, the chaos within threatening to spill out. But then, all at once, the portal shut. As if, without anyone left on the path, it knew the ritual to be complete.

Emory helped her mother to her feet. "Are you all right?"

"I'm fine," Luce panted. She eyed the muted silver veins on Emory's wrists. "It's you I'm worried about."

"I'll be all right."

Luce reached a hesitant hand to Emory's cheek, a soft smile gracing her features.

"Where are the others?" Sidraeus asked, breaking the moment.

Only then did Emory realize her friends weren't here to guard the portal like they were meant to. Virgil, Nisha, Ife, Javier . . . where had they gone?

Sidraeus suddenly doubled over, his runes flaring bright silver. Whatever pain he was feeling brought him to his knees. Emory fell with him, hating that she couldn't help him, that she was the reason he felt this pain to begin with.

"Emory!"

A man in a charcoal uniform was suddenly behind her, pulling her roughly off Sidraeus. There was the cold sting of metal at her wrists. She looked down in bewilderment to see damper cuffs there. Her mother screamed her name again as she fought against another man's hold.

The Regulators had found them. There were at least a dozen of them, dragging along Virgil, Nisha, Ife, and Javier, who were clearly Glamoured to stay silent and docile.

"Let my daughter go," Luce growled, fighting with everything she had.

"Daughter? Well, isn't this a lovely reunion," cooed a familiar voice.

Appearing in the Regulators' midst was Romie, eyes shifting like all the colors of the universe, like diamonds refracting light. She was dressed in sparkling white, a beaded gown that made her look like moonlight on water, like the moon itself, shining at its fullest. At her feet, writhing in pain, was an Eclipse-born Emory recognized from the safe house. Tortured by Atheia to bring Sidraeus to his knees.

The smile Atheia wore was victorious and full of malice. There was no hint of Romie in sight.

Four people wearing porcelain masks, one for each of the Tides, filed into the room after her. They were all dressed to the nines, and though their faces were covered, Emory recognized Leonie Thornby among them—Keiran's great-aunt—and knew this was the Tidal Council.

"I hope you enjoyed the gift I sent you," Atheia said to Sidraeus. "She was a dead ringer for Tala, wasn't she? I'm sure the pain was excruciating." She eyed his runes with hunger. "I'm looking forward to seeing you suffer in person."

Sidraeus remained silent and unmoving, a storm growing behind his eyes.

"Nothing to say?" Atheia smirked. "I forgot how much I enjoy the magics of this world. The compulsion especially. Perhaps I'll lift it only to hear you scream."

She gave a jerk of her chin to the Regulators holding Emory, who shoved her to her knees right in front of Sidraeus and splayed her tattooed hand out so it was palm down on the floor. One of them crouched next to her wielding what looked like a hot iron.

A U-shaped brand.

Panic seized Emory. She tried to fight back against the Regulators' hold, but whatever compulsion Atheia was working on Sidraeus must have extended to her, too. She couldn't move a muscle.

"You know," Atheia said, coming to stand between the two of them, "Clover did have *one* decent idea, wanting to make everyone into a Tidecaller. Of course, that's not exactly what I want. I want to make magic unlimited as it once was, so that those who worship the Tides can touch all the magics at their disposal once more." Her fingers hooked under Emory's chin, tilting it up to look at her. "Your blood is going to help me achieve that. All the power you stole—I will spill it to restore lunar magic to its fullest."

Emory wanted to tell Atheia it had *never* been like that with her magic. The only people she had ever *taken* from were the keys, but that was when she didn't yet know how to control her magic. That was before she realized she could *borrow* from them if only she asked. If they lent her their magic willingly, they didn't experience the deadly leeching they had when Emory had forcibly taken from them.

But with lunar mages? There had never been such taking of power. Whenever she used lunar magic, she was manifesting the magic as her own, not pulling it from others. She was a mirror. A mimicker. Not a thief.

But not according to Atheia. To her, Emory was the reason lunar magic was so limited. Because, with Atheia's return, lunar magic *should* have been restored to what it once was—accessible to all, no matter their ruling lunar house or tidal alignment. That wasn't the case. And so surely, the Eclipse-born must be to blame, the Tidecaller in their midst enemy number one.

The Regulator holding the Unhallowed Seal came close, and the panic inside Emory grew until she found her voice, able to talk through Atheia's compulsion.

"Please, Ro," she begged, hoping Romie was still in there the way Keiran had been when he was possessed—and that she might have more influence over Atheia than Keiran had over Sidraeus.

"Begging mercy from Romie won't help," Atheia said with that vicious tilt of her lips. "She wants to eradicate Eclipse magic as much as I do."

Emory shook her head. "Romie wouldn't want that."

Not if it meant the death of her brother, her father. Of Emory herself.

And yet . . . hadn't Emory seen Romie's growing disdain for her Tidecaller magic?

Atheia smiled at her knowingly, as if seeing the doubt plainly across her face. "It's time you gave back what you took, Tidethief. All the power you stole—I will spill it to restore lunar magic to its fullest. But first, this."

Emory heard Sidraeus in her mind, calling out her name like a lifeline thrown hopelessly in a stormy sea, as the Regulator brought the hot iron down on her hand. The Unhallowed Seal singed her skin, and then Emory's own screams drowned out every sound.

The pain alone, she might have endured—she had suffered worse before—but it was the knowledge of what this was, what it meant, that drew tears from her eyes and hollowed out her very soul. The pain lasted less than a minute, but the loss she felt when the Regulators released her was unending. Like a part of her had forever been put to rest, and she was left a shade of herself.

On the back of her right hand, marring the surface of her newly modified tattoo, was the Unhallowed Seal.

She could no longer feel her magic.

She could no longer hear Sidraeus in her mind, either. And when she tilted her face up to look at him, the bleak horror in his expression reflected how powerless she felt.

But then—a flare of his ecliptic eyes, the whisper of a crowned shadow behind him. In a blur of motion, Sidraeus broke through whatever Glamour Atheia had held him in and launched himself at her. He was a vengeful storm of shadows that took Atheia by surprise. Her eyes bulged as the clawed hands of the umbra extended out of Sidraeus like a separate entity and closed around her neck. Regulators tried to stop him, but shadows shot them all back.

Emory didn't have to hear his thoughts to know he was going to kill Atheia for this, and part of her was resigned to it. Romie was gone, after all, and Emory was powerless. Neither of them could stop this now.

I'm sorry, Ro.

But just as Atheia was about to succumb to Sidraeus's power, he was forced to let go of her, shoved back by a strange rippling barrier that appeared between the two of them. It seemed to take both deities by surprise, as if this hadn't been either of their doing.

In a swift, furious motion, Atheia produced a dagger that had been strapped to her leg and swiped at Sidraeus's neck—only for the same ripple of energy to deflect the dagger. She tried again, aiming the dagger at his heart, but it stopped inches from his chest. And as she called on what must have been Reaper magic, as Sidraeus's own shadows transformed into a piercing blade arcing toward Atheia's head, that barrier stopped every one of their attempts.

They couldn't kill each other no matter how much they wanted to. Some fault in the design, perhaps, or maybe this was just as the gods had always intended. The fate and the ruin, made to balance each other out and thus unable to exist without the other.

Destined to circle each other in a lethal dance but never come close enough to end the other.

All the fight winked out of Sidraeus, as if he came to the same realization. Atheia seized the moment to conjure a damper collar and snapped it around his neck, making his lethal shadow disappear. Rendering him powerless once more.

"I'm sorry," he whispered as he was shoved to his knees beside Emory again.

If he was apologizing for trying to kill Romie despite his promise not to or for failing to do so, she couldn't tell, nor did she have time to consider how she felt about it, because suddenly the room was trembling with such force that part of the tree was uprooted and the glass dome over their heads cracked and burst, sending lethal shards flying toward them.

Emory shielded her face, but the glass never reached her, Atheia standing tall to erect a ward over their group. The Tidal Council and Regulators and their still-Glamoured captives had all been knocked around by the powerful quake and were now righting themselves, looking at one another with alarm.

From somewhere outside, screams drifted to them.

"No," Atheia breathed. Her mouth was agape, a storm of emotions flitting across her face, as if she could sense something the rest of them could not. "It can't be."

"What is it?" asked one of the Tidal Council. "What happened?"

"Clover has done the unthinkable." Atheia's kaleidoscope eyes homed in on Sidraeus. "Can you feel it? The chaos he has wrought, the mess he's created? The fault lies with you, Sidraeus." To the Regulators, she said, "Bring them to the quad. It's time we put an end to the eclipse."

BAZ

BAZ WAS SUDDENLY SPRAWLED AT THE FOOT OF A familiar tree, his limbs tangled with Kai's. Their hands were still clasped tightly, a testament to how scared they'd both been to lose the other. Despite the horrors they'd just escaped, Baz wanted to stay here in this desperate embrace and forget the world around them existed. Kai seemed to share the sentiment. His eyes dropped to Baz's mouth. Heat rose up Baz's neck.

Now wasn't the time for a proper reunion.

But oh, how he'd missed this—the way his heart galloped at a single look from Kai, how the two of them seemed to melt into each other like hot metal poured into a mold. They were a perfect fit as Kai's face nestled in the crook of Baz's neck and Baz pulled him in closer, arms winding tightly around him. They held each other in the quiet, not needing words or anything but this closeness, this brief moment of stillness in the chaos.

Noises sounded from afar. Reality crashing in. Too brusque an end to too tender a moment.

Neither of them let the other go even as they got to their feet, as if their interwoven fingers were the last shred of strength they were both holding on to.

Kai's gaze sharpened as he took in the Reaper room they were in. "What is this place? Where did that bastard send us?"

"Back to Aldryn," Baz answered. The room was in shambles—the tree half uprooted, the ceiling shattered—and it was empty, quiet. "The others should be here . . ."

Unless, he thought, they hadn't gotten out of the portal.

Baz reached for the familiar pocket watch he'd snatched from the god's workshop—the device that had helped him navigate time travel. He didn't know what compelled him to pick it up when he saw it there amid the rubble of the destroyed workshop, but it could come in handy now, to flick open the little magnifying glass that would allow him to view past events.

Before he could do so, noises echoed outside the room again—only this time, there was no denying they were *screams*.

Wordlessly, Baz and Kai hurried out the door toward the screaming, still holding hands. Down the corridor, students had amassed outside Decrescens library, their faces pressed against a large diamond-paned window. They all looked aghast at what they saw outside, hands covering their mouths, tears in their eyes, the air ripe with their fear.

Baz and Kai shoved their way through to see what they all stared at. The Aldersea wasn't entirely visible from here, as Decrescens Hall was set farther back from the edge of the cliff, behind Pleniluna Hall. But Baz could see enough of it to know *something* had changed. He couldn't make sense of it, only grew more and more confused the longer he stared at it.

Students around them were shouting, some of them racing through the corridors toward Pleniluna Hall to get a better view. Baz and Kai ran after them, and finally, on the very top floor of the Pleniluna library, they got a full view of the coast.

In the distance, a storm raged over Cadence, veins of lightning turning the dark skies a deep indigo.

Only it wasn't Cadence anymore. Not really.

Where the village had once been now stood twin peaks that were as different from each other as night and day: one, a snow-capped mountain of moss-clad rock; the other, a desolate, jagged black volcano. They seemed fused together in an impossible way, as if the peaks had merged to create one, but fell short of such a vision.

The quaint cottages of Cadence were still there, Baz realized as he swept a gaze down the length of the peaks, but instead of being neatly organized along cobblestone streets gently sloping toward the sea, they now clung to the side of the mountains. As if a giant had plucked them from their places and scattered them along the mountainside.

And the Aldersea that had hugged the Cadence coast was no longer a sea at all but a sprawling forest of ancient-looking trees, their branches twisting up toward stormy skies.

As Baz stared and stared, trying to make sense of what his eyes were seeing, a loud roar rent the night. The source: something large flying above the twin peaks.

Something that looked, impossibly, like a *dragon*.

Understanding hit Baz all at once. Clover hadn't blown up all the doors between worlds. He'd gone one step further and *combined* all worlds, fusing them together. Whatever he did had created this great cosmic shift that saw the four worlds overlapping in strange, chaotic ways. Forests growing out of the sea. Snowy peaks sprouting in the space between islands. Beaches becoming deserts with rivers of lava running through. Different shores colliding to make something new.

All the worlds' peoples and beasts and magics clashing in this one great space, so that Clover could easily rule over this new domain of his.

A world without borders. Without limits.

One endless shore, rife with infinite possibilities.

PART III
THE FATE & THE RUIN

THEIR STORY BEGAN WITH A DREAM AND ENDED IN A nightmare.

In this world they loved best, where magic evolved with every phase of the moon and the eclipse unveiled yet more wonders to behold, they would not be known as the Tides of Fate and the Shadow of Ruin for some time yet. They were just two lonely deities at first, idealistic artists seeking connection through creation. They were each other's muse, and their shared love of magic and desire for innovation inspired many, until they had a great following of devoted disciples eager to mold the world in their image.

There was none more faithful than the keen-eyed girl who followed them around like the little sister neither of them ever had. Two beauty marks on her cheek looked like a sun and moon in eclipse, denoting her love for both deities, her understanding of all magics, her curiosity about all things godly.

She was the first to see the cracks in the foundation of their relationship, the jealousy that set in like rot. The rupture that eventually occurred between them split the girl down the middle, her loyalties divided, yet neither deity seemed to want her by their side anymore. The Tides called for the expulsion of Tidecallers from the world, though they told the girl this separation would be for the best. The Shadow marched on the godsworld without her, claiming he'd cut her out of his plan to keep her safe.

All she heard from them was dismissal, and it broke her heart.

It was in this final hour that the girl was visited by a vision of what would ensue: the splintering of the Tides, the imprisonment of the Shadow, the shutting of doors between worlds with the blood of her own peers. There was no time to stop any of it, no way to warn anyone. The girl only had time to save herself.

She was alone now with the secret of a magic that the higher gods believed they had eradicated. A Tidecaller without Tides left to call on, nor Shadow to answer to. But they would one day return, this much she knew.

Fate and ruin, she had come to understand, were symbiotic. Intrinsically tied. Neither could ever truly be rid of the other, and this, she feared, would lead to their mutual demise.

ROMIE

ATHEIA EMERGED FROM DECRESCENS HALL TO FIND the world in shambles.

The skies over the quad bred a vicious sort of wonder, the kind that had anger churning in Atheia's belly. Where before, the night had been dark with the new moon's reign, now it was full of strange, dancing lights and veins of lightning, and ruling high above were a moon and sun in eclipse. The mark of a new, twisted era.

Bewildered looks followed Atheia as she wound her way to the fountain at the center of the quad, her faithful Tidal Council and Regulators trailing behind her with their captives. From here, Atheia couldn't see the extent of the damage Clover had wrought, but she could *feel* what he'd done, how he had made himself into a god and blended all her perfect creations into one realm of pandemonium.

A sudden panic spiked through the crowd as the sound of wings drowned out all the chatter. Overhead had appeared creatures

Atheia had never seen in her lifetime, though she knew them from Tol's memories. *Corvus serpentes*, eldritch beasts from the Heartland that were half raven and half snake. Monsters born of Sidraeus's magic.

Fury burned within her as the creatures swooped toward the quad, eliciting screams as people ran to avoid their sharp beaks and talons and spiked tails. Atheia called blinding light to her hands to ward off the beasts. She fashioned the light into sharp blades imbued with the death magic of Quies and sent them arcing toward the *corvus serpentes*. They fell in twos, threes, plummeting to their death, yet more of them remained.

These monsters weren't attacking, Atheia realized. They were trying to fly *away* from something.

Trying to escape the strange pocket of darkness that had opened up in the sky.

A deep, tenebrous bruise had appeared high above them, like a tear in a piece of fabric, a window opened onto an uncanny obscurity that could only belong to the sleeping realm. Faint, distant stars could be seen through it. And Atheia watched, as bewildered as everyone else, as it swallowed up a pair of *corvus serpentes* who'd been too slow to avoid its spreading stain.

Panic intensified as a second pitch-black blot appeared in the corner of the quad where Pleniluna Hall met Decrescens Hall. Part of the cloisters there were sucked right into the blooming dark–along with a student who'd been cowering against the cloister wall, and who never stood a chance.

Atheia's stomach dropped. She felt, for a second, like a leaf in a storm, doomed to be blown this way and that way by forces greater than her, unable to seize control. Stone crumbled all around as the pocket expanded, drawing more and more of the cloisters in its depths. People ran for their lives, running to the other side of the quad, heading inside buildings as the tear in the sky also grew, and the few *corvus serpentes* that remained landed on the ground seeking safety.

Shaking out of her stupor, Atheia made the light in her hands amplify, desperate to stop the spreading dark.

But then, all at once, the nightmare stopped. The pockets of sleepscape remained where they were but ceased their spreading. Not because of anything Atheia did, but rather as if answering someone else's whims, a conductor leading musicians to the abrupt end of a piece.

So this was what it had come to. The four realms of the living combined into one—and threatened into oblivion by the sleeping realm that was trying to tear its way through. As if the living and sleeping realms were now fighting for dominance, unable to survive in this space together. Devouring each other until, perhaps, everything was doomed to become dust.

This was what Clover had done.

Had it been his intention, she wondered, to destroy her worlds this way? To lead them faster to oblivion?

People were still screaming, scared, not realizing that the dark had stopped its senseless destruction. The *corvus serpentes* now in their midst were just as frenzied. And dangerous.

Atheia didn't hesitate. Sharpening her anger, she let loose more of those whips of light and death, and in one fell swoop killed all the monsters that remained.

She caught sight of Sidraeus as he fell limply to his knees, all the color drained from his face, his eyes glazed over in pain. Interesting—he must have felt the creatures' suffering the same way he felt the pain of Eclipse-born. At his side, Emory was looking at Atheia with an expression of incredulous horror. It stirred something in Atheia—Romie's consciousness slipping through.

Atheia gently nudged her back. This was no time for sentimentality from her vessel.

The courtyard had fallen quiet. All eyes were on Atheia now, faces so scared it broke her heart.

"Do not be afraid, my friends," she said loudly. She imbued as much calm in her voice as she could, sending out waves of soul-tending magic from Aestas to soothe their panic. "I am the Tides returned to your shores, and I have come here to fix this world and restore things to how they were. But it seems the blight of the eclipse has been festering here for far too long. These creatures are from another realm, allowed to pass through here because of Eclipse magic. But I will keep you safe from them. I will stop this spreading darkness."

"How?" someone asked shakily.

"By ridding the world of the Shadow's taint," Atheia said. She motioned to her captives. "I have here the Shadow himself and the Tidecaller who brought him out of the Deep, as well as the traitorous lunar mages who aided them. They are the ones to blame for this. And once I am finished turning them back to the light, I promise you, the world and your magic will be restored, and there will be nothing left to fear."

She could sense their unease, feel their doubts. They didn't trust her to keep them safe, even if they wanted to. They *needed* someone to believe in, given all the impossible things they had seen in the last few minutes alone. They needed something true, a force they knew to be good.

"Trust in Bruma and Anima and Aestas and Quies, in we the Tides of Fate," Atheia said. "Let me demonstrate to you how those who put their faith in the Tides will be rewarded."

She motioned to the Regulators to bring Emory to the fountain. While they dragged her there, Atheia crouched beside a still subdued Sidraeus and said, barely above a whisper, "You told me back in the godsworld that if I spilled another drop of her blood, you'd split me up into pieces. So let me tell you, dear Sidraeus, that

I plan to bleed her dry—and take my time with it. When I'm done, she will die, and maybe this bond you share means you will too."

Atheia lifted his chin with a finger, watching with satisfaction as all the light dimmed from his eyes. "If I can't kill you myself," she said, "I'll gladly settle for this. And I'll enjoy every second of your slow torture."

Emory stood in the shallow, freezing waters of the Fountain of Fate. Atheia stepped in after her, wielding a sharp dagger. She turned to the crowd and let them feel the weight of her gaze, willing their attention to remain on her.

The Tidal Council and other Selenic Order members—all of them wearing porcelain Tide masks—formed a circle around the fountain, looking up at Atheia like supplicants. Behind them, the quad was a quiet sea of fearful students and curious professors and dispirited protesters, some still wearing their abominable Shadow masks as they waited with bated breath for what came next, ensorcelled by Atheia's magic.

Atheia took hold of Emory's wrist and pressed the dagger to it.

"Ro, please don't do this," Emory begged. "Don't let her—"

Atheia did not let her finish. She slashed the dagger across Emory's skin. Silver blood spilled out—they had branded her with the Unhallowed Seal while she was still in the thralls of her power, a near-Collapsing in effect—and mixed with the water in eddying swirls.

For the tiniest of seconds, Atheia lost the battle of wills inside her as Romie's heart broke for her friend.

We need her, Atheia reminded her.

Romie knew this. But as she looked at Emory, fighting to stay conscious as blood pooled out of her too fast—as her eyes found the traitorous Selenic Order members they'd subdued, Virgil and Ife and Javier and *Nisha* . . .

They will all be all right, Atheia said. *This will be over soon.*

Romie had been in agreement with Atheia on getting rid of Eclipse magic, and though her methods had become increasingly twisted, curdling unpleasantly in Romie's mind, she had let Atheia's words convince her that it was necessary. That the deity was getting the justice she deserved, and that this would somehow avenge the keys who had died at Clover's hands.

Never did Romie imagine it would get this far. Or if she did, she hadn't wanted to believe it. In retrospect, she should have drawn the line at the Luaguan professor's torture. But the shock of it had made her passive, resigned to her forced complicity. What other choice did she have but to go along with what the deity inhabiting her body wanted to do? She was no longer in control, and so it was better to be of one mind with Atheia than to fight back and see herself erased entirely.

But seeing her best friend like this . . . This, she couldn't abide.

It has to be done.

Atheia wrested control of her vessel again as she slashed her own wrist so that her blood mixed in with Emory's. It was Romie's blood, the blood of a lunar mage combined with the silver blood of an Eclipse-born, and yet it was not *only* Romie's blood, but Atheia's own divine essence. Magic in pure form, mixing with the magic Emory had stolen from her. The lunar overtaking the eclipse. Reclaiming it. Reshaping it.

They'd needed a Tidecaller to take power from. In a complete reversal of how a Tidecaller called on Atheia's magics, depleting the keys of their life force, Atheia now called on *Emory's* power, depleting *her* of her magic—this power of liminality in her veins that went beyond anything Atheia or Sidraeus could have ever created alone, a power that the gods themselves had feared.

Atheia had gotten the idea from Clover, how he had attempted to make everyone into Tidecallers all those centuries ago. This, she had glimpsed from his memories during their brief encounter.

Maybe he'd had the right idea. Maybe Tidecaller blood could be spilled to make everyone limitless, just not in the way Clover thought. And with Atheia's divinity poured into that blood, no one would need to die.

Unlike Tidecallers, Atheia was not a thief. She was a *creator*. And she was only taking back what was rightfully hers—and redistributing it to those she had created this magic for in the first place.

Atheia raised her arms over her head, and droplets of glowing, silvery water lifted in the air with her. The air crackled with magic, with possibility, as those ethereal droplets—as their combined blood—swirled around her, and then in one swift motion went flying toward the Selenic Order and Tidelore members standing around the fountain.

There was a flash of brilliant light. A collective gasp as her faithfuls were drenched in the magical droplets.

A woman wearing a Quies mask produced light at her fingertips—a power that should not have been accessible to her. Leonie Thornby, a Wordsmith, wielded tendrils of darkness. A man with a Full Moon sigil used Sower magic to make the lunar flower buds floating in the fountain bloom beautifully. Magic of all kinds rose from hands that did not bear the proper sigil, that did not answer to the moon over their heads, that did not need bloodletting to be let loose.

Awed murmurs rose from the crowd, understanding rippling through them. Those faithful to Atheia now had full access to all lunar magics. Just as it once was.

There was a splash as Emory fell limply, her head half submerged in the shallow water. She appeared woozy as her blood poured and poured, her magic worn thin by Atheia's will. Atheia faltered as Romie's consciousness broke through the surface again with renewed force.

Sensing her anger rising, Atheia tried to smooth it over with reason once more. *The return of lunar magic will chase away the stain of the Eclipse,* she said. *Don't you wish to see your friend, your brother, and your father saved from the Shadow's taint? We will turn them all to the light.*

And how will you do that exactly? Romie asked. *By bleeding them all until they die? Look at her—you're killing her.*

Just think of all the lunar mages who will have magic because of her sacrifice. This is so much bigger than Emory. The world will be saved by the eradication of Eclipse magic, and it will be because of us—because of you, Romie. You'll be like one of the heroes from those books, the white knight who saves the day, who casts away all the darkness.

This isn't what I want.

Nor would it be what Aspen and Tol and Orfeyi would have wanted. This wasn't the way to avenge them.

Romie took a lurching step through the pool toward Emory, the first step she'd taken as herself in a long time. But her movements were stilted as Atheia fought back for control. Romie raged at her inability to operate her own body and fought all the harder to get to Emory, who was slipping away, seconds from becoming unconscious. Would Atheia let her go under, let her drown here?

Romie wrested control the second Emory's head went underwater. She pulled her friend up, desperation making her heart pound wildly. "Please, Em," she cried. "Stay with me. Just hold on."

Those stormy blue eyes opened to slits to look at her, and for a miraculous moment, it felt like they were just the two of them, those same girls they'd always been peeking through who they'd become.

"Ro," Emory whispered.

"I'm here. I'm—"

Atheia flung Romie's consciousness back, seizing control again. The deity sensed a slight unease running through the crowd now, but most of them were too preoccupied with the Selenics' display of magic to care about the scene that had unfolded. Still, Atheia pulled Emory out of the fountain, holding her weakened body against hers.

"There now," she cooed, brushing wet strands of hair from Emory's face as she sent a healing wave to close her wound. "You're all right."

She couldn't appear cruel to those watching, had to be the benevolent and just Tides they all wanted her to be. Atheia motioned to a pair of Regulators to grab Emory; one of them even wrapped his jacket over her trembling shoulders, silently Glamoured by Atheia to do so.

Dripping with blood and water, Atheia stood tall as she addressed everyone in the quad. "This is how magic will be reclaimed and the world saved from the Shadow of Ruin. Drop by drop, what the Tidethief took will be restored to lunar mages, starting with those most faithful to the Tides."

The Selenic Order and Tidelore members who had been reveling in their newfound magic bowed to Atheia, a powerful sight to behold in their Bruma and Anima and Aestas and Quies masks. A reflection of Atheia's own might. She smiled at them dotingly, sensing a shift in the crowd—the vicious hunger of those who wanted to know this kind of power too. Yet there were still too many who doubted her, who were not swayed to her side in the slightest.

"Bring the Tidecaller and the Shadow to the Institute," Atheia instructed the Regulators.

"And what shall we do with them?" one of the Regulators asked, motioning to the captive lunar mages who'd helped Emory.

Virgil, Ife, Javier, and Nisha.

NISHA.

The feral, desperate scream inside her mind made Atheia stamp down on her vessel with more force than before. Compulsion had kept the captives quiet and docile while Atheia bled Emory in the fountain, though the four of them glared at her and the masked Selenic Order members—their former fellows—with admirable intensity.

Atheia was most intrigued by the fifth captive, the young woman who'd emerged from the Reaper tree with Emory and Sidraeus. Emory's mother, it seemed. Something about her called to Atheia, as if a distant echo of her own power flowed through her. Curiosity piqued, she looked through the woman's memories and realized why.

She'd been the key before Romie. The blood Atheia had sung to before her.

"Please."

The plea slipped from Emory's lips, barely above a whisper. Atheia had half a mind to cut down the captives where they stood to hurt Emory some more—and to warn others of what siding with the Tidecaller would bring.

But these were lunar mages, born with a sliver of *her* magic. They had been led astray and should be given a chance to see the error of their ways.

"We'll hold them in the prison wing with the rest of the lunar mages who've voiced their support for Eclipse-born," Atheia declared. She approached Nisha, tipping the girl's chin up to look at her, all while making sure Romie was aware of what was happening—that she saw the fear in Nisha's eyes. "I think they need to be made to atone for their treachery. Bled of their magic so that they know what it feels like to have their power stolen from them."

To Romie, she said, *Perhaps this will keep you quiet and pliant. I'm in charge of this body now, Romie, and if you don't agree with my methods, there is nothing you can do about it. It's for your own good. For the good of this whole world.*

Atheia's gaze swept over the Shadow-masked protesters. "Let

this be an example for anyone who stands with the Tidecaller and the Shadow. Your lack of faith in the Tides will drive the world to further destruction and bring about your own inevitable end. Choose to stand with the Tides, or we will send you to the Deep along with the Shadow and his ilk."

It mattered not that the real person to blame for this pandemonium was Clover. In Atheia's mind, he was still a Tidecaller, a product of Sidraeus, only now with the power of a god who'd rearranged the entire universe.

Clover, Emory, Sidraeus–she would destroy them all and hope it would not be too late for the worlds she loved.

BAZ

NO MATTER HOW LONG HE STARED AT IT, NO MATTER how much he turned it over in his mind, Baz couldn't make sense of this new multilayered world before him—especially not as those black holes appeared. They tore open the skies and swallowed whole sections of the cove below where the tide had started to come in, sweeping through the rotten trees of the forest that now stood there.

There were quiet gasps and quiet sobs and a desperate, quiet bewilderment as the students around him watched the scene unfold. From somewhere near, they heard screams and the sound of crumbling stone, and Baz suspected those hungry pockets of darkness must have appeared on campus, too.

He has fueled himself with death itself, and so death will keep eating away at this new world of his like termites until there is nothing left of the realms.

Equilibris hadn't lied. It was as if each dissonant puzzle piece of this new landscape Clover had created were vying for dominance over the others.

Baz thought someone might be speaking to him, but all he heard was a dull ringing in his ears, folded in with the echo of the hourglass breaking. He stared and stared at his bloodied hands, the cuts from the broken glass.

He'd *broken fate*. That careful pattern Equilibris had spent all of existence overseeing. All those intricate threads woven into a tapestry older than time. Gone. Undone by Baz's own two hands.

The barest thought had the threads of time around his wounded palms pulling back to when the gashes had never existed. His hands were clean and healed in an instant.

If Baz had thought the power his Collapsing allowed him was limitless, it was nothing compared to what he felt now. It was as if breaking fate had shattered the bottom of a far-reaching well inside him to unveil something even vaster, almost unfathomably so. Power thrummed in his veins like a steady vibration. He could see the threads of time all around him without even trying to— threads untethered from any sort of pattern, or rather choosing to make their own patterns at will.

Perhaps the fabric of the universe had changed completely with Clover's meddling, and maybe that applied to time, too, unbinding it from the constraints it used to answer to. Baz wasn't sure what that meant for his magic, and thinking of it made him sick to his stomach.

"Brysden. What now?"

The sound of Kai's voice brought him back to reality.

"We have to go find the others," Baz whispered.

They weaved through the gathered students, searching for their friends' faces, but Emory and the others were nowhere to be found. Baz had to believe they had made it out of the Reaper tree. He was of two minds about where they would have disappeared to: either they'd headed for the safety of Obscura Hall . . . or something terrible had happened to them.

Answers found him when he and Kai emerged in the quad. It was a jarring sight: part of the cloisters had been devoured by a pocket of darkness, and the ground was littered with the corpses of strange beasts. Small groups of students remained. There were a few Shadow-masked protesters here and there, but most were gone or in the process of fleeing.

"Baz!"

He spun around to see Penelope West heading their way, eyes wide with horror. "I've been looking all over for you," she said.

"What happened here?"

"Your sister did this—well, the Tides. They tried to stop the black holes from destroying everything and . . . and bled Emory of her magic. Right there in the fountain. Said this was how to fix whatever's happening to the world, by giving back the power she stole and sending the Shadow back to the Deep."

Baz's stomach dropped. "Where's Emory now? Is she—is she all right?"

"She's alive." Penelope's face was grave. "But she was given the Unhallowed Seal. The Tides drained her power and gave it to the Selenic Order who now have access to all lunar magics. They're not going to stop until it's restored for everyone. I'm scared of what they'll do to Emory at the Institute."

"The Institute?" Baz repeated with bleak horror.

"That's where they took her. Her and the Shadow and the others who were with them."

"What others?" Kai asked.

If Penelope recognized him, she didn't bat an eye at the fact that he was a fugitive of the Institute. "Virgil, Nisha, Ife, and Javier.

And a blond woman I didn't recognize. Had a Waning Moon sigil."

Kai's eyes squeezed shut, his face falling. "Luce." He swore. "We need to get them back."

"We already have people at the Institute," Baz said. "Maybe they can . . ."

The words died on his tongue. Jae and Vera and the others who'd gone to scope out the Institute would still be waiting for Sidraeus to magically appear with backup. That had been the plan: to use the protest as a distraction while they got Kai and Luce out of hell, then head to the Institute to break free the Eclipse-born prisoners while everyone was still occupied at Aldryn.

But now that plan was shot. Sidraeus wasn't here to whisk them back to the safe house. And with Atheia headed to the Institute, Baz could only hope Jae and the others would have the good sense to hide and find their own way to safety.

The sound of breaking porcelain caught his attention. Near the Fountain of Fate, a group of riotous students were smashing discarded Shadow masks on the ground and chanting hideous words.

"Down with the eclipse!"

"To the Deep with the Shadow!"

"Drop by drop, the Tidethief we will stop!"

"You should go," Penelope said, face blanching. She'd taken off her own Shadow mask. "It's not safe for you here."

Baz couldn't disagree. And with the remaining protesters fleeing and the other Eclipse-born he'd come here with nowhere in sight . . .

Penelope seemed to read the fear on his face. "Those assholes over there are only a fraction of who was here earlier. Most people saw just how vicious the Tides were with Emory and anyone who stood with her. And those pockets of darkness? This pandemonium? Everyone is left wondering why any of this is happening if the Tides are in our midst, when they were supposed to be our saviors."

Baz exchanged a glance with Kai. They both knew this had nothing to do with Atheia and all to do with Clover. And if the Tides were losing favor among some of the lunar mages, he could only wonder if they might start blaming the Shadow–and Eclipse-born–more intently.

His gaze drifted to the door to Obscura Hall, feeling torn. He had to make sure the rest of the Eclipse-born were all right before he even thought of helping Emory and the others.

He started toward Obscura Hall, but Penelope stopped him. "I saw Regulators rushing over there after you all left," she warned. "Be careful."

Baz nodded in thanks. They'd most likely find Regulators guarding the elevator. And if the Eclipse-born had managed to reclaim Obscura Hall, maybe the Regulators were trying to break past newly erected wards. Whatever the case, Baz wasn't scared of them. And neither was Kai.

But when they stepped through the doors, the small hall that led to the lone elevator was empty–except for the bodies of Regulators strewn over the floor.

Lights flickered ominously overhead. The hall was a bloodbath, as if the Regulators had imploded, as if their every blood vessel had burst. A single pair of bloodied footprints wove a path through the mutilated bodies toward the elevator, where they disappeared.

Someone had gone down to Obscura Hall after this gruesome scene had taken place. Either an innocent bystander, a survivor . . . or the person responsible.

All Baz could think of was his father and Professor Selandyn and the other Eclipse-born who'd gone to Obscura Hall. Had the same thing happened to them? He hurried into the elevator after Kai, not even taking the time to reach for the pocket watch that could let him see who or what had done this. The elevator jerked downward, and Baz could only hope against all hope that they weren't too late—that they wouldn't find such carnage at the bottom.

When the door creaked open, Baz felt the floor slip out from under him. He wasn't sure what he'd expected: the usual illusioned field of tall grass bowing toward the sea, or perhaps just a long, foreboding stone hallway, since the illusion magic must have shattered after the Regulators took over Obscura Hall.

The reality was neither.

Gone was the willow tree behind which stood the Eclipse commons. It was as if someone had blown open a wall, revealing the inside of the commons, like entrails spilling from an open stomach. The place they'd called home was eviscerated. The threadbare sofas and chairs were overturned, the fireplace was a mess of crumbled stone. The stairs leading up to the rooms stood precariously, as if they could topple at any second. Part of the ceiling had come down, along with the entire wall where the window had overlooked the cove and the secret passageway door had stood. The whole place was now open to the night sky above, the sea beyond.

Everything seemed to have been pushed aside by the appearance of objects that were entirely out of place. An ominous stone chamber, torches casting long shadows over its contents: some kind of alchemical workshop or laboratory, full of vials and jars, most of them empty, though some contained golden flames. Rusted metal chains were fastened to the wall, too big to be meant for humans. People were scrambling around, dressed in curious clothes that seemed plucked from a fairy tale, red robes and chain mail and gold-threaded doublets.

There was not a single Eclipse-born in sight, and Baz could only hope they'd gotten out safely before the commons got destroyed. There was, though, a man standing with his back to them, watching the scene with the same quiet stillness that Baz and Kai had been. He turned to them as if he'd sensed their coming. Baz wasn't surprised to see Clover's face. He braced himself, ready to reach for his magic, but something about Clover's demeanor made him hesitant to do so.

He looked almost . . . resigned. The wildness of the man he'd seen on the path between abyss and godsworld was gone, and what was left was raw, uncertain. Baz could almost imagine they were back in time, reminded of the Clover he'd spent long hours in the library with, the Clover who'd cared about his sister and his friends and his fellow Eclipse-born.

Baz might have believed this was that Clover if it weren't for his eyes—a shade of turquoise so luminous, there was no doubt it came from his unnatural godhood.

"You know," Clover said, a wistful note in his tone, "I never got a chance to step foot in Obscura Hall before. Doomed to the secrecy of being a Tidecaller, denied a chance to be my true self. Now here I stand a god."

"A monster, you mean," Kai seethed. "You've destroyed everything."

"Not destroyed," Clover said. "Remade into something viable for all. A new world order."

"What about those Regulators you killed up there?" Baz shook with barely leashed anger. "Is that the kind of *order* we can expect from our new god?"

Clover's nostrils flared angrily. "Those *Regulators*," he nearly spat the word, "had it coming for how they treat people like us, the Eclipse-born they deem too different to fit into their sacred lunar system. Enough with their tyranny. What I'm proposing is a world where no one is better than others, where everything and everyone work in balance with each other. Under my rule, everyone will be safe."

Kai laughed darkly. "Tell that to the people you hurt to get here, and everyone watching the literal black holes swallowing up the world right before their eyes. Was that part of the plan, *Cornelius*?"

Doubt seemed to flicker in Clover's unnatural eyes.

"I'll tell you what I think," Kai pressed further. "I think you're too absorbed in your own godhood to see your downfall coming. You think you're invincible, but you have no idea, do you?"

"No idea about what?" Clover said with a note of disdain, as if trying to mask his own ignorance.

"That the gods you tried to take power from are out here right now, gathering their strength so they can come after you. I might have a bone to pick with the bastards for abandoning me in the abyss, but I'll gladly cheer them on when they end you."

"They won't," Clover said with a confidence that might have sounded forced. He glared at the disparate pieces of worlds laid out before him. "I'll hunt them down myself and absorb whatever's left of their power so that I can fully embody the four worlds of the living. Then everything will be as it should be." Clover studied Kai. "I am glad, you know, to see that you survived. Losing you and Luce was . . . Well. I never thought I'd see either of you again."

"We had your boyfriend to thank for that."

Baz's head snapped to Kai, wondering who he meant.

"I wonder if you'll recognize him when the gods come for you wearing his face," Kai continued, voice taunting. "He might not look like Thames anymore, but I can assure you, his reincarnation remembers what you did to him just fine. I hope he gets the revenge he deser–"

In a flash of anger, Clover was on Kai faster than Baz could call on his magic to stop him. But his magic, it turned out, wasn't needed. No sooner had Clover wrapped his hands around Kai's neck than he let go with a cry of surprise, pain flashing across his face. As if he'd been burned by the tattoos on Kai's collarbones, which had come to life in a faint silver light.

There was a second of complete surprise where all three of them remained still, too stunned to react. And then Kai pulled back his fist and swung at Clover.

Before his punch could land, Clover disappeared in a cloud of billowing dust.

KAI

"WHAT THE HELL WAS THAT?" BAZ SCREECHED.

Kai stared down at his tattoos, which had already faded back to their normal black lines as soon as Clover disappeared.

"I have no idea," he breathed.

And yet he had a sneaking suspicion. This had happened in the abyss, too, when one of the gods had grabbed him. The four gods had stared at the tattoos as if they could sense a power there. Because surely that's what it was: some kind of protection against gods, perhaps. Though why that was or how it worked was beyond Kai. It wasn't as if he were the one controlling it, nor had it ever happened before, but then again, he'd never had the displeasure of meeting a god until recently.

He would have loved to have never met a single one of them.

Before either he or Baz could say another word, two figures wobbled their way from the rubble of the Eclipse commons. Kai recognized Theodore at once, as well as Rusli, whom he'd briefly met before going through Dovermere. Theodore was leaning heavily on Rusli, one of his legs a complete bloody mess.

Baz ran toward them. "What happened?"

"He got caught in the wreckage," Rusli panted as he set Theodore down on the floor. "I managed to pull him out with a little help."

At this, he gave a nod of thanks to a young boy who'd appeared behind them. The boy flushed. He was lanky and still growing into his teens, with green eyes and strawberry-blond curls. The rust-colored surcoat he wore was similar to the strange clothing of the other people running around, bearing a faded crest as though this were an old hand-me-down that had seen better days.

Baz fussed over his father, who tried to swat him away. "I'm fine," Theodore said with false bravado. "Really, it's—"

His leg healed before their eyes. The blood disappeared, and his shredded pants leg was whole again.

They all stared at Baz, who hadn't even blinked as he pulled back the threads of time.

"Well," Theodore mused, "that's a handy trick." He turned to Kai then, his face splitting into a smile. "I see they managed to pull you out of hell."

"Glad that part of our plan was successful, at least," Rusli said.

A swell of emotion rushed through Kai. He was hit with the realization that it wasn't just Baz and Emory who'd fought to get him out of the abyss, but a whole group of people who actually gave a shit about him.

"Where is everyone?" Baz asked, eyeing the rubble of the commons with worry. "Professor Selandyn . . . ?"

"She's fine," his father answered. "We managed to get everyone down to the beach after . . . whatever it is that's appeared here eviscerated Obscura Hall." He glanced at the strange boy. "What did you call this place of yours again?"

"The Chasm," the boy answered. "The seat of the Fellowship of the Light. The Golden Helm were in the process of raiding it when there was this big shift like the world was exploding. And all of a sudden, here we were."

Nothing he said made any sense to Kai, but the names must have sparked recognition in Baz and the others, because they all shared a knowing glance.

"You're from the Wastes—the Heartland, I mean?" Baz asked.

The boy nodded.

Theodore gaped at him. "How is any of this possible?"

Baz went on to explain what had happened—how Clover had risen as a god and fused together all the worlds. When he mentioned that Atheia had brought Emory and the others to the Institute, the boy's head snapped up, his eyes going as big as saucers.

"Did you say Emory? Emory Ainsleif, the Tidecaller?"

"You know her?"

"Yes, I—wait here a second."

The boy sprang off, and Kai had half a mind to follow him, but the others seemed to trust him.

"We need to get out of here," Rusli said. "Go back to the safe house, regroup there. Obscura Hall's useless to us now that it's in shambles. And if they've captured some of our own, we need to get them back."

Purpose sang within Kai. "Count me in."

The Institute had kept him locked up, had tried to tear his magic from him. He wouldn't stand idly by as others were subjected to the same harrowing imprisonment.

"How do we get to the safe house?" Baz asked. "And what about Jae and the others? It's not like we can just jump on a train back to Threnody. The Regulators will be looking for all of us."

"I could change our appearance with an illusion," Rusli suggested. "And maybe everyone will be too busy worrying over what's going on to even notice us . . ."

"With everything that's happened, I doubt the trains will be running," Theodore said grimly. "Maybe there are no tracks anymore, if the worlds have all been rearranged."

Before despair sent them spiraling further, the boy came running back with two other people in tow. Two women with umber skin, armed to the teeth, dressed in the same rust surcoat as the boy, though the crest on theirs was more visible. It depicted a gold dragon and a black winged beast all twisted up together, forming a perfect circle.

"You're Emory's friends?" asked the younger of the two.

They all nodded. The two women exchanged a glance. The older one said, "Any friend of Emory's is a friend of ours."

"You're Ivayne and Vivyan, aren't you?" Baz said with recognition. "Knights-errant of the Golden Helm."

The two women bowed in confirmation.

The younger knight clasped the young boy on the shoulder. "Caius here told us Emory's been captured. Whatever you've got planned to set her free, you can count us in." She winked at the boy. "You're proving yourself useful, page. I'm glad the Golden Helm took a chance on you when you left the Fellowship."

The boy flushed, a smile on his lips.

"What we need is a way out of here," Baz urged. "We have friends down on the beach below, others at the Institute a few miles from here, and the people of our world are going to be after us. We have a safe house, but it's too far to get there on foot, and we don't know if the trains are still up and running."

"I don't know what a *train* is," the older one said, throwing a glance behind her, "but we do have someone that could help."

As if on cue, a massive, winged beast appeared in the night sky behind her, talons digging into masonry as it clung to what remained of the torn-down wall that overlooked the cove. Its roar split the night.

It was a Tides-damned *dragon*.

ROMIE

THE VESSEL KEPT SCREAMING, DEEP IN THE RECESSES of her own mind, but Atheia was getting good at ignoring her. She wouldn't make the mistake of allowing Romie to share space with her anymore, not when she was so close to achieving her goal.

As her feet led her past the part of the Institute where dissident lunar mages were held—where Emory's friends were to be bled of their magic—Atheia stopped at a narrow window where a handful of Regulators were stationed, whispering to themselves at whatever they were watching outside. One of them saw her and beckoned her over.

"There's a—a *dragon* out there."

The Regulators parted to let her through. Outside, dawn was lightening the skies, making the pockets of sleepscape more evident. A magnificent dragon flew low over the woods that bordered the Institute.

"Should we do something about it?" asked a Regulator.

"No," Atheia breathed. "Leave it be."

Dragons were creatures of the Forger—*her* creations. The sight of it now brought a tear to her eyes, a fond smile to her lips, and a renewed sense of purpose as she wound her way through the prison.

There was one other stop she had to make before getting to work on drawing Emory's blood.

"I don't think I'll ever tire of seeing you on your knees, Sidraeus."

He glared up at her, hands bound behind his back, damper collar stark on his neck. Atheia ran a finger along one of the spiral runes on his collarbone, delighting in the way he shuddered and jerked away at her touch. Her smile grew.

"This place must be torture for you, in such proximity to so many Eclipse-born experiencing pain both physical and mental. Did you know I managed to capture a *corvus serpentes*? Now that the worlds are combined, I look forward to hunting down other creatures born of your magic to see how hurting them affects you. What's the one that's considered the Night Bringer's emblematic beast? Ah yes, the *panthera noctua*. Maybe I'll go after every single version of your abominations, one of each world. If I'm to save the realms by ridding them of all traces of Eclipse magic, none of them should be spared."

Sidraeus's silence—forced onto him by compulsion magic—was delectable. "What, nothing to say?" Atheia teased, finally lifting the Glamour.

His throat worked as if testing out his ability to speak. "Why don't you just end it?" he said roughly. "Do what it is you've been longing to do and kill me already."

"You saw what happened when I tried." The memory still infuriated her, how something had prevented her from ending his life back at Aldryn. "It seems we cannot kill each other."

"Then get someone else to do it."

"Oh no. I've decided that would be far too easy for you."

"You want every trace of my magic gone, so end me and see if it erases all of it. See if it does anything to save your precious worlds. I'd wager it doesn't, but if you promise to let Emory go, I'll accept the risk." He squared his shoulders, as if ready for the deadly blow they both knew Atheia couldn't give him. "Go on. Take what it is you want."

Atheia's blood boiled. "You have no idea what I want," she hissed. "I want you to admit you were wrong back then. I want you to take responsibility for what happened. I want an *apology*."

Sidraeus laughed. "Then I'm afraid you'll never get what you want, Atheia. Because I want the same things from you, but I at least know it's a lost cause."

The fury inside Atheia became a hurricane. "I'm going to make you regret ever stepping foot in the realms of the living."

She stormed out of the room before he could see the tears in her eyes. She wiped them away furiously, at war with these feelings inside her. The hurt she hadn't fully acknowledged yet, the heartbreak that echoed from over a millennium ago. She wanted none of it.

So she would break him before it broke her.

EMORY

EMORY GROGGILY OPENED HER EYES. THE STARK LIGHT that met her was disorienting. She tried to move, but found her wrists and ankles tied to a gurney. Panic shot through her, sharpening her focus. She was in a sterile room that was faintly familiar, wearing some kind of hospital gown. In the crook of her arm was a bandage. Beside her, syringes and vials full of blood.

Her silver blood.

The Institute. She'd only ever been here once, when she'd snuck in with Baz to see Kai, but she recognized the grimness of the place with painful realization.

How much blood would Atheia take from her? How long could she be kept here, weakened as her very *life force* was taken away from her to give to others?

"Hurts, doesn't it, to feel so powerless?"

Emory's head snapped to the side, the quick movement making her dizzy. Romie stood in the doorframe. No, not Romie. *Atheia,* face twisted in cruelty. She was still wearing the dress she'd worn at Aldryn.

"What did you do to them?" Emory asked, voice coming out weak from disuse. "Virgil, Nisha . . ." The rest of the names died on her lips.

Luce.

Her own mother, caught up in something that should never have involved her.

"There, there," Atheia said placatingly. She came to stand beside Emory, gently wiping at a tear on her cheek. As if she cared. "I said I'd give them the opportunity to atone for their traitorous alliance with Eclipse-born, didn't I?"

The way she said it made it sound like this method of atonement was the sort of painful torture Emory couldn't fathom.

"Your Eclipse friends, on the other hand . . ." Atheia tutted. "They'll get what's coming to them. Just imagine: your blood, used to power lunar mages who will bring about the end of your fellow Eclipse-born. There's an exquisite irony there."

"No one's going to let you get away with this."

A laugh that was so unlike Romie spilled from her mouth. "Who will stop me? The world has fallen to chaos. Anyone with a sliver of power and influence answers to me, the Tides who so generously restored their magic to its full might. No one's coming for you, Tidethief. You may as well be dead to what's left of your friends."

Emory had to believe she was wrong. Baz would come. The Eclipse-born would find a way to her. Her friends would be all right.

But another face occupied her thoughts, eyes of silver and gold, hair the color of autumn leaves, voice like the night clinging desperately to the dawn. When she called out to him in her mind, no answer came. There was only empty silence. She couldn't bring herself to ask Atheia what she'd done to him.

Atheia smiled as if she could read her thoughts all the same, and maybe she could. "That bond you share is quite an interesting one. For him to feel not only your pain, but that of all Eclipse-born . . ." She picked up a syringe, examining its sharp point. "I expected this place to be the worst sort of torture for him, but he's too stoic for my liking. It's tiresome."

She gave a long sigh and plunged the syringe in Emory's arm unexpectedly, drawing a whimper of surprised pain from her. The lights in the room flickered in and out, as if the raw power being drawn from her veins was affecting them.

The door opened as two Regulators dragged someone in. Sidraeus hung limply from their arms, head bowed, eyes closed. Emory fought against her restraints, his name slipping from her lips as the Regulators pushed him to his knees and forced his head up. Finally coming out of whatever groggy spell they had him under, he settled his gaze on her. He composed his features into stony neutrality, but his eyes held something of an apology, a trace of fury.

Emory hoped to hear his voice in her mind, but again it was only silence.

And then her ears filled with screaming—her own or his, she wasn't sure—as pain seared across her skin. Atheia's hands were grasping Emory's arms, emitting a bright, burning light. As if she were concentrating rays of sunlight, focusing them as a mirror or magnifying glass might, so that it burned through Emory's flesh. The smell invaded her senses. The pain was worse than any she remembered feeling. Tears streamed down her face as her screaming turned to a whimper, too weak was she to muster much else.

When Atheia drew her hands away, giving her a second of reprieve, Emory realized that her magic was truly gone. The healing power that had always saved her, that had made any hurt feel like a distant dream once it took away the source of it, was silenced by the Unhallowed Seal on her hand. The pain kept going in throbbing waves, yet she sought Sidraeus with her gaze, knowing he would have experienced it too. He was trembling on his knees, biting down on his own fist as if to keep from screaming, his eyes shut as if he couldn't bear the sight of Atheia's torture.

Atheia merely smiled and motioned for the Regulators. "Take him to see the other creatures," she ordered them. "I want to see if hurting them will hurt him too, or if this curse branded on his skin binds him to Eclipse-born of this world alone."

"Stop it," Emory breathed as she watched Sidraeus being dragged away. He didn't fight back, and that alarmed her more so than the burned handprints on her skin. "Haven't you done enough to him?"

Fury flashed in Atheia's eyes. "Typical of you Tidecallers to defend him so willingly. After everything he's done to your kind, I'm surprised you even care. Oh, but I suppose he's made you believe he had no choice, that he regrets everything he did."

Atheia smiled wickedly at whatever expression flickered over Emory's face. She tucked a strand of Emory's sweat-soaked hair behind her ear, the tender gesture made perverse by the cruelty seeping into her words.

"I too have been swayed by his honeyed words and brooding charms before. But here's a secret for you, Emory." She lowered her face close to Emory's ear, whispering, "Sidraeus will never care for anyone but himself, and if he has made you believe otherwise, it's only to get something from you."

With that, Atheia exited the room, leaving Emory alone with the pain.

Days might have bled into night without Emory's knowledge, the passage of time marked only by the comings and goings of those who took her blood. Groggily, she was aware of faces hovering over her, some she recognized as members of the Selenic Order. There was Vivianne Delaune, the Memorist who'd wiped Penelope's memories. And there was Leonie Thornby, Keiran's great-aunt, whose greedy expression as she took a vial of silver blood in her hands cut through the fog in Emory's mind.

"Why?" Emory asked, voice so weak she thought for certain Leonie wouldn't hear.

The older woman turned to her, hovering at her side for a moment. "I'm sorry, child."

But there was no remorse in her eyes.

Perhaps seeing Leonie is what made Emory dream of all the ghosts in her life. She hadn't seen Keiran's face since the abyss, but here he now was, sitting with her in a pile of broken glass. They were in Dovermere, she realized, the hourglass of her dreams already shattered. It was so quiet, Keiran's voice startled her.

"You should have listened to me, Ains." His face didn't have the distorted pallor of the ghost she'd seen in the abyss, nor the one that had haunted her in the Wychwood before that. He looked like he had the night of the bonfire when she'd first returned to Aldryn, alive and bright with that gold-hued charm of his. "None of this would have happened if you'd become the Tides' vessel like I'd planned."

And he was right. Instead, Emory had evaded that fate and pushed it onto Romie. Now her best friend was lost to the whims of a deity, Emory was going to die giving up all her power, and Eclipse magic would be eradicated.

"She's still in there, you know."

It was no longer Keiran sitting beside her, but Aspen. The witch looked as alive as she had been before Clover sacrificed her, except there was an open cavity in her middle showing her rib cage. A single rib bone was missing.

"Aspen," Emory cried, reaching toward her to heal her, before she realized this was only a dream, and she had no more magic besides.

Her eye caught on the other two people sitting beside the witch. There was Tol, who gave her a sad smile. His chest was open, his golden heart missing from where it should have been. And then there was the boy with blond curls whom Emory had only seen briefly in the godsworld. Orfeyi stared glassy-eyed into the distance, his vacant face hinting, perhaps, at his missing soul.

The sight of the three of them brought tears to Emory's eyes. So much had happened since the sea of ash that she hadn't fully processed their deaths. What happened to their souls, she wondered? She hadn't felt them among the restless ones that had escaped the abyss, but if no soul could find eternal rest with the fountain being depleted of magic, she couldn't fathom what might have become of theirs.

"I'm so sorry." Her words got caught in a sob. "I should have listened to Romie, should have stayed away from the sea of ash. Maybe then you wouldn't be dead and Romie wouldn't be— wouldn't have to—"

Aspen grasped Emory's hand, squeezing it tight. "There was no stopping the fate that awaited us. You can't keep blaming yourself for something you had no control over."

It was Emory's own words echoed back to her, but she couldn't bear to hear them here, not now. It wasn't just the keys' fate she felt responsible for, but everyone else's, too. The friends she knew were imprisoned here with her, and those whose fate remained unknown to her, like the Eclipse-born left behind at Aldryn, and Vera and Jae and the others who'd been scoping out the Institute perimeters. If her plan had led to their capture—or something worse—she would never forgive herself.

"I've failed you all," Emory insisted. "Everything's hopeless now."

"No, it isn't," Tol said gruffly, reaching over Aspen to grasp Emory's wrist. "Romie wants you to know she's fighting Atheia with everything she has."

Emory blinked at him. "She is?"

"She needs you to hang on a while longer." Aspen's gaze drifted sadly to the still silent Orfeyi. "We all do."

"I don't understand . . ."

"You can bring us back," Tol said. "We know you can."

The dream suddenly felt too real, his words slicing into Emory's awareness. Could it be that their souls were truly here, finding her in the realm of sleep? Desperate for her to help them. To save them, perhaps, from the hold Clover had taken of their wayward souls. "I don't have my magic anymore," Emory said defeatedly. "And even if I did, resurrecting you wouldn't be possible . . ."

It was Orfeyi who spoke next, his voice flat, his gaze still unfocused.

"It's not resurrection if we're not entirely dead."

Before she could ask what that meant, the dream dissolved.

ROMIE

ROMIE EXISTED ONLY IN DREAMS.

Atheia had banished her consciousness from her body after her outburst at Aldryn, like a mother sending an unruly child to their room and throwing away the key. But in sleeping, Romie was free.

Aspen, Tol, and Orfeyi were still here, those threads wrapped around Romie's pulse points like a lifeline. It was like their consciousness was kept locked away with her own. Or perhaps it was just the parts of them that were Atheia that lived on–the parts of them that were divinity, fused into Romie to bring Atheia back.

But *they* were dead, she reminded herself. Their personhoods erased, no matter how alive they appeared to her. Aspen would never get to hold her sister Bryony again, would never get to prove her mother wrong or follow in the High Matriarch's footsteps. Tol would never get justice for what the Knight Commander and all the masters within the Fellowship of the Light had done to draconics like him and the dragons they claimed to worship. Orfeyi would never return triumphant to the people who'd put their faith in him, nor would he ever get to play music again.

They were dead, they were dead, they were dead.

And Romie might as well be dead with them.

"You can't give up," Aspen pleaded with her, a note of anger in her voice. "Where's the girl who kept pestering me for answers in the Wychwood? Where's the girl who crossed through worlds and stopped at nothing to bring us all together?"

"She's gone, just like you."

Aspen shook her head, adopting a stern expression that could have rivaled her mother's. "You're wrong. This"—she tugged on the thread that connected them, sending a little jolt of feeling through Romie, as if waking her senses— "this is proof we're still here, still connected. So use those connections."

Romie didn't understand. Until, slowly, she tugged on the thread that connected her to Aspen and found herself able to use the witch's magic, much like when she, Aspen, and Tol had shared power in the Wastes. With a hitch of her breath, Romie found herself seeing the world through someone else's eyes. The person felt familiar, and as she saw the faces at her side—Virgil, Ife, Javier, Luce—she realized who she was scrying through with Aspen's residual magic was *Nisha*.

Her heart broke all over at seeing the pain Atheia had inflicted on Nisha and the others. They were being held now in another part of the Institute. Being drained of their blood—of their magic— for Atheia's twisted idea of repentance. All it did was keep them weak and disoriented and in pain. She could feel it in Nisha, this hollowness.

And it lit a fire in her she thought had been snuffed out.

Aspen was right: she couldn't give up. Maybe, if she tried hard enough, she could get a message across to Nisha and the others, tell them to hold on—

But the dream ended, the connection severed, and Atheia once more took over.

As soon as Atheia slept, Romie tried again, and again, and again.

This was how she spent her existence now: trying to contact others in dreaming, or through scrying, using her own magic as well as that of the keys to get a sense of what was happening in the waking world. She couldn't even be sure any of it was *real*—for all she knew, she was imagining Aspen, Tol, and Orfeyi, and they really were dead, and everything else was just her own sad, frightened imagination trying to provide comfort.

But she was done giving up, done being afraid.

Fear of failure's the bitch that holds you back from success, Romie used to say. It was more so Atheia now that kept her from successfully contacting others—and she was indeed a bitch.

The extent of Atheia's cruelty hit Romie in full when she finally got eyes on Emory. Using Aspen's scrying magic, she'd flitted into the consciousness of a Regulator just as they entered a sterile room where Emory was strapped to a gurney and people were taking vials of her blood, like vultures to a corpse.

Something in Romie snapped.

She'd known this was what Atheia had planned, but seeing it . . . Romie realized fully then just how far she'd been swept away by her need for a cause, this need to justify her actions. Because if all this time she'd been following the call of a destiny that was so very *wrong*, the song of a goddess who wasn't *good*, then what did that make Romie?

She had searched for validation in Atheia's promises. Had made excuses for all the things she'd had a hard time agreeing with. She'd let the splinter of fear and resentment she'd felt as a young girl turn into a blade twisting into her wounds by her own hands.

And now she was watching her best friend get hurt. She heard the screams of Eclipse-born who were being similarly tortured into giving up their blood and screamed right back in her own mind, raging against Atheia, against herself. Maybe it wouldn't have changed anything if she'd come to her senses sooner; she was, after all, trapped in her own body, powerless to stop the deity using her as a vessel. But maybe it would have. Maybe she could have prevented some of this if only she'd realized sooner how wrong it was.

Romie had always thought she could do everything on her own. Finding the epilogue. Following the song to Dovermere. Sacrificing herself to be Atheia's vessel.

Rosemarie Brysden never asks for help, does she? The accusation Emory had flung at her not so long ago resonated inside her mind, stinging of regret. How right she'd been to say those words. How wrong Romie was to have kept thinking she could do it all alone.

She needed help now more than ever. Not for herself–surely she was a lost cause, forever to remain Atheia's vessel. But she needed to help Emory and all the other Eclipse-born here. She needed to stop Atheia from taking their power.

And she needed a way for Atheia *not* to know what she was planning.

The idea came to her, naturally, in a dream.

Every chance she got, she found Emory's consciousness in sleep. Her best friend's dreams were nightmares, darkness pressing in so thick it threatened to consume Romie. Something she found herself considering for a split second, wondering if it might rid her of Atheia somehow. If she made herself become an eternal sleeper, if she doomed her body to a catatonic state, would it affect the deity, too?

The answer didn't matter. She had to stay strong for the others.

And so Romie stayed as long as the darkness would let her. She tried her hardest to turn the nightmares into dreams. Something she'd never thought possible, but as she imagined seagulls and the lapping of waves, laughter in dorm rooms and long talks late into the night, the scenes shifted. Took on the shape of what Romie visualized. They were shared memories between her and Emory, scenes that had shaped their youth. It was almost like Romie was drawing on Memorist magic—something that might be possible with Atheia's power coursing through her—so that it melded with her own Dreamer magic. Chasing away the nightmares with pleasant memories pulled from Emory's subconscious.

I'm here, Romie thought, hoping it would bring Emory comfort. *I'm here, and I won't let you down this time.*

One time, there was a figure hiding at the edge of the dream, cloaked in shadows so Romie couldn't see his face. His presence was a comfort, and as he drew away the darkness from the nightmare, she knew it had to be Kai.

"I need your help," Romie called out to him.

And here they were, a girl of dreams and boy of nightmares convening on the path of stars. An idea became a concrete plan, and the feeble hope Romie had been clinging to grew and grew.

There was a way out. Not for her, never for her, but for those she loved, there was hope.

Before Atheia could wake, Romie slipped into Nisha's dreaming, if only to see her one last time. It was a beautifully familiar scene—the old greenhouse where they'd first let their romance flourish among the plants they'd tended to. They were lying on a blanket Romie had brought, staring up at the windowpanes above them as bright sunlight filtered through.

Nisha held Romie's hand, their fingers interlaced above their heads, dancing through the sun rays. "I remember this day," Nisha said. "I'd been meaning to tell you I thought I was falling in love with you."

"Why didn't you?" Romie asked, a lump forming in her throat.

"You started talking about Dovermere, the initiation ritual. I could see how much it consumed you, and I was so scared to lose you." Nisha turned her head to peer at Romie. "Would you have said it back, if I told you then?"

Romie let the question wash over her. She wanted to say yes. Wanted to tell Nisha that she had felt the same way—had always felt the same way—and would have said she loved her back without any hesitation.

But that would have been a lie.

The Romie she'd been back then had already been so obsessed with Dovermere and doors and dreams, had already been pushing everyone she loved away. Hearing those words would have done nothing but scare her into running away from reality sooner than she had.

But she couldn't bring herself to tell Nisha the truth and ruin this sun-dappled dream. Instead, Romie swept a hand over Nisha's cheek. "Say it to me once we wake, and I'll tell you my heart belongs to you and always will."

She only wished they'd gotten more time together. That she'd gotten to tell her in person, in waking, every day for the rest of their lives. They'd never have that now.

Nisha kissed her, the barest brush of lips. The warmth of the sun on her skin, the lingering sweetness of that kiss . . . it was enough for Romie to want to stay here forever. But she pulled away from the dream, and hoped Nisha would remember this goodbye when she woke.

KAI

KAI WOULD HAVE LIKED TO IMAGINE THAT BEING PULLED from the abyss would be like emerging from the longest of nightmares–that being back in his own world again, in his own time, with people he knew to be true and trustworthy, would make it easier to distinguish what was real from what was not.

Unfortunately for him, the world was quite literally being devoured by the sleepscape, and if he hadn't known about the realms being merged, he would have taken one look at all the strange beasts and people who seemed plucked from storybooks and assumed they were all trapped together in someone's truly fucked-up hallucinogenic dream.

He'd ridden on the back of a *dragon*, for Tides' sake. They'd flown to the Institute to retrieve Jae and Vera and a handful of Eclipseborn who'd been hiding in the woods nearby, and now they were at a safe house near the sea that was no longer just a sea, planning a prison break with people who could sprout dragon wings and wore actual armor and wielded genuine swords.

How the hell was Kai *not* supposed to question his reality.

But it was real. He had Baz at his side to remind him of it.

Kai didn't want to leave reality behind for one second, but his presence was needed in the sleepscape. No one had been able to make contact with those who'd been taken to the Institute—even Louis, the only Selenic Order member who'd stayed behind at the safe house, couldn't reach them through the spiral mark they all had, as if the wards rendered that trick powerless. And so Kai let himself be pulled into nightmares in the hope that his own magic would prove more useful.

Hers was the first nightmare he sought, knowing the bond they shared could not be stopped by wards. He felt responsible for Luce. No one should be subjected to the horrors of the Institute, but she, least of all. Not after all they'd been through.

It pained him to see how haunted she appeared in her nightmare—a cruel scene in which her newborn child was ripped from her arms by Clover, a representation of how powerless she must feel, unable to save her daughter from the very monster she'd once sought help from.

As the nightmare faded, Kai drawing the worst of its darkness into him, Luce noticed him with all the awareness of a Dreamer, recognizing him as real. She launched herself into his arms and broke down into sobs, asking if he'd managed to reach Emory, despairing over the fact that she couldn't use her own Dreamer magic to find her daughter in sleep.

"We're going to get you all out of there," Kai promised her. "But we need to know where everyone's being kept, how many Regulators there are, every detail you can think of. I need you to help us piece all of it together. Can you do that?"

Luce gave him a determined nod. "If you do find Emory . . . tell her to hold on. Make sure she knows we're all here for her."

Kai did find Emory. Her Tidecaller power—even put to sleep by the Unhallowed Seal—called to him as it always did in sleep, a magnet pulling on his soul. Yet it felt like she was just out of his reach. He tried to talk to her, to make his presence known, but she couldn't hear him. Whatever they were doing to her must be horrific.

But Romie was there too, and Kai knew this was *Romie*, not Atheia. A glimmer of hope in the dark, because if she was dreaming, if she was *talking* to him and helping him plan this jailbreak just as Luce had been, then surely there was still a chance for her. A way, perhaps, for her to get rid of Atheia's possession.

Two Dreamers trapped in a waking nightmare. A Tidecaller without her power. Countless Eclipse-born forced into a soulless, magicless existence that Kai remembered all too well for having lived through it himself.

They were going to save them all—and tear the Institute to the ground.

BAZ

Baz woke to the steady sound of rain and the feel of a body pressed close to his.

Everything was faintly blurry without his glasses, but Kai's face was close enough to his own that it stood out in stark relief. Kai hadn't opened his eyes yet, his features peaceful in sleep. Baz studied him openly, every line of him familiar yet tinged with a newness seen this close. Baz breathed him in, the smell of his freshly washed hair and that midnight scent wrapping around him like a blanket. The actual blanket they shared was tangled around their intertwined limbs.

Heat crept up Baz's neck as he suddenly recalled, in vivid detail, the kissing that had led to such entanglement. Slow and languorous. Making up for lost time before sleep inevitably won. And while that was all they'd done–sleep–the intimacy of it still struck Baz. They were sharing a bed–had been for days now. Sleeping in each other's arms, something he had feared they would never get to do.

After they'd returned to the safe house a few days ago, carried here on the back of a dragon named Gwenhael—an actual dragon!—their group had spent hours going over what the plan was to rescue their friends from the Institute. By the time they'd all gone to bed, exhausted from what felt like a never-ending night, it was well into the morning hours. Baz had led Kai to his room, and alone at last, they lay in the dark, talking until there was nothing left to say, then kissing if only to keep sleep at bay, to bask in each other's presence a while longer. They had done the same every night since.

Gently, Baz brushed a dark strand of hair from Kai's brow. He wished they could stay here forever, but he could hear voices downstairs, the clang of activity, and a thrum of nervous energy he could feel creeping along the floorboards and invading the safe bubble that had enveloped this room for a moment.

The world was falling apart at the seams, and here he was contemplating the merits of stopping time so he could exist with Kai outside of it.

"It's way too early for whatever you're worrying about."

Kai kept his eyes closed as he sleepily muttered the words. Baz's heart hitched, his fingers freezing where they'd still been toying with that supple strand of hair. Kai angled his mouth to press a kiss on the inside of Baz's palm, sending a delighted shiver up his spine as his eyes finally opened, dark and heavy with sleep.

"Hi," Baz whispered.

"Hi."

"You know it's actually well past noon, right?"

Kai grumbled in response, nestling in closer to Baz. "I don't care."

Baz couldn't say he cared very much either as Kai kissed his neck. But the voices downstairs grew suddenly louder, pulling them both out of their haze. There was a jailbreak to keep planning, and with Kai's recent sleepscape encounter with Romie—the thought of her fighting against Atheia's hold brought Baz so much hope—they were closer than ever.

Kai heaved a sigh and sat up in bed, pressing his palms against his eyes. "All right," he said. "What's on your mind?"

Baz stayed quiet awhile, not wanting to let the peace of this moment come to an end. "I keep coming back to what Equilibris said about Emory not being strong enough to stop Clover," he said at last. "His exact words were, 'Your Tidecaller will never have the kind of power Clover imbibed.' Meaning the keys, right?"

"Or the gods," Kai said. "Hell, maybe even the souls of the dead."

"Maybe. But it all started with Clover imbibing the keys. It's like he shed a piece of his humanity with each one he consumed. If we forced his humanity back onto him, so to speak, it might allow us to take away his godhood, his monstrosity. And if he were just a man again, we could defeat him for good."

"What are you saying, Brysden?"

"You heard Equilibris. As the last Tidecaller, Emory is the only thing stopping him from resetting the worlds. But if she can defeat Clover, then there would be no need to reset anything. All this madness would end, and everything would go back to normal. But she needs the kind of power that could rival Clover's. I think that power lies with the original keys."

"But they're dead. I saw the bastard kill one of them right in front of me." Realization seemed to dawn on Kai's face as his eyes landed on the pocket watch sitting on the bedside table. "You want to turn back time."

"Yes."

"And what, bring them all back to life just so Emory can kill them, too?"

"No, of course not!" Baz exclaimed. "That's not—I don't think that would be necessary. And you know I won't mess with death. Ever."

"You pulled *me* out of hell."

"You weren't dead."

"Technically speaking."

"Look," Baz said with a sigh, reaching for the pocket watch. He ran his fingers over the familiar grooves of its surface. "I've tried to change the past before, and it did absolutely nothing. Then I broke fate so the worlds wouldn't have to be reset, just for Equilibris to keep threatening to do just that."

"Asshole," muttered Kai.

"That, he is," Baz agreed. But at least Equilibris was unmoored, he thought. As adrift as everyone else now that fate was shattered. The worlds being reset didn't *have* to be the fate they were barreling toward; Baz could feel it, the sheer possibility in the air, all the different outcomes that could now become reality.

"Ever since I broke fate," Baz said, "my power has grown. Almost like it's not bound by the same constraints as before. I think I can travel to the past and breathe life into the keys again, so to speak. Not *keys* as in people—but the pieces of them that held magic. The bone and the heart and the soul."

"No blood?"

"Clover never imbibed the blood, did he? Luce is at the Institute. Which means that maybe Clover's at a disadvantage. He never completely absorbed Atheia's power, never made himself as limitless as he wanted to. But if Emory were to wield all four of these pieces—make herself master of keys, in a way—then I think she might stand a fighting chance against him."

He could tell Kai was skeptical about it; knew how wild a theory it was. But his gut had told him to break the hourglass. His gut had him swiping the pocket watch from the god's workshop. And his gut was telling him this was the path he needed to take now.

It wasn't just the god's offhand comment about Emory. When Baz thought of it, it was almost like Equilibris had been leaving crumbs for him to follow. The sketch of fate's core he'd let Baz see.

The teacup he'd shattered, which had then given Baz the idea to break the hourglass of fate. Impossible that this was on purpose, given where Equilibris stood in all of this. Unless he never thought Baz would pick up on these crumbs to begin with. A god who never imagined he might be outsmarted by a human.

Or a god who knew exactly what he was doing, for a purpose Baz couldn't yet see.

Regardless, it was a risk he had to take. After all, he was the lungs, able to breathe in time and breathe out stories–and stories were a form of *life*, weren't they? They were creation. So he would breathe life into these keys again. Gather them all to him and pray they would serve Emory well when it mattered most.

A stab of guilt went through him at the thought that he wouldn't play a part in Emory's rescue. But if there was anyone he trusted to break her and everyone else out of the Institute, it was Kai.

As if reading his thoughts, Kai said, "You plan on doing this now."

"Yes."

"Why not wait until we come back from the Institute? None of this will matter if we don't get Emory out."

"I don't know how long it's going to take me, and, ironically, given my powers, we don't really have the luxury of time, do we?"

Kai's throat moved as he swallowed, as if fighting to find the right words. "I don't want to lose you again," he whispered at last.

"You won't." Baz cupped his cheek. "Besides, I think what we've gone through proves we'll always find each other, don't you think? Nothing can keep us apart, not hell, not time, not gods."

"I'm going to hold you to that promise, Brysden."

"Good."

They sealed it with a kiss.

When Baz told a select few people of his decision–namely his parents, Professor Selandyn, and Jae–the latter, who'd been wearing the same clothes they'd slept in, disappeared for a moment before coming back fully dressed and carrying a bag full of books and journals.

"What?" Jae said at the quizzical looks they all shot them. "If you're going back in time to live through the events of *Song of the Drowned Gods* and find the original keys, I'm obviously coming with you. Call it academic research."

"What about the Institute?"

So much of the plan hinged on Jae's Illusion magic. But Jae only waved Baz's concern off. "Rusli is more than able to handle that. Besides, you're hilarious if you think any of us will let you go alone."

"Jae's right, Basil," Theodore said. "It's not that we don't trust you, but with so much uncertainty, it's best to have help."

"I would offer to come with," Selandyn said from where she sat, fiddling with her cane, "but I'm an old woman with unforgiving bones who wouldn't want to slow you down."

"Beatrix," Jae said, "you can't be serious. This is a once-in-a-lifetime opportunity. A scholar's dream!"

"Those books have always been *your* dream. Besides, someone needs to document what's going on *here*. This combining of worlds . . . the potential to converse with people from all over, write their stories down . . . That's *my* calling. I am, after all, an Omnilinguist." She winked at Baz. "Take note of everything you see for me, though, will you?"

For a second, Baz was transported back to Aldryn, to simpler days where he helped Professor Selandyn with her research. He'd come a long way from running mundane errands for her; it felt like she was finally letting her fledgling soar on his own.

Jae rubbed their hands together excitedly. "So how about it?"

Baz couldn't help but smile at Jae's enthusiasm. He felt the same way, excitement thrumming at his fingertips at the thought of what they were about to do.

"Whenever you're ready," Baz said, holding out the pocket watch that would take them to the location and time of their choosing—which Baz hoped extended to any *world*.

"Oh, I'm ready. I've been ready since the moment I first opened that book." Jae clasped Baz's shoulder. "Let's reclaim this adventure and make the story our own."

ROMIE

TRYING TO STOP THE DEVOURING DARKNESS WAS A futile exercise, yet Atheia persisted.

It enraged her to see all these blotches of sleepscape swallowing pieces of the world whole. They kept appearing all over, faster than they could be stopped. Lightkeeper magic seemed somewhat effective in slowing the process down, and Wardcrafters had succeeded in creating barriers over affected areas. But their magic was still too thin, too weak, able to flourish only with the help of synths that could not be produced fast enough and in large enough quantities.

Even those who'd first had their magic restored by Atheia–the Selenic Order and Tidelore members who'd been with her at Aldryn–saw their power dwindling with each day that passed, so much so that they, too, had to rely on synths again to access other tidal alignments.

So it fell to Atheia to step in however she could to protect her worlds from succumbing to the seeping dark.

She'd been doing so ever since these black holes had first appeared, sometimes alone in the middle of the night, with no one there to bear witness to her efforts, and sometimes, like today, she was in plain sight, surrounded by her Tidal Council.

They'd been alerted to a cluster of pockets that had appeared in and around Cadence—or rather, what used to be Cadence, no longer a quaint seaside town but a collection of houses and cottages that grew along the base of twin peaks, as if they'd been dropped haphazardly from the skies.

Atheia had been told that, before this, most of Cadence had suffered great damage by the flooding swell of the tides. But they'd been rebuilding, safely hidden behind wards meant to protect them from the unpredictable Aldersea. Those wards hadn't protected them from this sudden fusing together of worlds, nor had they held up against the pockets of sleepscape now threatening the town. They had appeared all over: in the skies above, eating a sizable chunk of the moss-clad mountainside; in the streets, obliterating countless thatch-roofed cottages and little gardens and shops; and at the edge of the town proper, where the Aldersea had once hugged the coast but now stood the Wychwood itself, a portion of its ancient trees swallowed by the dark.

People screamed and cried for their losses, the homes and loved ones that had been ripped away in front of their eyes. No one who had entered these rifts had gotten out. They would likely not survive the sleepscape, a place made uninhabitable for anyone but gods and Tidecallers, Dreamers and Nightmare Weavers, and the few who might be Veiled Atlas compass-bearers.

As Atheia walked the destroyed streets—all the pockets contained, for now, by her magic—she couldn't help but feel for the the victims. Their pain was her own. This destruction had to end. Yet for every rift of darkness that was stopped, a dozen others seemed to appear elsewhere. They couldn't go on like this.

These were thoughts she kept to herself as she molded her vessel's features into that of the capable deity. The Tides these people could count on, with the powerful Tidal Council at her back. Yet the quiet glares sent her way told a different story: these people, despite her eagerness to help, did not trust her as they might have once. Their faith in her was dwindling, and quickly.

A little girl appeared in her path, holding a stuffed animal. She appeared lost. Atheia glided over to her, kneeling in front of her to be at eye level.

"Dearest," she said kindly. "Where are your parents?"

The girl merely pointed at a pocket of darkness a few houses down, where it had devoured half of a squat cottage.

Bleak understanding ran like ice water through Atheia's veins. When she looked up, dozens of villagers were watching her. The hardness of their faces revealed an anger directed solely at her. It didn't matter to them who was to blame for this chaos; it only mattered that she was supposed to help keep them safe, and could not.

"Come on," a young couple said to the little girl, grabbing her by the hands and turning her away from Atheia. They glared at her as they did.

Behind her, Atheia heard her Tidal Council whispering among themselves. She spun to them to see a flash of that same doubt on their faces, before they schooled their expressions into stony masks.

"Head back to the Institute," Atheia barked at them. "Grab as many Tidecaller synths as you can and get the Regulators to come help these people erect more wards."

She didn't wait for their reply, only stormed off down an alley. She needed a reprieve from all this attention; needed to gather her thoughts and emotions before she succumbed beneath the weight of their disappointment.

She turned a corner and came to a vista overlooking the

sprawling Wychwood below, the distant Aldersea where it had been pushed back, the skies split open by constant lightning storms and patches of starry darkness that should not have been there.

Atheia wanted to cry at the mess of it all, for once at a loss about how she would fix this.

From behind her came a voice. "Excuse me, miss? Are you the one they're calling the Tides?"

Atheia shut her eyes. "I am," she bit out without turning. She didn't want anyone to see her in such a state, and wasn't sure she could stand another villager's ire. "Did you lose people here today?"

"No. I'm not from here. I came up from the Wychwood looking to understand what's happening. If you're the Tides, I wondered . . . well, I've heard stories of you before, and I thought perhaps you could help. My daughter, you see, she's been in a coma for weeks now, after being possessed by a demon."

Demon. This girl must be a hellwraith, then, a witch sullied by the mark Sidraeus had left on the Wychwood. A perversion of the magic Atheia herself had created there. This girl was one of *his*, just like the Eclipse-born were. The idea crossed her mind to follow the witch to her estate, if only to snatch up her daughter and bring her to the Institute to torment as she had the Night Bringer's beasts.

Atheia finally turned to the witch. The woman was middle-aged, and her manner of dress was different from that of the residents of Cadence, pulled from a different world. Her eyes widened at the sight of Atheia, something desperate and wild and hopeful on her face.

"Romie?" the witch breathed.

Atheia froze, trying to search Romie's memories to determine who this was. There was magic to the woman. It smelled of verdant things, of damp soil and ancient trees. The name came to her in a flurry of memories.

Hazel Amberyl. The High Matriarch of the Wychwood.

Something inside her fought to the surface with surprising rigor. It was Romie but not. It was an echo of the bone key, the witch whose name had been Aspen. Atheia could feel memories surge behind her eyes: a bond between two sisters and their authoritative mother, a sense of fierce protectiveness she had rarely felt before. It rooted her in place, made her vessel's consciousness slip between the cracks enough for her to shout a warning.

"RUN, MRS. AMBERYL. I'M POSSESSED BY–"

Atheia fought to control the reins again, but the damage was done, the witch stumbling back from her as if she'd seen a ghost. Atheia tried to move in her direction, but Romie took over once more, making it impossible to take a single step.

The witch *ran.* By the time Atheia stomped her vessel deep down and was about to follow, going after the witch didn't matter anymore. Because a voice that felt like the moon itself, quiet and mercurial, rose from behind Atheia, so impossible that it knocked her entire world off its axis.

"Hello, daughter."

Atheia turned, thinking she must have imagined it, because there was no way that the being that voice belonged to was here, and no way she would call Atheia *daughter* despite her somewhat motherly inclination toward her.

Indeed, it was not the goddess of the moon who stood before her but a young man, a boy really, with blond curls and a fair complexion. There was a Waning Moon tattoo on his hand, marking him as a lunar mage. His eyes were like quicksilver, flashing too unnaturally to go unnoticed. And paired with the lilt of his voice, the words he'd used . . .

The goddess of the moon, wearing the face of a vessel much like

Atheia was, smiled knowingly at her quiet realization. "We are so pleased to see you."

She pulled Atheia in for an embrace, and when Atheia breathed her in, she could smell the moon itself, feel the goddess as she remembered her, as if the goddess's very essence had erased every bit of the vessel until it was only her, despite the unrecognizable features. Atheia couldn't help but fold into her embrace, realizing just how starved for affection she had become since being put back together in this body.

When the goddess pulled away, her eyes shifted, her essence changed, so that in quick succession the vessel became each of the other three gods of the living. The goddess of the earth smiling fondly at her; the god of the sun giving her a stoic nod; the god of the air winking at her as if they shared a secret. And then it was as if all four of them shared space at once in this vessel of theirs, his eyes bright with power, his features an amalgamation of these presences inside him.

"How can this be?" Atheia breathed. "I thought Clover had destroyed you all."

"He took our godly might from us, yes," they said in a voice that was layered and beautiful, a mixture of all their voices. "But even he could not kill immortal gods. And yet we find ourselves not quite immortal anymore, either."

Atheia gaped at them. "Not immortal—what does that mean?"

"The false god took our immortality when he stole our power. So long as we were confined in the abyss, we remained invulnerable, but here in the mortal realms? We could very well meet our end if we're not careful—which is why we have our emissary here to act as our vessel until we find a way to stop the false god for good."

They gently touched Atheia's cheek. "Will you help us, daughter?"

There was such genuine affection in that gesture, such hope shining in their shifting eyes, that Atheia could almost believe it to be sincere. She *wanted* it to be. This was what she had craved all her life, she realized. To be loved by these gods who had created her instead of being a mere instrument through which they ruled over their realms.

But the sincerity behind their words and expressions turned foul. Atheia knew they did not love her. They simply needed her, just like they'd needed her to splinter herself into pieces back then to save them all.

Atheia guarded her heart against this gutting realization. "How would you propose I help you?"

"Only the joint forces of the living and sleeping realms can defeat the false god now. We can't access the godsworld we've been cast out of nor wrest our godhood back without you and Sidraeus." A tilt of their head. "Rumor has it you've captured him. We would very much like to . . . say hello."

"Sidraeus is mine and mine alone to deal with." Vehemence seeped through Atheia's words. Doubt shadowed her thoughts. Was there another angle to their desire to see him–to this plea for her to cooperate? "I refuse to work with him, and trust me when I say he would do the same."

"From what we remember, you could be very persuasive," the gods said. "Have you lost your edge, Atheia? Have you given yourself so completely over to revenge that, like mortals, you are unable to keep a level head? Surely you can put such emotions aside to help us. Surely you can see that only by restoring our godhood, reclaiming the godsworld, purifying the fountain, we can save these worlds you so dearly love."

They looked around pointedly at the broken worlds before them, the haunting skies, the pockets of darkness. "Because clearly, your methods have not been successful so far. The people who once worshipped you are losing faith in you with each day that passes without you bringing them a viable solution to their catastrophic problems. Don't you wish to save them before it's too late?"

Atheia felt like a child being put in her place. Anger boiled inside her as she could see her agenda slipping, all her hard work swiped aside for these gods, just as it had always been. They called, she answered. Their needs, she saw to. Their will was hers, and she could not deny them even if she tried.

So you do know how that feels, Romie's voice echoed in her mind.

Atheia had lost focus—had become unbalanced with the arrival of the gods, letting Romie's consciousness slip through the cracks. She shoved her back with a hissed *Quiet*, her mind racing to come up with a plan. She refused to let Sidraeus go free. And yet the gods could help expedite her plan to eradicate him and his magic.

"Equilibris wants to send these worlds into oblivion and start fresh," the gods pressed. "You see? The realms are already fighting for dominance because of what the false god has done, and it will only fuel Equilibris to put an end to all of it. We must restore things to what they were before he can do so."

Atheia clenched her fists. "I thought I stopped that from happening the first time around when I splintered myself. When *you* convinced me that so long as a piece of me existed in each world, Equilibris could not wipe the board clean."

"It seems we may have been wrong."

She couldn't fathom the idea that her splintered existence might have been for nothing. But hearing the gods admit fault swayed her. "If I help you," she said slowly, "if I get Sidraeus to assist in defeating Clover, will you help *me* eradicate him and his abominations?"

"Of course," the gods said, stroking Atheia's cheek again. "We will trap him forevermore in the sleepscape, unable to visit the realms of the living, if this is what you desire. We will give you a bigger role than you've previously had, if you ask it of us. Anything for you, daughter of ours."

Atheia saw the truth beneath their honeyed words, that they

were still using her as a means to an end. But if it meant their goals were aligned, then it was worth becoming their instrument once more.

If they held up their end of the bargain.

Atheia lifted her chin. "I'll help you," she said. "But not before I finish what I've started here."

Something like anger flashed in the gods' eyes. "The more we wait, the more the worlds of the living will suffer."

If they had possessed the kind of power they did before Clover stole it from them, Atheia might have been scared of them. They could have forced her to do what they wanted. Could have dragged her to the gates of the godsworld without so much as lifting a finger. But they'd lost so much power, all they had left was this ability to manipulate their emissary. To all but *beg* for Atheia's help.

The thought sent a little thrill down her spine.

"Surely saving the worlds can wait until the evening," Atheia said sweetly. "Meet me at the Institute at sundown, and I will come with you to the godsworld." She turned her back to the gods' dumbfounded emissary, smiling to herself as she added, "I have business to take care of until then."

The gods had one thing right: her methods were not successful. The blood she'd taken from Emory, the power she'd restored to her faithful lunar mages . . . It was not the solution she hoped it would be, so perhaps it was time she put an end to the Tidecaller. And once Sidraeus was thoroughly broken by the pain of such a loss, then she would turn him over to the gods and gladly help them reclaim their power.

Atheia was on her way to Emory's room when an explosion rocked the Institute.

Her first thought as she righted herself in the ensuing chaos—clouds of dust and debris hanging heavy in the corridor, a buzz in her ears, muffled shouting nearby—was that a slew of sleepscape pockets must have appeared.

Her second thought was for her prisoners: if they had been swallowed up in these black holes, if she'd *lost* them, all her plans would be disrupted.

Atheia stumbled to the nearest prisoner wing, every nerve within her strung with anxious tension. A couple of Regulators emerged from the heavy dust clouds, coughing and bewildered.

"What happened?" Atheia urged them.

"We don't know," one of them wheezed. "Our security systems went dark, and then—"

There was a loud roar from somewhere deeper in the Institute. The Eclipse wing? Fury swept through Atheia. "Gather all the guards," she told the Regulators, "and make sure no one leaves."

She stepped into the veil of dust, using her magic to clear it as she went. What she found made her stop short, fury mounting to its highest peak within her.

Two figures dressed in charcoal Regulator uniforms stood before the cell where Emory's friends were being kept. But they were no Regulators. One was a Luaguan boy she didn't recognize; the other, a girl Romie had known as Vera, crouched over the lock of the cell as she tried to pick it open.

The Luaguan boy was the first to notice her, his head snapping in her direction. "She's here," he said in useless warning.

Everyone looked at her except for Vera, who kept picking at the lock, tongue trapped between her lips in concentration. Atheia didn't waste any more time. She gathered power around her—tendrils of dark and light and death—and snarled as she angled it toward them, ready to unleash it.

The lock clicked open. One of the prisoners burst out of the cell, putting herself directly in the line of fire of Atheia's magic, hands extended out, yelling at her to stop. It was Nisha. Somewhere deep within her, Romie screamed as Atheia moved to unleash her magic, delighting in the way Nisha simply closed her eyes, as if accepting her own death.

"I love you, Romie Brysden," the girl whispered, opening her eyes again to peer at her. "You said to tell you when we woke, so here I am, begging you to hear me."

The magic at Atheia's fingertips died as those words reached Romie like a hand pulling a drowning girl up onto solid land. All at once, Romie was present enough to wrest control of her own body, pushing Atheia's consciousness down, down, down.

"What did you say?" Romie croaked, stumbling over her own voice.

Nisha's face shone with bewilderment. A sob escaped her lips as she reached for Romie, hugging her close. "I love you." She said it again and again in Romie's ear like a prayer, impossible words Romie had heard in a dream and had stopped hoping she would ever hear in waking. Words that had coaxed her out from the unfathomable depths Atheia had pushed her into.

Romie's arms wound tightly around Nisha, fearing this was all going to be swept away from her at any second. Wanting to hold on to her forever yet knowing forever didn't exist. "I love you, too," she whispered, nestling her nose in Nisha's hair, breathing her in, branding this moment into her very soul so she would have this, at least; so she could revisit this in her dreams, again and again.

Atheia's rage was growing inside her, threatening to overthrow her control. Romie pulled away, her gaze landing on the woman hovering close who looked so much like Emory.

"You're Adriana," Romie whispered. Or Luce, as Kai had called her when he'd told Romie she'd been helping him with the escape plan.

Emory's mother gave her a wobbly smile. "Can you believe the nightmare boy actually came through for us?"

A disbelieving laugh bubbled past Romie's lips. The thought that this had all started with Romie and Kai venturing into the sleepscape together to find the epilogue that had been in Adriana's possession...

"Where is Kai?" Romie asked, noting his absence.

"He's taking care of the Eclipse wing," Vera said with a crooked smile. "Along with some help."

"And Baz?"

"He's fine," the Luaguan boy said. At Romie's quizzical brow, he added, "Sorry, I'm Rusli. The Illusionist who's going to get you all out of here undetected."

The sudden reality of it all fell in Romie's stomach like a weight. She turned to Nisha. "You have to get Emory out." She took the key that hung around her neck and pressed it into Nisha's hand, telling them where Emory was being held.

Nisha frowned at her. "You're coming with us."

Romie shook her head, holding back tears. "I can't. Atheia's already fighting for control, and I can't have her ruining your escape."

"No," Nisha said. "I'm not leaving you."

But Romie had already backed up into the open cell, motioning at Vera to lock her in.

Nisha launched herself at the bars. "Romie, don't do this."

"I have to." She felt Atheia clawing inside her, getting closer and closer to the surface. She wouldn't be able to hang on much longer, not against the will of a deity. "This won't hold her for long, but it'll give you all a head start."

There was the click of a lock. Romie reached through the bars for Nisha's face, wiping away her tears, forcing the girl of her dreams to look at her one last time. "I love you," Romie said again, desperately holding on to herself long enough to go in for a hasty, fervent kiss, to feel the salt of tears on her tongue and the silky feel of hair through her fingers.

Romie broke away with a frustrated gasp as Atheia's consciousness began to dawn. "Go!" she yelled at Nisha, at all her friends.

The last thing she saw was the girl she loved tearing down the corridor with the others before Atheia took control once more.

In the confines of her own mind, Romie couldn't help but smile at the luck she'd had to have this one win.

Luck. Or perhaps something greater.

EMORY

SHE SAW NO ONE IN HER SLEEP AFTER THAT FIRST VISIT from her ghosts. There was no reprieve to be found here from the pain she experienced in waking, no one to lean on but her own self and the darkness that was pressing in at the edges of this endless, empty nightmare.

Sometimes, that darkness taunted her with words meant to be encouraging. "Don't give up hope," it said. "We'll find a way out of this."

It was laughable, the way her subconscious wielded her loneliness against her. The way it made her crave the dark nothingness beyond the dream, made her wonder what it would be like to step into its embrace and simply disappear.

"WAKE UP."

Emory jerked awake but found herself restrained by binds tying her to the gurney. Her own face was leaning over her, hands shaking her gently. Was this a dream, still? Or was she dead, seeing a copy of herself, her soul perhaps, as it left her mortal body behind?

Tears welled in the copy's eyes. "She's awake."

Emory blinked away the grogginess of sleep and realized that this was no copy of herself. This was her mother, her features so similar to her own that it was no wonder she'd mistaken her. But surely this couldn't be real.

A second face appeared next to Luce's. Nisha. Another impossibility.

"How did you manage to get free?" Emory croaked, her voice broken from disuse.

"They had a little help," a third voice piped in.

Vera. Vera was here, but she couldn't be. Had she been captured that night everything went wrong, along with Jae and the other Eclipse-born?

Emory peered at the door, where her other friends stood. Virgil and Ife and Javier. And—Rusli? The Illusionist gave her a wink. It was hard to reconcile the Eclipse boy she'd come to know at the safe house with this version of him here, wearing a Regulator uniform. Vera, too, wore a similar uniform.

Emory felt the faintest hope blossom as she began to understand what was happening.

Help had come. She wasn't alone after all.

"How did you get past Atheia?" she asked.

"I got through to Romie," Nisha said while Vera tried to pick open the metal binds around Emory's ankles. "She let us go."

Romie wants you to know she's fighting Atheia with everything she has, the ghost of Tol had said to her in a dream. Her subconscious trying to find hope to latch on to, however false. But could they really trust Romie's good intentions if Atheia was still running things? She said as much to Nisha, but Nisha wouldn't hear it.

"We can trust her," she said with conviction.

"Damn it," Vera cried, still trying and failing to pick through the metal restraints. "I can't—"

"Move over, darling," came another voice, and suddenly Virgil was at Emory's side. There was a flash of something like pity in his eyes as he took in the sight of her, the blood vials next to her. Pity turned to fury, his nostrils flaring. And then, without a blink from him, without even the need for bloodletting to access whatever meager Reaper magic he might have left, he rusted through the metal restraints.

Emory gaped at him as she sat up, rubbing at her sore wrists. "How..."

"We sort of had to resort to synths. The Tidecaller kind made with your blood."

The kind that let them access all magics.

Virgil made a face. "Sorry. If it's any consolation, it's really watered down. I can already feel it fading after using it just once."

"It was either that or attempt this jailbreak powerless," Vera said matter-of-factly. She grabbed one of the vials containing a Tidecaller synth and slipped it to Emory. "Take it. We need you powered up more than anyone."

Emory stared at the vial in her hand. The U-shaped brand scarring her sigil glared back at her. She knew the synth would make any lunar mage super-powered, but the thought of having to resort to it now... this ghost of her own magic...

Her mother squeezed her hand, the gesture so full of understanding that it almost made the pain of losing her magic bearable.

"We're running out of time," came Ife's voice. She stood in the doorframe with Javier, both of them throwing nervous glances down the hall. "We need to move. Quickly."

With some help, Emory got down from the gurney. She wobbled on unsteady limbs, holding on tightly to her friends, as Vera injected her with the Tidecaller synth. Emory winced at the needle—then felt a trickle of magic go through her, familiar yet so *wrong*, twisted by Atheia's own power. Emory called on the healing magic she'd always known, willing strength back into her body.

Virgil was right: the power in the synth was incredibly diluted. This was nothing like the generous dose of power Atheia had given to her faithfuls back at Aldryn. Emory could already feel the magic slipping away, so she used it sparingly, keeping it for when it was needed.

"Someone's coming," Javier whispered. Looking at Emory, he asked, "You ready to run?"

She gave a weak shake of her head. "If Atheia's out there, we're not making it out of here." Especially not if their escape plan hinged on this diluted magic.

"Oh, we're getting out of here," Virgil said with a forced airiness in his tone. "And then we'll have a nice meal and the rest of that moonbrew back at the safe house and pretend all this unpleasantness never happened."

A shout echoed down the hall. Rusli blanched. "Let's go."

Adrenaline shot through Emory, enough that she could keep up the pace with Nisha and Virgil, who were still holding her upright as they darted out of the room. At one end of the corridor were Regulators coming their way, forcing them to head in the opposite direction—only to come face-to-face with more Regulators.

Vines shot forth from one, wrapping around Ife's ankle and making her fall. When Javier swung at another, his fist connected with a protective ward that the Regulator put up. And yet another told them to "stop moving," his voice laced with Glamour magic.

A quick glance at the Regulators' hands was proof enough that none of them should be able to wield these powers that did not belong to their lunar houses. They must have taken synths. And now Emory and her friends were unable to move.

Another Regulator appeared, his walk slow and deliberate as he advanced on them. There was an air of authority about him, and his beady eyes shone with gleeful malice as he called magic to him.

Emory would recognize the cold power of death anywhere. A Reaper's touch, even if a fabricated one. He was going to kill them—and the other Regulators were going to stand there and let it happen.

She didn't pause to think. She might have been Glamoured not to move, but no one said anything about not using magic. And so, before the beady-eyed Regulator could unleash death upon her and her friends, she called on every bit of synthetic power inside her, molding it into her very own Reaper magic, and sent it flying toward the man.

He fell with a grunt, clutching at his chest. And as the other Regulators flocked to him in concern and shouted for help—he wasn't dead yet, the synthetic magic not strong enough to give him a swift death—Emory waited for remorse to seize her, but all she felt was numb. *I did what I had to,* she told herself. She caught Virgil's eye and knew he understood.

Everything happened too quickly then as more Regulators surrounded them. Someone compelled them not to use magic, but it didn't matter now anyway, because Emory had no fight in her, not a drop of synthetic power left. All she could do was watch, defeated, as one of the Regulators reached for damper cuffs, knowing she would be brought back to that sterile room, and her friends to wherever prison they'd been held in. And if it was true that Nisha had broken through to Romie, Emory doubted she would be able to do so again.

They were going to die here, she thought.

Her eye caught on a sign that pointed toward the Eclipse wing—the one where those who'd Collapsed were held. She knew others must be here. Maybe even those she'd come to see as allies and friends. Had Baz been taken? His father? Jae? Kai?

And what of Sidraeus?

If her fate was to remain here with them all, then so be it. She was one of them, and she wouldn't leave them behind even if she could.

Before the cold metal of the damper cuffs could touch her wrists, chaos erupted around them, the floor beneath their feet trembling and sending them all tumbling. The power went out; darkness swept over them, the air full of dust. It had Emory thinking of Clover's ash-umbrae. But as a familiar face materialized in the chaos, a man she recognized climbing out of the dust and dark holding an everlight lantern, she knew these weren't allies of Clover.

Baz's father heaved a sigh as he spotted them. "Thank the Shadow." His mouth tightened as his eyes landed on the Regulators who'd been knocked by the blast. The beady-eyed one Emory had used Reaper magic on apparently refused to die; he was already up on his feet, still clutching painfully at his chest.

Theodore blanched. "Drutten."

The Regulator blinked at the name, gaping at Theodore. His dazed expression sharpened into one of fury. "I know you," he said. "Eclipse scum–"

Before he could utter another word or reach for his damper cuffs, a dagger embedded itself in his chest, drawing a muffled whimper from his lips as he toppled to the floor.

Behind Theodore, arm still outstretched from where she'd thrown the dagger with lethal precision, was a girl armed to the teeth, draconic wings tucked close against her back. And at Ivayne's side stood Kai in armor of his own, looking like a vengeful warrior pulled from a nightmare.

Emory watched, half thinking she was still dreaming, as Ivayne made quick work of the other Regulators. None of this was possible, and yet the blood staining the floor red was real, and so was the feel of Kai as he reached for her, grabbing her by the arms to force her to look at him. He was saying something to her, but all Emory could hear was the sound of her own heartbeat, the ringing in her ears, the little voice inside her that kept telling her this was all in her head, that no one was here to rescue her, that all of this was false, false, false.

A loud roar sounded from somewhere in the Institute, snapping Emory out of it.

"That would be Gwenhael," she heard Ivayne say with a toothy grin as she wiped her daggers on her shin. "Tore the roof off the Eclipse wing. Couldn't pass up the opportunity to be part of another jailbreak."

Emory couldn't begin to make sense of this. Draconics and dragons here in this world . . . "How is this possible?" she breathed, looking up at Kai.

As if satisfied she'd finally snapped out of her daze, Kai let her go. "Haven't you heard the worlds got fused together?"

"Fused together?" Virgil repeated. "As in—"

"As in there's no time to explain," Ivayne interrupted, "just accept that we're here to save your asses."

"Come on," Theodore urged them all, eyes darting to a corridor where they could hear the sound of Regulators coming their way. "We're getting all of you out of here."

They started toward the Eclipse wing. There, all the cells had been opened and people were flocking toward a tear in the wall at the end of the corridor, where gray skies promised freedom. Over their heads was Gwenhael, the dragon resplendent and so entirely out of place it might have been funny under any other circumstance.

While their group started to climb atop Gwenhael's back, Emory turned frantically to Kai. "Where's Baz?"

"He's not here. We're meant to reconvene at the safe house."

As Kai started to move away from her—away from Gwenhael and the promise of freedom—desperation seized her again. "Where are *you* going?"

"I'm not letting a single Eclipse-born stay in here." Fury was written all over Kai's face. His eyes cut to the Unhallowed Seal on her hand. "And once I'm sure everyone's out, then I'm gonna tear this place down. No Eclipse-born will ever again go through what we did."

Theodore extended a hand to Emory, motioning for her to get on Gwenhael next. But Emory shook her head, taking a step toward Kai. "I'm not leaving here without getting Sidraeus out too."

"Then I'm staying with you." This came from her mother as she slid off Gwenhael and landed next to Emory. "I'm not abandoning you again."

A swell of emotions rose in Emory—and then, a wave of power hit her. She fell to her knees with a scream. She recognized this power as Atheia's before that cold voice of hers sounded behind her.

"You're not going anywhere, Tidethief."

Emory turned pleading eyes to Luce and Theodore and Kai. "Go," she managed. "Leave before she—"

But Theodore was looking wide-eyed at Atheia.

At this deity wearing his daughter's face.

"Rosemarie," he breathed, taking a careless, mindless step toward her. "My brave girl, if you're still in there . . ."

Romie's features contorted with Atheia's hatred. Power gathered around her. And Emory, fearing she would unleash it upon Theodore, threw herself between them.

"Ro, please." She knew Romie would never forgive herself if any harm came to her father by her own hand. She had already hurt enough people she loved; this would be too much, the drop of water that would make the whole dam explode.

She might have imagined the flicker of brown in Atheia's kaleidoscope eyes, a moment of horror that was all Romie's, before Atheia's anger took over again. In a flash, she was standing a hairsbreadth from Emory, both hands wrapped tightly around her neck, squeezing with a force that lifted Emory off her feet. Distantly, Emory was aware of Kai and Luce and Theodore trying to reach her, but they froze, held there by some kind of compulsion wielded by Atheia.

"I should have killed you the moment I took your blood," Atheia snarled at Emory. "Keeping you alive is more trouble than you're worth."

Emory flailed against her hold and then sputtered out a scream as that bright, burning light shot out of Atheia's hands, singeing the tender skin on her neck. She couldn't muster up words now, could only claw at Romie's arms, hoping against all hope that her friend was still in there; that she would wrest control of her body and stop Atheia.

But the pain was too much. The hunger in Atheia's eyes too real.

Emory was going to die at the hands of her best friend, with both of them powerless to stop it.

Her feet struck the ground, her limbs folding beneath her, sending her sprawling on the floor. Emory gasped in pained breaths, scrambling backward to get away from Atheia. But Atheia wasn't paying attention to her anymore. In her slip of attention, her compulsion on Kai, Luce, and Theodore must have severed, because they were kneeling at Emory's side. The four of them watched Atheia snarling at the object of her distraction: a boy with blond curls and eyes of shifting colors who seemed to have appeared out of nowhere.

The sound that spilled from his lips was unnatural, a layering of disapproving voices that slithered down Emory's spine. "So this is the business you said you'd take care of? Revenge is such a mortal emotion. We thought you'd rise above it."

"You had no right to stop me," Atheia hissed. "Now get out of my way so I can finish what I started."

"We can't let you hurt the girl." The boy studied Emory with interest, and she couldn't help but think she'd seen him before.

"Why not?" Atheia said through gritted teeth. "She's a Tidecaller— the last remaining one."

"And it's come to our attention that Equilibris wants her dead for that very reason. If she perishes, he'll find a way to finally end the worlds, reset everything. Surely you don't want that any more than we do."

Fury distorted every feature of Atheia's. She looked like she was about to hurl herself at Emory again, until Kai drew himself to his feet in front of Emory.

The boy smiled wickedly at Kai. "We see you've found a way out of the abyss."

"No thanks to you assholes," Kai sneered. "I'm including Farran in that statement, in case your vessel can hear me."

Emory's sneaking suspicion solidified at their exchange. These were the *gods*—and this boy they were using as their vessel was Farran Caine, who was meant to be dead.

The gods squinted at Kai as if trying to figure him out, that smile never slipping from their face. "Those tattoos of yours," they said. "Where did a mortal like yourself learn the language of the gods?"

Kai arched a brow. "They're old Luaguan symbols."

"No," the gods said. "That's the divine alphabet of our language. No one is meant to know it but those who are divine. Unless someone introduced it in these worlds long ago."

Their eyes cut to Atheia at this. She watched Kai's tattoos with knitted brows, a flash of something like guilt in her eyes. She steeled herself, jutting her chin out.

"Why are we discussing this?" Atheia asked. "I said I'd come with you after I wrapped up loose ends here." She looked at Emory, her intention clear: *she* was the loose end that needed tying.

Before the gods answered, their head whipped to the side, as if they sensed something coming down a corridor. Their face turned white as a sheet.

"He's here," they said, voice full of terror. "The false god."

An unnatural cold suddenly swept over the corridor. A foul current that felt like death, like the abyss itself.

The gods lunged for Atheia, grabbing her wrist in a desperate plea. "Enough of this," they hissed at her. "Tell us where Sidraeus is and let us finish this before the false god comes."

But they were too late. Specters appeared all around them, wraithlike and translucent and skeletal. They were more terrifying than any umbra, ash or otherwise, and more haunting than any ghost, somehow a nightmarish combination of the two.

And at their helm was Clover, looking like the vengeful god he was.

KAI

CLOVER AMBLED OVER TO THEM, WATCHING FARRAN'S face closely. If he recognized any part of Thames's soul there, he didn't let it show. "You must be the gods of living," Clover said. "A bit rude of you not to show your faces to welcome me in your midst. I would even say cowardly of you not to appear in the flesh."

"We call it self-preservation," the gods said, plastering on a pleasant smile that rang false.

Kai knew fear intimately. And it was fear he sensed coming from the gods. They were properly scared of Clover–of what he might do to them, whether they were in a vessel or not. It was a risk for them to be here at all, not knowing the full extent of Clover's new godly powers. And they were still weak–still at a disadvantage.

Clover seemed to sense that. He didn't waste any more words. One second, he stood in the corridor surrounded by ghosts, and the next, he was standing in front of the gods, trapping them in the middle of a whirlwind of spectral monsters, about to deliver a death blow.

"Please." The sob that escaped Farran's mouth was so human, it took Kai aback. "Don't kill me again."

And it *was* Farran staring back at Clover, with eyes once more a deep blue—as if the gods had been cast out of him.

Clover stumbled back. "Who are you?"

It was Kai who answered: "He's the reincarnation of someone you once claimed to love. Someone you chose to betray at the last, before you watched him die."

Clover actually blanched. "Thames?"

"Yes," Farran confirmed. "It's me, Cornelius."

For a second, all of Clover's monstrosity seemed to fade away, replaced by a storm of emotions Kai wouldn't have thought him possible of feeling anymore. The spectral whirlwind around Farran disappeared as Clover lost himself in his memories, staring at the face of a boy that was unrecognizable, yet held something so familiar.

Farran took a hesitant step toward Clover, just as many emotions playing on his face. "You lost your humanity long before what you did to me, but I always thought there was hope for you. I always believed in you. But now look at you."

"Now I'm a *god*," Clover said defensively.

"A god who shed layers of his humanity with each life he took. You've lost yourself. If Cordelia could see you now . . ."

The sliver of humanity that had appeared in Clover was gone again in a flash. He slammed a fist on Farran's chest, and a rush of power blasted through him, making Farran's head tilt backward with a scream. Clover pummeled him again and again with deadly vengeance, with wild abandon, until Farran's face was a bloodied mess and he fell limply to the ground, unconscious.

Over his body, as if ripped from their vessel by the force of Clover's attack, were the faint outlines of the four gods as they had appeared in the abyss. They seemed like ghosts themselves, faint echoes of their true forms, and as Clover locked eyes on them, realizing that he hadn't killed them—that he'd only managed to hurt their vessel and separate them from him in the process—he turned his sights on them instead. Ready to imbibe the last echo of their power and rise as the one god, the sole ruler of the living realms.

Atheia stood between Clover and the vulnerable, untethered gods. And while their powers clashed, the gods dissolved, turning into specks of colorful dust just as they had in the abyss. Faster than any of them could stop them, they swept out of the corridor, disappearing out of sight.

Clover swore as he tried to get past Atheia to go after them. But there was nothing to go after; the gods were as immaterial as the wind, until they could find another vessel. Clover fell to his knees at Farran's side, something like regret flashing on his face.

From where he stood, Kai couldn't tell if Farran was still breathing. *Please be alive,* he thought, all the anger and resentment he'd felt toward him fading. Because damn it, even if Farran had hurt him, even if he'd played right into the gods' plans and got Kai and Luce trapped in the abyss, Kai couldn't *not* care.

And as he watched Clover's expression turn raw and vicious and monstrous again, Kai understood this would only fuel Clover to hunt down the gods even more. Because if Farran—Thames—was dead once again, Clover would blame the gods. They had forced his hand. And now he would get revenge.

Clover turned to Atheia, hissing, "You're wasted on them, you know. What did they tell you to get you to do their bidding this time?"

The answer slipped from Atheia's mouth as if under compulsion. "That only I and Sidraeus can defeat you."

"And how will that work, do you think?" He didn't give her the chance to answer. "The gods mean to spill both your blood into the fountain and take the invaluable source of power you form together for themselves. *That's* how you defeat me. By bleeding for them. *Dying* for them. All so they can make themselves powerful enough to defeat me."

Emotions played on Atheia's face like shifting waters. "You're lying."

Clover's mouth curled. His silence seemed like enough to sow seeds of doubt in Atheia, whose breathing was labored as her world came crashing down around her.

Footsteps sounded down the corridor. Regulators were barreling toward them. They stopped short as they took in the scene: Kai, Emory, Luce, and Theodore cowering in a corner; Clover kneeling in Farran's blood; Atheia standing over them, looking distraught.

Clover rose to his feet and turned to the Regulators. As if needing a release for his fury, he unleashed his specters on them.

They perished in a cloud of dust and death, their screams filling the hallway until they were no more. And when it was done, Clover was gone.

Kai didn't care about anything then. He rushed to Farran's side, checking for signs of life. Relief washed through him as he felt a pulse. "He's still alive." To Emory, Luce, and Theodore, he said, "We need to get him out of here."

"We have no use for him now."

Kai's head snapped up, dread making his blood run cold. The multilayered voices of the gods had come from Emory's mouth.

They had found a new vessel.

EMORY

EMORY GASPED AS AN ANCIENT, POWERFUL PRESENCE filled her mind. Every fiber of her being felt *alive*, burning with a power too great for her to contain, a divinity as endless and enduring as the moon and the earth and the sun and the skies, as every living thing nature had ever contained.

"Take us to Sidraeus."

The words spilled out of Emory's mouth in the voices of the gods, sharp and quiet and rough and mercurial all at once. Shock and betrayal shone on Atheia's face as she stared at Emory–at the gods now overriding her.

"Is it true?" Atheia breathed. "What Clover said–is that what you intend to do with Sidraeus and me? Sacrifice us so you can defeat him?"

"Of course not." Emory felt herself take a step toward Atheia, spreading her arms in a gesture of innocence. *"Don't listen to the false god's lies, daughter. You are a part of us we do not wish to see harmed."*

Their honeyed words seemed to appease some of Atheia's doubts, but Emory could feel their deceit on her tongue.

"*Take us to Sidraeus,*" the gods said again, "*and we will let you do what you please with this one once we have returned to the godsworld and are strong enough to take our own forms again.*"

This one.

They meant Emory.

The hunger on Atheia's face made it clear she was on board. She stepped over Farran's body, silencing the pleas from Luce and the angry protest from Kai with her magic. Emory tried to look at Kai, tried to convey to him to leave with her mother and Theodore, to get out of here without her before it was too late. She wanted to scream at Atheia that the gods were manipulating her, that Clover had been right. But she wasn't in control of her body. She was powerless to do anything as her feet moved of their own volition, as the gods followed Atheia down the foreboding corridor littered with dead Regulators.

Sidraeus was held in a dark cell, in a part of the Institute that felt older than the rest, like catacombs beneath it, cold and damp and chilling. He stood there suspended by chains, hands and feet bound, limbs drawn taut. His head hung limply, as if he'd been put to sleep, or worse.

Pain and misery hung thick in the air. There were no visible wounds on Sidraeus except for the raw, burnt skin around his wrists and ankles—because woven with the metal chains were veins of the same bright, burning light Atheia had used to singe Emory's own skin.

Emory wanted to go to him, wanted to lash out at Atheia for what she'd done to him, but the gods inside her wouldn't relinquish control.

"*It seems you've been having your fun with him,*" they said, tilting Emory's head quizzically to peer at Sidraeus. "*What kind of spell do you have him under that he remains so weak and docile?"*

"I have him trapped in his own mind," Atheia said. "Living in the prison of his own worst memories." She hesitated to unbind him, turning to Emory—to the gods. "How can I trust you'll let me kill her when earlier you didn't want me to? You said Equilibris needs her dead to reset the worlds."

Yes, Emory thought. *Poke holes in their logic. They're lying to you.*

The gods spoke through her. *"By then we will have regained our godhood, and the false god will be dead. The worlds will be restored, and it won't matter then if the Tidecaller is gone. Equilibris will have no reason to reset the worlds if we set them right ourselves."*

Still, Atheia hesitated for a beat more before steely resolution had her turning to Sidraeus, hands extended to untie him.

Panic seized Emory. If the gods got what they wanted, they would kill Atheia and Sidraeus. They would kill *Romie*. And once they were done with Emory as their temporary vessel, it wouldn't matter if she lived or died, because her best friend would be gone.

Romie had fought back against Atheia in order to get her friends freed. And if she could fight, then Emory could do the same for her.

She had no magic. She had no power against the gods impressing their will on hers. Still, she fought for words, a desperate plea, a shot in the dark. It rang in the echo chamber of her mind again and again.

Please help me.

She didn't expect it to slip past her lips, to hear her own voice sounding in her ears. There was a familiar prickling at her wrist, where the Selenic Mark shone in a light she had never seen from it before. It echoed the spirals on Sidraeus, which suddenly flared with the same bright light.

She felt them then—an echo of the souls of the very first Tidecallers rising around her. As if her plea had called on them, just like the syrinx had done.

Perhaps the bargain she'd made tied their essence to her just as much as it tied them to Sidraeus, and they were here to help her now. To help them both.

Symbols appeared all over her skin, looking, she thought, like the tattoos Kai had on his collarbone.

The language of the gods.

They burst with a light so bright it hurt her eyes, and the scream that tore from her throat was somehow her own voice and the gods' combined. But she felt the gods' presence receding, shying away from that light, as if the symbols that the souls of the Tidecallers had manifested on Emory were a mark of protection against them. A ward that cast the gods out of her entirely, until she was just herself again.

Herself, but not entirely alone, and not at all powerless.

Emory flung herself at Atheia, gripping her wrists tight, hoping against all hope that whatever power had evicted the gods from her body could free Romie, too.

"Let go of me." The words slithered out of Atheia, those kaleidoscope eyes burning with the fury of a thousand suns.

"Not until you give her back to me."

But the symbols on Emory's arms were already extinguished, their presence gone as quickly as it had come. She could no longer feel the souls of the Tidecallers.

Atheia seemed to realize this—how powerless Emory now was—and sent her flying across the corridor. Death magic gathered in her hands as she towered over Emory.

"The gods lied to you," Emory said in a desperate attempt to stop her. "Clover had it right. They mean to kill you and Sidraeus."

"I don't believe you."

"I *felt* their lie on my tongue. Heard their thoughts in my mind."

Atheia didn't seem to care. But before she could deliver her death blow, a resounding "No!" erupted from her.

From *Romie*, who had wrested control of her body and was staring at Emory now through big, brown eyes.

"Go, Em," she said. "Leave now before—"

Her eyes shifted to that kaleidoscope again, indicating Atheia had taken over. *"Quiet,"* she seethed, seemingly talking to herself. Her eyes shifted back to brown again as Romie screamed, and again back to Atheia, in a painful looking battle of wills.

"Emory!"

She whipped around to see Kai and Luce barreling toward her. Her heart sank. They were supposed to leave her here and escape with the others. Where Theodore and Farran had gone, she didn't know.

"What are you—"

It came without sound, a spot of darkness right behind Kai and Luce that bloomed and grew. It swallowed part of the ceiling, swallowed the corridor they had emerged from, the everlight lanterns fixed to the wall. Rock crumbling all around it, sucked *into* it. Like a pocket of sleepscape that was looking to devour the living.

Kai and Luce jumped out of the way with not a second to spare. When Emory locked eyes with Atheia, it was Romie staring back with horror. There was so much Emory wanted to say to her. *Don't stop fighting. I'm not giving up on you. We'll find a way out of this.* From the way Romie looked at her, the slight nod of her head, she understood. There was no time, might never be enough time, and this would have to be enough.

"Go!" Emory yelled at her, just as Atheia took control again.

Even Atheia wasn't foolish enough to stay put with the beckoning darkness threatening to swallow them all whole. In a flash, she dissolved into a great swirl of shimmering water that darted out of sight, much like she had done in the godsworld. Leaving Emory and her mother and Kai to scramble against the farthest wall away from the blooming dark.

It stopped spreading, only an inch from them. It had engulfed nearly all of the corridor, leaving only a tight space for them to go through. They needed to get out of here before the way out disappeared. Emory wasted no time. She stepped over to Sidraeus, who had remained unconscious through all of it. She took his face in her hands and tried to wake him, saying his name, but he wouldn't open his eyes.

I have him trapped in his own mind, Atheia had said. *Living in the prison of his own worst memories.*

How could Emory get him out without magic? She tried calling on the Tidecaller souls again to no avail. Would she and her mother and Kai be able to carry him out of here?

"We have to go," Kai said, eyeing the crumbled roof over their heads, the precarious stone that could still rain down on them at any second, the maw of darkness that could resume its spreading and devour them whole.

"I'm not leaving him," Emory said through gritted teeth.

She braced herself to untie Sidraeus's bindings, knowing this was going to hurt—that the threads of divine light woven through would burn her as it had before. She screamed as her skin came into contact with the white-hot bindings, fighting against the pain as her fingers worked to untie them. She got through both ankles first, biting back sobs, and when she was through untying one of his wrists, she felt his fingers wrap around her own wrist.

The pain—*her* pain—must have gotten through to him. His eyes were on her, like blazing suns one minute, a flash of silver the next, black as pitch and all over again. A perpetual eclipse. He gently pushed her aside to untie the last binding himself. It was only when Emory crumbled to her knees, her hands trembling in front of her a burned, bloodied mess, that she truly registered the pain. It was like when Romie had grabbed a star in her hands when they'd first crossed the sleepscape together. She could feel the shock starting to set in, had never wished for her healing magic more than in this instant.

Sidraeus was suddenly crouched in front of her, holding her face in his hands, speaking words she couldn't hear. She tried to focus on him, aware that he must be feeling her pain as his own, and yet he was fighting through it to calm her down.

Slowly, almost awkwardly, as if unused to offering such tenderness, Sidraeus pulled her toward him. She let her head fall against his shoulder as he held her there. Her breathing slowed, and she convinced herself the pain was nothing, numbing herself to it. There was only her and him and the weight of these wounds shared between them that felt lighter somehow.

Distantly, she heard Sidraeus saying something to her mother and Kai. Felt them standing on either side of her, resting a hand on each of Sidraeus's shoulders. Stars began to swirl around them, and she knew Sidraeus was teleporting the four of them out of the Institute. She closed her eyes, nestling closer to Sidraeus. She kept them closed long after everything stilled again, when the brine of the sea enveloped her and a gentle breeze tugged at her hair. Kai left them with the promise of getting help. A healer, perhaps. Emory wasn't sure, didn't care, not as she and Sidraeus stayed like that for a while yet, holding each other in this clumsy embrace.

And she felt safe.

ROMIE

A<small>THEIA STOOD IN THE RUBBLE OF THE INSTITUTE, MIND</small>less of the rain that fell on her through the torn roof.

Night had fallen since the destruction wrought by the prisoner escape. Crews of Regulators—what remained of them—were working tirelessly to extract bodies from the rubble, salvage Tidecaller blood vials and synthetic magics, and erect wards around the pockets of darkness that had appeared all over the decimated buildings.

Every single one of the Eclipse-born prisoners had escaped. And once they were free, the entire Eclipse wing had been swallowed up in one giant black hole. Almost as if the sleepscape had taken vengeance on the Institute in Sidraeus's name. A sort of divine retribution.

Atheia felt the Tidal Council hovering behind her before any of them spoke, their displeasure sharp as a knife in her back.

"If you have something to say to me," Atheia intoned flatly, "then say it."

She turned to face them at their prolonged quiet.

"What happened here?" Leonie Thornby asked, face full of devastation. "There are dozens upon dozens of Regulators dead. The Eclipse-born prisoners have all escaped..."

"It was an ambush," Atheia seethed. "There was nothing to be done against the gods waging battle here."

"I hear they came for you," Vivianne Delaune said with a hint of accusation in her voice. "Asking for Atheia and Sidraeus. The Tides and the Shadow. You're supposed to protect your people, and yet you chose to stand there and let them kill so many Regulators, so many lunar mages?"

"You have no idea the lengths I am going to in order to save this world and you people," Atheia said, feeling power rising within her, pent-up anger and desperation and *shame*. Because they were right: she was failing them all. There was a glint of fear in their eyes, and though it broke something in her, it also made her all the more furious that none of them could understand the righteousness behind what she was doing; the necessity of it all.

That's what happens when you're driven by revenge, Romie said. *You lose track of yourself. No one here trusts you. You're the Tides that were supposed to bring magic back to them, and look what you brought them instead: misery and death.*

Stop talking, Atheia shot back.

She must have spoken aloud, because the Selenics tensed, watching her like she was a feral animal.

"It's not just about those who died at the Institute," Leonie said bravely. "We know what you did to the lunar mages who allied themselves with Emory. Virgil, Nisha, Ife, Javier. You told us you would only lock them up to teach them a lesson, yet you tortured them. Bled them to keep them weak. Regardless of their betrayal in siding with the Eclipse-born, their blood runs with the hallowed magic of the Tides. They bear the sacred Selenic Mark, and that, to us, means something."

Atheia barked a disbelieving laugh. "Like you people weren't doing the same before I came? Imprisoning everyone and anyone who spoke out in favor of Eclipse-born, be they lunar or eclipse mage."

"That was different," argued Leonie. "These kids were members of our Order. Word of what was done to them has already spread within our network. Virgil Dade's parents were especially interested to hear what their son has been subjected to. Powerful people, the Dades. They blame the Tidal Council for letting it happen, are threatening to sail here from the Outerlands as soon as they're able to hold us all accountable and call for a change of leadership. I can't say I disagree with them. We're the ones who put our faith in you, after all. I see now that we were wrong."

"I am the Tides," Atheia hissed. "You all bowed to me once, and I had the power to choose who to share my magic with. Only the most worthy. I get to decide that still."

"Then maybe this is where our allegiance should end," Leonie said, tilting her chin up. "Perhaps we have outgrown the need for such archaic worshipping of a deity who does not care for us. Perhaps it's time we in the Order took matters of magic in our own hands."

Both the New Moon and Full Moon Council members produced damper cuffs. Atheia laughed. "I see. I give you access to all lunar magics, and this is how you repay me?"

"What power you did give us was only ever temporary," Leonie said. "And with the Tidecaller gone, you won't be able to give us anything at all."

"What will you do, chain me up in the ruins of your Institute?"

"Maybe we'll call on other gods to come and claim you, since they want you so badly."

At this, Atheia snapped. She called on a maelstrom of magic to put an end to these thankless people, but Romie broke through the surface, taking advantage of her lapse in control to yell out a warning.

"Run! She's going to kill—"

Atheia wrested back control and unleashed the magic that had been growing at her fingertips with a scream that sounded like a song pouring out of her. The Tidal Council standing before her tried to cover their ears, to run, to pull on their own magic. But she was divinity, had the power of creation at her fingertips, and they were nothing against her wrath.

She was so tired of feeling like she was losing everything. Her bodily autonomy, her plans for revenge on Sidraeus, the love of her gods, if they'd ever loved her at all, and now the trust of her lunar mages, too. If she couldn't have this, then she wanted none of it.

The Tidal Council doubled over in pain, their screams bloodcurdling, as blood-soaked lunar flowers blossomed in their throats and their lungs and their hearts, growing faster and faster as they erupted from their mouths and ears and eyes and wrapped around their bodies like vines around a tree trunk, rooting them to the floor where they stood.

Silence settled. Not a breath remained.

From the recesses of her mind, Romie's shock and horror reached her. Each Council member killed by vines of flowers from their respective lunar house. Even death was a creation of sorts, and this was nothing short of a masterpiece. Their corpses like statues, made beautiful by the bloodied blooms. Atheia reached for one, her hand coming away slick with blood.

No wonder the gods never loved you, Romie breathed, digging into Atheia's psyche and pulling up all the darkest bits. *No wonder the moon goddess suggested you splinter yourself when I'm sure she knew it would do nothing at all, that there was a better alternative. No wonder Sidraeus chose his magic over you.*

You're no better, Rosemarie Brysden. So easily swayed by my words and my will that you would turn against your own flesh and blood, against everyone you love. They will never forgive you for siding with me.

I'm fighting back now, aren't I?

But they will never know, dear Romie, because you're too late. The damage is done. When Emory sees your face, she will see only the person who tortured her. When your father sees you, he will be haunted by the ruin you sowed. When your brother looks at you, he will see only the girl who fought to eradicate everything that he is. You are as alone as I am.

Quiet followed. Atheia couldn't feel her vessel's presence anymore, and it made her own words burrow into her, like a dagger digging into her gut.

She was alone.

The gods who claimed to care for her wanted her dead. She had lost both Sidraeus and Emory. And she had just killed the only allies she had left.

There was a sound behind her. A pair of Regulators appeared, their faces full of terror as they beheld the scene. Before they could piece together what she'd done, Atheia disappeared, becoming one with the elements as she ran from this place of destruction. She needed to feel alive, to feel rooted, to feel in control for one damn second.

She found herself at the water's edge, where the rising Aldersea swept through the tree trunks of the Wychwood. Her feet squelched in the wet sand. She fell to her knees and let the frothing waves lap around her, washing away the blood on her hands. She tasted the salt of tears on her lips, mixing with the raindrops.

She didn't want to cry. Didn't want to break. Didn't want to admit defeat.

And yet.

She felt his presence before she saw him. Cornelius Clover crouched in front of her, close enough to snap her neck and end her right here if he wanted to. But there was something raw and open on his face. Not pity, but understanding. A loneliness that mirrored Atheia's own.

"You want revenge on the gods," he said.

It wasn't posed as a question, but Atheia answered all the same. "Yes."

"Then help me defeat them. And once I become ruler of the living realms, I'll make you an undeniable queen at my side, a goddess in full."

Atheia had been tricked too often to fall for such promises. Yet there was no trace of trickery in his voice, no hint of malice on his face. Here was someone who had been searching for a specific brand of companionship all throughout his long life; waiting for someone to be on his level, to rise as his true equal.

It seemed outlandish for them to put aside their previous differences. A Tidecaller turned monstrous god. A creator who kept destroying things instead of saving them.

But that was the thing about loneliness: there came a point when what it reflected back at you was too ugly to sit with. Until someone just as flawed sat beside you, and suddenly it wasn't such a burden.

When Clover extended a hand to her, the black spiral that flashed on the inside of his wrist a dark twin to her vessel's silver one, Atheia did not hesitate to grab it.

And together, they rose.

EMORY

THE SAFE HOUSE ON THE SHORES OF THRENODY FELT like home after the horrors of the Institute.

Emory slept and slept and slept, all those days of blood loss and captivity finally catching up to her. Louis tried to tend to everyone's wounds in Emory's place, but his own Healing magic was still a faint, ever-waning thing. He could only do so much, reverting to traditional healing methods where he could. He healed Emory's wounds to the best of his ability, but her recovery was slow without her own magic aiding her. The synth she'd taken had long since faded to nothing in her bloodstream.

Every time she saw the Unhallowed Seal on her hand, she wanted to claw it off. No one could reverse such a curse—except for Baz, who wasn't here.

"He and Jae went back in time to fetch the original keys," Kai told her when she was lucid enough to understand where she was and what had happened. There had been worry behind Kai's carefully shielded exterior; Emory could tell it ate him up to not have gone with Baz.

She'd watched him as he sat at her bedside, expression far away. This was the cost of being a hero: to wonder if the choices you'd made were the right ones, no matter the outcome.

Emory had reached for his hand and squeezed. "Thank you for rescuing me. For saving all of us."

His dark eyes had met hers, an understanding passing between them. "I know what it's like to be kept in that place. It was about time someone burned it to the ground."

Swallowed up by a pocket of sleepscape. Nothing could have been a more fitting end to the Institute.

After Sidraeus had whisked Emory, Kai, and Luce away—Theodore and Farran, she'd later learned, had been lifted out of there by Gwenhael, along with Emory's other friends—Kai had convinced Sidraeus to go back to the Institute with him to make sure they'd left no one behind. Together, Shadow and Nightmare Weaver had watched the blooming sleepscape devour what was left of the Eclipse wing.

Emory wished she could have seen it.

Days went by without Baz reappearing, without a whisper of Clover or Atheia or the gods. When Emory wasn't sleeping, she was visited by her friends. Nisha spent a lot of time curled up at her side, telling her how Romie had fought against Atheia's hold, wondering how—*if*—they would ever get Romie back. Virgil found ways to make Emory laugh as he always did, trying his best to shake away the dark memories of the Institute. Vera, Emory couldn't help but notice, was a near constant presence at his side, and it was obvious to everyone that there was something blooming between the two.

Others Emory never thought she'd see again came to visit her too: Ivayne and Vivyan, accompanied by Caius, the young draconic page who'd been a part of the corrupt Fellowship of the

Light, and who'd since left them to join the Golden Helm. Emory often saw him through her window, sitting on the beach writing in his bestiary—a compendium of creatures he was having a tremendous time filling with all sorts of animals and insects foreign to his own world—while Gwenhael soared over the Aldersea, terrorizing the seagulls.

Then there was the newcomer: Farran Caine. Emory didn't see much of him, but Kai told her all about his miraculous recovery—chalked up to the fact that he'd been touched by the divine—and all the groveling Farran had been doing to prove how sorry he was for getting Kai and Luce trapped in the abyss.

"And you forgive him?" Emory had asked him dubiously.

"Hell no." Kai had let out a long, frustrated sigh. "But he's been manipulated by gods all his life. Guess we can't really blame the guy for it. That's what your mom thinks, anyway."

Emory thought she might never get used to those words. Mom. Mother. *Parents*, plural, because by some miracle, both her parents were with her. The father who'd always been her shore, a sure place to land. And her mother the sailor, who'd fought her hardest to pull Emory from the stormy seas trying to claim her and bring her back to safety.

Sitting by Emory's bedside, Luce had told her everything. About her vision, the reason she'd left Emory, her journey through time—all of it a desperate attempt to save Emory. And though Baz had already recounted much of this to Emory, nothing could compare with hearing it in her mother's own words.

"I'm sorry about everything you've been through," Luce had said through tears. "I'm so sorry I couldn't do more for you. If I could go back—"

Emory had embraced her, trying to convey how much her presence meant to her. Her mother had hugged her back, and every resentment Emory had ever had toward her vanished. It didn't matter that Luce had abandoned her. It didn't matter that she'd left Emory wondering about her all her life, missing a mother she had never known. Because she was here now, in the flesh. No longer a simple myth, a story Emory clung to, but a real person she could finally know.

Her mother the sailor, Emory the sea. Together, they had somehow made it back to the shores where it had all begun, to Emory's father, the lighthouse keeper who had always been here as a beacon waiting, and maybe the three of them could finally be a family. There was comfort in that thought.

But it was odd, seeing them together. Time had run in a straight line for Henry, but in a loop for Luce, leaving him in his forties and her in her early twenties, frozen in a version of herself that was not much older than when Henry had first laid eyes on her.

The distance between them was a strange one, bridged only by their shared love and concern for Emory. After their first visit at her bedside together, they mostly came to her separately. She knew her father well enough to see how much Luce's return had destabilized him. He'd always been a quiet man, content with the quiet life he'd chosen. But part of Emory always wondered if he was that way because he was holding out hope for the intrepid sailor's return. Frozen in time himself as he tended his lighthouse and watched the horizon.

And now, at long last, she had reappeared.

When Emory asked him what might happen between the two of them, her father gave her a sad smile, rubbing at his beard. "I don't know. Things are complicated, aren't they?" He stared off in the distance for a while, perhaps imagining what a future might look like between them, or maybe accepting that what they'd shared would forever be trapped in the past. At last, he turned to Emory and patted her hand. "All that matters is that you get to know her. And I'm so glad for that."

So was she. Having Luce here was like a dream made reality, and Emory cherished every moment of it, these quiet conversations, the memories and tears they shared, lamenting all the lost time they wished they could have had together. Vera and Alya sometimes came to see her with Luce, sharing stories of the Kazans, the two sisters laughing loudly together as if they'd never been apart.

Between the visits and the sleep, Emory felt a constant dread in her stomach at the thought of losing Baz and Jae to the threads of time, at the thought of Atheia and Clover still out there.

At the thought of Sidraeus, somewhere in this safe house, keeping his distance from her.

She didn't blame him for it. She'd been doing the same thing on her end, not ready to face him just yet after everything that had happened at the Institute. But when she finally felt good enough to venture out of her room, her feet led her straight to him, as if pulled to him by an invisible string.

She found him alone in the old office they'd used for their radio transmission, with its fraying tapestry and bookshelves collecting dust. Sidraeus stood on the other side of the room, staring out the window. He glanced at her when she came in, tracking her movements, his face limned in the soft light of a single desk lamp. He looked like a blood moon sky, like a boy riddled with ghosts carved into his skin.

Emory sat at the desk, still unsteady on her feet.

"I owe you an apology," she said, staring at her hands. The words were easier to get out this way. "When I used the syrinx, I knew exactly the kind of bargain I was making on your behalf, the curse I'd force on you. And I did it anyway, without an ounce of hesitation, because I was so desperate to save Romie and the others and so sure this was the only way. But all this pain you've suffered . . . I truly am sorry."

"The pain *I've* suffered?"

The bite of surprise in his voice made her head snap up. Sidraeus looked angry, jaw tight and nostrils flaring.

"Emory... I'm not the one who was tortured, at least not directly. I'm not the one who was bled dry for my power. Everything that happened, everything Atheia did to you, is because of *me*."

Their eyes held. They'd been down this road before and had given each other the gift of forgiveness. Emory was about to remind him of that—ironic, she knew, after what she'd just said—but Sidraeus wasn't done.

"You could have left me behind, but you didn't. You pulled me from the darkness I'd resigned myself to, and I won't soon forget it."

His face was a complexity of emotions she could spend an eternity trying to parse and it still wouldn't be enough. Yet the stark truth beneath his words burrowed inside her. He'd spent so long with his guilt and regrets, he never expected anyone to fight for him. To stand by his side. The capricious god who'd shaped him never had, and neither had Atheia, in the end.

But Emory had.

She realized with a pang that her reasons for doing so hadn't been out of pure necessity like they had been before. Yes, she needed him. But somewhere between the bargain she'd made and now, she had started to value him not for what he might bring her, but for who he was and how he felt and how he made *her* feel. She had started to care about him. *Wanted* to stand by his side.

Maybe, beyond forgiveness, what Sidraeus truly longed for was loyalty. Companionship. The certitude that someone would stand by him in the dark, hold his hand on the tortuous road to redemption, and help him mold a better version of himself out of that darkness.

And maybe Emory, so used to hurting others before they could abandon her, had always craved the same thing.

"We're in this together," she said, needing him to understand, wondering, despite his words, if he felt the same.

He held her gaze with an intensity that made her aware of every fiber of her being. And when he looked away, it was down at her hands, as if seeing again the burnt flesh as she undid his binds.

"The souls of the Tidecallers cast out the gods from my mind," Emory said. She described to Sidraeus the markings that had appeared on her. She'd puzzled over it ever since it happened. "How could those marks have had power over actual gods?"

Sidraeus seemed lost in thought for a while. "I learned something at the Institute. About the last Tidecaller, who defied the gods and survived the sacrifice. I told you about Tala, the Luaguan Tidecaller who was like a sister to me. It turns out she escaped Equilibris's culling by boxing away a portion of her power—putting a damper on herself to hide her limitless well of magic. A damper that she would have had to Collapse to get rid of . . . which is a practice that lived on in all Eclipse magic that came after her."

A fond smile played on Sidraeus's lips. His eyes were distant and full of wonder as he kept speaking, as if he could see Tala before him. "She was always far too intelligent for her own good. It doesn't surprise me in the slightest that she would have not only evaded sacrifice for herself but also made it possible for Eclipse magic to remain. For those born with it to survive. She was such a force."

There was so much love in his voice, it made Emory's heart ache to imagine the relief he must have felt knowing she'd been the one Tidecaller to escape. Knowing there was at least one death he hadn't caused.

"I believe Tala went one step further than this damper she placed on her magic by also tattooing herself with wards that would keep the gods' notice at bay. Wards written in the language of the gods themselves, symbols she'd learned from Atheia and me, which I've seen here tattooed on Luaguan Eclipse-born." He shook his head as if in disbelief. "I wondered why those symbols were so familiar. How they would have found their way into this world at all. And now I'm sure of it: it's because of Tala. She wanted to protect herself and her peers, and so she found a way for the practice to remain long after she was gone."

A way to ward against the Shadow's curse—that was what Luaguans believed of their tattoos. But more than anything, it was a way to ward against the gods who'd sought to eradicate Eclipse magic from the start.

Tala was the reason Eclipse magic had survived at all.

"How did you learn all this?" Emory asked.

"The souls of the Tidecallers spoke to me," Sidraeus said. "When the pain and suffering I felt was at its worst, when I was delirious from it . . . They told me how I could put an end to this bargain I'm cursed with."

Emory blanched. "How?"

"By releasing them from their own curse," he said after some time. "Finally putting their souls to rest, something they've been denied since the moment Equilibris sacrificed them to seal the doors. They are cursed as much as I have ever been. And they want to be free."

"Is that something you have the power to do?"

"No." His eyes bore into her. "But you do."

Emory's brows shot up. "Me? I don't even have my magic."

"You'll get it back. And their curse is . . . tied to you, in a way. To a Tidecaller. It all goes back to Tala, the one Tidecaller who survived the sacrifice and escaped the god's punishment. So long as a Tidecaller existed in the world, Eclipse magic would endure. Not as Tidecaller magic, but as the Eclipse magic you know today. Except on rare occasions, of course."

He studied Emory. "When Tala put a damper on her magic, it left her with only Healing power going forward. Which is why, every time a Tidecaller was born, they were born as a Healer. And this brush with death they needed to unlock their true power, to become a Tidecaller in full, was a Collapsing of sorts. An eradication of Tala's damper. And every time a Tidecaller rose into their power, they heard the call of the doors. Not only because of Atheia's pieces that called to their magic, but because of the Tidecaller souls that were waiting for them to release them. They've been waiting for *you*, Emory."

A million thoughts raced through Emory's mind. "So that's why you're still here," she said flatly. "Why you've stuck by me. Because you need me."

"That's not—"

"No, I get it. I made this bargain against your will. Of course you want me to end it. I want to end it too. I just thought—I don't know. That maybe this *thing* between us was more than that. More than us using each other to achieve something else, I mean."

Fitting, she thought, that she should get a taste of her own medicine.

Sidraeus withdrew as if her tone had slapped him. "Is that what you still think of me, after all we've been through?" When she didn't respond, he breathed, "Did he really break your trust so completely?"

Her gaze snapped to his. She knew who he spoke of. And he was right. Keiran *had* broken her ability to trust her feelings—to trust in her attraction to this deity before her who had done nothing but save her time and time again, only for her to still question his motives.

Sidraeus will never care for anyone but himself, and if he has made you believe otherwise, it's only to get something from you.

Atheia's taunting voice sounded in Emory's ears, her warning so similar to the one Lizaveta had once given her about Keiran. The difference was, Emory hadn't believed for a second that there was any truth to Atheia's words. But now . . . had she been fooled again?

Sidraeus's nostrils flared angrily. "I can't say I appreciate being lumped into the same vile category as that sorry excuse of a person," he said, voice low and rough. His eyes went to her throat, as if he could see the imprint of Keiran's fingers there. He sighed, meeting her eye with a gentler expression. "But I can't fault you for how you feel, and I'm sorry that I've given you reason not to trust me in the past." His tone turned almost pleading. "I promise you I'm here to make it right. And it kills me that you might not believe that."

At her silence, he started to leave.

"Wait." He turned to her, and the devastation on his face fractured any resolve she'd had. "I don't want to do this alone."

He was by her side in an instant, kneeling where she sat. His hand covered her own, resting on her lap. "You're not alone."

She realized that, other than their embrace after escaping the Institute, it was the first time he'd really touched her since he'd regained his true form. As if realizing the same thing, he made to take his hand away.

Instead, Emory pulled him close and kissed him.

Damn whatever resolve she'd had. Damn the doubts in her head that popped up whenever she thought of him. These doubts were not about him. They were born out of Keiran's betrayal. But Sidraeus was not Keiran. He'd proven this to her time and time again. He'd taken swords for her. Had nearly died for her. Had suffered the sleepscape and the abyss and Atheia's wrath *for her*. And while she had mistrusted her own instincts where he was concerned, all of them had been proven right.

This thing between them, this attraction, this sense of belonging . . . She knew he felt it, too.

But perhaps she'd read him wrong, because the second their lips touched, he froze. Didn't reciprocate the kiss.

Emory pulled away, cheeks burning with the sting of rejection. "I'm sorry," she said. "This was a mistake."

But then—his hand touching her cheek. Her name spoken like a prayer. His thumb ran over her bottom lip as his eyes peered into hers, and in the vulnerability etched on his face she could only see a boy, not a deity. As scared as she was to do the wrong thing, take the wrong step.

He tilted her chin up with the tip of his fingers, ever so gently, as if still scared to touch her. And when his lips met hers, they were light as a feather, as a breath of air against skin. It was unlike anything she would have expected of him. The deadly deity motivated by vengeance. The wry humor that had set her aflame. No. Here was someone who was as touch-starved as she was, as eager to be seen for all that he was, yet still so very scared to put his heart on the line. To give in.

Emory was done being careful with her heart and her trust. She wanted this. And after what she'd gone through, she needed to feel alive—needed to feel *something*.

She ran her hands through his thick curls, drawing him closer. His hands snaked over hers, pulling them from the back of his neck down to his heart, before breaking the kiss to look at her.

"We shouldn't," he said. The words lacked conviction.

"Why not?" she asked.

"I—" He swallowed visibly, gaze trailing down to her mouth. His eyes were molten when they flicked back to hers. "To be honest, I'm running out of reasons."

"So am I."

Emory pressed her lips against his hands, still cupping her own, and held his gaze as she did so. He made a sound deep in his throat, and then his mouth was on hers again, setting her aflame.

The kiss was slow, indulgent. Emory melted into him, breathing in the vetiver and blood-orange and cedarwood scent of him as her hands fisted in his shirt to tug him closer, wanting to feel him against her. Sidraeus's hands were everywhere. They remained delicate as they gently cupped her face, the nape of her neck; as they found their way to her hips, the small of her back. He touched her like she was an ice sculpture that might melt away in his grasp, like she was crystal that might break and shatter into a million pieces.

"Sidraeus," she breathed, holding his face in her hands. "Sid." The way his dark lashes brushed against his cheeks as he closed his eyes, leaning into her touch, made her heart flutter.

"Emory." His eyes opened, intent on hers. Searching for an answer in them. "Are you sure this is what you want?"

"Is it not what you want?"

"It is. More than you can know. But I–" His jaw worked as he fought for words. "Can you ever forgive me, for making you feel so unsafe while I was wearing his face? For taunting you with the trauma he inflicted on you?"

She understood then that this softness was him not wanting to bring up the ghosts that plagued her, the memory of Keiran's hand wrapped around her throat, the insecurities that might forever linger. And this–the tender way he was treating her, the unspoken power he was giving her by letting her lead–it made her want to curl up in his embrace and never let go.

"We said we forgave each other, remember? I trust you," she said, and she meant it. She had never felt safer. "I want this."

The words unlocked something in him. Her name escaped his lips again, and then they were crashing together like two burning stars, hands clenching into hair and shirts without reservation now. They kissed like they were chasing the last bit of the sun's light. Like there would be no tomorrow. Like there would never be enough time between them to savor this.

As if they knew they would be interrupted a minute later, ripped apart by the creak of a door and a squeal of surprise.

"I didn't see anything."

Vera stood in the doorway, staring pointedly away from Emory and Sidraeus. Emory felt heat rise to her cheeks as she pushed Sidraeus away, mortified at what her cousin had walked in on.

"Just letting you know Baz is back," Vera said. "He's fine, before you ask. Waiting downstairs to speak to all of us. I'll, uh, give you two a minute."

Vera winked at Emory as she left. No judgment, no questioning Emory's choices. As if what happened here was an inevitability. Something she'd seen coming all along.

Emory and Sidraeus looked at each other in the quiet, swollen-lipped and panting. She wondered how much further they might have taken things if Vera hadn't interrupted. Images of what could have been played in her mind, making heat coil inside her. Sidraeus's burning gaze on her mouth didn't help. She didn't need to hear his thoughts to know he was imagining the same things, and if they didn't get out of this room soon, he wouldn't hesitate to turn them into reality. And Emory would gladly let him.

"We should head down," she said, trying to break the spell, to convince her own limbs to move.

But she wanted so badly to stay in this room, even as relief coursed through her at Baz's safe return, even as his voice reached her from downstairs and she yearned to see his face. Because if Baz was back, and if he'd succeeded at what he set out to do, then what happened next might change everything.

She wanted more time to explore what this was before they set out to save the worlds again.

But at least they'd had this moment, which had briefly felt like eternity.

BAZ

IT WAS A SHOT IN THE DARK TO BELIEVE THE TIME TRAVEL pocket watch could truly take Baz *anywhere*, including a different world. He was going on a hunch based on what Kai had told him of Farran–the god's old apprentice–and how he would use his pocket watch to travel out of the abyss. If he was able to do that, going from the deepest recesses of the realm of death to one of the realms of the living, then surely traveling from one living realm to another wasn't that big of a stretch.

Baz knew his hunch had been right when he and Jae found themselves in the Wychwood. And it truly was the Wychwood, Baz was certain about it. He'd seen it often enough in illustrations, had glimpsed it briefly in his own time, superposed against the fabric of his own world. Here and now, the Wychwood was still only the Wychwood, a separate world from his, a very real place pulled from a storybook. It smelled of moss and earth and subtle decay. It felt like a dream come to life.

"This is . . ." Jae spun in slow circles, staring wide-eyed at the thick woods around them. They looked like they wanted to document every fragment of their surroundings. They'd devoted their life's work to Clover's imaginary worlds, and now here they were, standing in the real version of one. "This can't be real."

Let's reclaim this adventure and make the story our own, Jae had said before Baz pulled the two of them through time. And now it was time for them to do so.

"We need to find the door," Baz said, trying to catch his bearings. "It should be nearby."

At least, he hoped so. He'd willed the pocket watch to bring them to the exact time and place he knew they needed to be.

Jae knelt to point at something on the ground. "Fresh tracks," they said. "Four sets. Could be Clover, Kai, Luce, and the witch."

Baz gaped at them. "Where did you learn to track?"

Jae shrugged with a secretive smile. "I'm full of surprises, Basil. Thought you'd know this about me by now. Their tracks get muddied around here, though." They jerked their chin at the pocket watch in Baz's hand. "Can't you use that device of yours to see where they went?"

Baz flicked open the magnifying glass. Indeed, it showed Clover, Kai, Luce, and Asphodel going through here less than an hour ago. A million thoughts ran through Baz's mind. He had the power to stop what he knew would happen: Clover murdering the witch, Kai and Luce falling into the abyss. But he'd been down this road before, trying to change the past. With fate broken—its threads all jumbled up, out of order, in chaotic shambles—there was no knowing how much more tangled things might become if he tried changing these big events now.

Still, his new unbound power was a marvel. It was as if the universe were at his fingertips, as if he had the power of the god of balance himself running through him, making him master of time and fate if he wanted to.

But he knew what he had to do. So he would hone that power like a needle, small and precise and effective.

"Over here," Baz said, starting in the direction the magnifying glass showed him the others had gone.

They came upon a hollowed-out tree trunk Baz would have recognized even without the magnifying glass, having heard it described by both Emory and Kai. It led to the basalt column cave deep below the earth. And there was the door, closed now after the others had gone through mere moments ago.

The rib of the original witch was still embedded in the spiral groove. Carefully, Baz picked it up. On the floor was a mound of clothes that could only have belonged to the witch. To Asphodel. Before Clover imbibed all that she was.

Looking away from the gruesome sight, Baz pulled on the threads of time around the bone—a lifeless, magicless bone now that it had already opened the door . . . But there. As he breathed in time and breathed life out, the bone became what it once was. It had life again, *magic* again, full of the witch's essence. It was warm in his hand, thrumming faintly with power, as if the witch herself were whispering to him.

Baz couldn't bring Asphodel back from the dead. But he would make sure her death had not been in vain.

He pocketed the rib bone, tucking it safe. The first key he needed, acquired. The first piece that would undo the mess Clover had made.

Baz looked at Jae. "Ready for the next world?"

They could have stayed in the Wychwood forever to explore this place they'd both dreamed of for so long. But time was of the essence, even with Baz holding its reins.

And so they found themselves in the third world, the scorched landscape of the Heartland a jarring sight after the lushness of the

Wychwood. They stood at the foot of a volcano Baz knew to be the Sunforge, surrounded by rivers of fire that made the air unbearably, swelteringly hot.

A loud wail sounded at the heart of the volcano. For a second, Baz thought it would erupt—that he and Jae had walked themselves right to their fiery end. But the sound was not that of lava and rock. It was pain.

They ran into the Sunforge just in time to see a blond head disappear through the door to the fourth world. *Clover.* They had missed him by a second, could see the carnage he had left behind. The discarded golden armor and sword of the warrior, whose body must have dissipated like Asphodel's did. And sprawled in front of the door, wheezing its final breath as blood pooled from horrid wounds, was a colossal dragon.

Baz and Jae stood rooted to the spot at the sight of it. Its eyes were fixed on them, as if they were the last thing it had seen before death took it. And Baz hated Clover all the more than he already did in this moment, to see the kind of monster he'd already let himself become at this point.

Jae laid a delicate hand on the dragon's snout, bowing their head as silent tears spilled from their eyes. The door had closed behind Clover, revealing the solid gold heart of the warrior fitted at the center of the golden spiral on the wall of black stone. Baz picked up the heart of this warrior Clover had killed and breathed life back into it. He pocketed the heart and felt the bone hum even more as it came into contact with it.

And Baz could *feel* the stories these two keys told. The witch's story with her twin sister and the demons and the honeyed promises of Clover. The warrior's tale with her induction into the draconic knights and this dragon that had bonded itself to her.

It was as if, as he pulled back the threads, made these pieces alive again, they shared their stories with him in exchange. They were the characters of the book he had first fallen in love with, the book he himself had written; but they were real people, too, people he was discovering under entirely new lights. Baz considered them old friends and new acquaintances all at once, and it was the strangest thing, but he felt like he was something of a hero, too, carrying these two legends who had lived in his mind for so long, who had shaped his childhood and everything that came after.

Baz couldn't bear to leave here without trying to make something of the gruesome carnage Clover left behind. He took the warrior's armor and sword and propped them up against the dragon's chest, near where he assumed the beast's heart would be. Jae illusioned a wreath of wildflowers that they laid atop the armor and wove around the gold sword.

"A warrior sprang from this world as improbably as the flowers that bloom in its arid wilderness," Jae intoned.

Emotion caught in Baz's throat. *"She is the heart of her world,"* he added softly, *"the bright burning core of it."*

And she had died at the hands of a monster who took that brightness for himself.

They couldn't let her death be in vain.

Just as Baz wielded the pocket watch that would bring him and Jae to the next world, taking them ahead in time to Clover's next victim, he thought he glimpsed someone watching from the shadow of the slain dragon. A stout frame that called to mind mismatched suits and peculiar goggles. But the pocket watch took him away before he could be sure.

The fourth door atop the snowy peak was one Baz had seen in countless illustrations, yet it still managed to take his breath away. There were no signs of vicious carnage here, only the heavy snow, the whistling wind, and the quiet beneath. It somehow made the place all the more foreboding.

Jae pointed to the discarded clothes half buried in the snow. All that was left of the guardian Clover had slain. The door was closed, and in the spiral in the middle of it swirled a curious, immaterial substance that must be the guardian's soul.

"How exactly are we going to carry that?" Jae asked.

An astute question that neither of them had thought to consider.

The snow pelted them harder, the cold seeping through their bones as the light quickly faded from the sky. Night was coming, and with it came that curious sensation of being watched again. Baz tried to spot Equilibris—he was certain it was him he'd seen back at the Sunforge, though why the god would be following him, he had no clue. He could see nothing through the blizzard.

They needed to grab the remaining key and get out of here before he lost his composure.

Jae suddenly moved with the certainty of someone driven by an idea. They pulled something peeking out of the snow: the guardian's lyre. Except the instrument wasn't gold like it was depicted in the book, but plain, humble wood. This wasn't the lyre that would be used by Clover two hundred years from now to bring Atheia back.

Jae looked the instrument over. "This world's magic is tied to song, right? If this lyre was the guardian's, it held meaning to him, is connected to him. Maybe we can use it to trap his soul somehow..."

The sound of flapping broke through the howling blizzard as a winged horse landed beside the gate. It was magnificent, its coat a dazzling white, its dark eyes full of keen wisdom. Baz gaped at it. Jae nearly dropped the lyre as the horse padded toward them, tucking its wings against its side.

A dozen more horses landed around them, silent and observant—and *mournful*. They all bowed their heads, facing the spot where the guardian's clothes remained, and Baz swore there were tears in their eyes. It was as if they'd come down from the skies to pay their respects for the fallen guardian, this boy who might have tamed these divine creatures just as he had in the book.

One of the horses gently nudged the lyre in Jae's hands, and it was the oddest thing, but Baz knew it was its way of telling them they'd been right about how to capture the guardian's soul. Indeed, when Jae plucked at the instrument, the wisps of the guardian's soul lifted from the door and wove around the lyre's strings. Baz breathed life back into the soul as it fused into the lyre, and the guardian's life played behind his eyes, so similar to the story he knew from *Song of the Drowned Gods.*

As Jae handed Baz the lyre, the power of the three keys he now carried hummed through every part of him. The urgency to get back home amplified, almost unbearable as adrenaline coursed through him. A younger Baz might have succumbed right here under the pressure, forgetting how to breathe as anxiety took over. But he retained his calm, kept breathing in and out and in again as he'd been taught.

And with a final glance at this impossible world, these ethereal creatures, the gate he'd imagined himself guarding so often, Baz whisked Jae and him and the three ancient keys home.

PART IV
THE GOD OF BALANCE

THE WEIGHT OF DREAD WAS SOMETHING THE GOD OF balance had never anticipated. It sat like a millstone around his neck, leaving him with leaden limbs and an ache in his chest he could never quite soothe. It was constant dissonance in his restless mind, threatening the harmony he was made for.

This was the price of being tied to fate. He was as powerless against it as any mortal, yet burdened with the knowledge of it. Alone to wait for the inevitable, surrounded by ticking clocks that grew more maddening with every second they inched closer to the dreadful conclusion that fate had concocted.

He wanted to be free of it.

He was a god, but he was a servant of fate above all, a ruler of nothing, not even his own nature. He was tired of feeling so caught between duty and desire. He wanted to carve out a fresh start, paint a better outcome, even if it went against everything he had ever stood for. What he was made for.

Balance was meant to keep him impartial, neither good nor evil. Defying fate would tip the scales in favor of the latter, but perhaps villainy would be a lighter burden to bear than the gravity of inaction.

At least then he would be free of this forced equilibrium, and fate would no longer be his concern.

EMORY

THE THREE KEYS ON THE TABLE CALLED TO EMORY WITH undeniable force.

As Baz told them how he'd retrieved them from the past, everyone at the safe house seemed mesmerized by them—the rib bone stark white, the heart of solid gold, the cloudy wisps of a soul trapped in the strings of a wooden lyre. The original keys that Clover had imbibed. The one thing that might make Emory strong enough to face him.

Emory's hands were tucked between her thighs, as if that might stop her from reaching out to grab the keys. On the back of her right hand, the ugly *U* mark that had sullied her freshly combined New Moon and Eclipse sigils was gone, and with her magic returned, its floodgates open wide, it was hard to resist the keys' pull. Harder still to focus on anything that was being said around her.

Only a few minutes after Baz's return, he'd taken Emory aside, his face white as a sheet. "Kai told me what they did to you. I'm so sorry, Emory. I should have been there, I should have—"

"Baz. You're here now, and that's all that matters."

His mouth had been a tight, downturned line as he took her branded hand and ran a thumb over the jagged Unhallowed Seal. "I can unmake it. Like I did for everyone else."

"Yes," Emory had said eagerly. Not a trace of hesitation.

Baz had watched her fondly. "You've come a long way from the girl who wanted nothing to do with Eclipse magic."

"Says the boy who used to be too scared to call on his magic for the simplest thing, and look at you now."

They were no longer those people acting out of fear.

Baz had wound back the threads of time like it was nothing. Barely a breath from him, and it was as if no brand had ever touched Emory's hand, no seal had ever put her magic to sleep. Her veins had run silver for a moment, her near-Collapsing no longer frozen in place by the brand. She didn't fall into a proper Collapsing, but as the full might of her power rushed through her again, so had *theirs*, their pull on her so strong she thought she might succumb to them right then and there.

She'd gripped Baz's arm so tight he'd yelped. "What's wrong?"

"I can feel them." The words had been strained, her breath labored. "The keys."

They bore a trace of Atheia's power that called to her the same way Romie, Aspen, and Tol had called to her, inviting her magic to borrow from their own with a force that demanded attention, that asked to be claimed. To be devoured.

"I don't want to turn out like Clover."

At her whispered words, Baz had gripped her shoulders tight. "You won't. Just hold off, resist the keys' pull awhile longer." Fierce determination had burned behind his glasses. "We're going to bring Clover down for good."

They had since been discussing plans to do just that with everyone at the safe house. There were too many unknowns surrounding how exactly the keys might help Emory defeat Clover. They didn't even know where Clover was, nor the gods who wanted him dead as badly as they did.

An idea crossed Emory's mind as she watched Farran. He was properly healed now–as was everyone else at the safe house, Emory having used her magic as soon as she got it back to heal away any lingering injuries, including her own. But there was a haunted look in his eye, an awkwardness to the way he held himself. As if he didn't quite know what to do with himself now that the gods had abandoned their emissary.

What are you thinking?

Emory's heart somersaulted as she caught Sidraeus's eye. The telepathic connection between them had reopened with the return of her magic, and hearing him in her mind felt suddenly much more intimate than before. She tried not to think of his lips on hers, the memory begging for as much attention as the keys, as she told him of her idea.

Do you think we can trust him? she asked, meaning Farran.

Your mother and the Nightmare Weaver seem to think so.

Emory recalled the words Kai had said at her bedside–that Farran had been manipulated by gods all his life, and they couldn't keep blaming him for it.

Deciding to take the leap, Emory finally spoke, interrupting whatever conversation the others had been having. "I have an idea how we can get to Clover." Her gaze swept the room and landed on Farran. "But it involves something you might not like."

Emory, Baz, and Kai stood in the tall grass overlooking the beach below. Emory's magic rendered them invisible in case the wards they stood behind didn't suffice. On the outside of the wards, walking toward the water's edge, was Farran–dragging a bound Sidraeus.

They heard Farran shouting at the skies. "Gods of the living! I've got what you want—so come and claim him. Use me as your emissary again, I implore you."

The skies thundered ominously above. For a while, nothing more happened as Farran kept shouting his invocation of the gods. And then something rippled on the wind, and Farran gasped, his head tilting up, his mouth open, the muscles of his neck tensing. He stretched his neck in an odd, languorous motion, and when he opened his eyes again, they were the ever-shifting colors of the gods.

"Let's go," Emory whispered to the others.

Baz and Kai stepped out of the wards in tandem with her just as Farran—the gods—grabbed Sidraeus by the throat, a wicked, hungry smile on their face. Seeking their chance to grab the one half of the equation they needed to sacrifice to the fountain.

With Baz's magic speeding up time, they were on them in a second, Emory lifting the invisibility around them just to see the shock register in the gods' eyes. The tattoos on Kai erupted in bright silver as he shoved Farran back from Sidraeus. The gods snarled at him, at the three of them standing as a protective barrier in front of Sidraeus.

"You're not going to lay a hand on him," Emory said. "But you are going to help us lure Clover. And then I'm going to defeat him."

They scoffed dubiously at her. "The keys won't be enough for you to defeat Clover, especially now that he and Atheia are working together." They sneered at the shock on Emory's face. "So you see? Sacrificing Sidraeus and Atheia to the fountain so *we* can take our power back is the only option there is."

"No. You're going to do this our way."

"Why would we do that?"

"Because you'll never be able to get to Atheia now," Sidraeus said, "not when you don't have your full power and she has allied herself with Clover."

"And because I'm not the only one with the language of gods on me," Kai added, "and we're more powerful than you give us credit for."

Out of the wards stepped Rusli and other Luaguan Eclipse-born, their own tattoos illuminated silver. Tala's safeguard against gods, activated while in their vicinity. A threat to the gods, a way to show them they had power in numbers.

Emory grabbed hold of Sidraeus's hand, feeling the souls of the Tidecallers all around her, alive as they had been when they'd ejected the gods from her at the Institute. "This is how we defeat Clover and put the worlds—*your worlds*—right again."

ROMIE

WORD OF WHAT HAD TRANSPIRED AT THE INSTITUTE traveled fast. When Atheia returned to Aldryn College a few days later, the reception she received was cold. There was another protest in motion calling for justice for Eclipse-born after those who'd escaped from the Institute shared their stories loud and wide. On top of that, whispered rumors ran rampant of the carnage that had taken place at the Institute, of the Tidal Council turned to stone by Atheia's own hand.

No one trusted her anymore, not even the people who'd previously been so loud about their views against Eclipse magic. She was here to put an end to that.

When the gods had called on her earlier that day and asked to meet here, Atheia had agreed, pretending she had seen reason and was willing to give herself up. But she had other plans in mind for them.

The gods stood in the center of the quad next to the Fountain of Fate, surrounded by people from all over who were calling for

Institutes to be shut down and Regulators and Tidelore leaders to be held accountable. Demanding answers from the Tides of Fate themselves—not only answers, but the magic she had promised them and failed to deliver on. No one seemed to bat an eye at the vessel of gods standing in their midst. They had reclaimed their emissary, who'd made a miraculous recovery.

In their possession was Sidraeus, bound at the wrists.

Atheia hadn't anticipated this. "Did you get yourself captured again so soon, Sidraeus?"

"I'm here of my own volition."

His unexpected answer gave her pause. "Why the binds, then?"

"It's to ensure he doesn't go back on his word," the gods answered. "But it is true: Sidraeus here has valiantly offered himself to us in sacrifice. The question is, daughter: Will you?"

"That's what I told you I would do, didn't I? It's why I'm here."

The gods gave her a pitying look. "Did you really think we would not see through your lies? We know you've allied yourself with Clover. We know you've lured us here so he can bring us to the sea of ash where we will be vulnerable."

Atheia's mind raced. She pressed close to the Fountain of Fate, adopting a nonchalant air as she ran a hand over the water's surface. "Then why show up at all?"

"To give you the chance to do the right thing. Call off your beast of a god and give yourself over to us so we can fix everything."

Atheia huffed a cold laugh. "I will do no such thing. And I don't believe for a second that Sidraeus has suddenly become so self-sacrificing."

"It's the only way, Atheia." Sidraeus swept a gaze over the onlooking students, the patch of darkness still open in the quad, the destruction of the cloisters it had wrought. "All of this started with us. The Tides and the Shadow and the choices we made. I'm done evading responsibility for what I've done. If our sacrifice is the only way to save these dying worlds—all these people who are suffering because of us—then I will gladly lay down my life."

"None of this is *my* fault," Atheia hissed. "Everything bad started when *you* stepped into the realms of the living and created your Tidecallers. It's *your* corrupt magic that coursed through Clover's veins and led to this. *You* are to blame, Sidraeus."

"If you want to play that game, then let's not forget you helped bring me into these realms. The first pebble in the landslide that followed." He shook his head slowly. "But it shouldn't matter who or where or how it started. We both had a part to play. We both made mistakes. We are both flawed, Atheia, like everything we created and everything that came after us. I finally understand that the flaws are what makes the good shine through. I'm trying to climb my way through the cracks of past mistakes instead of letting myself tumble deeper into darkness. Why can't you?"

"I will not die for them," she spat, gesturing to the gods.

"What about for your people?" Sidraeus asked. "For the worlds you love?"

Everyone was watching them. Murmurs in favor of the Shadow. Whispers of the Tides abandoning them.

Part of Atheia knew this was her chance to sway the lunar mages' opinion of her for good. If she went willingly with the gods, if she chose to sacrifice herself to save these people, just as Sidraeus had seemingly decided, then they would finally see everything she was doing was for them.

But she was in far too deep now to take accountability for something she did not see fault in. And she didn't trust Sidraeus or the gods in the slightest. Besides, the damage was already done. She saw the looks thrown her way. Knew she'd let her emotions get the better of her, and now they'd seen the truth of her, plain and simple.

The Shadow was willing to die for them; their beloved Tides were not.

And this, perhaps, was a bigger shift in their world than every other horror it had endured.

Atheia had lost their belief. And without it, she had nothing—except for her determination, and a plan that would ensure both their survival and her own. If they hated her for it afterward, so be it.

Too quick for the gods or Sidraeus to know what she was doing, Atheia dipped her hand in the fountain, just past her wrist. Her spiral mark shone faint silver as the salt water activated it, and as she called on Clover through his own blackened mark, a maelstrom of ash opened behind her on cue.

She smiled wickedly at the gods, at Sidraeus. "There is only one way to save the people and the worlds I love. And it's not with my death, but yours."

The maelstrom swallowed her and the gods and Sidraeus whole, bringing them into the sea of ash.

Right to Clover.

KAI

IT SHOULD HAVE COME AS NO SURPRISE TO ANYONE THAT the godsworld would be accessible in Dovermere. With all the worlds overlapping one another, the sea caves were no longer underwater, and they did not resemble the caves they'd come to know at all.

In fact, they looked like a patchwork of all the caves and grottos and deep places where a door had stood in each world. The algae-slick walls of Dovermere in some places. The basalt columns of the Wychwood tunnels under the yew tree in others. The cavernous, fiery insides of the Sunforge spread in the spaces between.

Where the Hourglass should have stood—where the door of each world now overlapped, Kai supposed—stood the icy gate of the fourth world, thrown wide open onto the sea of ash beyond.

"This is going to work," Emory said with more conviction than Kai felt as she stepped through the door ahead of the group.

Kai, Baz, and Luce followed. It had been a hard-fought battle to keep their group small. Everyone had wanted to come along—Jae,

Theodore, Virgil, Vera, and Nisha especially—but they'd ultimately agreed the fewer people, the better.

If this didn't work, there needed to be people left to pick up the fight.

As they walked up the steps toward the fountain, Kai could scarcely believe he was here, after all he'd been through. He'd seen the Wychwood with his own eyes, had gone to places that went beyond anything ever written of in *Song of the Drowned Gods*, yet somehow it felt incredible to him that the sea of ash actually existed. Bare and desolate and chilling, with a monster waiting in its midst.

Clover had his back turned to them, staring at a rift of ash through which emerged Farran and Atheia and Sidraeus. Clover wasted no time in trapping Farran in an onslaught of power. The gods were brought to their knees, no match for Clover here, in a world he had made his own, next to a stagnant fountain overspilling with ghosts eager to fuel their master.

Emory took the keys out of her pocket. Asphodel's rib bone and the warrior's gold heart in one hand, the guardian's wooden lyre in the other. While Clover was preoccupied with the gods, she unlocked their power—and absorbed it.

The bone and the heart began to shine in a brilliant light, and as Emory plucked the strings of the lyre, all three keys erupted into a maelstrom of earth and greenery, of flame and molten gold, of lightning and wind, and swirled around Emory, seeping into her.

Clover faltered, wincing in pain, as if *he* were losing that same power. Emory smiled victoriously. But it only lasted a second before Clover seemed to regain control of himself, smirking at her as if she were nothing but a small thorn in his side, and drew on the restless souls around him.

A tidal wave of translucent ghosts swept over the temple. Desperation and anger filled the air along with the cloying smell of sulfur. Kai's skin burned as the spirits brushed past him. He'd been through this before, he thought. In the hellfire stream down in the abyss. With these same restless souls that reminded him of the umbrae as they drew not on his fears, but on every single regret inside him, all the things he had ever hated himself for and wished he could take back, all the resentments he held for others, the anger he never quite learned to let go of.

It was torment. It was a taste of hell. It was a call to join these angry spirits that *understood*, that *glorified* such pain and anger, that wanted him to keep it inside him forever and tend to it until it consumed him whole and made him one of them. Empty and angry, eternally so.

But Kai didn't want to be tortured like this forever. He had wasted too much of his life being weighed down by this anger and resentment he carried. He had seen what holding on to such emotions did to the souls of the dead, how it turned them to stone deep down in the abyss, cementing them there forever if they couldn't let go. If they couldn't choose peace for themselves.

Kai thought of all the moments in his life that had brought him joy and love and serenity, these bright lights that had filtered in through the cracks of his anger. Waking up next to Baz. Finding community with the Eclipse-born. Helping to free them from the Institute. Even finding Farran again had been a blessing in disguise, a chance for Kai to understand the weight of resentment and forgiveness and second chances. To see someone refusing to be held back by the baggage of two lifetimes, persevering on and on despite everything he'd been subjected to by gods and fate and monsters and his own inner demons.

Kai would choose the same for himself now. These restless souls could not deter him.

At his side, Baz screamed and cried, plagued by the souls' torment. Kai reached for him, gripping his hand tight in his. "Don't let them win, Brysden. They feed on anger and despair and hate. I'm right here with you, and I'm not going anywhere."

Slowly, Baz seemed to come back to himself, sagging against Kai. His breathing was labored but his eyes were clear. Around them was chaos, but the souls seemed to have moved on to other targets to feed on and torment.

Kai caught sight of the gods in Farran's body, fending off these angry souls keeping them down, and Clover trying to draw on what was left of their power. But Clover finally turned his attention away from them, spinning toward Emory as she fought off a gaggle of souls and advanced on him now, ready to end him, fueled as she was by the three keys . . . no, *four* keys, because her mother had come up to her side, and Kai could see that Emory was drawing on the residual power of Atheia in Luce's blood.

Near the empty fountain were Sidraeus and Atheia, locked in a fruitless battle, neither of them able to die by the other's hand. But they could die by another's. And the gods, making use of Clover's distraction, moved against them.

"No!" Kai yelled.

The gods were supposed to let Emory kill Clover, but they'd made it clear they didn't have faith in her ability to do so. The fountain was right there, Sidraeus and Atheia right beside it, so why not sacrifice them and regain their godhood to put an end to Clover themselves, take matters into their own hands?

Farran's steps seemed to slow. Baz's magic, Kai realized, trying to stop him.

Baz was gritting his teeth. "I can't hold them—they're too strong—"

His magic might be powerful, but they were still gods, despite the faint trickle of power they had.

Kai moved in front of them, his tattoos activating as the wards they'd always been, and shoved the gods out of Farran's body again. It rendered them vulnerable—the gods in their true forms, not immaterial as they had been in the living realms, but as material as they had been when Kai first met them in the abyss.

Clover's head whipped to them, as if he could sense that they were here in full now, not hiding inside a vessel. Here, at last, they could be killed. The restless souls amplified their assault on the gods, driven by Clover, who could probably taste victory at hand. Kai pulled a dazed Farran out of the way, wondering if he'd just handed Clover the win without meaning to.

There was a scream, followed by a flash of movement. Sidraeus was on his knees, doubled over in pain. And Atheia, freed from their clash, was unleashing a wave of death magic toward the four gods. The gods managed to evade it, but Atheia was still advancing on them, wrath twisting Romie's features into something otherworldly and ugly.

Kai looked Sidraeus over but found no wound.

"It's not me who's hurt," Sidraeus gritted out, his eyes fixed on a point behind Kai.

Where Baz lay in a pool of blood.

BAZ

IT HAPPENED QUICKER THAN BAZ COULD STOP IT.

In truth, he was too shocked by Atheia running at him to even *think* of stopping it. Because this was his sister–this face he hadn't seen in almost a year, except in dreams and nightmares and hellish hallucinations. He knew it wasn't actually Romie; there had been no trace of her as Atheia and Sidraeus clashed in a dance of power, two deities circling each other like predators, a thousand years of rage brewing between the two and no way to put an end to each other. And there certainly was no trace of her as she drove the knife into Baz's middle.

He couldn't understand it at first, why she would turn on him at all. But when he saw Sidraeus doubled in pain, he realized she'd hurt Baz to get away from *him*–a distraction she was using now to kill the gods.

Anger flashed on Clover's face. A flicker of betrayal. *He* was supposed to kill the gods, not Atheia. Whatever truce had been between them was broken. Atheia wanted to claim power for herself, to end these gods that had been so very ready to sacrifice her.

As blood pooled out of him, as Kai reached for him, trying to stop the bleeding, desperate words and angry tears spilling from him, Baz could see with utter clarity how this would all end. Baz would die here by his sister's hand. Clover would kill Atheia, and by extension, Romie. He would destroy what was left of the gods. He would squash Emory like a fly and get his army of restless souls to devour them all whole.

What is hope in the face of a tyrant god? What is hope against the kind of destruction there is no coming back from?

Chaos would win, just as Equilibris said. The damage was irreversible.

But Baz had practice reversing things that would otherwise be irreparable. Reaper magic he could send back into the hands of an unsuspecting Tidecaller. Collapsings he could stop by reverting silver blood back to red. Unhallowed Seals he could undo so that magic flowed again in the veins of those who had been cut off from it.

He reached for Atheia with his magic. Willed the threads of time to pull her back, away from the gods, away from Clover, until she was standing in front of him with her dagger brandished toward him, its surface unbloodied, the wound in his middle yet to be inflicted.

Before she could plunge the knife into him, Baz said her name.

"Romie. Please."

She faltered, pausing. He fought back tears. Part of him wanted to gather her in his arms and never let go, to assure himself she was really here—that she hadn't died at Dovermere like he'd spent all those long months after her disappearance believing. She had simply disappeared through a door to other worlds, and now she had returned, and everything could be right between them again.

For a moment, he truly believed this was his sister. She looked the same, after all. But her eyes shifted colors like a prism, the curve of her mouth like a cruel dagger, and Baz was suddenly reminded of the hallucination he'd seen on the path between heaven and hell, where Romie had bled Emory and every Eclipse-born of their silver blood. Where she had sliced his own neck open with another dagger.

If his sister was still in there, if she still had some form of control over Atheia, it was clear that she no longer did in this moment. That Atheia alone held the reins.

And yet, she was still hesitating. Still had not plunged the knife into him.

"Romie, I beg you, if you're in there—don't let her do this. Don't let her destroy you by destroying those you love." Baz swallowed thickly. "We can go back home and be a family. It's not too late for that, Ro. Everything you've done—everything *she's* done through you—it isn't your fault. I forgive you. We all forgive you. There is nothing to forgive. Please, just come back to us."

Those kaleidoscope eyes glimmered with anger, her knuckles white around the dagger she still held. Power gathered in her free hand, Reaper magic dark and foreboding, as if death by knife would not suffice.

Baz's stomach fell. It was too late to get through to his sister. But at least he had tried.

He closed his eyes, breathed one last "I forgive you," and waited for death to strike.

ROMIE

I FORGIVE YOU. WE ALL FORGIVE YOU. THERE IS NOTHING to forgive.

The words reached into the depths of Romie's subconscious, the dark hole she'd been thrown in by Atheia. For a second, the death Atheia was so close to unleashing on Baz, just like she had the Tidal Council, paused.

But they'd been here before, the two of them. Romie had fought and fought against Atheia only to be pushed deeper in the dark after she did. And this—Baz waiting with his eyes closed for her to strike him down—it was inexcusable. There was no coming back from this. She'd failed at wresting power from Atheia when it mattered most and knew there could never be such a thing as forgiveness for her.

She was alone, as Atheia had said. And it was her own damn fault. The dreamer who'd reached too far, who'd been seduced by the call of a destiny she had believed to be pure and only saw how corrupt it was when it was literally invading her body.

Alone, alone, alone.

But she wasn't, not entirely.

If you let her win, that's when you become truly alone. That's when you go beyond forgiveness.

The voices of Aspen and Tol and Orfeyi—these voices she had so far only heard in dreams—called out to her in the dark. Romie felt them right there with her, holding her fraying mind together as her hands shook around the dagger she held in one and the power still accumulating in the other.

So fight, their voices urged. *Fight for yourself, and for them, and for us.*

And they were right: Romie wouldn't, *couldn't*, let Atheia win. She wouldn't let anyone else guide her actions but her own heart. Never again.

So with Aspen, Tol, and Orfeyi lending her strength, Romie pulled herself up to the surface and felt herself expand within her own mind.

You are the one who's alone, she told Atheia as she pushed the deity down and down and down. *So desperate to achieve perfection with your creations, you forgot the beauty in sharing, in collaboration, in friendship and love and accepting all the flaws that make things beautiful and unique. You chose to stand alone. I would rather die for those I love than to follow in your footsteps for one more second.*

Atheia raged and fought back, but Romie fought harder. Because that was *Baz* she was standing in front of. Romie was face-to-face with her brother for the first time in nearly a year, and she wanted so badly to run into his arms. She wanted to hear all his stories, see how much he'd changed over the past year—Tides, he even *looked* different, so much more assured of himself. She wanted to tell him all the things she'd seen as well, the stuff pulled from the very book that had shaped his childhood.

More than anything, she wanted to say sorry. Sorry for all the secrets she'd kept from him. For the grief and heartache he must have felt after she'd first disappeared. She wanted to apologize for pulling away from him after the incident at the printing press, because she knew now that, while she told herself she was above everyone else's fear of Eclipse magic, that hadn't been true. She'd been just as scared as anyone, if not more. She'd resented their father for what his Collapsing put their family through, and she'd feared Baz for his susceptibility to do the same.

Her gaze landed on Emory, who was fighting so hard to stop Clover, her power chipping so slowly at him, at this god she couldn't possibly defeat, yet here she was still trying.

Enough. Romie was done being a puppet for Atheia, this deity she'd put her trust in and who'd ended up being vile and hateful and ugly. She was done following the whims of fate, of a destiny that made her into a murderer.

She was done sharing her body.

She thought of Nisha. Of her father and mother. Of Emory and Baz and Kai, all these people she'd let down and who had fought for her anyway. Now it was her turn to fight for them.

You're not in control anymore, she told Atheia, pushing her consciousness to the same depths *she* had been imprisoned in.

With one last shove, Atheia's screaming subsided—and in a sudden, dizzying breath, Romie was free.

The magic Atheia had been about to unleash faded just as quickly, the dagger slipped from her hand, and all the fight left Romie as she fell to her knees. "I'm so sorry," she breathed.

Baz gaped at her. From the look in his eyes, she knew he saw *her*. Not Atheia, not the cruel deity, but his sister. He swallowed her up in a hug, and she broke down against him. A sob escaped her lips. "I'm sorry for everything."

"I'm sorry too," Baz said.

"You? For what?"

"For Collapsing that day at the printing press. Sending Dad to the Institute. Breaking our family apart."

"That wasn't your fault. I'm sorry it took me so long to tell you that."

They clung to each other. There was nothing to forgive for either of them. They were family—and that meant they would love each other no matter what.

Romie drew away from Baz to look at Emory. Her friend appeared utterly spent, but she was still trying. Clover barely spared a glance at her, too caught up in his efforts to kill what was left of the gods.

Until Emory erupted in brilliant light that made Clover falter.

EMORY

POWER COULD BE TAKEN, AND SO EMORY WOULD TAKE it away from Clover once and for all.

She tapped into the essence of the keys as she might have once done with Romie, Aspen, and Tol, felt them coursing through her veins. Her mother stood at her side, and Emory could sense the residual echo of Atheia that her blood carried, a hunch they'd all had that proved true now. Luce told her to take it—to tap into this faint trickle of power she carried—and so Emory gently pried it from her, careful not to weaken her mother like she had weakened Romie in the past.

Fueled by the old keys, she called on the ungodly power within Clover, desperate to take it away from him—all the magic he'd stolen from keys and gods and every soul he had ever done violence to or betrayed.

Clover was too strong. The gods had been right: even with the power of the previous keys fueling her, Emory was no match for him.

But if she were to sever his link to his source of power...

The souls of the dead were as relentless as they had been in the abyss, and more so now than ever. They did not whisper to her as they did then, begging to be used, to be *freed*; they were Clover's now, and his alone, trapped in a sort of twisted symbiotic relationship with him. They made him the god that he was, and through him, their power continued to flow. Through him, they got to taste magic–*life*–however corrupt. They grew angrier, more restless, feeding on his own anger. And he grew fouler with that venom coursing through him.

Emory hadn't wanted their ghostly power, and she was glad she hadn't let them anywhere near her. But this couldn't go on. She needed to stop them, to stop him.

She caught sight of *his* features among the throng of ghosts. Keiran. It didn't matter then, the bad choices he had made, the vile things he had done. He and all of these souls deserved a second chance. An opportunity to rest, if that's what they desired, or to try again.

In her mind, Emory heard Sidraeus telling her she would have to put to rest the sacrificed Tidecallers, much like she had healed the umbrae that first time she'd crossed through the space between worlds.

Maybe it was what she needed to do with these souls, too, for balance to be restored, for Clover to be destroyed.

But they were an unshakable force against the small power she wielded, even with the three keys she was drawing on, even with her mother at her side lending her strength. Emory needed more, so she opened herself up to powers that went beyond the keys, calling on the magic of every being who bore a trace of Sidraeus's might–not only the Eclipse-born, but their otherworldly equivalents, too, the hellwraiths and eldritch beasts and Songless who were all a result of the clashing vision between two creators, products of liminality that would never have existed without Sidraeus and Atheia both.

They were all the same, in the end. Desperate to not only survive, but to belong.

Emory could feel their familiar magic rush through her, making her shine with brilliant light. She wasn't stealing power from them; it was like when she had borrowed power from Romie, Aspen, and Tol at the Forge, a friend calling out for help and receiving it.

Fueled by all their combined power, Emory faced the specters with a single thought.

Heal.

She erupted in brilliant light, and every specter it touched seemed to quiet, shucking off all the pain and hate and resentment and unsettling thought they had let fester inside them. Theirs was not an unmaking, but a release. They did not vanish, but flowed gently into the fountain, where they swirled and eddied like oddly glowing water, like fog over a calm river. The fountain, at last, was being replenished.

From where he stood fighting the gods, Clover faltered as if suffering a fatal blow. Power rippled and fizzed around him in an unsettling way, as if he were a live wire cleaved in half, cut off from its source of power. The more and more souls pooled into the fountain, the weaker he seemed. He looked like Quince Travers had the night that started all of this on Dovermere Cove, deteriorating before their eyes. He looked like Lia Azula whose tongue became emaciated, and Jordyn Briar Burke who had turned into an umbra. He looked like the witch whose bones had broken and the warrior whose heart had stopped and the guardian whose soul was sucked out of him.

It was as if Clover's body was going through every such horror. As if, without the sustenance of the souls that had made him a god, he was becoming monstrous again. Veins turning black along pale skin. Turquoise eyes losing their otherworldly glow, flashing with hurt as he contorted in pain. He turned to face Emory, seeming to realize what was happening, what *she* was doing.

Emory felt how close she was to taking everything away from Clover—her own wretched ancestor, even if only distantly so. She could see it on his ashen face that his power was dwindling ever closer to extinction, until he was again just a Tidecaller, and perhaps not even that.

Just a man, painfully mortal.

And very, very angry.

His face contorted with a vengeful, vicious rage. Dust gathered around him, his faithful ash-monsters flocking to him as if to protect him. And just like that, Clover was gone—as if willing such power to him one last time—before he reappeared right in front of Emory.

She knew this would be the end. He looked like he was about to Collapse for good and take the whole universe with him in a killing blast. Maybe she had been too late. Maybe taking power away from him, cutting him from his corrupt source, hadn't worked one bit, and he would bring them all to ashes anyway.

Emory barely registered the body moving in front of her. She only made out the back of Sidraeus's head before he barreled straight into Clover and the two of them tumbled farther away, rolling in the ash. And then Sidraeus was crouching over Clover, holding him down, his runes flaring bright white.

Everything seemed to happen in slow motion. Clover's power building around him, ready to scorch everything in its path. Sidraeus meeting Emory's eye over his shoulder. His voice in her mind, soft as falling leaves.

You are a light, Emory Ainsleif. And it's been the honor of a very dark and lonely lifetime to know you.

"NO!"

Clover's magic erupted. But it did not sweep over them like a tidal wave of death. It concentrated around Sidraeus, *into* Sidraeus, making the runes on his skin come alive with electric light that flared brighter and brighter until the world was flooded white.

Emory couldn't see anything but light, couldn't feel anything except for the hole ripping open inside her, the loss so poignant it was unfathomable. The blast of power did not reach her, did not hurt her, because Sidraeus was containing it. Sidraeus was taking on the brunt of the attack, the full weight of Clover's deadly residual magic. Sidraeus was saving her, saving *all of them*.

And this would be his end.

When the light at last subsided, when everything quieted, Sidraeus's body was splayed out on the ground next to Clover's. Emory rushed over, tears streaming down her face, to find all the spiral runes on him gone, as if they had been wiped away by Clover's magic.

Sidraeus's skin was unblemished. No runes, no wounds.

A blast like that should have reduced him to cinders. But he opened his eyes—those beautiful, ecliptic eyes—and looked right at her. He reached a hand to her face, fingers so very delicate as they brushed her cheek, her lips.

"How?" Emory breathed.

He has fulfilled his bargain.

It was only then that Emory realized she and Sidraeus were surrounded by a familiar spiral of shadowy clouds, as if they were in the eye of a great cyclone frozen in time. The souls of the Tidecallers, whispering in their many-layered voices.

By being willing to die for the last Tidecaller, Sidraeus has put right what he broke so long ago, and so we protected him. They seemed to draw closer to Sidraeus, addressing him directly. *Phoebus. Bright one. Sidraeus. You brought us to ruin, cast a shadow upon the magic you left behind, but you have redeemed yourself here, and we the souls of those you first abandoned forgive you. Your bargain is ended. Your curse is lifted.*

Sidraeus's eyes shut as silent tears caught in his lashes. This was the redemption he had been looking for, and here it was granted.

The souls drew closer to Emory now, and when they spoke, their voices were full of yearning. *And now for our curse, Tidecaller. We wish to be free.*

"You deserve to be," Emory whispered, and gave the souls what they asked, healing them like she had the umbrae. They began to dissipate, rushing into the fountain like the other ghosts Emory had laid to rest.

When all of them disappeared, the world around them was still— except for the blur of motion in the corner of her eyes.

Clover had pulled himself to his feet, alive but ashen, his face lined and sunken as if the years were finally catching up to him. He must have been making his way toward Emory and Sidraeus, intent on killing them while they were trapped in the cyclone of souls. But Luce got to Clover first, plunging what looked like the first witch's discarded rib bone into his chest.

Clover's face contorted with shock and pain, his eyes falling on Luce as if he couldn't quite believe what was happening.

"This is for my daughter," Luce seethed, stabbing him again. "This is for everyone you lied to and used and brought to their deaths." Again. "For Asphodel and Thames and Cordelia most of all, whom you robbed of a great love, but not her legacy." Clover slumped to the ground as Luce pulled the rib out of him. She fell to her knees with him and held the bloodied bone over his heart. "Let my face be the last you see, knowing that it's your sister's own flesh and blood who put an end to you."

It happened fast. One moment, Luce was holding the bloodied bone over Clover's heart, and the next, *he* was the one holding it and slashing it wildly in defense.

A wet sound slipped from Luce's lips. A strained gargle as blood sprayed all over Clover's face. Luce stumbled backward, her hands going to her neck, where rivers of red rushed from a deep, horizontal slit.

A visceral scream tore from Emory's throat as she caught her mother in her arms. She didn't register what happened to Clover. Didn't register anything beyond the light fading too quickly from her mother's eyes, the way she fought to look at Emory as blood gushed out of her, pooling around them both. The hot, sticky feel of her hand as she touched Emory's cheek.

The faint smile that stretched her red-stained lips, as if she wasn't afraid to die if it meant her daughter lived.

Emory rejected it—this notion that anyone should have to die for her. Sidraeus had been willing to give up his life to save her, and now her mother, too, this woman who had already given up so much to protect her . . .

Enough.

The healing magic she'd grown up feeling so mediocre with poured out of Emory like a song echoing across the oceans of time that had once separated her and her mother. "Stay with me," she pleaded. "Don't leave me again."

She felt like the young girl she'd once been, who'd looked out her lighthouse window time and time again, waiting for the sailor she'd always known would never come back.

But Luce had come back, and Emory refused to let her go.

BAZ

THE RIB BONE WAS STILL IN CLOVER'S HAND WHEN KAI ripped him off Luce and shoved him to the ground. Baz couldn't begin to make sense of it—Luce, dying in Emory's arms. Emory's cries, slicing through his heart. But then, a gasp. Luce's throat patched up, healed by Emory. The two of them clinging to each other in a pool of blood. *Alive.*

The sight of Kai pummeling Clover with all the rage and grief of someone who hadn't yet realized the Dreamer wasn't dead broke through Baz's paralysis. He moved in tandem with Farran, both of them pulling Kai back from the wretched monster before them.

Weakly, Clover drew himself to his knees. His face was painted in red flecks from Luce's slashed neck, and his own blood spilled from his mouth and the wounds in his chest, black and oozing. His gaze landed on Luce, the sight of her alive making his shoulders slump. Not in defeat, Baz thought, but *relief*.

Clover had never looked so helpless as Cordelia's name tumbled from his lips. It stirred something in Baz, to know that after all this time, until the very end, Clover still thought of her. This was still his twisted way of protecting her. Of trying to better the world for her.

Cordelia had been the one person he'd wanted to save in this world, and the person he'd ended up becoming a monster for.

Farran knelt at Clover's side and grabbed hold of his hand, his face devastated. Clover looked at him as if he could see through the unrecognizable features to the boy he'd known at Aldryn two hundred years ago, the boy he'd used and manipulated and killed. The boy he might have loved if he weren't so very monstrous.

"Do you think I'll see her again?" Clover asked, quiet tears running down his cheeks.

Farran didn't answer him, only stayed there, holding his hand as Clover's breath rasped. Even after everything he had suffered through as Thames–even after trying so desperately to stop Clover as his reincarnated self–Farran still found it in him to be there for Clover in the end.

"Forgive me," Clover breathed, looking up at the sky.

Whether he meant the words for Thames or Cordelia or Luce or all the world, no one would ever know.

Clover disintegrated to dust. Like a manuscript burnt to ashes, all of its words and thoughts and stories forever lost to the flame. Swept away on a breeze, never to return. Any trace of the magic he had stolen–from the keys, from the gods, from the souls he had bound to him–returned to the fountain in a murmuration of bright specks, free from their captor at last.

Everyone stood still as the gods breathed in their recovered power, appearing more solid than ever with their full divinity returned to them. The silence that lingered was punctuated by the soft, teary words Emory and Luce were exchanging as they clung to each other, their clothes soaked through with blood. At Baz's side, Romie watched the tender scene with shining eyes, though something like remorse shadowed her features.

Baz turned to look at Kai but found the Nightmare Weaver hovering over Farran. Farran looked entirely stunned, kneeling in the ash where Clover had been. Tentatively, as if fighting against his better judgment, Kai rested a hand on Farran's shoulder.

"He's gone," Kai said in a voice so soft Baz almost didn't hear him. "It's over now."

Farran slowly lifted his face up to Kai, eyes red-rimmed and haunted. He looked once more at the empty spot beside him, his breathing labored, his lip trembling, as if he were only now realizing that Clover had been defeated. That this person who'd been such a fixture in not one of his lives, but two, was gone.

Not a person anymore, Baz reminded himself bitterly. A monstrous, soulless god who had wrought unspeakable destruction.

Farran seemed to come to the same conclusion. He nodded as if to convince himself, took hold of the hand Kai extended to him, and rose to his feet.

"If it's over," Farran said to no one in particular, "then why doesn't it feel like it?"

He was right. The sea of ash was as quiet and desolate and ominous as ever. Clover was gone, but there was an evil that persisted, a feeling of decay that gnawed at the edges of Baz's senses.

The ground beneath them lurched. A hole opened in the ash to reveal an endless darkness full of stars. In the distance, a tear in the air itself through which they could see a battering sea and rotten vines and storms trying to claw their way into the godsworld. It was like the godsworld was disintegrating before their eyes, pieces of the living realms and the sleeping realm breaking through.

Baz could see the familiar outline of Aldryn College through one of these openings–and the many faces pressed in windowpanes as students peered, wide-eyed, into the sea of ash.

"What's happening?" Baz exclaimed. "I thought getting rid of Clover would fix everything!"

Even the gods looked stunned. The goddess of the moon leaned over the fountain, where the souls that had been appeased by Emory swirled and swirled, nearly overflowing past the lip of the fountain.

The goddess's face paled. "It's the fountain. It may have been replenished with Clover's power, but it hasn't been restored to its former glory."

"That can't be," Luce said weakly as her daughter helped her to her feet. "Clover's dead."

"And I severed his link to the restless souls he was fueling himself with," Emory added. "I healed them all, put them to rest."

"Yet they remain stagnant in the fountain," the goddess said. "They aren't being reincarnated, and so the worlds aren't being replenished with pure magic like they should."

They had all thought that killing Clover would heal the worlds, return magic to its people. That it would make everything as it should be. But it didn't. Clover's death had fixed *nothing*.

The worlds seemed to be crumbling faster now, all fated to become ash. Almost as if Clover had put a curse on everyone: that if he should meet his end, then everything else must too.

Baz paused time just as the wave of chaos was about to hit them. The vastness of this power made him falter with the threads of time, had him scrambling to contain more and more and more. The tears in the fabric of the universe—the sleepscape sinkhole that had opened up at their feet and the dark pockets in the air through which the rest of the world poked through—they were all trying to expand, to consume the godsworld whole. It was as if the universe itself were trying to shatter around them, water pushing against a dam, and Baz couldn't hold it back, not as more and more force built behind the flood wall, threatening to burst.

"Clocks, this escalated quicker than I anticipated."

Equilibris's voice startled everyone as he sauntered up to them, looking for all the world like he was late for nothing more than a tea party. This was not the energetic, frenzied god Baz had come to know, but someone who seemed to have given up entirely. It was rather shocking, the difference between him and the other gods. While the four gods of the living had an aura of divinity to them now that their power had been restored, Equilibris had never looked so human, as if *his* power were still dwindling–had been since fate was broken and the worlds were fused together.

He took one look at the chaos Baz was keeping frozen in time and shook his head with a mournful look, mouth downturned. "A pity it had to come to this."

The god of the air narrowed their eyes at him. "And where have you been all this time, while we tried to stop it?"

"Languishing in his workshop, no doubt," the sun god said gruffly. "Leaving us to suffer as always."

Equilibris lifted a brow at the four of them. "Centuries we haven't seen each other, and this is the reception I get?"

"You threw us into the abyss."

"To keep you safe from Clover, yes. We've been over this before. It was never meant to be permanent. And here you stand, back in the godsworld with your power restored."

"So what is this, then?" The goddess of the earth gestured to the fountain, to the sea of ash breaking at the seams. "Why is nothing fixed?"

"Because the magic that was in Clover has been twisted and tainted by being inside him. It may have been returned to the fountain, but it is no longer a pure source of power like it once was. The darkness from this magic will continue to spread across realms as it has." Equilibris sighed. "I told you all it would come to this. The chaos is too great to be defeated by anyone."

"But you're a *god*," Baz spat. "Can't you do anything?"

Equilibris met his gaze square on, something playing behind his eyes that Baz couldn't decipher. "I told you you'd be begging me to reset the worlds in the end, didn't I?"

The one thing the god of balance had always been designed to do: wipe clean the board should it ever come to this point. Restart the whole tapestry from scratch and pray that fate would be kinder the next time around.

"No," Baz breathed. "There has to be another way." He'd broken fate, damn it; he was not letting everything happen the way he had seen it play out.

"I have to agree with the boy," the god of the sun grumbled. "To have gone through so much only to reach the same inevitable outcome as before . . ."

"Perhaps that is exactly why we should let Equilibris wipe clean the board," the goddess of the moon said with bitter resignation. "If eliminating Clover couldn't restore our realms to their former glory, then starting anew may well be our only choice." She fixed Emory with a predatory stare. "Of course, the Tidecaller would first need to die."

The last remaining failsafe preventing Equilibris from resetting the worlds.

"That's not going to happen," Sidraeus seethed, moving in front of Emory. "There has to be another way to fix things."

"There *is*," Equilibris said slowly, "but it is not something we gods can do." He motioned to all the dark rifts around them, these cracks of impossible power that Baz was trying to hold back. "This chaos will spill across the realms of the living and sleeping until death and creation become so at odds with each other that they obliterate us all in a wink. Unless the magic that flows through the fountain is fixed. It needs to be purged of its darkness for it to flow properly again, and that darkness needs to be taken far away from here, to a place where things go to be unmade."

The void.

The place beyond the abyss that was oblivion itself.

"But . . . how would that even be possible?" Baz asked.

"Isn't it obvious?" the god said with a gruff laugh. "You wrote the words yourself, Timespinner. *Blood and bones and heart and soul, combined to keep chaos and death from spilling across all worlds.*"

Baz blanched at the words from *Song of the Drowned Gods*. The scholar, the witch, the warrior, and the guardian had *become* the drowned gods, joining forces to face this darkness at the center of all things, just as the gods before them had done for centuries. A life for a life. The cycle starting anew. The sea of ash needed its keepers to guard the deadly beast within.

Blood and bones and heart and soul, combined to keep chaos and death from spilling across worlds.

His gaze snapped to Sidraeus, who was frowning at the fountain as if he were slowly putting the pieces together; then to his sister–Atheia's vessel–whose brown eyes were open wide, her mouth agape, as she understood.

The god of balance confirmed Baz's inkling when he said: "The only ones who can contain such chaos are the two beings who were made for such a thing. Sidraeus, the ferrier of souls, embodiment of sleep and death–and Atheia, who embodies life and healing."

As above, so below.

There was no way to properly restore the realms, to undo the chaos spilling across them, so the two deities had to take it with them into the void, the dark beyond stars.

Jumping into the void would unmake them. But it would also unmake the chaos. Restore balance. Wipe clean the slate without actually obliterating the worlds and everyone in them, as the god was compelled to do.

"So," the god said, clapping his hands together. "These are your options. You either fix this mess by taking the chaos out of here and into the void, thus restoring balance . . . or the Tidecaller has to die so I can reset the clock, so to speak, and start everything anew."

An impossible decision, here at the end of all things.

ROMIE

THE HORROR ROMIE FELT WAS MIRRORED ON EMORY'S face. Because no matter what they chose, at least one of them would die.

But Romie was not going to let it be Emory.

She felt Atheia's consciousness raging inside her at this conclusion, screaming about the problem being Sidraeus and his creations, not her. She refused to see everything she'd worked for be for nothing, refused to suffer such an end. Even now, faced with the destruction of the worlds she so loved, Atheia was unwilling to admit defeat.

Romie understood Atheia's anger and reluctance. She understood her refusal to die. And she understood, bleakly and all at once, that if Atheia were to die, then she would too.

Their fates were tied.

Once, Romie would have gladly embraced such a destiny. But now . . .

Now she wanted her own life, her own fate. To carve her own

path. Because she had realized that the destiny she'd been chasing all this time hadn't been hers at all, but Atheia's. Always Atheia's, this deity whose song Romie had followed until she was no longer herself but a vessel for someone else—whose song Aspen and Tol and Orfeyi had followed to their death.

They had lost everything because of their unwavering faith in Atheia, in this shared destiny of theirs. And after the fight Romie had put up to reclaim her body, to take control of her actions, she wanted to know what it would be like to keep going.

She wanted to earn the forgiveness her brother offered, wanted to set things right between her and Emory and all the people she had hurt under Atheia's influence. She wanted to build a greenhouse and spend her days in it with Nisha. She wanted to travel and make connections of her own free will, not ones dictated by a deity. She wanted to let her feet wander aimlessly instead of marching on a path set by a god.

Romie desired nothing more than to live outside of this senseless quest she'd gone on. To find her own destiny outside of that one. To do something *she* longed to do, not something her blood was predestined to *make* her want to do.

But she was done being selfish, too.

There would be no convincing Atheia to sacrifice herself. To carry this burden and follow this bleak path that would send her into the void. And though it made Romie sick to her stomach to decide such a thing for someone else, even someone as twisted as Atheia had become, she had to.

If she didn't, then the universe would perish. Her friends would die. Her family, too. And Romie couldn't have that.

What do you think? she asked Aspen and Tol and Orfeyi. Atheia's opinion might not weigh on her decision, but theirs did. They were a part of her; and though they were dead, they deserved a say.

We're with you, the three of them answered in unison. *Every step of the way into the dark, we'll be with you.*

It was all the confirmation Romie needed.

"I'll do it," she said aloud, though her voice was so soft no one seemed to hear. Louder, she repeated, "I'll do it."

Everyone turned to her, wide-eyed. She didn't blame them for their shocked looks; the decision was just as shocking to her, or rather the steadiness of her voice, the certainty in her blood, was what surprised her.

Atheia was pleading now, *begging*. But it didn't matter what Atheia wanted anymore. Romie stood resolute, unwilling to let Atheia be a driving force in her decisions. Because this was *her* choice, one she was making of her own volition, even if it went against all her broken dreams, because she was resolved to do what was right. To follow her damned destiny one last time, straight into the void if she must, if it meant those she loved would live.

At least this time, it was a destiny *she* was choosing.

EMORY

EMORY HAD JUST SAVED HER MOTHER FROM THE BRINK of death—could barely still believe how close she'd come to losing her—and now her best friend was talking about flinging herself into the void.

"I accept this fate in Atheia's place," Romie repeated in the wake of everyone's dumbfounded silence. "If this is what's needed to save everyone from oblivion, so be it. As Atheia's vessel, I'll do it. I accept."

"No," Baz breathed, shaking his head. Every muscle in him seemed to strain against the weight of the world, the chaos he was holding back as he slowed down time. "I can't let you do this, Ro." He looked at Emory with unshed tears. "I can't see either of you die."

Yet that was the choice Equilibris had presented them with, and Emory couldn't see another way out of this mess. She wasn't willing to die only for the worlds to be wiped clean, for everyone she loved to stop existing. What would be the point?

But the alternative was unthinkable. For the worlds and everyone in them to survive, two people she couldn't fathom parting with needed to die.

She looked at Sidraeus, his features set in valiant determination, and knew his choice would echo Romie's. He had just laid down his life for them all and had been spared by the runes on his skin, the bargain struck between him and the Tidecallers. No such bargain would save him now.

He met her gaze with such peaceful resignation, it speared through her heart like a knife. *I am not afraid of death, Tidecaller,* his voice echoed in her mind. *There is peace in endings, and if mine allows for survival to flourish from it, then it must be done.*

He accepted his fate. Atheia's, too. And while Emory wanted to beg him not to, wanted selfishly to keep him here by her side, this deity who had been her tormentor, her ally, her friend—who had found her in the dark and shown her there was beauty in it—she knew there would be no convincing him. It was his choice to make, and she understood it. She accepted it, even though it broke her heart to do so.

But she would not accept such a fate for Romie.

Sidraeus looked at her as if he knew exactly what she was about to do. He stopped her roughly by the arm as she took a step forward.

"Don't do this," he said in that low voice of his. His eyes blared with the wild beauty of the eclipse.

Emory touched his face, smiling through the blur of tears. "You've sacrificed yourself for me time and time again. I'm not letting you do it again." In her mind, she said, *We're accustomed to the dark, you and I. If you're not afraid of it, neither am I.*

His eyes closed, his cheek pressing into her hand. Accepting her choice just as she had his.

There was a great tremble around them as the chaos temporarily broke through Baz's defenses. He struggled to keep it contained outside of time, to keep it frozen, but the strain on his face, the way he was leaning against Kai, so weak from holding back this impossible thing . . .

"Time is running out," the god of balance said, looking between Emory, Sidraeus, and Romie. "What will it be?"

Without thinking twice on it, Emory reached for Romie, pulling her friend in a tight embrace. "I love you, Ro."

Romie's arms wrapped around her middle. "I love you, too. But you understand why I have to do this, right? You dying would accomplish nothing. But Atheia and Sidraeus . . ."

"I know." Emory held her tighter, not willing to let go, not wanting Romie to see the tears in her eyes and guess her intentions. "They have to go. But that doesn't mean you have to."

"What—"

Romie gasped and sagged against Emory as magic rushed through them. She shoved out of Emory's arms, confusion stark on her face. "What the hell are you doing?"

"It's all right," Emory whispered. "This is how it has to be."

With the power of the previous keys still coursing through her, Emory sought to separate Atheia from her vessel.

Being her vessel should never have been Romie's burden to bear, but Emory's. That's what Keiran had wanted from her from the start. That's what Emory had expected for herself too. But Romie had been forced to take on that role instead.

Emory, Emory.

Romie, Romie.

Emory and Romie. Their names practically an anagram, as if their destinies had always been entwined. Interchangeable, in a way. Emory, who thought she'd be the Tides' vessel. Romie, who had become just that. And Emory who would now take Romie's place when it counted most.

She had sacrificed parts of herself to save Romie before, but this wasn't the same. This felt right. Because she knew, had suspected for some time now, ever since they'd come to her in a dream, that Aspen, Tol, and Orfeyi weren't entirely dead. There was a way to restore them, she was sure of it. But not if Romie flung herself into the void, carrying them inside her—dooming them, unknowingly perhaps, to a truer death, one that could not be undone.

If Emory restored the keys and took Atheia's essence into herself—made herself into the vessel she was always destined to become—then she would be saving four people she cared about, and an entire universe in the process.

She could feel the magic working, powered not only by the three keys she'd taken into herself to defeat Clover—the original bone, heart, and soul—but her own mother's blood, too, thus completing the four-part symphony that was Atheia, all four keys swirling inside her in an echo of the power that was inside Romie.

She knew, though, that by unbinding Romie, Aspen, Tol, and Orfeyi from Atheia's essence, Atheia would die. She would go back to being a splintered thing, only this time, she would be gone for good.

Unless Emory took Atheia's essence into herself. She was a Tidecaller, after all; her ability was to call on the Tides' magic, to wield it as her own. And so she called on Atheia's power, her very essence, and consumed it.

She drew in a sharp breath as it settled inside her. It was ice cold in her veins. It was strength in her bones. It was fire in her heart and a gentle wind blowing through her soul.

With that divine power, she gave the keys back their lives. They had never been dead to begin with, had only been fused with Romie, kept tethered to her by their lifelines. She could see them suddenly: all of them surrounding Romie, connected to her pulse points by shimmering threads. Their lifelines tying them to the blood that coursed through everything like water.

So Emory called on her oldest magic and begged it to heal her friends.

Those threads shimmered brighter as Aspen, Tol, and Orfeyi solidified, going from translucent, ghostlike things, to flesh-and-bone living, breathing beings. And Romie—Romie's eyes were a definitive brown once more, not a single trace left of the cruel deity she had housed.

The keys were no longer keys. They were human, entirely themselves and so very much alive. And the deity whose essence Emory had taken inside her *raged*, and cried, and finally quieted, molding herself to Emory's insides.

For a terrible second, Emory heard Keiran's voice in her mind, telling her she would become the Tides' vessel and finally be rid of the Shadow's stain inside her. And she'd thought, perhaps, that taking Atheia's essence into her would indeed unmake her identity. She feared that she would lose being what she had now accepted she was: Eclipse-born, a Tidecaller, wielding the magic Sidraeus had created against all odds.

But no. She felt oddly complete, like this was what she'd been barreling toward all this time. And she didn't feel any less Eclipse-born than she did before. If anything, Atheia's magic transformed inside her to fit *her* identity.

The Tides. The Tidecaller.

Emory met Sidraeus's gaze. The way he looked at her made it clear he saw *her*, not Atheia. He knew she was still the same. That she'd molded Atheia's essence into her own, until Atheia was only another sort of magic pulsing through her veins, nothing more.

"Emory." Her mother looked at her with utter devastation. "What have you done?"

The words to make her understand escaped Emory. How could she tell her mother that this was, in a sense, her way of repaying Luce for the sacrifice she'd made all those years ago—leaving her child, interrupting her whole life to journey into the past and across worlds and into the pits of hell itself, all in an attempt to save not only Emory but all the worlds, too.

Now it was Emory's turn to do so.

Heart fracturing around her resolve, Emory drew Luce in for a tight embrace. "I wish we'd had time to know each other better," she whispered against her mother's ear, inhaling the scent of her, committing everything about her to memory.

When Luce pulled back, holding Emory's face in her hands, she didn't argue, didn't try to sway Emory from her decision; it was too late to do so anyway. Through tears, Luce mustered a smile and said, "But I do know you, my brave, incredible girl. You're everything I'd always imagined you'd be, and so much more."

Emory gave her a tearful smile of her own. "So are you. Take care of Henry, will you? Tell him—tell him I love him, and I'm sorry I had to leave him like this."

Luce nodded. "I will."

Her mother the sailor and her father the lighthouse keeper. In so many ways, Emory was the sea that had brought them back to each other. And now, like any tide, she would ebb outward again, leaving them both on a shore she wasn't destined for.

Before her resolve could shatter, she turned away from her mother, meeting Equilibris's gaze. Making it clear what choice she'd made.

The thought crossed Emory's mind that she had done what Clover had tried to, in a sense. She had imbibed the essence of a god. Did that make her a deity? Perhaps, in another time, she would have let herself become drunk off this knowledge, would have let herself sink into this deep well of power inside her. But she was changed. She didn't want such power. She had never needed it.

Now it was only a burden to bear, at least until the void unmade her and this power inside her and the chaos that threatened to destroy all the worlds and those she loved.

It was her sacrifice to make.

But not hers alone.

As Sidraeus took her hand, the fear that had started to take root inside her receded. They would face the void together, and that made it bearable.

ROMIE

ROMIE WAS USED TO HER LIFE FRACTURING INTO *befores* and *afters*, but nothing could have prepared her for the pain of being splintered from Atheia—from the keys, especially. These bonds that had united them and tethered them to Atheia *snapped*, and Romie felt like screaming, the loss so poignant she thought she would never be whole again without them. But when she opened her eyes, Aspen and Tol and Orfeyi were all here. Alive, in their own bodies.

And so was she.

The four of them held on to one another, embracing as if they couldn't quite believe that they were here, that this was real, that against all odds they were *alive*. But as Romie watched Aspen nestle her head against Tol's arm, saw the love in the draconic's eyes as he whispered something in the witch's ear; as Orfeyi squeezed Romie's hand with a wide, triumphant smile, all she could think was that there was something missing.

The echo of the song they'd all followed, this link to Atheia they had all shared that had made such inexplicable kinship bloom between them, was gone. There was an emptiness inside Romie that felt like grief, even though they were standing right here with her.

Maybe it wasn't emptiness. Maybe there was simply more room to be herself now that she wasn't sharing her body with someone else's essence. This was all her.

Because Atheia was gone.

And as Romie looked at Emory, her friend smiling at her through tears, Romie felt a wild rush of relief and hope. If her fate was severed from Atheia's, it meant she wouldn't have to sacrifice herself. Wouldn't have to throw herself into the void. She would get to *live*, and fight every day for Emory's forgiveness. They could move past this, she was sure of it. She understood now that they couldn't go back to those two girls they'd been before, because they had changed too much. Had gone through so much together. And perhaps that made their friendship stronger. The future could only make it stronger still.

Because they would get to live.

But then reality tore down her hope and her smile as she made sense of the tears in Emory's eyes, of the resignation on her face.

Romie might get to live. But Emory wouldn't—because she had taken Atheia's essence inside her.

I love you, Emory mouthed, her eyes full of apology.

Romie wanted to tear Atheia's essence out of her friend with her bare hands and take it into herself again. She couldn't let Emory sacrifice herself in her stead. She wanted to rage against whatever cruel destiny it was that they should each choose to sacrifice herself for the other. That this should be the moment where they finally understood each other's motivations and all the hardships they'd gone through. That for a brief moment, Romie had let herself hope that they could save the worlds together and go home and be friends again, laugh as they once did, forgive each other and accept all the parts of their selves they felt ashamed of. That they could grow from this experience, their friendship becoming stronger than ever, because they finally, fully understood each other. Fully accepted each other.

But it was too late.

It was too late.

BAZ

BAZ COULDN'T BELIEVE HE WAS HERE AGAIN, WATCHing helplessly as Emory was about to leave to horizons he could not follow her to. And he hated it. He wanted to keep her here, to beg her to stay. Last time, he hadn't. Last time, he'd let her go because that was what was needed.

His resolve wasn't so sturdy now.

Because this time, he knew there was no coming back for her.

But watching Romie and Emory break down in each other's arms as they said goodbye, seeing Luce hug herself as she tried desperately not to fall apart, Baz knew he had to remain strong. He saw it on Emory's face, how fraying her own resolve was. He had to be strong for her, for everyone else around him, for the worlds themselves.

But his strength was dwindling. Kai was holding him steady—as he always had, in more ways than one—but Baz's magic was taking a toll on him. He wasn't made to contain such chaos, to hold back the weight of a universe tearing at the seams. If he faltered even slightly, they would all perish.

He swallowed back his tears as Emory turned to him. They both knew there was no time for a proper goodbye. Both knew that if they were to embrace, to share words, both of their resolves might break. And yet Emory did so anyway. She pulled him in for a hug, and Baz couldn't help but press his lips against the side of her head, inhaling the scent of her one last time.

"I don't know if I can do this," Emory whispered, so low he barely heard her.

Whether she meant saying goodbye or healing magic or stepping through the void, Baz didn't know. It didn't matter. What she sought from him was reassurance, and this much, he could give her.

"If I've learned anything from you, Emory Ainsleif, it's that you can do anything you set your mind to. There has never been a darkness you couldn't face or a door you couldn't walk through or impossible odds you couldn't overcome."

Her arms tightened around him, her body spasming in a silent sob. "I'll miss you so much."

"Maybe this isn't the end," Baz whispered, needing this glimmer of hope to hold him steady, to give him the strength to let her go.

Emory smiled at him sadly, not believing his words, perhaps, but clinging to them anyway. She wiped at her eyes, looking at Kai. "Take care of him. Of all of them."

"You have my word," Kai said.

Emory drew back to stand next to Sidraeus. They looked at each other, a silent exchange passing between them. When Emory met Baz's gaze again, the stormy seas of her eyes were quiet and sure.

"You can let go now," she said.

With a breath, Baz did—and watched as that chaos wove infinity circles around Emory and Sidraeus, a vortex of death that only they could contain.

Wait, Baz wanted to say. *Stay.* But he knew that this time, it was impossible.

He may have broken fate, but this was still the only ending left.

EMORY

IT STARTS AT THE ROOT, NOT THE LEAF, BAZ HAD TOLD her once, when helping her work out how to use Sower magic in Romie's greenhouse.

Emory realized that this was where they'd gone wrong. They'd been trying to fix the problems that stemmed from the root of the issue, but not the root cause itself.

To restore the balance of the universe, they couldn't just revive the wilted leaves—defeating Clover, returning power to the gods, healing the restless souls. They had to address the root, this darkness that had corrupted magic itself, that had set like rot in the source of all creation.

The fountain needed to flow freely with magic that was made pure again, with power that could reincarnate all the souls that found themselves there and flow back out into the worlds, feeding into the ley lines like blood vessels to revitalize them.

This most vital of cycles needed to be restarted. Death feeding into life feeding into death, over and over, like the phases of the moon and the ebb and flow of the tides.

After darkness, light; again and again.

And Emory had practice drawing on such darkness. She reached for this corrupt source of power, felt it through the ley lines that spiraled through all worlds, which had become one thanks to what Clover had done. The ley lines were entwined in ways that should never have been possible, blocking the flow of even the trickles of power left there, and all it wanted was death and destruction and chaos.

Emory called on all the magics at her disposal to cleanse the rot. She had tried before to heal the ley lines and had failed miserably. But fueled as she was now by the original keys and Atheia's own essence, failure wasn't in the cards. And she understood what she hadn't back then: that for this darkness to be purged, it needed somewhere to go. Someone to hold it.

Her veins glowed silver even as the darkness wove around her, thicker and thicker. She felt Sidraeus's hand reach for hers, and suddenly the weight of the darkness wasn't so heavy. It seeped into him, drawn away from her at his touch as he had done so often before. But the more corruption she drew away from the fountain, the heavier that burden became, and neither of them could hold it forever.

When Emory thought she might break, Sidraeus drew her into a tender embrace. She wished they would have had more time together. A chance to explore what was between them. To share more than that kiss, so fleeting in hindsight. A stolen moment that would never be enough.

There was only this now. Everything else fell away: the sea of ash, the death and chaos all around them. The shape of her name yelled in the chaos, a voice that told her to *wait*. And she knew that voice. Had been in this very same predicament before. Only this time, she did not turn. She did not stop for one final goodbye with those she loved. It was already done.

All of it faded until there was only her name murmured on Sidraeus's lips, brushing against her ear, her magic, her soul. A promise that they would find each other again, if such a thing were possible.

We are born of the moon and tides, and to them we return, Emory thought.

Except there was no returning for her. Not this time. She'd not only been born of the moon and tides, but of the darkness and stars, too. Caught somewhere in the space between them. That was where she was bound—the dark oblivion that was the void beyond stars.

Together, she and Sidraeus drew the last of the darkness inside them, all the ash and death that was destroying the universe. It amassed in a maelstrom of power around them. The more and more it gathered, the more the godsworld changed before their eyes, and as those pockets of the living and sleeping realms closed, Emory knew that the worlds had been unfused, and order had at last been restored.

With the final bit of rot swirling around them, Emory and Sidraeus took a step into the last pocket of darkness that was closing up.

And plummeted through the dark.

ROMIE

AS ROMIE WATCHED EMORY TAKE ALL THAT DARKNESS inside her, the sun came out. A singular ray of hope in all this chaos. Emory smiled at her, as if she too could see it. As if she too was daring to hope that this might not be the end. That she might survive this, and they might see each other again.

The sun shone brighter. It pierced through the clouds of ash and flooded the godsworld as all evil was chased away, seeping into Emory and Sidraeus.

In a burst of light, Emory and Sidraeus shot across the sea of ash and into the darkness of the sleepscape just before the rift closed behind them, swallowing them forever, like stars winking out of the universe.

And though the sun had never been brighter, the godsworld restored to a flowering garden, Romie fell to her knees and screamed, feeling a hole inside her she knew would never be filled.

PART V
THE VOIDBOUND

THROUGH DARKNESS THEY FELL, AND FELL, AND fell. Past the bridge of stars that connected the four living realms like points on a spiral. Past the path between heaven and hell. Through the deep abyss where souls turned to stone were tortured for eternity.

They had seen it all, every facet of these realms. It was a comfort to know they would be restored with their unmaking. The two held on to each other as they plunged toward this inevitable end, hoping to remain forever bound like binary stars orbiting around the darkness held between them.

The void opened below, inviting them to drown in its infinite nothingness.

They dissolved in a whisper, a hush.

And here, at last, was the end.

But there was peace to be found in endings, beauty in imagining where they might lead next.

BAZ

IT WAS BAZ'S FIRST DAY BACK AT ALDRYN, AND ALREADY he was in the library.

He had just been to Dean Fulton's office, discussing the terms of his return. Spring was here, the school term was almost out, but Baz would catch up on the time he had lost so that he could graduate. Which explained his trip to each of the four libraries, where he gathered all the textbooks he would need.

It felt incredibly mundane, after everything he'd been through. And yet there was comfort in it too.

The world was its own again. No dragons soaring in the sky, no pockets of darkness appearing like bruises on skin. The tide ebbed and flowed in steady fashion, the moon went from new to waxing, full to waning, and new all over again. Everything was as it should be, magic following the rules it always had now that the mythic forces it drew on had been repaired.

But the scars left by the chaos remained. Shores were still ravaged. The lighthouse still lay at the bottom of the cliff Aldryn stood on. The campus itself was in a state of disrepair, battle-scarred yet holding strong.

As Baz walked through campus, hugging his stack of books close, nothing felt the same. Students waved at him in passing, gave him a kind nod or a smile, even a friendly word. He was not a ghost, no longer someone whispered about behind hands. He was the Timespinner who'd been there when the Tides and the Shadow left, when the Tidecaller sacrificed herself to save their world and restore their magic.

To most, he was a hero. To others, few though they were, he was still Eclipse-born, still someone they did not trust.

Lunar magic had been restored, though only as they had always known it—splintered between lunar houses and tidal alignments, with all the same rules that had always dictated it. And Eclipse magic remained the same in that it was accessible always, not reliant on moon phases and tide levels to be used by its bearers.

But the real change came from the eradication of Collapsing. They no longer had to deal with this barrier put on their magic; they had access to all their limitless power the way the original Eclipse-born did.

It was as if, once the souls of the original Tidecallers had been lain to rest, perhaps the memory of Tala, who had first created this damper on Eclipse-born power to shield them from the gods, found peace. And the Shadow's curse as they knew it came to an end.

No one had to fear them anymore. They never should have to begin with—should have always trusted the Eclipse-born to handle the risks of Collapsing, just as Reapers were trusted not to misuse their own deadly magic. But perhaps this would open the eyes of more people to the fact that Eclipse magic belonged. That it posed no danger.

It certainly felt like most people believed this, as Baz walked through campus. A lot of them had reconsidered their stance on Eclipse-born after seeing the lengths to which Atheia had gone and hearing Sidraeus be willing to sacrifice himself for them all while she was not—and then glimpsing what had happened through the pockets that had opened up to the godsworld during that final fight. But Baz knew there were those who stuck to their hateful beliefs.

The Tidelore cult and what remained of the Selenic Order that hadn't been destroyed by Atheia were still running about, though no longer fueled by the magic Atheia had given them. The horrors they'd been committing at the Institute—taking power from Eclipse-born held captive there—had come to light, and now they and every hateful Regulator involved were under harsh scrutiny. They had Virgil's parents to thank for that, as well as other prominent members of the Order who claimed not to have known what the Tidal Council was up to. All of them were now risking their reputations to help expose the Order's every dark secret.

It was a start, Baz thought. But maybe everything couldn't be fixed overnight. Maybe the best they could hope for was that they were headed for better days. There was still work to be done—and maybe there would always be.

Baz hopped into the elevator that would lead him down to Obscura Hall, wondering if there would be a need to keep it behind wards going forward. The wards had kept lunar mages out to protect them from accidental Collapsings, making it a safe haven for Eclipse-born. But maybe, once they had properly reclaimed it for themselves, they could open the doors to others. To those who wanted to learn at their side.

The familiar rush of the elevator going down made Baz's heart catch in his throat. Suddenly everything seemed to slow. He blinked—and found he was no longer in the elevator, but in a familiar workshop.

It was not the destroyed workshop he had last seen, with all its time-measuring instruments broken and shattered and the loom toppled over on its platform. Everything had been restored and put back in its place. The loom stood in the center once more, but it spun no threads, weaved no tapestry. A sheet had been thrown over it, as if to cover something no longer needed.

And it wasn't needed. Threads wove over and around the workshop, dancing between the stars, knotting and twisting together of their own volition, making patterns more intricate and beautiful than Baz had ever seen. As if, unbound from the fate that had dictated their movements, they were free to move as they wanted.

"This was always the outcome I had hoped for, you know."

Baz spun at the rough voice. Equilibris stood behind him, looking more at peace than ever before as he surveyed the dancing threads, a fond smile on his lips.

His words were slow to reach Baz. After Emory and Sidraeus had disappeared into the void, after the rest of them had been sent back to their world, Baz had been too numb to care about the whims of gods and the events that had led them here. Not when Emory was gone forever.

But he had thought about it in the days since. Everything Equilibris had done had been a great manipulation. Letting a single Tidecaller survive back then, a girl named Tala who created a damper that would shield her magic from godly eyes and allow for other Tidecallers to be born, every now and then, each one preventing Equilibris from resetting the worlds. Bringing Baz into his workshop, introducing him to the inner workings of fate so that he would eventually break it. Painting himself as the villain who *wanted* to wipe clean the board, all so Baz and his friends would find another way to fix things. A way that ended in Emory and Sidraeus sacrificing themselves to make magic pure again, ensuring the preservation of an entire universe.

"You never wanted to reset the worlds and start over, did you?" Baz said. It was formed like a question, but it wasn't really. He knew it to be true in his gut. "You wanted me to break fate so you wouldn't have to do what you were destined to do. You wanted us to save the universe instead of having you destroy it."

The god's eyes were bright. "Yes."

Baz studied him, recalling how painfully human Equilibris had looked next to the gods of the living. He appeared stronger now, as if he'd gotten his spark back once the chaos had been eradicated and the fountain restored. And yet, Baz couldn't shake this feeling that Equilibris still didn't seem as powerful as he had when they'd first met.

"Would you even have been able to reset the worlds, in the end?" he asked on a hunch.

Equilibris gave him a sad, knowing smile. "I lost that ability the moment you broke fate."

Baz should have known—should have put it together that destroying fate would untether the god from his, free him from his destiny. "Yet you let us all believe it was still an option. Why?"

"I find that people are more accepting of their fates when they believe they have a choice. But that was my last manipulation, I assure you," the god said sheepishly. "Everything I've done, it was to allow humans to take control of their fates. I could never make that happen on my own. It went against my very nature. So I had to take small rebellions, create strategic snags in the tapestry that would weaken it enough for you to break it." He sighed. "I was chained to fate as much as you all were. Have been since the dawn of time. And I was so very tired. I wanted to be free of it. Now I can be, and so can you."

Baz swept a gaze over the workshop again. The sheet over the loom. The instruments on the shelves. Everything appeared to be put away for good. "So, what, this was just a long con for you to retire?"

The god burst out laughing. "In a way, I suppose it was. We gods have had our time at the helm of our realms. But control over the worlds should belong to those who live in them, and no god should ever have the power to obliterate them on a whim. I've always agreed with Atheia and Sidraeus about that. Now that fate lies in mortal hands, we gods are . . . well, if not obsolete, then certainly not as needed as we might once have thought ourselves."

Baz lifted a brow. "And your fellow gods agree with that?"

"They want to see their worlds thrive. You might not see that, might not agree with how they've shown it in the past, but believe me, they do care, in their own way, about what happens next. We've had long talks about it since the restoration of magic. And on this matter, we are all in agreement."

Equilibris laid a hand on Baz's shoulder, peering into his eyes. "It's up to each world to control the narrative now. It's up to the people to write their own stories, not gods, not fate." His other hand rested on Baz's chest. "You have the power to change things for the better. Don't waste it."

Before Baz could reply, he was suddenly back in the elevator shaft, the grate opening as it reached the bottom. With a start, he realized a weight was missing from his neck; the time-traveling pocket watch that had hung there was gone. The god must have swept it from him. Maybe it was for the best.

Baz took a lurching, disorienting step into Obscura Hall, which had been illusioned once more to take on a scenery from the most senior student's memories. He ached at seeing the familiar tall grass sloping toward the sea. He could almost imagine he was back at the safe house, that somewhere just past the swaying grass sat Emory, watching the horizon.

But it was only an illusion, like everything else. A falsity.

Because underneath it, Baz knew the corridor must still bear the destruction it had suffered when the worlds were laid on top of one another, and when the Regulators had ransacked the commons.

He parted the willow tree's mane and stepped into the commons, where Kai stood next to the torn down wall that overlooked the cove below. Everything was still a mess, the blasted ceiling open to the sky above, barely anything usable in the rubble. Dusk emerged from somewhere and perched on a pile of debris, staring at Baz with those keen cat eyes of his.

You have the power to change things for the better. Don't waste it.

Baz remembered a time when he had never wanted to make waves. He had thought the world was as it was, and there was nothing he could do about it. He was done being so complacent. Done thinking he didn't have the power for change. Change was collective. Change would be slow. But he was ready to fight every step of the way, without a care for his own comfort or need for peace.

The old Baz wouldn't have wanted to let anything disturb the calm he felt in solitude and in books, wouldn't have wanted the real world and all its problems to affect him. But he had experienced true chaos. Had held it in his very hands. And he'd seen evil succumb to change. To good.

He hoped those who still had evil in their hearts could change too.

Kai kicked forlornly at a broken piece of furniture, catching Baz's eye. This home of theirs was unrecognizable, destroyed almost beyond repair.

"It'll take forever to rebuild," Kai said, dejected. "And I don't think it'll ever be the same."

Baz had the same thought. It wasn't just about the physical destruction, which Baz could easily turn back time to undo. It was the memories that lingered like a stain, sullying their haven in an irrevocable way.

Could they still call this a home, feel a sense of belonging here, after everything that happened?

He thought of everything they had shared here. It was the place where their friendship had begun. Where it had evolved into something more. They had been interrupted again and again in their progression—Kai being sent to the Institute, the two of them going back in time, getting separated not once but twice by forces both divine and monstrous.

Now they finally had the chance to rebuild Aldryn into what they wanted it to be. They could make it into a safe place for Eclipse-born in a way it never fully was before. Baz could take up Professor Selandyn's mantel and become a professor like he'd always intended. Kai could resume his studies, help Jae Ahn teach Eclipse-born how to control their now stronger powers—something Baz had heard them both talking about already, full of excitement and hope at the prospect.

Baz and Kai were here, in this place that had always been theirs, and their whole life unfurled in front of them. And they'd get to do it all together.

Baz took Kai's hand in his, kissing his knuckles. He smiled at him, feeling hope take root inside him for the first time since the sea of ash.

"We've got time," he said.

A promise, a vow.

After all, he was the Timespinner. And time ran in his favor.

ROMIE

THE LIGHTHOUSE CAME INTO VIEW ON A CLOUDLESS afternoon.

It was Nisha, standing at the bow of their sailboat, who saw it first. She turned back to Romie to shout an enthusiastic "Look!", her face splitting into a smile so brilliant, it was all Romie wanted to look at. Hard not to, when Nisha appeared so at home on the water. The sea air suited her, with the color on her cheeks deepened by the sun, her long hair tied back with a bright kerchief, loose strands dancing in the wind. Eyes like amber reflecting all the light around her.

Romie craned her neck from where she sat at the stern steering the ship. The sight of the coastline made her heart swell and ache in equal measure. The late summer saw harebells in full bloom, a veritable sea of purple wildflowers growing in the shade of the jack pines and spruce trees that hugged the cove. And towering over it all, weathered yet firm, was the Ainsleif lighthouse.

Six figures spilled onto the smooth gray rocks of the shore to wave their hands in greeting, and though they were too far still to make out their faces, Romie would recognize her brother's gawky frame anywhere.

Romie laughed, excitement pulling her like a taut string toward the coast. She was home at last, after months of traveling with Nisha. They'd been wandering aimlessly together, sailing wherever they felt like it–to Trevel, the Constellation Isles, anywhere that was far from Aldryn and the Institute, these places riddled with bad memories for them both.

Returning to Elegy now, they found those memories didn't seem as dark or as daunting. As if they had left them behind somewhere in the Aldersea.

The moment her feet struck ground, Romie was swept into Baz's embrace. Her brother's hair was shorter, and he had the faintest scruff on his face. He looked downright professorial; fitting, Romie supposed, since he was meant to start as a teaching fellow once the new term started. At his side, Kai looked more serene than she'd ever seen him, as if he'd peeled back several layers of sullen anger to uncover someone who seemed genuinely *happy*.

Nisha was caught between Virgil and Vera, who were bickering like an old married couple. Rumor was they'd spent most of the summer together in Trevel–Virgil mentioning something about horse racing the last time Romie had spoken to him–but Romie wasn't sure what the future held for the two of them, what with Virgil heading back to Aldryn for his last year of studies and Vera splitting her time between Trevel and Cadence, where the Kazan sisters lived.

And Harebell Cove, Romie supposed, spotting the youngest of the Kazans standing close to Henry. Adriana. Luce, as she preferred to be called still. The very Dreamer that Romie had chased after in dreams at the start of all this. She looked so strikingly like Emory–only a few years older than her, thanks to whatever paradox had pulled her through time—that Romie felt the breath knocked out of her. Luce and Henry made an odd pair, to be sure, but she was glad to know Henry wasn't alone in his lighthouse, since Luce had moved in.

Still, Romie couldn't help but note the new lines around Henry's eyes, the thinner frame of his face. He seemed to have aged years in the wake of losing Emory. But the smile he gave Romie as he greeted her with a hug was genuine, and so very fond.

Once, Romie had believed a life devoid of adventure would be a boring one. Now she understood the merit of a quiet life. Or at least of quiet moments. She still couldn't bring herself to stay still for very long. She still wanted to see the world, to carve her own path in it. But she finally understood how to live in the present. To not always be looking toward the next thing, but to be here and now, savoring every second of it.

It was never the destination she should have had her eye on; it was the road along the way, the people she met along it, the things she saw—that was the real adventure.

She wished she'd been so present when Emory was still around, but she took solace in the idea that everything she was seeing, every moment she soaked in, Emory was there somehow. The world had been restored by Emory's hand, after all. It was the least Romie could do to appreciate it for the both of them.

It had become a bit of a tradition for everyone to meet up at Henry Ainsleif's lighthouse as often as they could. Romie and Nisha had stopped by once before setting sail when they both decided they did not want to return to Aldryn College, at least not for now. And she knew that Baz visited Henry every month without fault.

Today was special, because they were all here. Romie and Nisha; Baz and Kai; Virgil and Vera; Ife, Louis, and Javier, who, along with Virgil and some help from Nisha, were all fighting tirelessly to bring what remained of the Selenic Order to justice; even Romie and Baz's parents were here along with Jae, Professor Selandyn, and Alya Kazan.

And perhaps best of all—a slight exaggeration, but not really—was *Dusk*, brought over in a cat carrier by Baz and Kai, who had unofficially adopted him while Romie was traveling the world.

Romie's heart was full as they all sat around the lighthouse swapping stories and eating Henry's famous brown bread and chowder. Dusk purred on her lap, Nisha's hand was warm in hers, and everything was fine. Romie was content.

Content was something she was learning to appreciate. *Content* was safe.

And yet.

The scroll of parchment was tucked into her pocket. It had appeared on the sailboat one night as if by magic—two identical scrolls, one addressed to Romie, the other to Nisha.

An invitation from the gods themselves.

The doors between worlds were open for those who knew where to look for them. But there was no way to travel between them; not without a Tidecaller, not without keys. The gods themselves were bound to their godsworld once more, powerless to meddle with human affairs. Which was why they were calling on people from each of the four worlds to act as their emissaries, granted the power to travel between all the realms.

The Veiled Atlas reborn.

Romie wasn't sure how she felt about it yet. It had the weight of a secret, like when she had been tapped for initiation by the Selenic Order, and she had promised herself she would no longer keep such secrets from the people she loved.

As it turned out, there was no need to bring it up to Baz; her brother did it for her.

"I'm assuming you received an invitation from the gods?" he

asked her when things were dwindling down for the night and they found themselves alone.

Romie scrunched up her brow. "How did you know?"

Baz gave her a sheepish smile. "Because I got one too. So did Kai. Virgil and Vera, too."

Of course they would have. After everything they'd been through, the worlds they'd traversed, the horrors they'd fought, it only made sense they would all of them receive the call to join the Veiled Atlas. It was as if the gods were extending an olive branch. As if they knew they'd all be longing for adventure again at some point.

Romie grasped Baz's hands, heart soaring as she realized he'd finally received the call he'd long fantasized about. "This is great," she said excitedly. Truly letting herself imagine what it would be like to answer the call for the first time since the scroll had appeared to her. "We can all go and—"

"I'm not going," Baz said.

Romie blinked at him. "But . . . isn't this what you've always wanted?"

"Maybe it was, once." Baz glanced to where the others were talking—to where Kai sat peacefully stroking a curled-up Dusk in his lap, a quiet smile on his face. "Not anymore."

As if sensing Baz's gaze, Kai looked up and winked at him.

They both were choosing to stay here, Romie realized. Choosing each other over the call of gods. And why wouldn't they? They had been separated by time, by monsters, by the Deep itself. They deserved to be done with it all, if that's what they wanted.

Romie wasn't sure what she wanted. Or she thought she knew but was mulling it over more so than she ever would have before. She'd never been one to think things through—she'd always just acted on a whim.

Things had changed.

On one hand, she was eager to be reunited with Aspen and Tol and Orfeyi, these people she'd forged unbreakable bonds with—bonds that seemed to defy all logic now, as she could still find them in dreams, even when they were worlds apart.

Maybe it was the time they'd spent joined together as Atheia's vessel that made such a thing possible. It was how she knew that Aspen's sister, Bryony, had made a miraculous recovery from her coma, that the Amberyls were happily reunited, the witches thriving as their Wychwood became lush and green once more. It was how she knew that Tol had helped disband the Fellowship of the Light as it once had been, that the knights were now following the old ways of the Golden Helm, where dragons and eldritch beasts and draconics lived in mutual respect of one another. It was how she knew that storms had ceased in Orfeyi's world, that music soared once more, that sometimes one might glimpse a winged horse soaring through clouds, their divinity restored.

These dream encounters were how Romie knew the three of them had also been chosen to be part of this new Veiled Atlas and were going to accept.

This was where Romie's trepidation lay: the idea of following the call of another destiny.

Yet this wasn't some unshakeable song that pulled them all forward. It was a choice that Romie was free to make on her own. There was no sense of predestined obligation. Just . . . curiosity. A desire for something new.

Perhaps it would always be in Romie's nature to want such things—adventure, the unknown. Only this time, she would be in control of who she was and where such an adventure would take her.

And if she accepted, she'd do better this time. She wouldn't fail the people she cared about like she had before.

Later she found Nisha dozing in front of the fireplace with Dusk in her lap. Romie curled up beside her on the sofa. And here in front of the fire, with her arms wrapped around this girl she loved who had stuck by her from the start, Romie knew her choice rested on wherever Nisha was.

"You know," Nisha mumbled drowsily, her eyes still closed as she pulled Romie's arms around her tighter, "I never did get to properly see the Wychwood."

"It's like one giant greenhouse. You'd love it."

"Maybe they need help restoring all those plants after the rot set in." Nisha cracked an eye open. "I seem to recall you'd developed somewhat of a green thumb."

"Not as green as yours, surely."

"What I'm trying to say is . . . maybe we could go."

"Are you sure?"

Nisha nestled her face in the crook of Romie's neck. "As long as I'm with you, I'm happy."

The words settled something inside Romie. She thought of the little greenhouse they'd tended to at Aldryn. Thought of the mess of withering plants she'd never gotten around to fixing. She had tended instead to another dream rooted inside her—the call of Dovermere, of a destiny she felt so certain of and ended up being so wrong about—choosing to ignore the dream that had already blossomed all around her. The budding relationship with Nisha that she had let shrivel up before it had had any real chance to bloom.

She wouldn't make the same mistake again.

Whatever dream they chased after, they would do so together.

KAI

Kai found solace in nightmares. There was a sense of peace in them now. Perhaps going to the very depths of hell had left a mark on him, giving him a better appreciation for this realm of sleep and death.

Or maybe it was that he had shucked away all his anger, so that it did not weigh on him as it once did.

He realized this when he visited Farran in a nightmare, not long after they'd come back from the godsworld. The nightmare seemed to be a blend of memories drawn from both Thames and Farran: They stood in what looked like the Treasury and the Belly of the Beast combined, with the foul stench of the abyss in the air and the incessant ticking of clocks filling their ears, like an echo of the god of balance's workshop. All the places where Thames and Farran had died and come back and been taken advantage of, imbued with such horror and despair, it had Farran hugging himself like a scared child as tears ran down his face.

Kai pulled on the nightmare's darkness, gathering it into him until it wasn't so frightening anymore. His shoulder brushed Farran's, who looked up at him with relief, unsurprised at his presence.

"Thank you," Farran breathed, the lines of him relaxing a bit as he took in the scene around them. "You'd think as a former Fear Eater, I'd be better at confronting my nightmares."

"You were never as skilled as I am."

That drew a smile from Farran, but it quickly vanished as he looked at Kai with stark sincerity. "I truly am sorry, you know. For everything I've done."

"Not your fault," Kai said with a shrug, and realized he meant it. "You were compelled by fate, after all."

Farran's brows shot up in surprise. "I didn't expect to get off that easy from someone who's repeatedly told me to go to hell. Thought you hated my guts."

"If there's one thing hell taught me, it's to let bygones be bygones. Time to move on."

"Speaking of which." Farran scuffed the floor with the tip of his foot. "I, uh, have decided I'm done with this iteration of my life."

A weight fell in Kai's stomach, a chill going through him at those words. "What the fuck does that even mean?"

Farran gave him a wry smile. "I'm not technically alive, am I? I've died before. *Twice*. And now I want my soul to go into the fountain and be reincarnated for good this time. Equilibris denied me a life of my own when he made me a puppet on a string, all my actions playing into fate's design. I was made a dupe by Clover, an errand boy for gods, and I'm tired. I want . . . I want to start over fresh, make my own choices knowing they're entirely mine."

Kai understood. And yet, it felt bittersweet to say goodbye. "See you in another life, maybe," he told Farran.

Farran smiled. "You've got a good one here. Don't waste it."

Kai did not intend to.

It was part of the reason he'd decided not to take up the gods' invitation to join the Veiled Atlas. The gods might be eager to turn the page on everything that had happened, to prove that they cared about their worlds in their own fucked-up way, but Kai wanted no part in it.

Turning the page for him meant turning his back on the gods. Choosing to lead a life that was all his own, just like Farran had. It meant advocating for the Eclipse-born harder than ever, because the strides they had made were a start, yes, but nowhere near good enough. It meant packing up his many copies of *Song of the Drowned Gods* and giving them all away. Letting go of this book that had shaped him, this story that was darkened now by the ugly truth that had shaped *it*. There were plenty more stories out there just waiting to evoke wonder in him again.

Turning the page meant sitting quietly with Baz at nightfall, drinking tea instead of gin—Kai's trusty flask forgotten, because there was no need to keep the nightmares at bay anymore—and seeing Baz scribble in a notebook, a spark of inspiration behind his glasses.

"I know for a fact Selandyn didn't give you any research to work on over the summer," Kai teased him. "So what are you writing?"

Baz looked up from his journal with a smile. "I don't know yet. And that's the beauty of it."

A story all his own, perhaps. Not one bound to him by fate.

There was one thing Kai could not turn the page on, one thing he mostly kept to himself. That often, he tried to search for Emory and Sidraeus in the folds of darkness beyond the path of stars, and sometimes, he thought he felt them, always just out of reach. But it was like a phantom wind, there and gone again in a flash, making him wonder if he'd imagined it.

They were gone. Yet Kai spoke to the darkness all the same.

"Everyone misses you," he would say, imagining it might bring some comfort to Emory to know this. He told the darkness of all the things Baz had accomplished, of Romie's travels, of what he himself was striving for with Jae and the Eclipse-born. He told Emory of how her parents still grieved for her, but assured her they weren't alone–that Henry had struck up a close friendship with Theodore and Anise and Jae; that Luce had finally been reunited with the other Kazans; that together on the shores of Harebell Cove, the two of them kept Emory's memory alive between them.

Kai communed with the faraway void in the hopes these words would reach her, if she was there at all.

And when he woke in the bed he shared with the boy he loved, he wrapped his arms around Baz a little tighter.

Not out of fear, but gratefulness for what they had, and hope for what was to come.

EPILOGUE

THE STORYTELLER

THE NIGHT SKY WAS UNLIKE ANYTHING BAZ HAD ever seen over the lighthouse at the end of the world.

Stars here were so bright and plenty, there was barely any darkness between. Baz had made it a habit of watching the night sky every time he visited Henry and Luce. They would sit together on the shores of the Aldersea, Emory's presence always with them.

Tonight, as the three of them watched stars dart across the skies in spectacular blazes of white, Baz remembered what Emory had told him once, so long ago: that her father believed shooting stars were souls trying to find their way home.

Baz imagined now that one of them was Emory. He knew it wasn't possible; knew there was no coming back from the void. It was a nice thought to have all the same. That perhaps this was not the end of her story, but the start of a new one.

An adventure that would carry her to the most distant of shores, before one day returning her to the ones she'd called home.

ACKNOWLEDGMENTS

WRITING THE DROWNED GODS TRILOGY HAS BEEN quite a roller coaster. The first book poured out of me like a swift tide; the second nearly drowned me; the third was a lifeline, pulling me from the dark depths of creative burnout. It made me find joy in writing again, and I'm proud of the result.

I can hardly believe I am now the author of a finished trilogy! There are so many people I need to thank for bringing me to this point:

To my agent, Victoria Marini, and my editor, Sarah McCabe–what a journey it's been. I can't thank you both enough for all the hard work and dedication you've poured into this series, and for helping me grow as a writer. You heard me out when I came to you with this wild, last-minute idea for a third book, and now I couldn't imagine the Drowned Gods ever not being a trilogy. I appreciate you both beyond words. And to Anum Shafqat–I am so grateful for your editorial assistance over the course of this series. I couldn't have asked for a better editorial team with you and Sarah.

Thank you to all the incredible people at Simon & Schuster/McElderry Books who had a hand in the making of this book: Justin Chanda, Karen Wojtyla, Anne Zafian, Jennifer Strada, Elizabeth Blake-Linn, Greg Stadnyk (I can't thank you enough for these book covers you designed; they are an absolute dream), Chrissy Noh, Caitlin Sweeny, Alissa Rashid, Bezi Yohannes, Perla Gil, Remi Moon, Amelia Johnson, James Akinaka, Saleena Nival, Elizabeth Huang, Trey Glickman, Shannon Pender, Kayah Hodge, Amy Lavigne, Julia Ashley Romero, Lisa Moraleda, Nicole Russo, Samantha McVeigh, Christina Pecorale and her sales team, and Michelle Leo and her education/library team. Thank you also to the Simon & Schuster Canada, UK, and Australia teams, and to all the publishers abroad who have translated the Drowned Gods series in so many languages and gotten it the recognition I always dreamed it would get.

A special thank-you to the booksellers, librarians, and bloggers around the world who have helped these books find their audience. And to all the artists I've commissioned book-related art from over the years and those who have shared with me fan art of my characters—in a time when true artistry is being threatened by the rise of generative AI, I hope you remember how precious and inspiring your work is. Thank you.

Because my memory is foggy and I don't want to forget anyone, please accept this blanket thank-you to everyone within the writing community who has shown up for me and this series over the last five years. Your support, friendship, and help have meant the world to me. Special thanks to Kapri Psych and Adrian Graves, the Crying Emoji Club, without whom I wouldn't have written a word of this book and would still be crying over all my "book 3 problems"; to Hannah Laycraft for the helpful feedback (a certain character thanks you for their life); and to Lara Ameen for the thoughtful sensitivity read and heartwarming hype.

Thank you, as always, to my friends and family. You keep me going when the times get dark.

Finally, to my readers–thank you for your enthusiasm over the years, for trusting me with these characters you've grown so fond of, and for sticking with this trilogy until the end. It's been an honor to share this story with you. I hope your final journey through these worlds is a memorable one. And remember: some endings are also beginnings.

PASCALE LACELLE IS THE *NEW YORK TIMES* bestselling author of *Curious Tides* and *Stranger Skies*. A longtime devourer of books, she started writing her own at the age of thirteen and quickly became enthralled by the magic of words in both French and English. She lives in Ottawa, Canada, with her beloved dog and an ever-growing library of books waiting to be read. You can find her online at PascaleLacelle.com or on Instagram @PascaleLacelle.